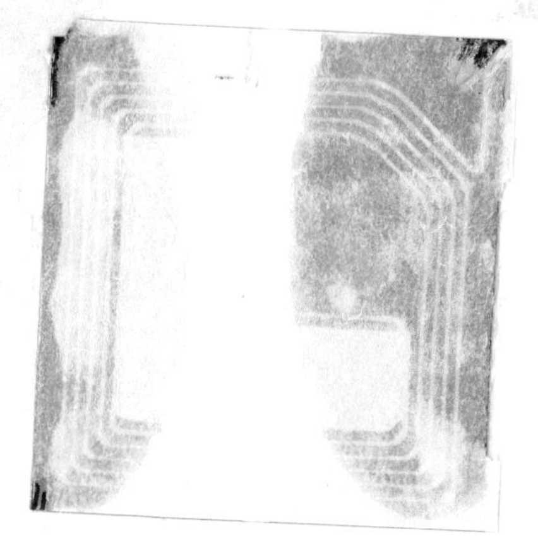

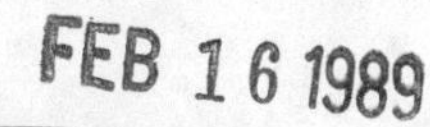

EVAN GREEN

ALICE TO NOWHERE

St. Martin's Press
New York

 For information, address St. Martin's Press, 175 Fifth Avenue, New York, N.Y. 10010.

Library of Congress Cataloging-in-Publication Data

Green, Evan.
Alice to nowhere / by Evan Green.

p. cm.
"A Thomas Dunne book."
ISBN 0-312-01384-1 : $16.95
I. Title.
PR9619.3.G72A79 1988
823—dc19

87-27363
CIP

First published in Australia by James Fraser Publishing Pty Ltd.

First U.S. Edition

10 9 8 7 6 5 4 3 2 1

CHAPTER ONE

He walked from the shadows and stood on the footpath. No one was about. He turned up the collar of his jacket, for he felt colder now. A vast cloud, crinkled with strands of grey where it blocked the full moon, sprawled high above the town. The only bright light came from the street lamp at the corner and it glowed frostily, through a sphere of mist. From another street came the hum of a car's motor. He prepared to move back into the shadow of the building but the sound faded. He waited, listening for some new noise to challenge him, but none came. It was quiet. That was just what surprised him. Despite all that had happened, the place was still quiet. He began to breathe heavily, for he had been holding his breath. It seemed unbelievable. The town still slept, and yet, only a few minutes before, he had beaten a woman to death.

He turned and signalled his companion to join him. The other man was shorter, and fat. He walked down the steps, glancing nervously about him. Together, they walked to the corner, stepped through the glowing zone of mist beneath the lamp, and crossed the road towards the parked utility truck. The fat man was reaching for the keys when they heard the sound of an approaching car.

'Keep walking,' the tall man said. 'Act normal.'

They continued beyond the truck. Behind them, there was the faint rub of brakes, and headlights swung around the corner, throwing their shadows against a shopfront. It was a taxi, roof emblem alight. The driver saw them and pulled towards the kerb, ready to stop if summoned. The tall man shook his head without turning his face, and the taxi accelerated away. They watched it disappear and then doubled back to the parked truck. The fat man unlocked the door. His hand was shaking. The other man stood clear. He was looking back, towards the hotel.

'Get in and wait,' he said. 'I've just thought of something.'

He walked back to the hotel. He was thinking more clearly now. The chill air helped. That and the fact that things were so quiet outside. So different to the last thirty minutes, back inside the hotel office. There, the two men had hardly dared breathe as they worked, and every sound had torn at their nerves. They had been so careful and yet they had been discovered. They had left too quickly, and now there were things he should do.

The hotel was still in darkness. He climbed the steps and pushed open the unlocked glass door. It swung noiselessly on its hinges. He pulled his gloves firmly down to his wrists and felt his way past the reception desk and along the wall to the office door. The key was in the lock, where they had left it. Gently he opened the door and pocketed the key. He slipped inside and pressed the door closed.

The room was dark and silent. He felt his jacket. He knew the opals would still be there but it was an involuntary movement, an act of self assurance in the overwhelming darkness of this room. He patted the case and pulled out his torch.

For one horrifying moment he thought she had gone. Then the light shone on her feet and he ran the beam along the body of the old woman he had killed. She was partly under a table. He hadn't remembered that. Maybe she was still alive. He bent down. She lay on her back, dressing gown twisted around her body, exposing one leg to the hip.

There was no doubt she was dead. Her head was a pulpy mess. One eye was visible, wide open, and he stared at it in fascination. He had never seen a dead person before and she didn't look real. He wasn't sickened, or even nervous anymore. He thought about that and was pleased.

He remembered the way she had come into the office. He had

almost cried out with fright. His fat companion had just opened the safe and begun to withdraw the opal case when the woman had suddenly appeared at the door. She must have been terrified, he reflected. She had stood there, waving her stick at him but saying nothing. And when she had opened her mouth as if to scream, he had seized the stick and beaten her with it. She had fallen and he had rained blows on her, until he was sure she would not cry out.

He stood up. He was glad he had come back. They had fled the first time. That was bad. They shouldn't have run from a planned job like this. There was too much chance of spoiling things, of leaving something behind to identify them.

Carefully, he directed the light around the room. The safe door was wide open. He moved across and closed it. From his new position he examined the floor, checking it thoroughly until he was satisfied they had left nothing. The torch was small, casting a narrow pencil beam, and he spent almost a minute searching for something he had glimpsed earlier. The patch of light floated past filing cabinets and over a typewriter on a wide bench, flashed at him in a wall mirror, and crisscrossed a large table piled high with papers before he found what he sought. It was a small clock, standing on a desk near the safe. Beside it was a calendar, celebrating the arrival of March, 1957, with a glossy picture, all reds and blacks, of the Sturt Desert Pea. He picked up the clock and with gloved fingers, fumbled to wind the hands until they showed five thirty. He put the clock face-down on the floor, next to the woman's body, and knelt on it until he heard the crack of glass. He held his breath; there was no other sound. Applying more weight, he ground his knee into the back of the clock until there came a deeper, crunching sound. He put his ear near the clock to make sure it had stopped.

With one hand, he rolled the woman on her side and with the other pushed the shattered clock against her body. He brushed the glass fragments into the same area and let the body slump back into place. The clock was hidden. He checked to make sure no pieces of broken glass were exposed.

The torch flashed across the woman's face, making her eye appear to wink. He looked away. Rolling the body had further dislodged her dressing gown, exposing her body even more. Her thigh was bruised and wrinkled. The sight offended him and he pulled the gown over her knee.

Johnny Parsons stood up. He patted the opal case again, made sure his pistol was in place, and checked his watch. Nearly two o'clock. It was time to leave Alice Springs.

Barbara Dean gave up the struggle to sleep and glanced through the window of the railway carriage. Grey shapes were flitting past in the pre-dawn light. The familiar, shadowy outlines of motor trucks gave way to strange silhouettes of mechanical devices frozen in the posture of insects under threat. She looked more closely. They were giant earthmoving machines, blades raised, scoops poised on long metallic stalks. Must be a town, or some sort of depot, she thought, and closed her eyes again for a few seconds. Her back ached. She sat up, stretching to ease the stiffness in her body. The man beside her grunted, but continued to sleep. He was sprawled awkwardly across the seat with his head and shoulders covered by a coat, a blanket-substitute into which he pumped a sour but warm breath at deep, regular intervals. He broke wind and she concentrated on the moving view beyond the window. Neither the sound nor the man offended her. She was a nursing sister. And having decided to spend the next twelve months of her life serving in one of the most remote mission hospitals in Australia, she was prepared to ignore such things and to accept even the occasional kicks this sleeping stranger had aimed her way during the night, with the tolerance of one who expects worse to come.

The train had slowed. It was the change in pace, the interruption to the monotonous rumbling and swaying that had finally stirred her into wakefulness. Not that she had had much sleep since leaving Adelaide. The foot of the sleeping man touched her knee. Gently but firmly she pushed it back to his side of the seat. She had been travelling all night and half the previous day, but the man had boarded the north-bound train during the night, at Hawker. He was obviously a regular traveller. Being aware of the rigours of the journey ahead, he had come aboard well primed and had soon lapsed into a drunken sleep.

There were more bulldozers outside, then huts, long and dark in the grey light. The sky flushed in anticipation of the sun. Beneath it, the land seemed flat and stretched in an endless shadow. Barbara Dean had never seen such country. She had abandoned city life for the outback and this was her first glimpse of land that might resemble her future surroundings. She was heading for the Channel Country but had been told the land in this part of South Australia was similar. She caught the reflection of her own face in the window and smiled at herself. It was a gesture of comfort. Everything from now on would be new to her, and she needed reassurance — even if only from her own reflection. Plenty of her friends had warned her she was doing the wrong thing, leaving the city and all that it offered for a tiny hospital in a settlement that was more than one thousand miles from the coast. But none of them had been there and so she ignored them. Going there was what she wanted to do. No God-fearing missionary, she was nonetheless moved by a sense of wanting to do something for others, and to achieve some purpose in her own life. She had been nursing in the city for almost ten years. She'd been in a rut.

She was glad to be awake before the sun had risen. The land seemed soft in its shadows. She would like it. She was determined to like it. But she was glad the rising sun would reveal the outback gradually, as though by way of a gentle introduction.

The train rattled past a final cluster of bulldozers, shielding another row of huts and makeshift water-towers. It had been a camp, not a town. She pressed her face to the glass, watching the signs of habitation slide into the distance, to be replaced by the grey-blue of a flat and featureless plain. She guessed the camp had been a base for workers on the new railway line to Alice Springs. All the way from Port Pirie and along the western ridge of the Flinders Ranges, the train had passed near the new line, with its sturdier bridges, bigger stations and wider embankments testifying to the work of this army of men and their strange machines. They had a long way to go, for the camp had still not reached Marree and that was less than halfway to Alice Springs. That she knew, because Marree was where she was to leave the train.

She dozed again, and missed the dawn. When she awoke, the land had turned brown. It swept past her window, as flat and dull as painted blotting paper. She felt hungry and tired and apprehensive. The man alongside kicked her again. She pushed his foot away more firmly than before, causing the head beneath the coat to lift and speak, without revealing itself: 'Give us a kick when we're at Marree, will you mate?'

Mate. She took an apple from a brown paper bag and bit into it savagely. 'Why is Barbara going bush at her time of life?' her mother's friends had asked. She thought of them gossiping at tennis on a Wednesday. 'She won't get married at all if she leaves town now. What's she burying herself in the bush for? She won't find any doctors out there.' No one understood. She wasn't running, or hiding. This was something she was doing by choice. It was far better than marrying for the sake of appeasing her mother's friends and spending her days in tedium, gossip and tennis.

She hoped Sydney, distant, disappearing Sydney, would have a succession of wet Wednesdays. She smiled at the thought, enjoying her own, unusual touch of malice.

She was on the western side of the train and therefore shielded from the glare of the rising sun. The carriage's long shadow raced alongside. Far away on the horizon, the morning light had reached a low range of hills and bathed them in a soft wash of violet. The hills were old, and scalloped by weathering over the centuries. Wrinkled, like old men. The distance and their contrast with the plain made the hills remote and more beautiful because of their isolation. Would they seem so outstanding back home, planted at the edge of the Blue Mountains? She pondered the thought and imagined this ancient range scarred with houses, asphalt streets and telegraph poles. Beauty was in the eye of the beholder, and the beholder, she mused, was influenced by one's surroundings. Her eyes stared back at her, ghostly and pale in the faint reflection from the carriage window, and she wondered how she would be judged out here, away from a multitude of women. She was no beauty, but not bad. A good looking girl. Correction. Woman, for she was twenty-six. A good looking nurse, one of hundreds in Sydney, where nurses were regarded either as angels of mercy or easy pickings for unattached men. If you were not married by twenty-six, there must be something wrong. 'Is Barbara really going out to that terrible place? For how long? A year. Oh! Well that's not so long. A sort of handy time, isn't it.' She thought of tennis and those stupid women and was angry.

The carriages were shuffling, touching each other in the concertina-like procession of pushing buffers and straining couplings that meant the brakes were on. They were slowing again. She saw some buildings ahead. A guard was walking down the corridor, legs wide apart in the sailor-like roll of railwaymen.

'Is this Marree?' she asked.

He nodded without breaking the rhythm of his gait, touching the back of each seat as he went, as though counting to make sure none was missing since the last stop. She stood to straighten her dress and lifted her bags from the rack. Only two. They were remarkably light for someone who was moving into a new world. She grasped each handle tightly. 'It's funny how little I own,' she thought and searched for her reflection in the window but its comforting presence had gone, banished by a shaft of daylight. More than at any time since leaving Sydney, she had a sense of being uprooted, of drifting without a grip on the world, of being on her own.

Her carriage drew level with the buildings. They looked cold and bare, ranged in haphazard order on the far side of a wide street. One tall building, drab brown with its edging blocks painted white. A verandah with a man standing on it. Smaller buildings of iron. Iron fences. A few trees. Scrappy grass. Dust. The train, carriages bumping and recoiling with the slowing pace, entered a wide railway enclosure. Her staring face drifted past a sequence of sheds and platforms, and a string of rail tankers at rest in a siding. A row of empty cattle trucks. A few people were waiting, gazing up at the passing windows for a familiar face. She saw a man with red hair and a pipe in his mouth stare hard at her, look away and then glance back. She stopped opposite two men who were waving their arms in animated conversation. One was in railway uniform. The other man had a black beard and dirty face. She was fascinated by him. How he could be so filthy so early in the day she could not imagine. She still had more than three hundred miles to travel to her destination; if people in a town like Marree were as dirty as this, what would they be like at the mission, deeper in the outback?

Blackbeard was speaking in a voice that was unnaturally loud, as though the other man were deaf. 'They'd be up the back. They're great big tyres, for a bulldozer or something.' He caught sight of her looking at him. He smiled.

She gathered her bags and made for the door. The man with the pipe hurried from the other carriage door towards her. His red hair sparkled in the sunlight. He took out his pipe and called:

'Sister Dean?'

'Yes.' She paused on the step.

'My name's Black. Mr Crawford asked me to meet you.' He reached up to take her bags. 'Welcome to Marree.'

'Thank you.'

She paused, remembering something. 'Excuse me just a moment,' she said and returned through the carriage to her compartment. The man from Hawker was still asleep, but he looked more comfortable, for his legs were fully stretched out. She kicked his feet off her seat. 'Marree,' she said.

CHAPTER TWO

The early morning sun was casting a spider web pattern on the fat man's face. With every bump in the road the pattern changed. The light was angling across the windscreen, filtering through an etching of wiper scratches, dust and the splattered remains of insects. The sun danced with the bumps, and tormented the fat man's eyes. More than ever he felt sorry for himself.

Francis Raymond Gardiner had spent most of his life feeling sorry for himself. He thought about the sorry chain of events that had led to him being at the wheel of a utility truck, fleeing from Alice Springs. Oh God, or whoever it was who allowed things to go wrong, how he wished he could turn back the clock.

Gardiner had been born at the wrong time. He had been a child during the Depression. That in itself didn't worry him but his mother had suffered and she made sure he suffered too. She was a widow. At least she told him so; the children at school claimed otherwise. They called him words he didn't understand. That was part of his problem. Much that happened about him was beyond his understanding.

The truck hit a bump and he winced.

He thought of school. His time there had been a nightmare, a sentence to be endured. It was a time when adults spoke to him with envy, insisting those would be the best years of his life, grinding into him a sense of despair when he considered the future and shame at his singular inability to enjoy what were supposedly joyous times. He became confused, being told what he should believe and not knowing what he did believe.

Because of his initials, Francis Raymond Gardiner had been given the nickname Frog. He grew up in Sydney, at a time and in a suburb that demanded of its young a name other than that given by parents. It was a guide to social order in the schoolyard. A derogatory name was inevitable if you were low down the scale. Gardiner, being fat and confused, was near the bottom. He spent his years in primary school condemned to the company of Rabbit-ears Anderson, Tadpole Tindall and a German boy who brightly endured the corruption of his name into Shitslinger.

The track curled to the south-west and for a few moments his eyes were in shade. Geeze, he was tired.

He hated school and later he hated the fate that allowed him to grow into a fat adult, for that perpetuated the name Frog, and made the name Francis as remote as his dead or untraceable father.

He was good with his hands but not his head. It was inevitable that he should mix with criminals because, by his social status and lack of self-drive, he was automatically shovelled into their company. At first, it was just a mob of boys, the dregs of his former school mates. They used to pack outside the School of Arts on a Friday night, to bash someone coming out of the dance. Anyone. It didn't matter. He enjoyed those days because they gave him an unusual sense of belonging, and of being on the winning side. It was good to give and not receive. He stole a few cars, went to jail and made contacts that taught him the art of breaking and entering. He graduated to safes. Frog Gardiner was good with his own hands but pliable in the hands of others. It was this combination of skill and malleability that led him so often into trouble.

But he had never been in trouble like this. He had been lured into this job by the promise of easy money but now the man who had made the promise had killed a woman and that had changed everything.

Frog had driven since Alice Springs. He had covered more than two hundred and fifty miles. They had been rough miles for the Stuart Highway, the only road south from the centre, was a bone-shaking charlatan: a bush track masquerading as a national highway, with bulldust, rock outcrops and acute corrugations to punish any traveller. They had driven through no towns because there were none. Near the South Australian border, Kulgera, with a store and a police station to justify its name on the map, showed no sign of life as they drove through. The taller man, Johnny Parsons, had stayed awake, talking constantly, until they reached the border. The boundary separating the Northern Territory from the state of South Australia was marked by no more than a metal sign, pock-marked so deeply by bullet holes that it was difficult to read. This token of irreverent vandalism seemed to relax Parsons. The country to the south of the border was little different from that to the north. There was no river to cross, mountain range to climb or barrier to pass. But to Parsons, it was as though a gate had been met and found open. Once out of the Territory, he had fallen asleep.

With envy, Frog Gardiner glanced across at the sleeping man. His own eyelids felt hot and heavy and he longed to close them. The day before, he had driven the utility well over four hundred miles to Alice Springs and his eyes were beginning to swim in a head soggy with sleep. For a few delicious seconds, he closed them, but he imagined the vehicle was swaying and awoke, frightened. He thrust his head through the open side window and drove for several hundred yards with the wind snatching tears from his eyes. He felt a little fresher for that, but nothing he had tried all through the long drive could shake away the worry he felt over the way this job had gone.

He tried to make out the time on the other man's wristwatch but he couldn't take his eyes from the road long enough to see. Time was so important in Johnny's plan.

There'd been nothing about killing when Johnny had first explained the plan to him. It was going to be just a straightforward safe job and Frog was good at that. That was why the other man had come to him. Johnny knew all about the opals and had worked out a plan to steal them and get away with them, but he was no good at opening safes. Or pinching trucks, for that matter. So Frog was with him. He'd been promised a half share. Five thousand wasn't to be sniffed at but Frog was regretting his decision now. He'd never been mixed up in murder before and the experience frightened him.

He was feeling hot and he unzippered his jacket. 'Your plan had better be right,' he mused out loud.

As though responding, Parsons shifted his feet, stretching one leg so that his shoe touched the driver's left ankle.

Frog waited to make sure the other man was still asleep before continuing. His voice was softer. 'You didn't say you was going to kill the old lady when you got me to do this job.'

He had to slow for a rock outcrop and the brakes grabbed on one side. He cursed the truck. It was noisy and the brakes were uneven and the road was rough and he was sick to death of driving.

'It's all right for you,' he continued. 'It's your plan but I do all the work. I pinch the ute, I drive up, I open the safe and now I drive all the flamin' way back again. I reckon . . .' His voice trailed off as his companion grunted and turned in the seat. Johnny Parsons closed his lips to wet them and then let his mouth sag open again. He squirmed on to his back and began snoring.

How could he sleep with all the worry that must be on his mind? Frog had never met a man with so much confidence. This character had planned everything down to the last detail and seemed sure that nothing would go wrong.

Up to the time the woman had found them, everything had gone as Johnny Parsons had reckoned. They'd flown from Adelaide to Oodnadatta and found the truck, just as Johnny had said they would. The owner was away, like Johnny had said, and taking it had been dead easy. There had been no trouble driving up and they had arrived after dark. They carried petrol in drums in the back, so there had been no need for them to call in at a garage. As far as they knew, no one had noticed them arrive at Alice Springs. Everything had gone right. Even the safe had proved little trouble and they had found the opals, just as Johnny had said.

And then the woman had come in.

Again Frog was worried about the time. The rest of the plan depended on time. They had to be at Oodnadatta by four o'clock that afternoon to catch the plane. They couldn't afford to miss it. Not now.

That was a part of the plan that had worried Frog, but Johnny had insisted it was safe. It seemed unnatural to return to Alice Springs but Johnny had talked him into it. They had to get to

Darwin, that was certain. That was where Johnny had the contact who would take the opals and pay them the cash. The quickest way to get there was to fly and so here they were, going to Oodnadatta to catch the plane to Alice Springs and Darwin. Johnny reckoned the police wouldn't think of checking people flying into town. They'd check them going out, but not coming in. At least that's what Johnny reckoned. Frog hoped he was right. But time was so important. They had a long way to go and they couldn't miss that plane.

The motor spluttered, fired again and then coughed to a stop. Frog swore at the truck. Here he was, trying to make time, and the truck had run out of petrol. He hadn't noticed the gauge showing empty. He swore at the truck again.

Stiffly, he climbed out and walked to the back. He lowered a funnel and a four-gallon drum of petrol from the tray and began to refill the tank. A swarm of little black flies descended on his unshaded face. He tried to brush them aside with one hand, but jerked the upturned drum and spilled petrol on the bulldust.

He began to mutter to himself but the flies crawled on the moist inner part of his lips and he had to close his mouth tight. He emptied the first drum and opened a second.

The contents of three drums went into the tank and then he threw the empties into the bush and walked back to the cabin, waving his arms vigorously to keep the flies clear.

Johnny was still asleep.

'It's all right for you,' Frog whispered as he slid behind the wheel. 'You don't have to put petrol in this bomb with all those flamin' flies outside. Geeze, I'm tired.'

He caught a fly and crushed it slowly between his thumb and forefinger. He flicked it on to Johnny and pressed the starter button. The motor whirred dryly for several seconds before coughing into life. Frog crunched the gear lever into first and accelerated harshly. He drove brutally, as though he wanted to punish the vehicle, and changed gears with a wide-open throttle.

'By geeze, this plan had better work, Johnny. This is a hell of a way to get to Darwin.' He kept his foot hard down on the pedal.

The truck was travelling fast now, faster than they had gone all night. He glanced at the sleeping man. Johnny stirred. He wet his lips and stretched his legs.

A shuddering bump made Frog look up. A line of trees lay just ahead. Dry creek crossing. He was going too fast. He jabbed the brake but a front wheel grabbed and the truck started to skid in the loose dust. Suddenly he was frightened.

He could see the crossing now, a blur of sand and rocks. The truck's nose dipped into it, lifting him from the seat. He tried to change gear. He jerked the lever into neutral but the clutch pedal wouldn't move. He pushed vainly again. In panic, he looked down. The sleeping man's outstretched foot was wedged beneath the pedal. He tried to kick it away, but couldn't. The front wheels hit the first stones and sent a shock wave through the truck. The motor was roaring in neutral. In desperation, he jammed hard on the clutch. The other man woke with a yell of pain. They were sliding sideways, the tyres flipping stones into the side of the truck with the rapid beat of machine gun bullets. Frog, bouncing in the seat, struggled to control the truck. He swung past an uprooted tree, but a tyre hit a rock and the wheel spun out of his hands. His head hit the roof. He saw Johnny bounce towards him, felt an elbow crack his cheekbone. Dazed, he fell sprawling over the wheel. He tugged it hard to the right, back towards the track.

The wheel shuddered in his hands. They were bounding towards the creek bank, only yards away. His foot found the brake pedal again. He jammed hard down and the steering wheel dipped suddenly to the left. Johnny was shouting.

They rammed the embankment in a shower of sandy soil.

Just north of Marree, Fred Crawford was sitting beside the Land-Rover in the middle of the road because he knew there would be no traffic. He wore no shirt because he preferred not to, and the flying sand stung his back. He was hot, and annoyed because the tyre had punctured so close to town. Seeing the buildings in the distance and being out here, caught in a sudden windstorm when he could be sheltering at home or in the pub, made him more upset. Most people took time off — at the weekends, when they were sick, or for holidays — but Fred Crawford, changing the wheel in a windstorm at the end of three hard days out of town, and with the town in sight, mocking him, imagined at that moment that he alone worked all the time. He wiped some sand from his eyes. Immediately more sand replaced it. He strained to tighten a rusty wheel nut and automatically held his breath to avoid filling his nose with flying grit.

Seven years of living in this part of the world had taught him the danger of deep breathing, and of filling his lungs either with sand or flies. At least the sandstorm kept the flies away.

For the first few years, Crawford had enjoyed this sort of life. More than that, he had been fascinated by it, discovering the open spaces, the sunshine, the slow pace of life and the brooding, captivating majesty of the desert with the astonishment of one who opens a door and finds a secret, unimagined place beyond.

He was a contractor. That's what he put on his tax forms and as the taxman was the supreme authority in Australia that's what he was. It meant he had the contract for a mail run through country no one else was prepared to cross and he got contracts to sink a few bores and dig dams in places where water had never been. He was, he reflected, a fringe dweller, living on the edge of society, doing jobs other people found unpleasant or impossible. At least he was his own boss and that meant a great deal to him. He couldn't work for another man or a large company. He had tried that after the war. Never again. Fred Crawford had to work outside and this was certainly an out-of-doors occupation. He glanced over his shoulder, part closing his eyes to avoid the stinging slap of the windstorm; and saw the familiar horizon through the scudding layer of dust. There wasn't much to look at. He grinned. A man must be a masochist.

MASOCHIST: one who enjoys abuse or domination. He thought of the dictionary definition. It was a new word he'd learned. Words were his release. He always carried a dictionary with him because he read a lot and he needed the dictionary to understand what he read. He savoured some special words, rolling them within his mouth, not opening his teeth for fear they might escape. Masochist was a current favourite because in his present mood he felt it suited him. He was his own boss and yet he never stopped working. He must enjoy abuse because he made himself suffer. He finished tightening the last wheel nut. Mas-o-chist. It was a hard, punishing word; one you had to force out. He had been saying it to himself that morning, coming back to town from the job near Muloorina, just as he was recalling that he had never taken a holiday in all the seven years since he had moved to Marree.

One man worked with him on the mail run and another two

were out west of Muloorina, sinking a bore. That was his newest contract. He had spent a couple of days helping them fix the power plant driving the drill. Great way to spend a weekend.

He put away the jack and wheelbrace. The wind stopped as suddenly as it had started.

Crawford was a tall man and lean as a cattle dog. He walked slowly. 'If you want to survive out here, slow down,' was the first bit of advice he had received when he arrived in this district. It had come from a station owner who had made the gruelling journey from near-poverty before the war to great wealth in the wool boom that followed. A man like that was worth listening to. He used to yarn with Fred, telling him of the days when he and his small family ate only cockatoo, because they couldn't afford to slaughter a sheep. 'Take your pace from the sheep,' his friend advised him. 'If you don't walk any faster than a sheep, you'll learn to live in this country. People who hurry won't stand the heat.'

So Fred Crawford walked slowly, because he was determined to survive.

He had served in the navy in the war. That was where he had developed a hatred for confined spaces. He couldn't stand ships, with their narrow passageways, cramped quarters, low bulkheads and creaking metal. However, his years at sea had taught him a lot about machinery, given him a yearning for solitude and developed in him a love for space and the feeling of being surrounded by immensity. The desert was like that. It was a fossilised ocean, spreading far beyond the horizon to lap against shores so distant that they were beyond the limits of worry or imagination.

After seven years in this part of the world, he still liked the nights. Clear, moonlit nights were best. They occurred regularly in such dry country. On the main run he liked to walk well clear of the track, after his companion fell asleep, to gaze at the infinite landscape. If the moon was bright, the rocks and sand ripples cast shadows like waves, fortifying the illusion of standing in a motionless sea. The experiences made time and ambition meaningless. This desert had been here long before man trod the earth and would remain long after him. Towns would be unrecognisable in another century — he imagined what Maree would be like in 2057 — whereas the desert would be virtually unchanged in another million years. Maybe a little more worn, and even more peaceful.

On moonlit nights he would breathe in the cool air and imagine he was the only person on earth. It was beautiful, his empty desert. Something like the moon itself. Untouched. Vast. Clean.

The days were different. He was now finding the heat harder to endure, the dust storms more annoying and the work more taxing. If there had been a challenge at first, it had long been answered. All that remained was the effort and the monotony. Maybe he would get out soon. He was making a lot of money, enough to start up again in some place that had grass and trees and water; where there were other people, where the roads were sealed rather than non-existent, where the consequences of taking a wrong turning in the road were inconvenience and loss of time, rather than possible death. Travellers who wandered off or broke down still died up here. That wasn't right. Fred loved the solitude, but the brutality of the country offended him.

He was a loner who cared for other people. He might not have been so lonely if Betty had married him. Maybe that was why he worked so hard. He should leave. She still lived up the track and every time he headed that way — once a fortnight, up and back — he grew agitated. She was married now, so he should forget her.

He slapped dust from his shorts and from the brown army hat he had bought in a war surplus store.

The road from Marree looped around a curve in the railway line. He was wondering, with a pang of intense interest, whether the nurse had arrived on the morning train when he noticed the vehicle coming towards him. It trailed dust that corkscrewed like a red tunnel beneath the sky. He waited.

Another Land-Rover pulled up alongside him. Its doors bore the shield of the South Australian police force.

'How'd the job go?' the policeman behind the wheel asked.

'All right,' Fred said. 'How are things?'

The policeman's hands made a gesture which could have meant anything. Fred took it as a sign that things were normal. They usually were.

The two men were quiet for several seconds.

Fred broke the silence. 'Had a puncture.'

Sergeant Eric Wallis nodded. He had wondered why his friend

had stopped in the middle of the road.

'I saw your passenger in town a while ago,' the policeman said. 'Sister Dean. She looks very nice. Staying with John and Eve. You're off the day after tomorrow I suppose?'

Fred nodded.

'Nasty business up in Alice Springs.'

'What happened?'

'I don't know the full story yet but an old woman up there's been murdered. Happened only this morning apparently. Mrs Charles. Ran a hotel. Know her?'

Fred shook his head. 'No.'

'Robbery as well as murder, apparently,' Eric Wallis continued. He snicked the Land-Rover into first gear. 'See you later.'

He drove away and Fred Crawford climbed into his own vehicle. He pushed aside the small bag containing a shirt, his shaving gear, the book he had taken to the bore and not read, and his dictionary. He realised he hadn't asked the policeman where he was going, and now wondered. There wasn't much up that way.

The motor cranked into life with reluctance, for the Land-Rover was old. It was a hack, and not one of Fred Crawford's money making vehicles. He began wondering about the nurse and what sort of company she would be on the three-day journey that faced them. He also wondered if he would have a chance to start the book: *Collected Essays of Walter Murdoch*. It was not the sort of book many people in Marree would read. They liked their stories simple and gory. Suddenly he laughed. Here he was, about to act as chauffeur to a good looking girl from the city — and in a part of the country that had a chronic shortage of women — and he was wondering if he would get a chance to read a book. He was only thirty-five but he was starting to think like an old man. It was the monotony, the sheer tedium of doing the same thing, meeting the same few people, doing the same bone-cracking work under the same blistering sun. He needed a change. Maybe taking the nurse to Queensland would inject a little interest into his existence. The prospect, which had embarrassed him, now began to appeal.

He passed the old signpost with its two opposing blades leaning at uneven angles. 'Marree 1' read the sign pointing the way he was travelling. Seemed ridiculous having a sign so close to town, when you could see the railway yards and buildings so clearly. The only people who drove to Marree from the north-west knew the town anyway. The paint on the post was fading and peeling in dry flakes, making the other sign almost impossible to distinguish. There were three numbers that had long since ceased to be recognisable as the figures 279 and the word Oodnadatta had all but disappeared.

Further north than Oodnadatta was Alice Springs. Fred had never been there. He thought of the murder there that morning with a remote indifference and drove into town to start loading the mail truck.

Oodnadatta was four hundred and fifteen miles from Alice Springs, and the first town in all that distance. It lay well to the east of the Stuart Highway, away from any hint of traffic. It was a town that owed its existence to the explorer John McDouall Stuart who was forced that way in making a detour around the bulk of Lake Eyre. The Overland Telegraph Line followed Stuart's route and the railway, when it was pushed north, followed the telegraph line. Only the main road went elsewhere, to dodge the many watercourses scouring the land to the west of the giant lake. The primitive highway and the town it ignored were separated by a low range of dumpling hills that splotched the land in layers of raw reds and whites and gravelly tans, like high points in a bubbled and burnt pancake. Three separate tracks wound their way through the hills from the highway to the town. The middle one, the most direct link, was eighty-two miles long. It was a dusty roller-coaster which kinked, dipped and rose through a succession of jump-ups and dried watercourses, as it followed the way of the lower arm of the Neales, one of the principal river systems of the north. Lake Eyre, four thousand, eight hundred square miles in area and normally dry, was at the centre of a maze of tributaries, which ran to its hub like the fractured spokes of an old wagon wheel.

The Neales was one such spoke. It was bent and splintered in many places for it was as erratic in character as in direction, changing from a deep sandy bed, lacking nothing but regular water, to a tangled frenzy of channels, running shallow and wide across flat country in a frantic quest for somewhere to go. The

Neales was called neither river nor creek because it defied conventional terms. It was a floodway, a series of grooves and flats that scratched a path towards a lake that was usually dry. Its meandering channels linked low places, and were bonded by a common edging of trees, as though to give them direction. The Neales was a desert gutter, gouged by floods and ignored by gentle rains. It was created in moments of fury, but spent most of its life in ages of tranquil aridity.

The track along the Neales to Oodnadatta was rough. In fact, all the journey had been rough, but this was the worst part, and the utility truck, mobile again after its crash into the creek bank, shook and twisted like a creature in pain. The two men had spent almost two hours repairing it. Johnny Parsons, who had driven since the crash, originally had allowed fourteen hours for the total journey. He knew that was not a lot of time for a rough road. The average seemed reasonable, a mere 29.6 miles per hour. He had worked it out carefully, for he was meticulous with his calculations. They had carried fuel for the whole distance, not just to maintain security but to ensure they could drive all the way without a delay caused by some outback garage being closed or having run out of petrol. He had heard of that happening, when he was in Coober Pedy where the idea of the opal robbery had first arisen. Now he was angry. His plan was endangered because of the other man's stupidity. Of course he had known the tight time schedule would allow little margin for trouble. He was not a gambler. Just the opposite. He was scornful of people who took risks without doing what they could to nullify them. Some gained zest by a heady confrontation with chance. Not Johnny Parsons. His greatest joy came from achieving what he expected and planned to do. And here he was, with the whole venture in jeopardy because the other man couldn't steer a truck through a wide creek bed. They were mobile again, but the steering was bent and their progress was slow. The front tyres, knocked out of alignment by the impact, groaned with every turn and the steering wheel shook in his hands. He had never ridden a horse but he could imagine the wheel, shaking and fighting his hands, as the head of some powerful and cantankerous beast. With the intensity of one hostile animal confronting another, he hated that wheel and the truck that was carrying them too slowly towards Oodnadatta.

Getting to the airfield on time was essential, more than ever since that old woman had fouled things up by walking into the office. Her death would increase the intensity of the search. That concerned him. Not her death. Her dying was a worry to him only because it would sharpen the police effort and he had made all his plans on a given set of happenings. Her stumbling on to them had not been one of his assumptions and he cursed her for it. Then he forgot her. The stricken truck, shaking as though in its death throes, jarred every thought from his mind except the necessity to reach Oodnadatta. The track was awful, winding and dipping incessantly. His arms ached.

The annoying thing, to a man who prided himself on his organisational ability and forward thinking, was that the trouble had happened on the one truly risky segment of the venture. Fourteen hours was a tight schedule for four hundred and fifteen miles over such a road. But the essence of the plan, the guarantee of their escape and journey to Darwin being successful, was in the timing. He had always planned to leave some false clue to the timing of the robbery in the hotel office. The woman's arrival and subsequent happenings had made him forget — temporarily. But now the clue was there in the broken clock, and they had a three and a half hour start over the imagination of the Alice Springs police.

A driving time of fourteen hours to Oodnadatta was tight, but ten and a half hours was next to impossible. The timing had to be close, to give them that sort of margin. More time for the journey and they could be instant suspects. But not with ten and a half hours. They would never be suspected. Particularly as they were going to be flying back, returning to the town. Several times he let the logic tumble through his mind and it always fell right way up. Now all they had to do was catch the plane. It had better be late. He had given up checking the time for he knew it was close to four o'clock. Surely the plane would be late. Just a little. Everything ran late up this way.

The crash had broken one of the truck's headlamps and deranged a mudguard. Dirt clung to the battered grille and was packed tightly in pockets of metal at the front of the vehicle. Such disfigurement was merely cosmetic. The real damage was to the steering. A tie rod had been bent and the two men had worked desperately to fix it, removing the rod and trying to beat it straight on the rocks of the creek bed. They had been partly successful: the vehicle was driveable but the wheels nosed outwards at such an angle that driving it was hell.

Johnny Parsons had been at the wheel now for five hours. His wrists and arms ached and were becoming numbed from the effort of holding the utility through a succession of rock-strewn watercourses and rutted crossings. Even when the track ran straight, the truck tried to dart to the left with a stubborn insistence that was exhausting him. He was not a good driver and certainly not a keen one, but he was determined. His plan was in danger and therefore he was at the wheel, in control.

Frog had dozed at first but now sat slumped beside him, silent but awake. The utility shuddered drunkenly through a succession of pot holes, sending a cloud of fine white dust rising from the floor. Frog coughed himself upright. 'What's the time now, Johnny?' he asked.

The driver didn't move his eyes from the narrow road.

'We going to make it Johnny?'

'We'd better.' He sneezed mud on to a grimy handkerchief and lowered his eyes for a moment to inspect it. The cloth was flecked with dried blood, where he had been wiping a cut on his forehead, caused by the crash. He fingered the wound before speaking again.

'Only a few miles to go, I reckon. If only you hadn't bent the wheels back there, we'd have sailed in.' He blew his nose again.

The truck began to bump violently. It was nosing off the road and heading along two wheeltracks, baked deep in brick-hard mud. Johnny tried to swing to the right but the utility followed the tracks, like a tram on its lines. He swung harder. The truck started to climb clear then slid back and scraped to a stop with its belly on the high central ridge.

He swore violently and stormed out. The utility was caught in the tracks left by a bigger truck which had tried to blaze a detour after rain.

He climbed back in the cabin and wrenched the gear lever into reverse. The truck shook with power before painfully grating its way back through the ruts. He had no desire to save the vehicle. He wanted to punish it.

'You can't go on,' Frog called, having jumped out to examine the truck. 'Your wheels are way out of plumb again.'

'Bugger the wheels. Get in.'
'But you'll never drive it like that. You'll scrub out the tyres.'
'Bugger the tyres,' he roared. 'Get in, you stupid prick. Get in.'
The truck lurched forward. It swung hard to the left and stopped with a squeal of brakes.
'This blasted steering,' Johnny exploded. He let in the clutch again and steered hard to the right. The truck gathered speed and ran straight, on tyres wailing a low-pitched protest. He accelerated and the truck began to veer to the left. A harder turn to the right and the wail of the tyres became a shriek. The wheels hit a bump and jarred the steering wheel from his hand. The truck spun to the left and he braked hard.
Frog catapulted against the windscreen and then thumped to his knees on the floor. He pushed himself back to the seat, leaving one bracing arm against the dashboard.
His eyes were wide in distress. 'We'll never make it like this, Johnny,' he wailed.
'How long will it take you to straighten it this time?'
'Maybe half an hour.'
'We've only got minutes, if that. We'll go on.'
They rolled into a shallow creek bed and he lost control coming out. The truck steam-rolled a curving path through low bushes before Johnny dragged it back to the road. For two more minutes he drove a maddening, weaving path to the east. A silver reflection in the distance winked at them.
'Frog. Look. Oodnadatta. That's the sun on the tin roofs.'
'Are we going to make it, Johnny?'
He did not answer, but tried to go faster. Instead they began curling to the left. He started to ease off when Frog tapped the windscreen violently.
'Johnny. The roof. It's moving. Look.'
Johnny stared hard at the glittering object rising from the horizon. For ten seconds he followed its path into the sky. Then he stopped the truck.
'That's our plane, Frog. We missed it.'

'You were a sailor? Now what would a sailor be doing out here, in a town like this?' Barbara Dean could not disguise her astonishment. Fred Crawford shuffled his boots in embarrassment. Being introduced to the new sister while he was dressed like this, naked but for his shorts and boots and a coating of dust, was a big enough ordeal in itself without his life history being dragged into it. But that was like John Black. The Marree postmaster never talked if he could make a speech, and he had introduced Fred with a sixty second summary of his life.

'I could understand a sailor retiring to live on the coast,' the girl continued, 'but you could hardly be farther from the sea.'

'I haven't exactly retired,' Fred said.

She looked puzzled and John Black, his desire to please her wound as tight as a clock spring, mimicked the expression.

'I still work,' Fred said. 'You said something about retiring to the coast.'

Now she was embarrassed, and Fred immediately regretted the way he had twisted the conversation. Curse John. He had arranged this, making sure the new sister was stationed outside the post office as Fred drove into town. Must have been watching for the first sign of his Land-Rover coming back from Muloorina, and then trundled her out on to the footpath. Now the meeting had taken on the atmosphere of a jousting match, because of the postmaster's love of stage-managing things.

It was hot in the sun, and Fred would have preferred to have had a drink and to have washed himself and put on a few more clothes before meeting the sister he was scheduled to take up to Birdsville. He wondered if he should have shaken hands. She looked as though she might have offered hers, but he had hesitated because his hands were calloused and dirty and, anyhow, the moment had gone. Now they were talking about sailors, for God's sake.

'Well, I was in the navy,' Fred said, wondering why he was continuing this conversation. 'There's a difference.'

'Oh,' she said.

'Between that and being a sailor.'

'Yes.' She smiled. She didn't know what she should say. Every man out here seemed so sure of himself. Like the tall man in front of her. He was exactly as she had imagined a man of the outback would be. Tall, lean, a little remote. Very relaxed, the way he stood there, with a natural grace that his light coating of dust and salty, male smell accentuated. She was talking too much. Her mother used to tell her that she talked too much. Or rather, said too much. There was a difference, just like there was between being a sailor and merely being in the navy.

'It's so dry out here, and empty,' she said, waving her arm in an arc as though sweeping Marree's buildings out of the way.

'Yes. No sign of the sea. I see what you mean.'

She smiled and John Black laughed a split-second later. He spoke to Fred: 'Sister Dean came in on the train this morning.'

Fred nodded and she nodded and therefore Black nodded. 'I was telling her all about you and just mentioned you were in the navy during the war because you'd told me many times how much this country reminds you of the sea. It's the space.'

Space? That's not the correct word, Fred thought, but nodded. This girl was very attractive. Much better looking than Sister Jennings, whom she was replacing. There were two nursing sisters at the Australian Inland Mission hospital. Esme Jennings had retired early, before her stint was completed, and Barbara Dean was replacing her. Poor Esme had been friendly and efficient but fat. Sister Dean was going to cause quite a stir at Birdsville. He wondered how she would find life in such a small and isolated community. Not everyone could accept it. Esme hadn't. She had ended up hating half the town which, he reflected, was only a couple of people. The former sister had grown to detest the publican because of the time he refused to fix the washing machine, and she had been in constant conflict with the policeman's wife who wouldn't accept anyone who hadn't been born in the district and didn't like anyone who had. Esme's tirades against the townsfolk had grown more bitter until she had become sick and had to leave.

'Can you fix a washing machine?' he asked Barbara.

She looked surprised. 'Will I have to?' She smiled. My God, Fred thought, smile like that and you could get the publican to fix anything, even if poor, fat Esme couldn't get him to walk down the street.

'I was told we would have to be self-sufficient,' she continued. 'But I'm not too sure about mechanical things. I know one sister looks after the patients one week while the other does the housework and then we change. I suppose the housework includes fixing things. I didn't know the washing machine wasn't working.'

'Oh, it's working all right now,' he said, feeling more relaxed. He leaned against the wall of the post office. 'It's just something your predecessor had trouble with.'

'Fred fixed it for her,' John Black said.

'Oh,' she said. 'You'll be a very welcome visitor then.'

Fred uncrossed his ankles and took some of his weight from the wall.

'How often will we see you at the hospital?'

'Once a fortnight.' He paused and no one else spoke. He stood straight, clear of the wall. 'I'd better go and do some work or we won't make it this trip at all. Got a lot to do and only a bit over a day to get everything done.'

'Yes, of course,' she said.

'See you for dinner,' John Black said.

Fred got back in the Land-Rover and drove off. He wished he could have found the words that would have made it easy for him to have remained.

Eight miles north west of Oodnadatta, a squadron of hawks circled high in the air, wheeling and soaring above an expanse of clay and grass and scrub. They were town birds, who normally hovered around the fringe of the settlement and devoured rubbish, sniped at mice and occasionally pecked out the eyes of young goats. But Oodnadatta dozed in the afternoon heat and the hawks had drifted towards the horizon, to a place where their sharp eyes had detected movement. They circled above a cluster of trees and bushes, into which two men had driven a truck and were now trying to camouflage it behind a crude wall of branches. The hawks watched with interest, scanning the area for discarded food, or disturbed lizards. The men, concerned only with detection from ground level worked for several minutes, breaking limbs from bushes in the centre of the clump of timber, and stacking them against the sides of the vehicle. They ate no food, and discarded nothing. Then they crawled into the shadows to sleep, for they were exhausted.

Above them, the hawks continued to circle, their dart-like tails twitching and warping to hold the gliding patterns they followed in their quest for food. The birds stayed aloft, drifting, patient, searching, while the sun burned its way towards the horizon. The two men slept. The air pulsed with rising heat, and the hawks floated back towards town, like blackened leaves spiralling above a fire.

The sun was low, and Fred Crawford was still working. He had been loading the truck he used on the Marree to Birdsville mail run, and now he was filling the tank.

He was working in the backyard of his home. The house was small. It had a verandah that ran across the back of the building and contained his single bed, a couple of hanging water bags and odd pieces of machinery.

The yard had one large shed that served as a workshop, an outdoor toilet whose wooden door refused to close, and a couple of peppercorn trees. It was a big area, surrounded by a corrugated iron fence that kept out the sand when the wind blew.

Like the yards that sprawled from most outback homes, Fred's was a mess. One corner was a wilderness of worn tyres, broken timber and leaking drums. The soil around this area was black with oil. A row of empty forty-four gallon drums stood nearby. Beside them was an elevated frame that held a block and tackle he used to lift heavy items. A few paces away, near the fence, yawned a trench that served as a vehicle inspection pit. Years of oily rain, dripping from the engines, gearboxes, transfer cases, steering boxes and differentials fitted to a variety of machines, had left the bottom of the pit as sticky as treacle. Oxyacetylene cylinders leaned against the fence, next to a ramshackle pile of cartons and wooden crates that had once carried cans of soup, washing powder, bottles of beer, tinned vegetables and the other necessities of Fred Crawford's life.

A shirt hung from a clothes line strung between a verandah post and a tall radio mast at the fence. The shirt was so dry it had become as stiff as cardboard.

A broad water tank, made from corrugated iron, squatted between the house and the shed. The shadows cast by a peppercorn tree rippled across the tank's silver-grey wall, camouflaging its galvanised ugliness. Pipes ran to the tank from the guttering edging the roofs of both the house and the shed. It was a big tank. It had to be, because rain rarely fell but when it came, it was likely to be a deluge. When that happened, every cupfull had to be retained for the long spells of drought.

A number of vehicles stood in the yard. There was his Land-Rover, a tractor that didn't work and a small front-end loader that did, an ancient International with left-hand drive, a semi-trailer prime mover, an uncoupled low loader with a set of rear wheels missing, and the truck he used for the run to Birdsville.

The mail truck was big and square and worn beyond belief. It was a Chevrolet. Or it had been. Its badges and other signs of identity had fallen off or been worn away. The Chev had begun its working life with the Australian army, having been delivered in the final year of the war. In that time, it had covered ten thousand miles of nose-to-tail convoys, following and leading strings of identical vehicles. Since its military days, the square-nosed Chev had covered six times that distance. That was not an excessive mileage for a truck operating under normal conditions, but the mailman's ex-army Chev didn't operate normally. In its last sixty thousand miles, the truck had rarely passed another vehicle. It served in isolation in one of the roughest regions of the world. Its wheels created the track they now followed every two weeks. Not quite thirteen years old, the truck had a worn and battered look that suggested great age.

Fred Crawford took perverse pride in the fact that the truck looked bad, but ran well — if with some idiosyncrasies that demanded special care at the wheel. Like jumping out of four-wheel drive. He had to drive with his hand or leg against the lever to keep the drive engaged. He'd have to fix that one day. Maybe at the end of this trip.

Fred had bought the truck for three hundred pounds. He had found it in Adelaide, in a yard filled with scores of surplus army vehicles: big trucks, Bren gun carriers and jeeps that had been built in a rush to win the war and were being overwhelmed, at nature's leisure, by rust and paspalum. He had chosen the Chev because of its size and because it had four-wheel drive. He needed that, to operate in the Channel Country. He had also bought a set of oversized wheels and a stock of wide, bar-tread tyres, to increase clearance, and, through the wider spread of rubber, improve the truck's traction in sand.

The big wheels exaggerated the truck's ungainly appearance. Part loaded, it had the look of a child's toy, an out-of-proportion push-along truck with tall wheels, fat tyres and a stack of wooden blocks on its back. But it was functional. That was a word the mail contractor favoured.

FUNC—TION—AL: having some use. Well, his old Chev had certainly had some use, Fred reflected. An easy life in the army, serving the nation, and a hard life in civvie use, serving a few people in one of the loneliest parts of the country. None of the old military maintenance schemes for this Chev. He just kept in order those things that were necessary to keep the truck rolling. When things fell off, they stayed off, unless they were vital to progress. As a result, the Royal Mail went to Birdsville in a vehicle that lacked such niceties as one headlamp, the front number plate and even padding on the seats.

Fred heard the gurgling sound which indicated the tank was almost full and eased his rate of pumping. The tank was a forty-four gallon drum that lay flat and was strapped to the side of the chassis. He had converted the drum to a fuel tank by sealing the normal openings and welding a filling spout to the upper surface. It was a conversion that worked well. The original tank had fallen off.

In this truck, Fred Crawford drove up and down the Birdsville Track once a fortnight. Eight hundred miles or more, depending on the weather and his choice of detours, over a track that was so rough and potentially dangerous that no other vehicle and no other person — bar his assistant — tackled it regularly.

Fred tightened the petrol cap and looked at the vehicle with affection. It had a rough life, churning its way slowly over the sandhills, rumbling across wide stretches of gibber plain, following the grooved wheeltracks that its own tyres had carved in the desert. There were salt pans to avoid, basins of bulldust to drag at the wheels and, on some occasions, flooded rivers to cross.

Fred Crawford carried a lot of goods for private individuals along the track, but it was the government contract for hauling and delivering the mail that gave the job its financial backbone. He was paid by the mile and so he charged the Postmaster-General for a journey of four hundred and twenty miles. That was what the signpost at Birdsville said. The fact that the signpost here in Marree indicated three hundred and twenty-five miles was no more than a slight embarrassment. If anyone wanted to check the distance, he could drive to Birdsville himself. John Black, the Marree postmaster, had never been up the track and he was the man who counted because he authorised the payments. Anyhow, there was no set distance for the journey. Fred himself made the road. A grader had only been up the first ninety miles and from there on, it was just wheeltracks. Mostly his. His track was the definitive version. Definitive but of infinite variety. If there was rain and a salt pan became soft and too treacherous to cross, he had to detour around it. Sometimes, after a long spell of dry weather, the sand became so powdery on the crests of the dunes that he had to cut fresh tracks and, often, plate his way across. That was a slow, exhausting task, laying his stack of flat metal plates on the sand in front of the truck. He drove on them like a train following a railway line, only he had to drag the used plates from behind the vehicle and lay them ahead, to support the truck again as it inched its way across the soft sand.

Goyder Lagoon, up to the north, was flooded now and he was faced with the looping detour to the east, around Damperannie Well. That meant he would cover well over four hundred miles this journey, and be in the low gears for much of the way. Not much profit this time, he thought.

Using a long tyre lever, Fred tightened the cap on the drum from which he had completed filling the truck's tank, and then used the lever to tap on the row of drums already loaded on the back of the truck. They contained spare fuel and water. Their dull boom confirmed they were full. He knew that, but liked the reassurance of the sound.

A bearded man walked from the shed. 'I fixed the puncture on the Land-Rover, Fred,' he siad.

'Good. I'm through here.' Fred put the tyre lever on top of the part-empty forty-four gallon drum. He picked up a cloth and wiped his hands. Christ, they were calloused. He thought again of his meeting with the sister and was glad he hadn't shaken hands. He had felt rough and uncomfortable in her presence. What had she thought? That he was rough and dirty? Well, he was. He flung down the cloth. His mind could play with fancy words and he could imagine all the conversations he liked, but the fact was that he was rough and dirty, his hands had callouses like sea shells, and he had trouble stringing together sentences and meaningful words when it counted. He wiped his hands together. They were as worn and damaged and dirty as the truck he drove.

'Come on,' he said to his companion. 'Let's get over to the railway and collect those big tyres before it gets dark.'

CHAPTER THREE

Frog Gardiner drove the utility truck into town as quietly as possible, rumbling along Oodnadatta's wide and dusty main street at the slowest speed the vehicle would tolerate in top gear. The two men had waited for more than an hour after sunset before leaving their hiding place in the trees. They wanted to enter Oodnadatta unseen, and the night was obliging them, for its blackness hung over the small town like the drapes of a velvet curtain. A few buildings ruffled the base of the velvet, lifting it to reveal spangles of light glinting from doors and windows. No one was on the street.

They drew level with the store, a low, wide building on their right. A wedge of light issued from the store's open doorway. Frog slipped the gear lever into neutral and allowed the truck to roll quietly past the building. The cloud of dust pursuing them along the street reached the zone of light and transformed it into a rectangular shaft of brown that billowed and thickened as the dust grains swirled angrily in the air. Frog swung the vehicle to the right, so that the solitary headlamp beam swept the edge of the road. He saw no one. He stopped and switched off the motor.

Johnny Parsons struck a match and lit a cigarette. The sudden flare of light so close startled Frog. He was surprised to see how tired and dirty Johnny looked. Perspiration had glued a thick coating of dust to his companion's face. His eyes, concentrating on the cigarette, were sunken and looked sore. A thin stubble broke through his chin and his usually neat hair was unruly and dusty.

Johnny inhaled deeply, then pursed his lips and played the smoke down on the bag resting on his lap.

'You got a plan yet?' Frog interrupted. 'Decided what we should do?'

The other man stared at the reflection of his burning cigarette in the windscreen before replying. 'We'll have to go back, Frog. By road.' He turned to face his companion. 'Nothing else for it. Fix the steering and then head back to the Alice. No one would suspect us. Not this late. Least, they shouldn't. It's not the sort of thing they'd expect us to do, is it?' He sounded uncertain.

He paused to draw on the cigarette. Frog remained silent.

'In any case,' Johnny continued, 'there's nowhere to go from here.' He raised his free hand to his face, and squeezed the bridge of his nose, as though to press out the tiredness inflaming his eyes.

'How about the plane?' Frog cut in. 'We've still got tickets. Wouldn't that be easier?'

'It'd be easier all right, but a lot more dangerous by the time the next plane comes through.'

Johnny stopped suddenly. He realised he had been speaking loudly. He twisted his head to look back towards the store. Softly, he continued: 'No, the plane's too dangerous now. The whole point in catching the plane was the time factor. We'd have caught the plane too early for anyone to have connected us with the job. Too risky now. Anyhow, I'm not going to try and change the tickets. The bloke who sold them would get all curious. Especially with all the dirt.'

He thumped his jacket and dust flew out.

'But what about the ute, Johnny?' Frog asked. 'We were going to leave it where we found it, so's when the owner comes back he won't suspect nothing.'

'We've still got a few days until he gets back, Frog. We know that. By the time he reports it missing, we'll be clear of Alice Springs. We can dump it well outside the town if we like, where no one will find it for a while. The place is lousy with abandoned trucks and utes and things. We can hitch a ride on the bitumen with a truckie or even get on the bus to Darwin.'

'Christ, I don't like the sound of that.'

'Well, one thing's certain. We can't stay here. This ute's hot around here for one thing. We can't go near the pub because we stopped there on the way up. The only bloke I want to see in Oodnadatta this time is the storekeeper and he hasn't seen me before. We've got to have something to eat and drink.' Johnny rubbed his dusty lips. 'I'm dry, but we'll have to stick to soft stuff.' He opened the door. 'Stay here while I go and get something. All you've got to do is mind the bags and keep your head down. Don't talk if anyone comes by and sees you. Pretend you're asleep.' He slid out of the seat. 'See you later.'

Johnny groped his way around the back of the truck and made towards the lighted doorway. Inside, someone was whistling. The sound ceased as Johnny's feet grated in a loose patch of gravel at the entrance.

A bald, middle-aged man looked up. He was behind the counter, and had been reading a magazine. He wore a blue singlet. Above him a pressure lantern, studded with insects, blazed down on his bald head. His skin was burnt brown and looked like soft, rippling, aged leather. The lights cast shadows in the folds of his skin, making it appear too big and loose for his frame.

The man straightened up painfully. 'What a curse it is to be getting old,' he grinned. 'G' day.'

'Er, g'day,' Johnny answered. 'I want some drink and some food.'

'Who doesn't?' The man shut the magazine and turned towards the shelves. 'What, for instance?'

Johnny ordered bottles of soft drink and tinned meat.

The storekeeper began to collect the order. 'Just got in, eh? Staying long?' he asked, as he stretched for a top shelf.

'No.'

'You look as though you've had a hard day. Where are you making for?' He stacked a pile of tins on the counter and glanced at Johnny who was staring down at the floor.

'Alice Springs,' Johnny mumbled.

'Don't tell me you've driven from Marree.'

Johnny looked up sharply. 'Pardon?'

'I said have you come from Marree?'

Johnny nodded.

'What, on your own?'

'Er, yes. Not many come through from there, eh?'

'No, I'll say not. But the road's not as bad as they make out, is it? Lot better than it used to be when they drafted the road maps.' He picked a map out of a dusty display folder on the counter and waved it. 'Listen to this, will yer. "Motorists are advised to go by train between Port Augusta and Alice Springs",' he quoted. 'That's even for the main road. Lot of bullshit. You'd think they were talking about the Marree to Birdsville Track. That is bad, but it doesn't matter because it goes nowhere.'

Johnny took the map from him and opened it. His eyes searched for Marree. 'How does the road to Alice Springs compare with the one I've been on?' he asked slowly.

'Oh, you'll find it a lot better, especially when you reach the main road. Some of the creek crossings are bad though. Watch out for them or you could soon knock something off. But on the whole it's good. Come from Adelaide?'

Johnny nodded without looking up from the map. He had located Oodnadatta and found the road beside the railway line to Marree, below Lake Eyre.

The storekeeper was still talking. 'You've certainly come up the hard way. Must have been on business, eh?'

Johnny nodded. He could see two other routes from Marree. One still followed the railway south to Port Augusta and Adelaide; the other, a dotted line only, ran north to Birdsville in Queensland. So that was the road to nowhere.

'I suppose you were too early for the roadblocks,' the man was chatting on.

Johnny looked up slowly. 'Pardon?'

'I said I suppose you missed the roadblocks at Port Augusta. Oh yes, of course you would. Only set up today. You'll strike quite a few from now on. That's a mighty big search they've got on.'

'Oh, who are they looking for?'

'A killer.'

'Oh.'

'Yes, someone killed poor old Mrs Charles at Alice Springs sometime around dawn this morning. Did you know Mrs Charles?'

'No, haven't been up this way before.'

'Well, she was one of the real personalities at the Alice. Ran one of the pubs there — good pub, too. Now she's dead.' He thumped two tins of compressed meat together. 'Bashed to pieces. Came over the radio today. All day. They're asking all people along the way out of Alice to watch for vehicles going out. Keep your eyes open, will you? That enough meat?'

'That's good,' Johnny answered. 'And six bottles of drink. What should I look for?'

'Eh?'

'You said keep your eyes open. What's the man they're looking for driving?'

'Can't say mate. Lemonade do you?' He waited for Johnny's nod before bending painfully beneath the counter. 'Oh, my flaming back,' he groaned. 'Maybe it'd get better if I drank some of this stuff myself, eh? It's not real cold but at least it's not so warm you can't touch it.' His hand steadied the bottle and he disappeared below the counter for more.

'No, it's hard to say what you should look for. The police aren't even sure themselves. There are a whole lot of opals missing — belonged to a man staying at the pub, a Yank — so they reckon it's a cert the thief's shot through. Not that there need be only one man mixed up in it, I reckon. Could be a couple or even a gang. Goodness knows.'

He straightened himself slowly and thumped the last bottle on the counter. 'That'll be eighteen bob. Anything else I can get?'

Johnny had begun to screw the map in his fingers. 'Ah, no. No thanks,' he answered and fumbled for some money. He made a show of noticing the map. 'Oh, I'd better take this too,' he said, waving the crumpled paper. 'I've made it a bit second-hand.'

'That's another four bob. Want these wrapped?' He pointed to the tins and bottles.

Johnny shook his head and gave him the money. 'How long have they been watching the roads?' he asked.

'Well, we first heard they were setting up roadblocks about noon. Believe they've set up a check where the road from here joins the main north-south road. You'll strike that eighty miles or so on. Be a good place to have a rest. They'd be glad of some company. Not much goes through.'

'I reckon I'd go straight on. I'm in a bit of a hurry. They

wouldn't want to stop me, would they, coming this way?'

'Probably give you the once over. They're pretty wound up. You should have heard the calls going over the pedal radio this arvo. Just like a search for a lost kid, only different. A lot of these coves would probably shoot the bloke if they found him. Good thing, too.'

Johnny nodded agreement. 'Have they seen anyone yet?'

'Nope. Oh, a few truckies and that sort of thing but all accounted for. That is, all except one and, by gee, you might be able to help there. A rider reported in at one of the stations that he saw a couple of blokes in a ute stuck in a creek this morning. He was with a mob of cattle a fair way off and didn't speak to them, but he reckons they were in a fair bit of strife. They were belting away at something. That was on the main road, though, a fair way from here. You'd be there sometime in the morning.'

Johnny put the map on the counter, rubbing the wrinkles out of it and carefully folding it. 'What sort of ute was it? Did the bloke who saw it say?'

The storekeeper looked surprised. He scratched his stomach. 'Wouldn't have a clue. Hang on. Red. That's what I heard. He reckons it was red. There's a few red utes around, unfortunately.' He smiled. 'Even that burnt-out International near the last rail crossing. Used to belong to my brother. Bloody thing caught fire as he was driving along. Fuel line came off and sprayed petrol all over the exhaust. The thing had only done twelve thousand miles. The fire didn't leave much, did it? You'd have noticed it back there?'

Before Johnny could answer, a raucous blast pierced the silence. He spun round towards the door.

Behind him, the storekeeper smiled. 'Just the train pulling in mate. Diesel. Horn makes a helluva noise, if you're not used to it.' He looked up at an alarm clock perched on a biscuit tin on a shelf. 'It's late. They musta been checking it along the line.'

The sound came again, a blaring noise that grew in strength and then died amid a shrieking, metallic squeal. 'It's from Alice Springs, is it?' Johnny was calm again.

'Yeah. Going where you've come from. They're checking the train too. It's normally late of course, but this is later than normal. Bert Morgan's been waiting for it for the last hour or two. He's the constable. He's got to check the passengers.'

'He's down at the station, is he?'

'Yeah, otherwise he'd probably be up checking on radio calls from the homesteads or watching the road. He'll be up all night. Probably enjoys it, you know. Change from collaring nothing but an occasional black on the grog. Nice bloke, Bert. Anyhow, you're right now mate, aren't you?'

'Yes,' Johnny answered. 'I'll be shoving off.' He picked up his tins and bottles from the counter, balanced himself and then made for the doorway. 'Be seeing you,' he called over his shoulder.

'Yes, mate. Good trip,' the main said, 'and watch out, eh?' He scratched a loose fold of skin under his singlet. 'Call again,' he muttered to himself, and then turned back to his magazine.

Johnny stumbled out into the darkness. This time, with no light to guide him he kept close to the store wall beneath the awning. He took three steps and then his foot hit a low object. He stumbled and heard a gasp and a shuffling, down in the shadows. Someone was sitting on the path. 'Sorry mate,' came a voice.

Johnny ignored him. He straightened himself, tightened his grip on his purchases and stepped warily towards the utility. He could see its shape in the first feeble light of the rising moon. He walked up and tapped on the running board with the toe of one shoe.

Frog leaned across to open the door. 'Everything okay?' he asked in a whisper.

'We're okay, Frog. Here, take these bottles and stow them where they won't break. And keep your voice down. There's at least one bloke over there in the shadows. I just trod on him.'

'When are we going to eat?' Frog asked.

'While we're fixing the tie rod. We'll refuel from the last drums at the same time. Let's get out of here quickly.'

'Okay. Hang on while I turn the truck around.'

'We're not turning back,' Johnny replied. 'There's been a change in plan. We're going south. To a place called Marree.'

The storekeeper was still reading the magazine when he heard the utility's motor start. Footsteps crunched on the gravel outside and he looked up to see an Aboriginal stockman at the doorway. He lowered his head and resumed reading.

The stockman shuffled into the store. He raised his right leg and rested an elastic-sided riding boot on a sack propped against the counter. He began to rub his shin. 'Geeze, my leg's sore,' he said.

'Oh?' The storekeeper kept reading.

'Yeah, the cove who just came out of your shop trod on it.'

'What can you expect if you sit in the middle of the footpath.' He turned a page.

'Trod fair on the bone with his heel. Geeze, he hurt.' He gave his shin one final rub, then stood gingerly on his leg. He shook his foot and walked slowly to the doorway. Outside, the tail light of the truck had vanished in the night.

He turned and leaned against the doorway. 'What was he doing here, Mac, do you know?'

'Nope.' The storekeeper licked his finger and turned another page. 'Just come in from Marree.'

'No he never, Mac.'

'Well, he told me he did. And now he's off to Alice Springs.' He flipped over several pages.

'Well, he's just taken the Marree road. And I seen him and the other bloke drive in from the north.' He stuck his thumbs in his belt and leaned more heavily against the doorway. 'You got it the wrong way round, Mac.'

The storekeeper closed the magazine and slowly pushed himself upright. 'Now let's have all that again,' he said.

Twenty one miles south-east of Oodnadatta, the red International squealed to a stop with its headlight focused on a leaning signpost.

'"Railway STOP Crossing",' Frog laboriously read from the sign. '"Penalty for failure to stop, £50."' They mean business, don't they? It's so flat you could see anything coming for miles. Well, we've stopped. We don't want to break the law, do we Johnny?' He laughed and leaned out of the window to throw an empty lemonade bottle at the sign.

'We want to find that abandoned truck, that's what we want to do,' Johnny snapped. He peered into the darkness beside the road. 'All that lemonade you've been guzzling has made you a bit light in the head. They're looking for us in this ute and the way it is now you could run faster than it. We've got to find that other truck the storekeeper was talking about, and take its tie rod off and put it on ours. Then maybe we'll start to make good time.'

'You're sure it's an International?'

'That's what he said.'

Frog raised his hands from the steering wheel. 'Well, it's not on this side of the line. Hasn't been a sign of it up to now.' He snicked the gear lever into first. 'Will I go on?'

Johnny was still looking through the side window. 'We can't stay here all night.' He twisted straight. 'Yes, go on. It must be on the other side.'

Slowly the truck rumbled on to the crossing. It crunched over the loose metal and then swung left, sending its light raking through the sparse scrub flanking the curve.

Each man saw the wreck at the same time. It was a blackened shell. The wheels were gone, letting its belly rest on the edge of the grassless claypan. Frog drove to within five feet of the wreck, letting the light burn into the blackened and blistered body. 'Well, it's an International,' he said. 'But it's a wreck. Burnt right out.'

Johnny had begun to climb from his seat. 'Well, the tie rod should still be all right, shouldn't it?' he called, walking into the light. 'Come on Frog,' he beckoned with his head, 'have a look will you?'

The fat man climbed down. His legs were stiff, and he walked awkwardly to the wrecked vehicle. He kneeled beside the front mudguard. He lowered his head and peered in. 'It's not there,' he announced. 'Someone's stripped it. This thing,' he rapped the mudguard, 'is only a hollow shell.'

Johnny stamped his foot on the hard clay. He turned to Frog, staring at him for several seconds. 'Well partner,' he said, 'it looks like you fix the one we've got straight away.'

'Oh geeze, Johnny,' Frog pleaded, 'She's so bent and I've just about had it. I've had practically no sleep for two days. What say we have a feed and spend the night here and do something in the morning?'

'We do it now. We're too close to Oodnadatta for a rest. You sit on your blot here all night and you'll probably be sitting on it for the rest of your lazy life in the jug at Adelaide. Come on.'

'Can't we have something to eat first?' Frog persisted. 'I'm so hungry I feel sick.'

Johnny ran his tongue over his teeth. 'Yeah, I could do with something too. No use starving ourselves. We've still got a long way to go tonight. But we'll have to be quick. Where'd you put the tins?'

'Beside the seat.'

He reached into the cabin and took out two tins. He threw one across the bonnet to Frog. 'There's a key on the side to open it with,' he called. With his key he unrolled the top of the tin and shook the compressed meat into his left hand. He took a big bite and chewed wolfishly. 'By Christ,' he called, pushing an escaping morsel back into the corner of his mouth, 'I'd forgotten how hungry I was.'

Suddenly he walked to the utility's cabin, reached in and switched off the light.

'What did you do that for?' Frog protested.

Johnny didn't answer. Instead he turned towards Oodnadatta. He stood motionless, listening. Frog began to speak again but was hushed into silence. As if to test his hearing Johnny hurled the empty tin out on to the claypan and listened to its dull thud as it landed. Then he turned back along the road and stood in silence.

'What is it, Johnny?' Frog whispered.

'Thought I heard something,' Johnny answered softly. 'Like something coming.'

He listened again, turning his head and cupping one hand around his ear to catch any sound.

'There it is again. Listen, that rumbling noise.' He paused, frozen in an attitude of absolute concentration, and then slapped his knee. 'Of course, of course. The train.' He laughed. 'Just the train. I'm getting jumpy. Anyhow, we'll leave the lights off. We don't want anyone on the train seeing us as they shoot by.'

'Wish I was on it,' muttered Frog. 'They're going to get to Marree a long time before we do. *If* we do, with this bomb like it is.'

Johnny looked hard at the shadowy outline of their crippled truck and then peered intently along the line. In the distance he could just make out a faint light.

'Will they, by Christ,' he said, and turned towards Frog. 'Get up, quickly.' He slapped the squatting man hard on the shoulder, knocking the meat tin from his grasp.

'Get in the truck and drive it across the claypan to the first bunch of trees you see and park it underneath. Hide it from the road. And get back here on the double. Otherwise you'll miss the train. I'm going to try and stop it.' He looked back along the line. The light had brightened and was now a steady flicker of white in the distance.

'Move, Frog, move,' he yelled and then suddenly added, 'Oh for Christ's sake, hold on a sec.' He ran to the cabin and took the bag with the opals from his seat. 'Hell, imagine leaving these.'

Frog started the motor with a roar. 'Hold on,' Johnny yelled above the engine. He ran to the back and took off a four gallon drum of petrol. 'Okay,' he called. Frog didn't hear him. He dropped the drum and ran to the front. He thumped the driver's door with his fist. 'Okay,' he yelled, waving his thumb towards the claypan. 'Hide it — and be quick. And keep the lights off.' He glanced back at the line. The light was clear now and the rumble had grown distinct.

He picked up the drum. He ran, a slow, unbalanced jog, towards the level crossing. He reached it out of breath and with his fingers numb from weight. On the line, the rumbling of the advancing locomotive changed to a faint buzz; the rails were vibrating, as though shaking in anticipation of the great weight bearing down on them. The light was still a long way away, but sharply in focus now, aiming straight at him down the middle of the twin rails of steel. From far away, he heard the sound of the utility's motor die. He turned, but could see nothing but the faint outline of trees. Good. The vehicle was out of sight.

He dropped the drum in the middle of the tracks and unscrewed the cap. He splashed petrol on the sleepers and began jogging backwards along the line, still pouring. He covered ten yards before turning and stumbling down from the line through the metal into the dry spinifex. He sprayed petrol wildly about him. As the can emptied, he ran wide of the line, sprinkling the last of the fluid over a particularly thick clump of grass. He took out his matches.

'Frog,' he screamed. 'Hurry.' A faint cry, almost muffled by the rising diesel throb and vibration of the tracks, answered him.

Johnny stooped to light the spinifex. It erupted in a puff of blue. He jumped back, stumbled on a stone and sprawled on his back. He rolled to his knees to see flames reach the most saturated area of grass and leap upwards with a roar. He put one hand to his waist to hold the opal case in place and ran, crouched low, well wide of the track but towards the train. When he judged the locomotive to be half a mile away he stopped, lying face down on the earth.

He had come a long way from the fire. He called to Frog but the sound of the diesel's horn drowned any answer. The train's light now began to pick out the edges of the sleepers abreast of him. He began to run again. Keeping low, so that he was no higher than the spinifex, he now angled towards the rails. He heard the sudden jar of brakes. The light grew stronger. He flung himself on the ground. Behind him, he heard his name called. 'Get down,' he shouted over his shoulder, then pressed his cheek into the dust as the combined noise of horn, throbbing motors and screaming brakes hurtled towards him. For an instant, his body shook as a thundering vibration passed. Then it was darker and only the squealing remained.

He sat up and turned. The locomotive was sliding to a stop short of the fiery crossing. Flames were still leaping several feet into the air and the spreading blaze crackled fiercely in the spinifex below the line. Carriage by carriage the train jolted to a stop, the shunting noise echoing far down the line. Silhouetted against the fire, a man climbed from the locomotive and jogged towards the blaze. Johnny saw him turn and beckon to another man now on his way down.

Johnny couldn't see Frog. He looked up. A darkened passenger carriage loomed above him, its outline sharp against the moonlit sky. He counted four more towards the locomotive. He looked towards the tail of the train. Beyond the tall carriage above him stretched the low outline of freight trucks. He pushed himself to his feet and, bent low, began to move along the line towards the trucks.

A head was thrust from a carriage window above him. 'Bloody boongs, I'll bet,' grumbled a deep voice. Someone else laughed. Johnny stopped moving and stared, fascinated, at the outline of the man's head above him.

'What was it? A corroboree?' The deep voice yelled the question, obviously for the man who had stepped from the locomotive. Johnny let his body sink to the ground.

A voice shouted something in return. Johnny could see two men standing before the fire. One waved an arm.

'What did they say?' From above him came the voice of the man who had laughed.

'Couldn't make it out,' answered the deep voice, whose owner pulled his head back inside the carriage. 'Bet it was the bloody boongs, though. Full as farts, and set fire to their own metho. Hopeless with grog. Bloody hopeless.'

Johnny got to his knees and crawled away, towards the rear of the train. He reached the first goods truck. It was covered by a heavy tarpaulin, lashed down tightly. He stood erect and began to run, stumbling constantly on the rough surface. The next truck was also covered, and the next and the next. He ran faster. The tenth was a flat platform carrying a car being freighted south. In the shadowy darkness, he found a foothold in the spokes of a small brake wheel and clambered up, resting his body on the edge and then swinging his legs over. He rolled on to the wooden platform, lying flat as his eyes searched the shadows for Frog. Up ahead the glow had diminished.

He heard the voices again and then the metallic ring of a door slamming.

Still no Frog. The rumble of diesel motors rose to a powerful throb and then his platform shook, jerked forward, eased and started to roll. Behind him, the other trucks jolted into position with a succession of clangs.

He squirmed forward until his head and shoulders projected from the truck's edge. The side of the line, in the glow of the grass fire, seemed deserted. The train had gathered a little speed. 'Johnny, Johnny, where are you?' a soft voice was calling. It was behind him.

Johnny spun around. He saw a stocky figure jogging beside the next truck. 'Frog, here,' he shouted, scrambling to his feet and waving his arms. 'Here, on the next one.'

Frog began to run but stumbled and slid to one knee. He rose and ran harder. Johnny felt his way to the rear of the truck and lay down, holding out his hand to the runner. Frog was near, left arm outstretched. He tried to sprint to grasp Johnny's hand but his legs kept stumbling and sliding in the loose, uneven metal. Above the accelerating rumble of the wheels, Johnny could hear Frog moaning. It was a curious sound, caused partly from want of breath and partly through fear. The noise reminded Johnny of the sound made by a dog he had once run over and he was filled with disgust that a man should make such a vile animal noise.

Frog fell, stood up, and resumed running, making more noise, but travelling at a slower pace. He was being left behind.

The trucks rolled past the burning grass and the level crossing. Frog continued to drop back. Johnny looked at the next wagon. It was flat and carried another car. He stood up and leaped for the truck. His feet landed on a bracing rope, sending him pitching on to the splintery platform. He slithered forward until he was abreast of the tiring Frog. He reached out and grabbed an outstretched arm. Frog's free hand clutched the jacked sleeve, the movement spinning him off balance so that his body twisted and heels dragged in the metal.

With his other hand, Johnny lunged down and caught the trailing Frog by the collar. The truck was now swaying with speed. Johnny tried to lift Frog but almost overbalanced as the truck pitched suddenly.

He spread his legs wide apart, hooking one foot beneath the wheel of the car, and hauled again on the arm and collar. Frog's face appeared out of the shadows alongside his, eyes wide and mouth open but stifled. 'Let go my arm and grab the edge,' Johnny ordered, his voice high against the rattle of the wheels. Frog stared and held on. 'Let go,' Johnny screamed, tightening his throttling grip on the collar. Frog let go the sleeve and clutched the raised edge. 'Now your other hand,' Johnny shouted, releasing Frog's fist. Frog obeyed, his feet now swinging clear of the blur below. Johnny, his other hand free, reached down for Frog's belt, grabbed it and hauled. He could make no progress. He drew his knees beneath his body and pulled again, head back and teeth clenched in strain. Slowly the twisting hips of the fat man scraped across the edge. One threshing leg hooked itself over the platform. A final tug and Frog was on, sprawling on to his back, safe at last.

Breathing noisily, he lay there with his eyes closed. Above him, Johnny slowly stood and leaned for support against a door of the gently rocking motor car. He began picking at a splinter in his palm. 'Okay Frog?' he panted.

Frog put an arm to his forehead and nodded, without opening his eyes. 'There was too much light,' he gasped and spent several seconds gaining enough breath to speak again. 'I had to keep wide. I must have come in a long way behind you.' The train swayed, and Frog's head swung with the motion, his muscles too tired to resist. He groaned and breathed deeply several times. 'Christ I ran a long way.'

'Well, we're on our way to Marree, that's the main thing.' Johnny brushed his clothes. 'How's the ute? Well hidden?'

Frog nodded. 'Wedged in between some trees and scrub. I don't think you'd see it from the road. I had to leave our cases, but.'

'Hell, I'd forgotten them.'

'I started to carry them but they slowed me down too much.' He took a deep breath. 'Had to toss them into some bushes and then run for it. I'd never have made it with them, Johnny, honest.'

The tall man looked back along the train at the distant flicker that was the grass fire. 'All right. Too late now to do anything about it. We've got the opals, that's the main thing. Come on, we've had enough for one night. Let's travel to Marree in comfort.' He patted the car door. 'Hop into the car and we'll have a sleep.'

'It's probably locked.'

'Don't tell me that's going to stop a safe breaker, like you.' He spoke as one would to a child whom you wished to coax into action. He rattled the door handle. 'It's locked all right. Come on Frog, get up mate. What do you think I brought you in on this job for? Here's another lock for you to pick.'

Frog rolled painfully to his hands and knees and crawled to the car. He pulled himself up by the handle and groped in his pocket for the key tools he had used in Alice Springs. 'Thank heaven it's a big car,' he remarked. 'We'll be able to stretch out.'

He examined the car, and put his tools back in his pocket. 'No need for any of these,' he said. 'This model's dead easy. Just a bit of pressure here...'

He pressed hard on the flipper window in the driver's door. It broke at its base, allowing the glass to sag from its upper pivot. Frog pulled the window clear, inserted his arm in the triangular opening, and unlocked the door. 'The owner can blame the railways for this,' he said. 'Teach him to buy a car like this, anyway. My best time for one of these is fifteen seconds. That's from the time I touch the car to the time the motor's running. That's without a key.' What pride there was in his voice was eroded by a lack of certainty that the magnitude of his accomplishment was appreciated.

'I was the best on these,' he said.

Johnny was waiting for the back door to be unlocked. 'Terrific,' he said.

The long train rolled south.

CHAPTER FOUR

'Don't touch. He might bite.' The warning came in a soft voice but carried such a tone of authority that Barbara Dean pulled back her hand immediately. The camel tethered to the wire fence rolled its jaws.

'Give you a nasty nip.' An old man emerged from the doorway of a shanty made largely of corrugated iron, and began to walk across the dusty yard towards the fence. He looked as worn and decrepit as the building. He wore a torn felt hat that had long lost any semblance of shape. A checkered shirt trailed strands of thread from frayed elbows. His trousers were held in place by a rope belt. But he walked with dignity, adapting his pace to the stoop of his body so that he seemed to be bent in scholarly thought.

'Cranky thing,' he said when he had reached her, and stood on the other side of the wire. 'He'll let you get close, then bite you. Won't you.' He addressed the last words to the camel, which slowly turned its head towards him and blinked a heavy set of eyelids in acknowledgement. The jaws ground across each other.

'Yes, you'd like to have my fingers in there, wouldn't you?' the old man said. He was unshaven, with several days' growth of iron-grey stubble bristling from his lower face and throat. He noticed Barbara studying him, and touched his whiskers self-consciously.

'What's his name?' the sister asked pleasantly. She saw a young woman standing in the shadows beyond the doorway of the building. The woman had a slim, elegant face and dark hair that fell below her shoulders. A small child, naked but for a shirt, ran from the gloom behind her legs and headed for the old man. The boy stopped halfway to the fence when he saw the strange woman there.

'Abdullah,' the old man said. He glanced back. The dark haired woman stayed in the shadows. The boy was frozen by shyness in a patch of bright sunlight. The camel swung its head suddenly towards Barbara and she jumped back. The old man swung an arm at the animal and growled at it. The camel answered with an obscene gurgling, and displayed rows of large, yellow teeth. The dark woman moved into the sun. Her skin was the colour of weathered copper. She was smiling.

'You'd better stand clear,' the old man said, indicating a position further down the fence. 'He's a cunning old devil. Like nothing better than to give you a nip. You wouldn't forget it either.' He permitted himself a brief smile.

The small boy darted forward and grabbed the old man's leg. The man spread his legs a little wider to withstand the sudden leverage. A gnarled hand, weathered by age, dirt and hard work, fondled the boy's black hair.

'Grandson,' he said, glancing down quickly at the boy. 'Just as big a devil as Abdullah.'

'I'm Barbara Dean, the new nursing sister for Birdsville,' Barbara said.

'Oh yes,' he said, without introducing himself. He paused for several seconds. 'Been there before?'

'No,' she said. She meant the answer to sound matter-of-fact, but it came out weakly, as though she were defending herself.

'No,' he repeated softly, as though absorbing a wealth of information. He scratched the head of his grandson, who stared up at the sister. The boy's nose was running, she observed, but he was clean. 'Well, I don't know whether you'll like it or not,' the man added. 'Gets very hot. And it gets very cold. Not as big as Marree of course.'

'So I've been told.'

'There's no railway or telephone or anything like that.'

'You know Birdsville well? The only person I've met who's

been there is the mail contractor. Everyone else seems to regard it as the end of the earth.'

'Back of beyond,' he mused. Again there was a long pause. 'I've been there a few times. Not recently.'

He turned and saw the dark woman standing clear of the doorway. 'Go back to your mother,' he whispered, and aimed the child across the yard. The boy ran, revealing a glistening set of buttocks. Barbara smiled.

'Shouldn't be out like that,' the old man said, more to himself than the girl. The camel leaned towards a thorny bush and broke off a branch. The foliage disappeared into its mouth in a slow, crunching series of slides.

'That'll keep him quiet for a few minutes,' the old man said. His eyes smiled through a watery film that occasionally overflowed his lids, causing him to dab at his face, rubbing the fluid away with a broad thumb. He produced a crumpled handkerchief and blew his nose, an action that provoked a cascade of tears. 'Yes, I know Birdsville. Used to take camels there.'

She waited for him to continue. He was in no hurry. He mopped his face with the handkerchief.

It was the second morning of Barbara Dean's stay in Marree. She had risen early and gone for a walk, crossing the railway line and picking a path through the rubbish and abandoned car bodies that littered the eastern fringe of Marree. It was a curious, divided town. To the north-west, bright in the early morning light, she had seen the railway workshops and stockyards that were, collectively, the main reason for the settlement's existence. Then came the principal part of the town. Some houses, the two-storeyed hotel, the low and wide post office with its high fence to repel dust storms, the open fronted store and the railway station, with its sheds and water-towers. That was the main part of Marree, and that was the white part of town.

She had wandered into the Afghan settlement. Their buildings began boldly enough near the railway line, but soon degenerated into a squalid patchwork of shacks and lean-tos, made of corrugated iron sheets, wood and bags. The buildings were small and almost overwhelmed by the mounds of old machinery, rotting saddles, oil drums, rusted ice chests, metal springs and worn tyres that lay around them like ugly offspring. The Afghans were early risers and washing fluttered from several lines. Children were playing around the scrap heaps, improvising toys from the materials they found. Five youngsters, all trying to fit on one tricycle that had long ago lost its rubber tyres, had followed her, giggling and falling constantly.

Beyond the Afghan settlement was the Aboriginal camp. It was separated from the other buildings and the rubbish dumps by a wide expanse of raw earth and stones. The Aborigines' homes were less pretentious: low, flimsy structures of wood, scrap metal and canvas. She had seen a few squat, shadowy women moving in front of their humpies. They seemed remote. She wondered whether she should go there, but doubted it. The camp seemed in an alien world.

And so she had been walking through the Afghan settlement when she had seen the camel at a fence near a shanty that was ringed by a shady line of trees.

Having wiped the excess moisture from his eyes, the old man was gently drying his skin with a thumb, stroking the leathery flesh with the care of a painter brushing the final colours on a portrait.

'We used to take camel trains up there,' he said, when he was ready to resume. 'Seventy camels and six men. Hard work.' He pocketed the handkerchief. 'We used to go to Betoota, Birdsville, Arabury, Cordillo. Heard of them?'

'I've heard of Birdsville.'

His watery eyes examined the young woman. Her face was unlined and her eyes were eager. Hardship and disappointment had not dulled them yet. Her hands, lightly touching the fence, were smooth and soft looking. Not unworked hands, he thought, but not showing the cracks and sandpaper roughness that you found on women who worked all their lives in the outback.

'I'm going there to help at the Australian Inland Mission nursing home,' she continued. 'There's another nurse there already.'

He nodded. 'Did you know Flynn? John Flynn?' The question was a challenge, flung from the sanctuary of age.

'Flynn of the Inland? No. I never met him.'

'Good man.' He expressed the judgement slowly, as though he had just made up his mind about the founder of the AIM. 'Always used to wear a suit, no matter what the weather. With a collar and tie.' He touched his neck, to make sure she understood.

'Where are those other places?' she asked.

'Up that way.' He waved to the north, where a band of low scrub stained the horizon. His eyes glazed, and she imagined him deep in memories of old journeys. The camel made a sound like thick porridge simmering on a stove. The old man looked at the camel and then the girl. 'There's a pub at Betoota. That's a hot place. Hundreds of hawks. Thousands of them.'

He took off his hat and wiped his forehead. 'I've been there in summer when the heat's flattened the hawks. You see dozens of them lying on the ground, too hot to take off. We used to go up for wool. We'd load the camels with beer and produce and come back with wool. Bales of it.' He glanced at the camel. 'Hard days. We'd be out for two months.'

'How long ago was this?' she asked. The children on the tricycle came pedalling and pushing and tumbling around the corner of the fence and collapsed, in a tangle of legs and spinning wheels, near the sister. The old man waved his fingers at them and they moved away. He wiped a thumb across his eyes.

'That was between 1926 and 1934. The trucks took over then.'

The children fell off the tricycle again, and giggled.

'I'm going up in the mail truck tomorrow,' she said.

'Yes. No camels now. How long will it take you. Three days?'

She nodded.

'Things have changed,' he said. The camel, having digested all of the bush within range, made a deep wheezing sound and the old man began to untie the rope that secured it to the fence.

'How old is he?' Barbara asked, unwilling to see the man go, as seemed his intention.

'Four,' he said. 'About the best age for a camel. In the old days a good three- or four-year-old bull could carry six hundred weight.' Abdullah gurgled once more.

'He wants to move,' the old man said, and began to lead the beast across the yard. He didn't say goodbye.

Barbara was feeling hot and the flies were now troublesome. The Aboriginal humpies, the farthest outpost of the town, were beginning to shimmer in a heat haze that was advancing on the town of Marree. She headed back towards the railway line. A Land-Rover, which had been driving towards the rail crossing, turned and stopped near her. Fred Crawford was at the wheel. She recognised him with pleasure and smiled.

He reached across the cabin to push open her door. 'Hop in,' he invited. 'You're out early.'

'Just wanted to look at the town. I didn't see much yesterday. I was so tired.'

'Not much to see.'

'I had a most interesting talk with a man with a camel.'

'Old feller?' Fred grinned. 'Jimmy the Afghan.'

'He didn't look like an Afghan.'

'What did you expect? Basil Rathbone with a towel around his head?'

She smiled. 'I see you go to the pictures.'

'Used to,' he said. The Land-Rover bounced over the railway lines. 'Actually, he's not a real Afghan. All the people here, or their ancestors to be more accurate, came from Peshawar, which is in what you call Pakistan these days. Still, they were called Afghans when they came, so the name's stuck. I don't think one of them living here now was born anywhere but in Australia. Most of them were born here, in Marree. Nice people. Jimmy's a good bloke. He's lived here more than fifty years. His father and some of his father's brothers came out last century to look after a mob of camels.'

'He speaks . . . well, he's very quiet,' she said.

'He's hardly what you'd call loquacious,' Fred said.

She look surprised. 'Indeed not.'

Fred looked pleased. He doubted whether anyone else in town, barring the postmaster, knew what the word meant. He stopped outside the post office. He had arranged for the sister to stay there with John Black and his family, rather than condemn her to the rowdier atmosphere of the hotel.

'Ivan's just finishing loading the truck,' he said. 'We should be leaving on time in the morning.'

A loud horn blast came rolling into town.

'Ah,' said Fred. 'The train from Alice Springs.'

'All out please.' Johnny Parsons straightened his knees and stretched, pushing his feet into something soft and spongy.

The distant call came again, in the same flat, strange voice. He opened his eyes and stared up at beige cloth. The cloth merged into the frame of a car window, with the pillars picked out by sunlight. Recollection came sliding back into his mind. The car was steady. No rocking, no rumbling sound. The train had stopped.

He moved his feet from the door padding and slowly bent forward, raising his head to window level. The sun glared at him across a flat, pinkish plain, dotted by the shadows of thousands of stones.

A gentle snoring came from the front of the car. He looked over the seat at Frog, curled up in sleep, face pressed into the seat and one arm awkwardly looped through the rim of the steering wheel. His black hair was matted with grease and dust and his clothes were filthy. Johnny fingered the rough stubble on his own chin and looked at the dirt caking his clothes. He felt for the opals. His jacket zipper had loosened and the slim case had slipped from the inner pocket. He pushed it back, flat against his stomach, and drew up the zipper.

Voices coming from the front of the train made him look up quickly. He slid across to the other side window and pressed his face against the middle pillar. The train's elongated shadows stretched across a road towards a row of buildings, their stone faces bright and fresh in the early light. The rocky plain continued beyond the buildings to end in a distant row of hills. Johnny turned in the seat and, for the first time, saw the extent of the train they had jumped. A narrowing succession of shadowy goods trucks curved several hundred yards into the distance, around a bend to the west.

The voice drifted in again, louder now. 'I'm sorry mate,' it was shouting, 'but you've got to get out. Police order.'

Gravel crunched as someone jumped to the ground.

'We'll be as quick as we can, mate,' the voice apologised.

Johnny pressed his cheek against the glass and tried to see who was speaking. He could see several people walking aimlessly in the shadows between the train and a low, narrow, brown building. The station, he thought. He looked for an identification sign but could see none. His eyes followed the shadows across the road and searched for a name on the handful of buildings. Most were low and wide-browed; only the far one stood out, a two-storeyed place with fancy iron posts supporting an upstairs verandah. A whisp of grey smoke curled from a chimney. It looked like a hotel, but he couldn't read the sign.

One by one, he examined the buildings nearer him. They looked like old and weather-scarred homes, except one with a canvas front and barrels and drums beneath an awning. 'Store' was written across the front in fading paint.

The road was wide and sun-baked. Near him it forked, one branch following the curve of the railway line, the other disappearing at a level crossing beneath the train. For the first time he noticed at the fork a signpost, its leaning pole cut by the long shadow of the last passenger carriage. One narrow board pointed to Oodnadatta. The other, its sharpened end sagging, pointed towards the rail crossing. It was harder to read the wording. He concentrated on it for several seconds before making it out. 'Birdsville 325.' He withdrew the map from his pocket and hid below the window to study it.

Soon he rose and propped his chin on the back of the driver's seat. 'Hey, Frog,' he called softly. 'Wake up, Frog.' He gripped the seat and shook it. The curled figure stirred. A red-rimmed eye blinked open and gazed up at Johnny's face.

'Wake up, Frog. We're at Marree.'

Frog disentangled his arm from the steering wheel and began to sit up.

'Stay where you are a few minutes,' Johnny warned, and dropped to the floor. 'There are people moving about up front. They might see you. Are you properly awake?'

'Mmm.'

'Well stay there and listen. There's a search going on. At present they're making all the passengers get out. Next thing they'll probably check the freight so we've got to get out before they find us. We'll have to get out on the left side, where the sun is. I can't see anything but desert on that side. The other side's in shadow but the town's there and someone might spot us. There are a few people up front on that side too. Ready?'

Johnny heard Frog grunting with the effort of climbing from the floor. 'Keep your head down,' he whispered. 'I'll have a look first to see if it's still clear.' He slid along the seat and slowly pushed himself up, keeping his head close to the backrest for protective cover, until his eyes rose above the window. The rocky plain was still empty. He turned his head to look out the rear window and sucked in his breath in surprise. Two hats were bobbing towards him.

'Down,' he whispered. He dropped quickly, slapping his cheek on the seat and gripping the edge with tense fingers. From the front he heard Frog's foot thump the floor and wondered how far the sound would travel. He held his breath and listened. He could hear voices and the grating sound of footsteps.

'... well, we're going to do it again,' one voice was saying.

'But this'll be the third flamin' time since we left. There's no one in the freight.' The voices were beside the car now.

'We're still going to have a look. At everything.'

'We'll be here for hours. What about our schedule...'

The voices faded. Johnny began to raise his head but dropped back quickly when he heard more footsteps. They crunched past, after the other two men. He waited until the sound had gone and then peeped out. All was clear. He whispered to Frog: 'I'm going out the door now. If it's clear, I'll tap on the car. Stay down until I tap.'

He pressed the handle until the door sprung open. He held it ajar and listened. Nothing. Slowly he pushed the door open. It creaked alarmingly. He bit his lip and waited. Still quiet. He slid his feet forward and lowered them on to the rail truck's platform. The sun felt warm on his legs. He wriggled his body through the narrow opening and gently pushed the door shut. Still there was no one in sight. He lay on his stomach and squirmed his way around the back of the car to the other side. He could see the locomotive now and people milling around a brown station shed. Nearer, a man with a wide-brimmed khaki hat was beginning to untie the rope on the tarpaulin of the first goods truck. Behind him stood a darker man with a rifle.

A man in a railway uniform was walking away from them, towards the brown shed. Johnny crawled back to the sunlit side. He looked towards the front of the train but the locomotive and carriages were hidden by the curving row of goods trucks. He could see no one. With a raised foot he tapped on the side of the car. He heard a click, an almost noiseless shuffle and another click.

'What now?' Frog whispered, pressing his shoulder against the other man's.

Johnny wriggled back under the car, until he was well clear of the edge. 'We're going to walk along the train on this side,' he answered softly. 'The other side's in the shade just here, but anyone could see us from the train or the town. We're stopped on a curve, so if we follow the line back,' he drew a curve with his left hand, 'we should get more and more out of their line of vision. I think that was the guard that went by towards the front a while ago, so the back should be clear. They've started checking from the front. But they can't see us from where they are yet. Be ready to duck under a carriage in case someone comes. We just go as far as we can, and then cut across to come into the town from the back.'

The train was rumbling out of Marree as the tall, thin woman let the kitchen's flyscreen door slam behind her. She followed the dirt path that led to the garbage cans. There was only one guest at the hotel and she carried the remains of his breakfast. With her free hand, she began automatically to brush away the flies that greeted her emergence. The hand flicked back and forth with practised ease. The Marree Permanent Wave, they called it.

She reached the wooden staircase, still cool in its morning shade, and bent beneath it to lift the lid of the nearest can. A swarm of disturbed flies buzzed from it. She held her breath and dropped the greasy bundle inside. Up whirled a fresh cloud of flies. She shoved the lid in place, locking the flies from their new prize, and turned away. Long, sepia fingers pulled a piece of cloth from her blouse sleeve and she blew her nose. She inspected the wet patch of cloth with more interest than she had devoted to any subject so far that morning. She wedged the cloth back in the sleeve. The Permanent Wave resumed as she meandered back to the door. Going to be hot today, she thought, and for the first time looked up from the dusty yard.

Two men were staring at her. Startled, she took a step back. They were standing only fifteen yards away, where the long shadows of the hotel gave way to the glare of the plain. She rubbed a moist palm on her hip and began to walk on. Out of the corner of her eye she could see them, standing together, silently watching her. They were dirty, she thought. But interesting. Especially the tall one. At least they were new in town. Probably from the railway camp. She turned on the step, arched an eyebrow towards them and then disappeared into the darkness that led to the kitchen.

The noise of the slamming wire door swept out past Johnny and Frog. 'Well, at least we didn't frighten her,' Johnny said. 'Did you get the look she gave us?'

'Geeze, I'd want to be tired to go to bed with her,' said Frog, rubbing his parched lips in distaste. 'A touch of smoked log by the look of her. She seemed in a bit of a dream. For a while I thought she wasn't going to see us at all.'

'Well, she did and it didn't seem to worry her. That's good. Just act normal and no one'll take any notice of us. Let's go round to the front of the pub. And let me do the talking.'

They brushed their clothing in a futile attempt to remove the layers of dust and walked around the high stone wall that led to the front footpath. A bearded man, slumped in the sunlight on a seat next to the hotel entrance, looked up as they ambled towards him. He made no attempt to brush away the flies that crawled around the lids of his questioning eyes. Johnny halted momentarily at the entrance and stared down at the face. It was framed by greasy, matted hair and the skin was wrinkled and tormented by years in the sun. Yet it was the face of a young man. He smiled.

Johnny looked away without answering the wordless greeting and led Frog into the shadows of the hotel hallway. Ahead of them, a staircase rose into the darkness. To the left, light glowed through an open doorway. Beyond it a small man was bending beneath a counter. He saw the two men and straightened. He was young and wearing shorts and an open-neck shirt. 'Looking for someone?' he inquired. He pushed a box into a shelf and moved towards them. His face was freckled and looked freshly polished. He seemed friendly.

'We'd like a room,' Johnny answered.

The small man stepped into the corridor and turned his back on them to close the door. 'Like a clean up too, eh?' he asked, over his shoulder.

'Er, yes, we could do with one I reckon. Spent the night out. Me and my mate were, ah, coming up by motor bike from Port Augusta, and it conked out. We walked in this morning.'

'That's bad luck. What happened to it?'

'Out of petrol,' Johnny continued. 'We didn't know what it was, for a while. Got ourselves filthy trying to fix it.' He held up his hands in explanation. 'Funny how you never think of checking the petrol first, isn't it?'

The man's freckles crinkled in a grin. 'How far did you walk?'

'Fair way. We started about dawn.'

'Well, I can give you a gallon can to put some juice in. There's a pump outside. A gallon would take your bike further than you can walk in a couple of hours, I reckon.' Again he smiled pleasantly. 'No use walking back, though. One of the trucks from the railway camp will be in later for sure. They'll take you back. They're about twenty miles down the road, so they should pass your bike.'

'Good. When'll they be in?'

'About evening. If anything else turns up, I'll let you know.' He signalled up the stairs. 'Anyway, you'll want a clean up. Got any gear?'

Johnny shook his head.

'Left it with the bike, eh?' The man began to trot up the stairs and they followed. 'You'll find towels and soap in your room. You don't mind sharing a room, do you?'

'If we can share a motor bike, we can share a room,' Johnny answered. Behind him, Frog grunted agreement.

The man had reached the top of the stairs. 'That's your room there.' He pointed to a door across the corridor. 'If you've been up all night, you'll want to have a lay down for a while. Where are you two from?'

'Sydney,' Johnny answered. 'Thought we'd see a bit of the country. Sort of a working holiday. You know, travel a bit, work a bit.'

The freckles creased into another grin. 'Hard way to do it, on a bike.'

'First trouble we've had.' Johnny was wishing there really was a motor bike waiting for him down the road. He wanted to get away from this man and think things out, in the quiet of the room.

'Sorry I can't offer you a feed just now.' The man was poised on the top of the stairs. 'The girls have finished breakfast. You know what it's like with staff these days. Lunch is at twelve-thirty. Have a clean up and a rest and you'll be ready to ride a few more miles on that bike. What do you plan doing up here? Bit out of the way by road.'

Johnny's mind pictured the map. 'Thought we'd have a look-see. Might ride to Alice Springs or go up to Birdsville.'

'Birdsville!' The freckled face broke into a laugh. 'I don't think you'd make it on a motor bike. I've lived here most of my life and I've never been past the Cooper. If you ran out of petrol there'd be no one along to help you up there.'

Johnny lifted his shoulders and grinned in the manner of one who acknowledges having made a foolish suggestion.

The small man began to jog down the stairs. 'No one ever goes up the Birdsville Track unless they've got to. And the only one who's got to is Fred Crawford, and he doesn't take a motor bike. See you later.'

Johnny stared thoughtfully at the staircase as the man disappeared downstairs. 'Who's this Crawford?' he muttered.

Frog shook his head. 'Don't know him,' he said, as though he should have. 'Let's get clean, Johnny,' he pleaded. He stared repulsively at the dirt caked on his fingers and palms. He hated dirty hands.

They took the towels from their room and walked to the bathroom and showered. Then they shook the dust from their clothes and dressed.

'What now?' Frog asked as they entered their room. He was rubbing his fingers, easing fine rolls of grease from the sides of his nails. 'We can't stay here. This is like being locked up, waiting for the johns to collect us.'

'Do you feel like moving?' It was an accusation, rather than a question.

'No. I'm shagged. I could do with a sleep. I've done a lot of driving in the last couple of days. I've had it. I'm covered in bruises from trying to get on that train.' He started to lift his shirt, but the other turned his back.

'Okay, okay. Spare me that. I've felt better myself.' He touched the cut on his forehead. The shower had washed away the scab and fresh blood stained his finger. He sat on his bed with his dirty handkerchief pressed against the wound. 'Anyhow, we're probably as safe here as anywhere. Neither of us are in much shape for travelling. Get some sleep.'

Frog was pleased with the order. He wanted to be told what to do, and sleeping was what he wanted to do. He was soon asleep. Johnny took out the map, and pored over it for several minutes. He thought about the man called Crawford, and the road no one else used. He lay on the bed for a long time, thinking, and then he, too, slept.

CHAPTER FIVE

Frog was first to wake. The room was dark. He could hear the drone of a blowfly slapping itself against the window and the soft rise and fall of Johnny's breathing. He closed his eyes again. Faint voices drifted into the room. It was hot, and his skin was moist with perspiration. He ground his hands into his eyes to rub away the sleep and sat up.

The blind on the window glowed soft yellow. Must be late afternoon, he thought. He sniffed and looked across at Johnny. He was sleeping on his side, with the jacket stuffed beneath his pillow. The opals, Frog thought. What a mess they'd got them into. He stood up, tucked his shirt into his pants and walked over to his companion. He bent down to look at the time on Johnny's wristwatch, but it was obscured by the other arm. With gentle fingers, he touched the arm to lift it clear.

The arm jerked out of his tender grasp. Johnny's eyes were open and staring at Frog. Suddenly he sat up. One hand felt for the opal case. 'What are you up to,' he demanded.

'I just wanted to know the time.'

Johnny moistened his lips and looked around the shadows of the room. He raised his wrist and looked at the watch. Four-thirty, or was it five-thirty. He blinked and looked again. Five-thirty. Hell, they'd slept most of the day.

He strode to the window and raised the blind. The blowfly roused itself into a fresh attack against the glass. Johnny crushed it with his thumb and looked down on the street. Below him, through the railing of the balcony, he could see three vehicles parked on the far side of the street. He checked them: a jeep, a big utility and a car with peeling paintwork.

They stood bright in the afternoon sunlight, but the hotel's shadow was reaching for them, stretching elongated fingers across the road. Beyond the vehicles, the railway station appeared deserted. A couple of tanker trucks lay idle on a siding. Smoke was rising from the chimney of a house beyond the rows of rails that flanked the station. Unruffled by wind, the smoke climbed into a sky that was bleached of all colour.

He examined the rest of the street. To the left, a young Aborigine slouched on a horse that was picking its way through the dust. The horse ambled past a group of people gathered around a truck. The young horseman touched his hatbrim in a lazy wave. A tall man, naked except for khaki shorts and an old army hat and boots, waved back.

Johnny pressed his cheek against the window to inspect the truck more closely. It was parked facing away from the hotel, with its nose towards the signpost he had seen from the train earlier that day. The back of the truck was laden with a variety of items. He could pick out petrol drums, tyres, wooden crates, a stack of cardboard boxes — they looked like beer cartons — and a clumsily spread tarpaulin covering anonymous bulges. It was a huge load.

The man who had waved was leaning with one arm against the back of the truck. One foot was crossed over the other ankle in the classic Australian lean. Knock his arm away and he'd have fallen.

With his back to the hotel stood a smaller man, also in shorts but wearing a shirt. He had no hat and he stood with his hands on his hips. Beside him was a thin man whose face was almost lost in a mass of black hair. Johnny recognised him as the bearded man he had seen outside the hotel entrance. He wore a shirt and long trousers that were stained with oil.

As he watched, the tall man straightened and the others turned. A woman walked around the back of the truck and joined them. Johnny watched with renewed interest. From the back, she looked good. Her hair was short and dark and it accentuated the fair skin that showed above an off-the-shoulder frock.

Johnny turned from the window. 'Here's something more in your line, Frog,' he said. Frog walked to the window. 'Up the road, hard on your left,' Johnny directed.

Frog gave a low whistle. 'White, too. Who's the mob she's with?'

'How should I know? Better come away from the window before you dribble on someone down below. Come in, I want to talk.' He checked his appearance in the room's single mirror and gently touched the cut on his forehead.

Frog walked back to his bed. He sat down.

Johnny took the pistol from his pocket and began to clean dust from it. He spoke without looking at the other man. 'Do you realise the position we're in?'

Frog looked serious. He nodded.

'By now, every way out of this place will be blocked. We've got no truck and we'd have the devil's own job getting on a train without being seen and questioned.' He turned the gun in his hand. 'And yet we've got to get out of here tonight.'

'Johnny,' Frog interrupted, 'you got me into this and you've got to get me out of it. You misled me, Johnny.' He was leaning forward on his bed. 'You said it would be a straightforward safe job. You said you had everything planned. We should be in Darwin by now, rich, and instead we're cooped up in this stinking hole. Where are we anyhow? I don't even know where this place is.'

Johnny examined the gun for several seconds. He let the barrel point towards the other man. 'No need to panic,' he said. 'Do that and we've had it. Things look bad, but I've got a plan.' He lowered the gun and allowed his lips to curl in a slight smile. 'Here.' He threw the map across. 'Have a look at that while I explain.' He lay on the bed and gazed at the ceiling, as though to draw inspiration from its moulded plaster patterns.

'The bloke downstairs said a truck would be in from the railway camp late today. That could be it we saw down the road just now. It was loaded up with petrol and things. Here's what we're going to do. We'll go downstairs and get a gallon of petrol for the bike we're supposed to have down the road. Then we'll check on the truck. If that's it, we'll try and stall the driver till it's dark and leave town with him. A mile or two out, we'll take over.' He sat up, put the gun back in his pocket and buttoned down the flap. 'We'll wait a while, and then drive back around the town and go on up to Birdsville. Have a look on the map. You can go from Birdsville straight up to Mount Isa and then across to Darwin. From what the feller here said, only one bloke ever goes up to Birdsville, so we wouldn't have to worry about other traffic. Apparently the track's pretty rugged, so we'll ask a few questions about it downstairs. As far as I see it, this could be our only way out so we want to know all we can about it.' He lit a cigarette. 'That was my last one. We'll need more and some provisions too, although there may be some on the truck.' He stood up. 'Come on, let's go.'

'What was that again?' Frog asked. He was terribly confused.

'Christ.' Johnny said. 'Never mind. Just follow me.'

A steadily increasing volume of noise greeted them as they walked down the stairs. A man with elastic-sided boots and the swinging gait of a horseman entered the hotel and disappeared through a door on their left, without looking up at them. They reached the bottom of the stairs and saw the bar door on their right was now closed. Through it came the rumble of voices. Suddenly from the left came the thump, thump, thump of a guitar, the noise magnified many times. Then a voice came shrieking out at them, in a western yodel. It was deafening. Howls of protest came from the bar.

'What in the name of hell is that?' Frog had to yell the question to be heard.

The door of the bar burst open and the small man with freckles thundered across the hall. He brushed past them and swooped into the room. Three seconds later, the shattering music stopped abruptly. A cheer came from the bar.

The freckled man emerged from the now silent room, wiping his hands on his hips. He grinned when he saw them. 'I put in a gramophone to attract customers, not drive them away.' He nodded his head towards the room. 'He's been out riding for days without hearing the sound of another voice and comes into town and tries to make up for it in one hit.' There was a sudden look of concern. 'Didn't wake you, did he?'

They shook their heads.

'You fellows must have been pretty tired. Takes a lot out of you, having trouble on the road like that and being up all night. I let you sleep through lunch. Went up to your room to let you know it was on but you were dead to the world. I thought one of you was awake at first because I could hear a voice through the door, but it was just you talking in your sleep.' He nodded at Johnny.

'What was I saying?' Johnny smiled the question, but his face was white.

'Oh, I dunno. You were just mumbling. Didn't hear any sheilas' names.' He grinned. 'Anyhow, I've got to get back to the bar. Nearly closing time. See you at dinner.'

'Just a second,' said Johnny. 'Has the truck from the railway camp come in yet?'

'No.' The man opened the bar door and the rest of his reply was engulfed in a flood of loud voices.

Johnny raised his voice: 'What's the truck down the road, then? The one all loaded with petrol and stuff.'

'The big Chev? That's Fred Crawford's. You know, the Birdsville mailman. He's going the wrong way for you. He's setting off up the track first thing tomorrow. Look, I've got to go. See you later.' He closed the bar door behind him and the flood of sound subsided. Seconds later it burst out again and the freckled man's head reappeared.

'Come and have a drink. That way.' He shook his head to indicate they should enter the bar from the front, and then closed the door.

'Not a bad idea,' Frog said. 'My mouth feels like dry sand. Oh no!' The music had begun to thunder out again.

Johnny gripped Frog's arm and pushed him towards the door. 'Let's not miss this one. Come on.'

As they reached the gravel footpath, they heard the bar door slam and quick footsteps thud across the hall. They entered the bar as the thunder of guitar strings stopped. The mob in the bar cheered again. The noise bounced around the small square room. Everyone laughed. They were a tough looking mob, Johnny thought. Almost all of them were big, the young ones, anyway. Most of the young ones had beards, too. Everyone was sunburned and covered with a layer of dust.

They brushed past a youth dressed in boots, shorts and hat. He was thickly caked in a greyish dust which seemed to be broken only at his eyelids and mouth, where little streaks of mud were forming. A middle-aged man shifted his enormous stomach to make room for them at the wooden bar. An elderly man behind the bar was talking to a group of customers. He nodded at Johnny and Frog but made no attempt to serve them.

The freckled man re-entered, swearing and shaking his head with great emphasis for the benefit of the customers. Some of them laughed and he laughed back. He saw Johnny and Frog and pulled two beers. He put them in front of them. 'How'll that be for a start?' he asked.

'Fine,' said Frog. They paid and drank them quickly. Johnny ordered some cigarettes and then two more drinks.

The barman served the dusty young man and then beckoned to Johnny. 'I informed you wrong a while ago,' he confided. 'That young fellow comes from the railway camp. Drives a dozer for them. Can't see the cook, though.' He scanned the crowd. 'Short, dark Englishman with a real Pommy voice. Probably down at the store picking up supplies. He's in charge of the truck. Wait till he turns up and I'll have a word with him for you. No use speaking to the young fellow here. He's just come along for the ride. Excuse me.' He served a leathery-skinned man who was offering five empty glasses over their shoulders.

They drank their second beers and left. Outside, the long shadows were merging into a soft dusk. The air was stirring with the first suggestions of a breeze, and it was cooler. Johnny blew a fly away from his moist lips. They began to stroll towards the laden truck.

Two women were walking towards them. One was short and fat and black. The other was the tall, slouched woman they had first seen when they reached the hotel that morning. She recognised them and lowered her head as they approached. From below the protective brows, her eyes stared at Johnny.

A small Aboriginal boy ran up to the fat woman and wrapped his arms around her thigh, so that she couldn't walk. She smacked him hard on the bottom. He held on tighter. She waited until the two white men had passed and then smacked again. He let go and ran away. Johnny glanced back. The tall woman was looking at him. He turned his head and, feeling uncomfortable, strolled on towards the truck. There, he and Frog stopped.

He looked back again. The two women were disappearing around the far side of the hotel. 'Well, I'm glad she's stopped staring at me,' Johnny said. 'She'd give you the creeps.'

'Do you think she suspects anything?'

'No, I don't think so. She looks as though she's only got one thought in her head.' He turned his attention to the truck. 'This has had some hard work.' He slapped a rear tyre. The tread had been chewed away so that the great tyre presented a pitted but patternless surface to the road. All the tyres were the same.

They walked to the front. One headlight was missing and the other had a yellowy reflector and bulb showing, but no protective glass. A South Australian registration number was chalked on the front mudguard, just above a waterbag mounting. The driver's windscreen was open and jutted out over the short, pugnacious nose. The vehicle had no doors.

Frog glanced inside the cabin. The padding on the separate seats had long since rotted away, leaving just the shaped metal frames. The driver allowed himself the luxury of a rubber cushion. Frog peered at the floor. Bare metal. 'Christ, this must be a hotbox in the daytime,' he said.

A voice answered from above: 'It's cooler up here.'

Frog withdrew from the cabin so quickly he bumped into Johnny. Together they stared up towards the voice. Someone was perched high on the back of the truck. It was the bearded man they had seen in the group beside the truck, half an hour earlier.

'Didn't see you up there,' Johnny called out. 'Just having a look at the truck.'

'She's a beauty, isn't she?' The voice came down in a musical, foreign lilt. 'Had a good rest?'

Johnny was surprised by the question and didn't answer.

'I saw you come in this morning, remember? Roy — that's the publican — told me about your bad luck. Hang on, I'll come down.'

'This bloke's a bit of a nut, isn't he?' Frog whispered. 'Migrant of some sort. Cop the voice.'

Johnny hushed him and watched the bearded man slowly pick his way down through the bits and pieces of the truck's load. He certainly looked strange; and dirty. Maybe he never changed his clothes. Most of the oil stains looked old although his hair glistened with fresh grease slicks.

The man jumped to the ground and hitched his pants around his waist. Frog noticed that the flies, preparing to depart for the night, were peculiarly attracted to his hands. Then he saw that the knuckles on several fingers were bleeding.

'What were you doing up there?' Johnny said, preferring to ask the questions.

'Just checking the load. Tightening things down and that, you know.' He gave a shy, boyish grin and rubbed his hands together to brush the flies off. 'I work for Fred,' he continued eagerly in his singsong voice. 'Know the track very well. We're about the only two who do. That's the Birdsville Track, I mean. We carry the mail and stuff. This is his truck. Setting off first thing tomorrow. You've had a pretty rough trip, boys?'

'Not as rough as you're used to, I'll bet,' Johnny parried.

'Oh, the track's not too bad, just at the moment, you know. The sand's pretty firm on the hills.' He sucked a skinned knuckle, and examined the result as he kept on talking. 'Fred's taken a couple of days just to cross one sandhill, digging and plating all the way. You wouldn't make it on a motor bike, you know.' He sucked the knuckle loudly.

'We're not going to try. Much traffic use the track?'

'Only this.' He patted the truck. 'We make the trip once a fortnight. Oh, the people on the stations use it of course, if they've got to come into town. We're the only regulars, though. Might make half a dozen trips without seeing another thing on the road.'

'You take all this stuff to Birdsville?' Johnny indicated the load.

'Not all of it. Some of it's for the stations along the way.'

'There's a railway line up there?'

The man paused. A look of puzzlement erupted into a grin. 'Not railway stations; cattle stations.' He laughed. 'Without us they'd have to pack up and leave. We take just about all their food except meat. We've got a great stack of flour and sugar and stuff on now for Clifton Hills. They only get that once a year or so. Nothing grows out there, of course, except meat, you know.' He leaned against the truck and his voice raced on.

'We always take up fruit and stuff like that every trip, if there's room. And then there's drums of petrol and oil and the bits for their machinery — and the grog, of course.' He smiled. 'We've always got a lot of that.' He sucked another bloody knuckle. 'Most of it goes up to the pub at Birdsville. A couple of months ago when it was real hot, we had to leave the beer behind. Too much other stuff that was wanted and was more important.' He checked a rope and heaved on it, retying the knot. 'You know, were they crooked at the pub. A drover and his ringers had ridden in and they'd knocked off all the beer in town. They were waiting for us with their tongues hanging out. Should have seen their faces.' He walked to the other side of the truck to tighten another rope.

'Geeze, he can talk,' Frog complained.

'I want to hear him say more,' Johnny said, and followed the bearded man.

'What sort of place is Birdsville?' Johnny asked.

'Oh, well, it's not much of a place. Smaller than this, of course, you know. Used to be big once, last century, but it's only got one pub now. Had three then, they say.' He pulled on the rope, grunting with the effort. 'Not many people go there now, although it's a pretty important place in its own way. Important for the cattlemen. A lot of cattle come down the Birdsville Track from the stations near Birdsville and up north in Queensland and the Territory.' He tied a knot, and flashed a smile at them. 'They drive them down the track and put them on the train here to take them to market. Good cattle, too. Doesn't look it to you probably, but it's good cattle country, especially further north. Free from cattle pests, you know, tick and the like. Too dry for them or something.'

'How many people live there?'

'Where?'

'Birdsville, you were telling us about Birdsville.'

'Not many. There's not much for them to do now. It used to be a customs base before your Federation came in. That changed things. Did away with customs bases on the state borders. Birdsville's just over the border in Queensland, you know. All the drovers had to pay the customs men for the cattle that crossed the border. A lot used to try to dodge paying, of course, so they used to have men riding the fence to catch them. They all used to make Birdsville their base. Used to be a big place.'

'How many'd live there now?'

'Oh, about a dozen whites and twice as many Abos, I suppose. There's only a couple of buildings there, you know. Some of the old ones just crumbled and blew away with the sand. Even the pub's beginning to crumble a bit now. It'd be, ooh, I suppose about seventy or eighty years old. Made of mud and straw bricks in parts. When things got dry, the camels used to come in and nibble the straw.' He pulled hard on another rope and spent a few seconds in silence concentrating on a knot. 'You don't see many camels about now,' he reflected, when the knot was tied. 'They used to take the mail up before they put trucks on. Did a mighty job, too, they say. Just as well the camels are gone, though. Otherwise the pub would've probably fallen down.'

'Why?' Frog asked.

The bearded man seemed delighted by the question. 'The bricks,' he said.

He waited for Frog to laugh or show understanding but the fat man looked puzzled. 'When the camels ate the straw, the rest of the brick used to crumble. The camels ate half the town. The coming of the motor car saved the place.'

'Must be some town,' Johnny said and smiled, and the bearded man nodded, looking pleased.

He began to talk about wild camels, but Johnny interrupted him: 'Who lives at Birdsville now? A postmaster and a policeman?' he emphasised the final word. 'Those sort of people, I suppose. You know, government people.' Another smile appeared through the whiskers. 'There's the policeman and the postmaster and the coroner and the inspector of goodness knows what and they're all the same bloke. Carl Davis, the cop. I think he's got about seventeen different jobs. As far as Birdsville's concerned, he's the government.'

'Just one man, eh? With all those jobs, I suppose he's pretty well tied up in town all the time?' Johnny said. The bearded one looked puzzled. 'Busy,' Johnny explained. 'Has to stay in town?'

'Oh yes, but he's got the one big hell of a territory to cover. There's no other cop for hundreds of miles. He might be away for a week at a time, chasing some bloke or other, you know. Gets around in a Holden ute. Tough country for a thing like that. About the only other cars you see up that way are Land-Rovers and these.' He patted the truck.

Johnny looked at the stone-ravaged tyres again, and understood. 'Who else lives there?'

'Well, there's Bob Jackson at the pub and his wife of course, and the young school teacher and the two sisters at the mission hospital — there's only one at the moment, a new one's going up — and then there's the Betoota mail contractor and his family — he looks after things from the Queensland side — and a grazier who spends most of his time in town and that's about all. And the Abos, of course.'

'Must be lonely for people up there. I suppose they've got the telephone and radio, though.'

'Telephone!' He slapped the truck and walked to the footpath. 'That'd be the day. The nearest line's a couple of hundred miles away to the east.' He swung his arm to emphasise the distance. 'This is as far as you get the telephone, here. None of the stations along the track have got the phone on. There's only the one line up here from Leigh Creek, you know.'

Johnny's eyebrows arched in interest. 'How about radio?'

'Oh, they've all got the radio on, of course. Linked up with the Flying Doctor Service, you know.'

'Where's the main base. Here in Marree?'

'No. The stations on the track are mainly on to Broken Hill. Birdsville and the stations around there are on to Charleville.'

'So there's no link between here and the stations on the track.'

'No.'

'Pretty isolated, aren't they?'

'I'll say. Up there's really what you call the Dead Heart. You'd reckon you were in another world.'

'How does news travel up there?'

'What do you mean?'

'How do they find out what's happening in the rest of the world?'

'We take up the papers and magazines from Adelaide. They're about a fortnight old, though, by the time they get them. We tell them what's been happening around here. If anything has.' He grinned. 'They've got the radio, of course. They can pick up the ABC news from Adelaide or Brisbane. Relayed, of course, from Port Pirie or Charleville.'

'You know a lot about this area, don't you.'

The bearded man's eyes shone. 'You get to know these things. Besides, I like to find out about the place where I work. You know. A lot of them here couldn't care less, but I do.'

'Where do you come from?' asked Johnny.

'I was in Adelaide before I moved up here.'

'No, I mean before you came to this country. You're a migrant, aren't you?'

The answer came slowly, almost resentfully. 'I was a Russian.

Not a Communist, you know.' He paused, to make sure they understood. 'I fought the Germans, just like you probably did only they caught me. I was only a boy. I like it up here. No fences. Get awfully sick of barbed wire after a couple of years behind it, you know. Anyhow, I been here a long time now. Speak the language just like a native, as good as you, eh?' He smiled. His tongue came out and followed a bristly path around his lips. 'I'm thirsty. Going to have a drink?' He began to move towards the hotel.

'No thanks,' Johnny answered. 'We're going to have a meal. Bit peckish.' He went to slap his stomach in emphasis but instead hit the bag with the opals. He bit his lip at the sound.

'Certainly sounds empty,' the bearded man said and grinned. 'Well, I'll have a drink and a feed and see you later.' He walked away.

'See you later,' Frog echoed.

'Just a sec,' Johnny called after him. 'I suppose you'll be gone tomorrow, eh?'

The Russian stopped and turned. 'First thing. I'll see you tonight, though, and we can have a drink together.'

'Do you reckon a normal driver could get to Birdsville. With the track like it is now?'

'What in?'

'Oh, a utility, or something like that.'

'If he knew the track, I suppose he could.'

'And if he didn't?'

'He'd probably sit on a sandhill, stuck for a fortnight waiting for us to come along. Anyhow, he'd never cross the river now, unless it was a real big ute.'

Johnny stared. 'What river?'

'The Diamantina.' The word tumbled off his tongue. 'Just before Birdsville. It's coming down at the moment. I reckon we'll just get through this trip. It's a couple of feet deep, you know. And anyway, a stranger would be battling to find the way to get that far. The dry weather track's no good and you've got to double round the swamp now. There are tracks everywhere. If you shoot off to the left, you'd end up in the Simpson Desert and if you go off to the right, you're in the middle of the Stony Desert. Anyhow, I'll leave before the bar closes. You know,' he suddenly confided, walking back to them, 'he's a funny fellow, Roy. Here we are, the best part of five hundred miles from Adelaide and yet he tosses you out of the bar dead on six, just like they have to down there. I suppose the copper keeps him on the mark. Goodness knows. See you later.'

As he walked away, a Land-Rover, with headlights prematurely blazing, swung into the street and drove past the hotel towards them. Johnny grasped Frog's arm and pulled him against the truck, where they could not be seen.

The bearded man swung an arm lazily in greeting at the Land-Rover. As the vehicle drove by Johnny caught a glimpse of the driver. He was a policeman.

Eric Wallis stopped the Land-Rover outside the police station and walked past the gate that was permanently jammed in an open position. He dusted his uniform. What a waste of a day.

The row of faces on the faded wanted posters stared at him. He entered the office and headed for the broad brown desk that occupied the middle of the room. An Aborigine in police uniform was sweeping dust from the corner behind the door. 'G'day boss. Back already?' Albert Pantanjeela, whose special police skills involved the tracking of people, could not get used to the fact that motor vehicles covered long distances much faster than someone on foot, and smiled in admiration at the miracle Wallis had accomplished.

Much of the disturbed dust was in the air. Wallis sneezed. 'You're doing a good job,' he said.

'Bloody hard, boss, it's everywhere.'

'Yeah.' Wallis glanced at the desk. A fine coating of fresh dust covered the papers and envelopes that littered the desk. They were scattered across the scarred wooden surface like playing cards that had been dealt in a gust of wind. Christ, thought Wallis, he had two days work ahead of him in clearing that mess.

'Anything been happening?'

'No boss.' The man leaned on his broom, as though steadying himself to make sure he heard what the sergeant had to say.

'Any messages?'

'Yes, boss.'

'Anything urgent?'

'No, boss.'

'No one wants me to go dancing up the line again, like a blue-arsed fly, searching for someone that someone else thought maybe he might have seen? Nothing like that?'

'No, boss.' The pattern of a smile began to form on Albert's face, like chisel cuts in ebony. 'Good.' Wallis touched a pile of papers, thought about reading them, and decided against it. 'Do you mind hanging on here a bit?'

The black man shook his head and showed broad, tobacco stained teeth. Wallis smiled back. 'Good feller. I want to get cleaned up and have a bite to eat. Then I want to get over to John Black's place.'

As Johnny Parsons and Frog Gardiner reached the hotel, the sound of a wooden spoon belting a metal tray announced that it was dinner time. On their left, a chorus of moans recognised that it was also time for the bar to close.

Johnny led Frog up to the landing on the stairway. 'We'll wait here for a minute or two and see who goes in to have dinner.'

'Why didn't we go straight in and have something to eat?' Frog complained. 'We haven't had a proper feed for a couple of days.'

'Just wait.' Johnny peered down the hall out towards the road. He had seen a set of headlights pass. 'We'd skip this meal, only that'd arouse more suspicion than it'd be worth. Young smiling boy in the bar and the idiot with whiskers would be nosing around our room again to see why we hadn't eaten. Anyhow, we need the food.'

The sound of footsteps behind them made him turn suddenly. A freshly shaven young man in sandals, shorts and open-neck white shirt was coming down the stairs. He mumbled 'G'day' as he passed, but kept his eyes on the steps. They watched him enter the dining room. They waited another two minutes and then followed him.

Johnny opened the door and paused before entering. The room was rectangular, with a row of tables with bench seats on either side. The young man was seated on their left, his head bent over a bowl of soup. At the far end of the room, there was another door and a concealed entrance to the kitchen. He led Frog to the table nearest the other door. From where he sat, he could see both doors and the kitchen entrance behind the partition.

Staring at him from the kitchen was the tall woman he had twice encountered. She disappeared for a moment and then walked out carrying two plates of soup. She placed them on the table so heavily that they splashed on to the plastic cover. Halfway back to the kitchen, she said 'goodnight' and then she was gone. They heard the sound of giggling.

'Well, at least she can talk,' Frog commented. Johnny began to eat the soup.

The woman reappeared at the kitchen door. She was grinning at him. Occasionally she made a comment to someone in the kitchen.

When they finished the soup, she swooped out, took the plates and returned with two helpings of roast beef. 'Don't eat the Marmite,' she said, nodding her head at the jar on the table.

'Why?' said Johnny, who had started to butter his bread.

'It's George's.'

'Who's George?'

'A regular. He's away this week, but that's his Marmite.'

The hall door opened and the publican's head appeared. He saw them at once and smiled. 'How's everything. All right?' he enquired.

Johnny had his mouth full and nodded.

'Well, I'll see you later. And how are you tonight?' He had turned his attention to the young man who mumbled 'G'day' but kept his eyes on his food. The head disappeared and the door closed.

Johnny finished his beef first and the waitress sprung out to take his plate. She hovered beside Frog, waiting for him to finish. While waiting, she smiled at Johnny. He concentrated on the large metal salt shaker on the table, and the forbidden jar of Marmite. Frog put the last piece of meat in his mouth but before he could return the fork, her hand was on the plate. 'Such service,' he said.

She was off to the kitchen. 'You're welcome,' she flung back, with a slight emphasis on the first word.

'I think you've had your chips,' said Frog with a smile. 'I'm home and hosed.'

'You'd need to be hosed if you went home with her. What a bag.'

'Oh, I don't know. A couple of months here and she'd begin to look all right.'

'Well, tonight's the only night you'll be spending here, Frog.

And you haven't got time for any of that.'

Two plates of dessert were sliding along the plastic cover towards them. Johnny looked up to see her turning from her launching point at the end of the table. 'I think you've had it too, mate,' he told Frog.

Fred Crawford stared at his image in the mirror. It was indistinct, because the mirror was yellowed and flawed but an essentially clean man, freshly shaven and with his wet hair finely parted, looked back at him. He was going to dinner at John Black's place and he wanted to look good. Not that the prospect of eating with the Black's appealed. Certainly Mrs Black was a good cook but she made him edgy because of her constant criticism of her husband. And of anything to do with Marree. But Barbara Dean was staying with them, and that was the reason for the special dinner — a welcome and farewell to Marree in three courses — and the reason for his special concern. He picked at an erect strand of hair.

He had been invited back for breakfast too, and that had never happened before. 'Yes, all welcome,' John Black had said, so he intended taking Ivan, because otherwise his companion wouldn't get a feed before they set off up the track. Ivan had never been allowed inside Mrs Black's house. Fred wondered how she would respond when Ivan turned up. Nice as pie because the sister would be there, watching, or her usual bitchy self? You're a nasty bastard, he said to the mirror. The man in the glass returned his smile.

CHAPTER SIX

Having finished their meal at the hotel, the two men went into the hall. A buzz of sound came from a room on their left, the room from which the deafening music had issued that afternoon.

The publican emerged carrying a tray loaded with empty glasses. He crossed the hall to the bar door. 'Hi there,' he called out. 'Going to have a drink?'

'I don't think so, thanks,' Johnny replied. 'Can I see you for a moment?'

'Sure, come on in the bar.' He rolled the door open with his hip. Johnny followed.

'I'd like to fix you up for the room. How much do we owe you?'

'Oh, you can settle when you come back. You'll be staying here for a day or so I suppose, once you get your bike back on the road?' He washed the glasses rapidly, spending no more time than was necessary to remove traces of froth.

'Well, yes, I suppose so,' Johnny said. 'But I can fix you up now, if you'd prefer.'

'No, she's right. I can tell an honest face when I see one.' He flashed a smile at Johnny, and bent to refill the glasses.

'Well, there's one other thing. Have you seen the bloke with the truck?'

'The cook from the railway camp? Yes, he's in the lounge,

talking his head off. Come on in and I'll introduce you.' He swept past with the laden tray. 'Close the door behind you, will you?'

The two men followed him into the lounge. The room was crowded with tables and swarms of seated men. An electric light globe, flickering with the throb of a power generator, shone through a pall of cigarette smoke. A circle of moths surrounded the light. A wind-up gramophone stood in the far corner, issuing the sounds of a ravaged Tex Morton record. Its popularity must have been sustained by sentiment, for the words were indecipherable.

The bearded Russian was sitting just inside the door. The publican deposited a beer on his small table. 'There you are Ivan,' he said. Ivan paid and then saw Johnny and Frog and raised a finger in greeting. The blood on his knuckles had congealed. His hair was uncombed and still bore its fresh slick of thick grease, where he had apparently brushed against the chassis of the mail truck.

He flashed that curious, boyish smile. He'd only be in his thirties, Frog guessed, and suddenly felt sorry for him. He was the only man sitting by himself in the noisy room.

'He mightn't look much but he's not a bad bloke,' the publican confided, as he squeezed his way between two chairs towards the centre of the room. 'Ivan works like buggery, that's one thing I'll say for him.'

Johnny and Frog followed through the gap. There was a scraping of chair legs and a muttering of protests. Strange faces stared up at the two newcomers. 'Thank you, gents,' said the publican and then continued, in a lower voice, as though he were imparting a state secret: 'You couldn't pronounce his real name, I'm told, so everyone calls him Ivan. He's Russian, you know.' He placed the tray on a round table and handed the drinks to six men seated there. When he finished, he turned to Johnny and Frog.

'Fellows,' he said, putting an arm around the shoulder of each of them, 'here's a man who could help you, although if he does, you'll be the first he ever has.' He indicated a short fat man opposite him, with jet black hair and dressed, like almost everyone else, in singlet and shorts. 'His mother gave him some name or other but we call him Pommy because that's all he is.'

The group at the table laughed. The fat man, the cook from the railway camp, did not laugh but nodded his head as though adding that jibe to a long list of insults. The publican stopped laughing.

'No, all jokes aside, you'll find him a good bloke. You tell him what your trouble is. What'll you have to drink?'

They ordered beer.

'What's your trouble?' the English cook asked.

Johnny told him the story of the motor bike. When he finished, the cook said: 'Well, I hope it's still there. We didn't see any motor bike on the way in, did we Clarrie?'

The dusty young man sitting opposite shook his head.

'We ran it off the road and put it behind a bush,' Johnny said. Frog nodded in agreement. The cook lifted a cigar from a cheap metal ashtray and sucked on it, as though seeking inspiration from the inhaled smoke.

'How far back did you say it happened?'

'Oh, I'm not sure. Maybe ten miles.'

The Englishman scratched his chest, balancing the cigar delicately between his other fingers. 'Must have walked a mighty long way to find a bush back there big enough to hide a bike, eh Clarrie?'

Johnny didn't like the trend in the conversation. 'Well, if you'll give us a lift back, we'll soon show you which bush. When do you plan leaving?'

The Englishman lifted his beer. 'No hurry, mate. I can't leave till the train from the south comes in with some of the stuff for the store. It's late. Probably being searched like all the others.'

Frog moistened his lips.

The publican returned with the two beers. Johnny welcomed the break. 'Well, here's to your health,' he said. The Englishman drank with him.

'Where are you two bound for?' he asked when Johnny finished.

'We're just having a look around. Sort of a working holiday around the country.'

'Careful vot you say,' a big man with a red face warned. His accent was pure Hollywood German. 'He might kiff you chob at railway camp and poison you vit his cooking.' He burst into laughter.

The cook smiled, but he was looking at Frog's hands. 'The work there might be too tough,' he said. 'By the look of your hands, you haven't done much work in the country so far.'

Frog put his free hand behind his back and nervously drank some more beer. When he finished, he attempted to smile.

'We don't mind getting our hands dirty,' Johnny was saying.

'You should've seen them, when they bowled in this morning,' the publican butted in. 'They were a darned sight dirtier than I've ever seen you. The trouble with you is that you can't stand the sight of a clean Australian.' He laughed and slapped Pommy's dusty friend on the back but then grimaced and wiped the dust from his hand. He went to another group and began gathering the empty glasses. 'Same all round?' he enquired. The men nodded. One of them appeared to be asleep, for his eyes were closed and his head was tilted against his chest, but he nodded too.

When the publican had departed with the empties, Johnny said: 'I thought this place was supposed to close at six.' He smiled but received unfriendly stares in reply.

Clarrie spoke. 'That's only for the bar, mate. Roy can serve special guests in here as long as he likes.'

'As long as we're thirsty,' added the cook. 'You don't object or anything do you?'

'No, it does me.' Johnny tried to smile pleasantly. The group was silent. 'It's just that, what's his name, Ivan over there told me you couldn't get a drink after six.'

'Ivan wouldn't remember anythink vot happened after six,' the red-faced man said.

'Hey Ivan,' the cook called. The Russian, who had been sitting with his head bent over the corner table, slowly looked up. 'Come over here and have a drink with us and your new friends.'

'Yeah,' red-face said softly, 'and bring your vogs vitt you. Better you sit my side.' He grabbed a chair from another table. 'I couldn't stand you opposite me. I'd hatt to look at you.'

They all started laughing. Ivan laughed with them and spilled a little of the drink he was carrying. He sat down without saying a word.

'You know these two chaps, don't you?' The cook waved a hand at Johnny and Frog. Ivan nodded shyly.

'Come up by motor bike,' the Englishman continued and then swung his eyes slowly from Ivan to Johnny. 'What sort of bike did you say it was?'

Johnny hesitated. 'BSA,' said Frog. The publican swept back into the room.

'A British bike, see,' said the cook loudly.

'And it broke down,' the publican said, as he placed the drinks on the adjoining table. The man who seemed to be sleeping lifted his head but did not open his eyes. His hand groped for the glass.

The cook breathed deeply. 'Ran out of petrol, that was all, my friend. How's it been going?'

'Good,' said Frog.

'Where'd you fill up last?' The cook examined them along the barrel of his cigar.

Frog looked at Johnny. 'Port Augusta,' said Johnny.

'That's a long hop on one tankful for a motor bike. You should have carried a spare can.'

'I wish we had,' said Johnny and laughed. The red-faced man nodded and so did Ivan.

Frog was studying the Englishman's face. He felt uneasy. The man was either drunk and troublesome or he was suspicious. Or both. He wanted to get away.

'Johnny,' he said. 'Let's have a bit of a walk round outside to have a look at the town.'

'You will not see much in the dark, I am afraid,' said a tall Italian who hadn't spoken before. His English, though accented, was delivered with precision, each phrase being chipped square at the edges, and polished, like monuments to clear expression, before the next was delivered. 'It is not a bad place, but you are liable to walk right out the other end without knowing. It is very black. There are no lights outside.'

'The professor's right,' said the English cook. 'Besides, you'll be back tomorrow, won't you? You can see Marree in all its majesty then.'

'All the same, I think we'll grab a bit of cool air,' Johnny said. 'You'll be around for a while, won't you?'

'Till the train comes in.'

'We'll see you then.'

Chairs scraped on the floor as they made their way to the door. Beer was spilled. 'Jesus,' growled a voice.

'Can't like drinking with us,' said Clarrie. 'Gonna give them a lift?'

The Englishman examined the glowing tip of his cigar.

'Funny pair,' he said and blew smoke at the insects circling the light.

As the Italian had said, it was so dark outside that little of the town could be distinguished. The two men stood on the dirt footpath in the soft glow cast by the hall light. The only other lights they could see came from the lounge window on their left and from a lantern in the railway station opposite. Down the far end of the town someone turned on a set of vehicle headlamps and in the bright glow, they could see the untidy silhouette of the Birdsville mail truck, closer to them and still parked at the edge of the road. The distant headlights pulled on to the road and moved towards the hotel.

Johnny took Frog's elbow. 'Out of this light. Quick.'

They walked around the corner of the hotel. The headlights drew closer and then arced across the road as the vehicle nosed into the hotel. The two men heard a door slam. Feet crunched on gravel.

'There Roy?' a man called, in a loud and deep voice.

The publican's voice sounded faintly and then, a few seconds later, they heard it say: 'Hi there, Eric, what can I do for you. Care for a drink?'

'Not just now thanks. I'm a bit busy. Had a coot of a day. We're still out looking.'

Johnny moved to the corner and glanced around. A policeman was standing in the lighted doorway.

'What, for the bloke from the Alice?' Roy was saying. 'Haven't you fellows nabbed him yet?'

'No. They reckon there might be two of them now. I've been out all day up along the line and came back tonight to find a pile of messages for me. They think there might be two of them and it looks like they're down this way somewhere. That's why I'm here. Have you heard of any strangers around the place.'

Johnny fondled the gun in his pocket.

'Two men?' There was an air of incredulity in the reply. 'I thought there was only supposed to be one.'

'Well, we never said for sure there was only one, but a cove at Oodnadatta last night reported two blokes in a utility truck heading this way. Acted suspiciously. They tracked the ute to a level crossing not far out of town. It was abandoned there with no sign of the blokes so they think they might have jumped a train. The driver of the morning train reported a stop for a fire across the track in about the same place, so it could add up. Not that we found anything, as you know. Just before lunch I got a call up the line to Bopeechee. Been there all flaming afternoon.' He shuffled his shoes on the gravel to emphasise his frustration. 'They thought they saw someone up there near the line. Nothing in it, though. Have you heard of anyone strange in town while I've been away?'

'No.' The word was drawn out and hesitant. 'As you know, Eric, we get a lot of people round the pub in a day. You get so busy, you don't notice everything.'

The feet grated on the gravel again.

'Cut out the bull. What are you trying to tell me?'

'Well, we had two blokes come in here this morning, a fair while after breakfast. But they couldn't be the ones you're looking for. They came up from Port Augusta on a motor bike.'

'Where are they now?'

'About somewhere. I was just looking for a can to get some petrol for them. They were with the Pommy cook from the railway camp a while ago.'

'Where's their bike?'

'Oh, it's not here. It's down the road a few miles. They ran out of petrol last night and had to walk in.'

'You haven't seen the bike, then?'

'No.'

'Then how do you know they came up by bike from Port Augusta?'

'Well, they told me so. They seemed nice enough blokes and they looked as though they'd been walking for miles.'

'Anyone see them walk in?'

'No, not that I know of.'

'And where did you say they are now?'

'Oh, they're about somewhere. Only just left the party in there a few minutes ago. Might be up in their room. Like to have a look?'

'Yes. I would. Lead the way.'

The voices faded away. Frog spoke. 'Johnny, we're in trouble.'

'Not so loud,' Johnny hissed. 'Come on, let's get away from here.' He turned and gave a little jump of surprise. Standing only a few feet behind him was the tall waitress. She took a step back, then turned and began to run towards the rear of the building.

Johnny stepped past Frog and chased her. He caught her arm after only half a dozen steps and jerked her to a stop. She spun round and stood, loose-jointed with fear, staring at him.

He bunched his right fist and hit her as hard as he could in the face. Blood burst from her lips, and she began to topple backwards, her limbs suddenly loose as though the joints had been disconnected. He swung again, hissing with the exertion. The smack of the blow striking the falling woman sickened Frog. 'Johnny,' he pleaded, 'don't kill her, too.'

He grabbed the other's arm but was shaken loose. Johnny stood over the woman, watching for any movement. Then he spoke. 'Quick. Let's get her out of the way.'

They carried her off beyond the hotel, blundering through the darkness until they came to a small clump of bushes. They pushed her into the middle of them. Johnny and Frog stood there for ten seconds, as if expecting her to shriek an alarm. It was Frog who broke the silence. 'Is she dead?'

'What's it matter, as long as she keeps quiet until we can clear out of here.' His eyes now used to the darkness, Johnny could make out Frog's face, with his big eyes, wide open, staring at him.

'What's the matter with you?' he whispered. 'Why are you looking at me like that?'

'Why'd you have to hit her so hard? Aren't things bad enough without bashing her too? I'd never have joined you if I'd known things were going to be like this.' Frog began to shake. 'You never said nothing about killing. You seem to like it.'

Johnny grabbed him by the upper arms and pushed him away, so sharply that Frog stumbled and sat down. A small bush crackled under him.

Johnny glanced back towards the hotel. He could see no one. He knelt beside Frog and spoke softly to him. 'The trouble we've had has just been bad luck. We're still all right, aren't we? We're still free and we've got the opals.' He prodded the man to emphasise the latter point. 'Just think of the money. There'll be lots of it once we hit Darwin. I've got friends there, remember that. Wealthy friends and they'll make us wealthy, too.'

He looked back over his shoulder. 'Just pull yourself together. We've had a rough trot. We only got out of that pub just in time but the important thing is that we got out. What we've got to do now is plan our next move.' He paused, studying the outline of the town. He could distinguish a few buildings, and the tall outline of the mail truck.

'More than ever now, I think Birdsville's our only way out. You remember what the bearded bloke, Ivan, said about the track and Birdsville. They're isolated from here. Don't know a thing that's going on. Probably haven't heard about us yet. You remember what he said? It's like another world. That's for us, eh, Frog?' He poked the other man in the arm.

Frog didn't answer. He tried to stand but Johnny pushed him back on his haunches. 'Stay down. We'll be harder to see.' Johnny jabbed him in the arm again, harder. 'We're in this together, right? You know your only chance of getting away is by sticking with me. All right, you didn't like me hitting the sheila. What was I supposed to do? Let her go yelling her head off? If I had, we'd have been nicely caught by now. I did what I had to for our sakes, Frog, and you know it. She'll be okay. I only gave her a couple of taps. Anyhow, forget her. We've got to move quickly. If that cop comes flashing a light about here, we'll be a couple of sitting ducks.

'I've been thinking about what we've got to do. We can't go with that Englishman in the truck. That's had it now. Even if the cop hadn't busted in when he did, I think the Pommy was beginning to smell a rat and would have caused trouble. We might be able to pinch his ute but where would that get us? We'd probably lose our way in the dark or else someone would be after us.' He touched the fat man on the arm again to make sure he was listening.

'We've got to get out of here without anyone knowing. So that means someone has got to take us up the Birdsville Track without him knowing it and without the town knowing it.' He paused to make sure the other man understood. 'Now that's a simple problem because there's only one answer. Only one person goes up the Birdsville Track; the mailman. We just move over there now and bury ourselves in all that junk on the back. And then tomorrow, the mailman starts to deliver us to Birdsville. Come on. Keep down on your hands and knees and take it easy. That cop's just about due to start looking over the town for us.'

Sergeant Eric Wallis spent fifteen minutes searching the hotel.

He checked every bedroom, the showers, toilets, the kitchen and the store rooms. He probed the area at the back of the hotel, shining his torch up the fire escape and poking through some old timber near the garbage bins. He even lifted the lid on the largest bin. He felt foolish. There was a ninety per cent chance the two men were just drifters whose motor bike had broken down like they claimed. Alice Springs was a long way away. He himself had never been there, and that fact, in his mind, made it seem less likely that any fugitives from the Alice would travel to Marree. Still, he searched, for Eric Wallis was a persistent man, given to doing what he knew should be done.

He examined the front of the hotel again, spoke briefly with the publican and some men who were standing with him, and walked out into the soft light spreading from the doorway to the street. He walked to the middle of the road and looked both ways. He let his eyes grow accustomed to the dark once more, but could see no one. He returned to the Land-Rover.

Reversing on to the road, the policeman swung the vehicle's nose to the south and drove slowly away from the hotel. The shape of a building loomed on his right. It was the last structure in town, a shed that lay in darkness. Pulling up outside the building, Wallis got out and checked that its front door was locked. He returned to the Land-Rover and circled the building, driving far from the road so that his headlights swept the wide plain beyond the town. The policeman turned north and drove past the hotel. He swerved slowly to the right so the lights raked the yard and buildings adjoining the railway line. The area seemed deserted, although on the far side, two station attendants were talking. They were waiting for the train from the south. Wallis drove across to them. He spoke loudly, for one of the men was deaf.

A minute later, he returned to the road, just beyond the place where the mailman's truck was parked. He reversed his Land-Rover until it drew alongside the heavily laden Chev. With his torch in hand, he leaned across and checked that the cabin was empty. He sat in the Land-Rover for a full minute, pondering the situation. He took out a notebook and, by torchlight, printed several lines on a page. He wrote cryptically, in the style of a telegram. Wallis flashed one final glance at the truck and then headed north once more, weaving slowly along the street, using the lights to sweep alternate sides of the wide road in his search for the missing men.

After he left, the truck rocked slightly. High on its load, Johnny Parsons and Frog Gardiner resumed their efforts to burrow deep into a tunnel of truck tyres. From the distance came the blast of a diesel locomotive horn.

Fred Crawford was replacing his teacup in its saucer when he heard the train. He looked at his wristwatch. 'It's later than ever,' he said.

Beside him, Barbara Dean smiled and leaned back in her chair. 'I'm glad I came up yesterday,' she said. 'My train was just late on schedule, was it?'

They were in the post office residence. The couple sitting on the other side of the table grimaced. 'Late and unreliable all the time,' the wife said. 'Brings us things that have spoiled or gone bad or that we didn't order.'

'I don't know,' chipped in John Black, 'Now and then it brings us nice things, Sister. Like you.'

His wife gave him a sidelong look. 'Well, I mean it, Eve,' he continued, shaking his red hair in defence of his statement. 'Sister here is the best looking thing we've seen around these parts since we came three years ago. About the only visitors we ever get are Fred here and his bearded mate. And I don't think you could compare their looks with the sister, now, could you?' He put a pipe in his mouth and bit on the stem.

What an unhappy couple, Barbara thought. They were strained in her presence, as though trying not to fight but anxious to score points in some private contest they waged. Her own parents used to fight, when she was young. In some way, this room aroused half-forgotten memories. Faint aromas haunted the place, wafting from the dark corners to remind her of childhood visits to old people living in shadowy houses. There was a smell of tobacco smoke, burning kerosene and fine dust which combined to nibble at the shrouds enfolding those memories. And there was a tension that could be sensed, a familiar but half-forgotten awareness of tension that the house had absorbed, like daytime heat, and was now dissipating from its walls.

John and Eve Black were probably the age of her own parents, when they used to argue so bitterly. The Blacks were not an old couple, but the feeling around them was of great age or, more correctly, of lost youth, frustrated ambition and the decay of hope.

'I've been very glad to have you here,' said Eve Black, addressing the sister and speaking more loudly than was necessary. 'And John knows it. I'm only sorry you've got to go on to Birdsville. Heaven knows, we could do with you here.'

'They need her up at Birdsville, too, Mrs Black,' Fred said.

'Oh, I know that. But there's nothing here in the way of medical care. We've got Leigh Creek, I suppose, but that's almost seventy miles away and I've always got the feeling that if something bad happened to the children, it'd be too late by the time they were taken down there.' She stared at her teacup. An awful feeling of isolation gnawed at Eve Black. Why had she let her husband take her and the three children from the crowded security of their Adelaide suburb to this? It was a promotion, he had said. A certain stepping stone to better things. And for that nebulous promise, they had to endure the heat and the flies and the loneliness. Her eyes sharpened into focus on the cup. 'Well,' she announced loudly, 'no use just sitting here, staring at the dirty crockery.' She rose and began gathering the cups and plates. Barbara rose to help.

'Now you just stay where you are,' Mrs Black said. 'You've got a long trip ahead of you. Besides, why not take it easy while you can. Not many women get that chance out here. Goodness knows, you'll be busy enough once you get to Birdsville. If I want help I'll get John.'

John Black raised his eyebrows as a warning that he was about to speak. He began to take the pipe out of his mouth, but she had recognised the sign. 'Don't worry,' she said. 'You stay here and entertain Fred and the sister. I'll have these finished in a moment. Besides,' she added quietly as she left the room, 'you'd probably make such a fuss you'd wake the children.' It sounded like a well-worn line.

Raising his eyebrows once again, John Black removed his pipe and looked up at Barbara. 'Eve's not too keen on it up here, you know,' he said softly. 'It's a hard life for a woman, especially with young kids. Harder for a city woman like Eve. This is a lot different from the place we had in Adelaide.'

He gestured with his hand. 'Look what she's got to put up with — pressure lamp instead of electric light, fuel stove, always got to be sparing with the water, dust everywhere, flies by daytime and insects by night. It's not much of a life, Sister. You're a city girl, aren't you?'

She nodded. 'Sydney.'

'How do you reckon you'll make out? It'll be worse in Birdsville than here.'

Fred winced. John and his wife would have this girl back on the next train south. Barbara saw his expression.

'I hope I'll be all right,' she smiled at him. 'I like my work and I've always wanted to see the outback.'

'You're certainly going to see a lot of Birdsville,' Black said.

'Yes, I suppose I am, but I'm looking forward to it. I've been told the other sister in the mission hospital is nice, and besides, my term is only for a year. If I don't like it, it's not that long.'

'That's something,' the postmaster said. 'Eve's had three years here and I think she's got to the stage where she's hating each day a little bit more. Anyhow, I don't want to depress you before you even get to the place.' His face brightened. 'You certainly chose a rough way to be delivered to your new job. Why didn't you fly in? There's a fortnightly air service from Brisbane through Charleville.'

Fred liked the way she stretched her arms on the chair before answering. Her skin had the light, soft tan of a city girl, not the deep-burned, leathery texture of an inlander.

'I told you,' she smiled. 'I want to see the country. The Birdsville Track's pretty famous, even away in Sydney. Back at the Australian Inland Mission headquarters I met one of the girls who'd been at Birdsville who told me she'd flown in and never had the chance to see the Track and had always regretted it. So I decided to see it first.' She tilted her head, and flashed a smile at him.

'Well, good luck to you,' John Black said. He was embarrassed by the warmth of the smile and the thought of his wife washing up alone. 'You can be sure Fred'll take good care of you. You know,' he leaned forward, pointing the stem of his pipe at her, 'you've made quite a hit with Fred. He even put on a shirt to have dinner.' He threw himself back in the chair and enjoyed the mailman's embarrassment.

A knock sounded at the door. He rose and opened it. Eric Wallis entered.

'Hello, John,' the policeman said and brushed past him. He walked to the table where Fred Crawford was sitting. 'Fred, I want you to get Ivan to stand guard over your truck all night and I want you to get your rifle and come with me.' He noticed the girl. 'Good evening. Can you do that for me, Fred?'

'Hold on,' Black broke in, 'what's all this about?'

'Is Mrs Black out the back?'

'Yes. In the kitchen, Why? What's up?'

'Get her to lock the doors and windows, John. Now there's nothing to be alarmed about, but it's just a precaution.'

'What for?'

'Remember the message you had waiting for me this afternoon? About the two men.'

The red hair nodded.

'They could be in town. Roy says two men checked in at the pub today. One of them tallies with the description we got from Oodnadatta. They've only been gone from the pub for a little while. Don't know where they've gone, but if they're not out of the town yet, we want to stop them getting away.'

'What's this about getting Ivan?' said Fred, slightly bewildered.

'Your truck's stuck out on the road, just asking to be pinched. I checked it on my way down the street. It's okay but I suggest you haul Ivan out of the pub quick-smart and have him guard it. There are two men in town that the police might be looking for, and we don't want to present them with the means of getting out of here. If these are the men we think they are, they'll be desperate, so tell your mate not to take any chances. Get him to move the truck near the pub and give him the lantern. And Fred, make sure he stays with the truck. No ducking off into Roy's place. John, get the lantern for Ivan, will you? And Fred, have you got a torch?'

'Yes.'

'Well, after you set up Ivan, bring your gun and torch and join me over at the station. The train's just come in and I've got to duck back over there. There's a good chance these fellows may try to jump it. Be as quick as you can, will you? I've got a couple of the others from up the road joining us.'

Black returned with his wife and the lantern. 'We've locked the back,' he said. 'What do you want me to do now?'

'Send this will you please?' He gave Black a slip of paper. 'Hope you can read the writing. Send it straight away and then wait here, please. There may be a reply. I'll check back here during the night. Are you armed?'

'I've got a pistol. Never used it though.'

'Hope you don't have to. Don't forget to lock everything up.' He moved towards the door. 'If we keep them out of the houses there aren't many other places they can hide. Don't worry, ladies,' he added as an aside. 'Goodnight.' He left the room and slammed the door behind him.

'Goodnight!' Eve Black echoed. 'Oh that rude man. Just barges in.'

'What is happening?' Barbara said. 'What was all that about?'

Fred nodded support. 'I wouldn't mind a few more clues myself.'

'Oh, he got a message through this afternoon from Adelaide about the killing up at Alice Springs a couple of nights ago,' Black said. 'Seems two men passed through Oodnadatta last night and they think they might be the ones who did it. Now they think they're here.' He glanced suddenly at his wife. 'Are the kids right, Eve?'

'They're right, of course they're right. What do you mean?'

'The window in their room. Eric said to close everything.'

'It's closed. It's always closed to keep out the dust.' She eyed the sister to make sure she had noted the remark, and then turned again to her husband. 'What's the message you're supposed to send?'

Black held the paper near the lantern. 'It's to the police in Adelaide. He's asking them to send help. He tells them about the two men seen here and gives a description.'

'Are they Aborigines?' she asked.

'No. They're white men.'

'That's a change. Most of the trouble here seems to come from the blacks.' She was addressing the sister, as though explaining some fact of life. 'Filthy people. I just pray I can keep the children out of their way until we move back south. They're the most degenerate, dirty people you could imagine.'

Fred looked at the floor. You could learn something from the Aborigines if you bothered, he thought and, for a delicious moment, imagined Eve Black trying to live in a humpy on the edge of town.

'Well, I'll be off.' Fred spoke from the corner of the room where he had taken a torch from his small bundle of personal belongings. 'I'll go and get my rifle from the truck and then collect Ivan. See you later, John, Mrs Black. Goodnight, Sister.' He opened the door, looked carefully about him, and stepped into the darkness. Black locked the door. He turned to Barbara. 'Pity you're not staying longer. Something's happening here at last. This place will probably be swarming with police by tomorrow. That's if they don't catch these fellows tonight.'

CHAPTER SEVEN

The violet flush of an awakening sky roused Eric Wallis. A light breeze touched his face. He looked at Fred Crawford, asleep, slumped against the door on the other side of the Land-Rover. Painfully, the policeman stretched his legs beneath the steering wheel and envied Fred's peaceful sleep. Not that he had been asleep long. Only for a couple of hours, after the two of them had shared a long, tiring and frustrating night.

He rubbed his eyes and stared, without focusing, at the fringe of light beginning to glow on the eastern horizon. What a night. If only he had called into the hotel ten minutes earlier, he'd have caught the men while they were still there. He was sure now they were the men all the State was searching for. They had been here in Marree and it looked as though he had let them get away.

He pushed the half-open door fully out and swung his legs on to the roadway. He stood up, yawned and stretched his arms and shoulders. He reached back in the Land-Rover and withdrew his rifle. Fred was still asleep. No use waking him for a while. Still not enough light to resume the search. Anyway, it wasn't Fred's job. His friend had his own job to do, and goodness knows, it was hard enough. You wouldn't find many men who were willing to travel up and down the Birdsville Track to earn a crust. Fred was the best friend he had in Marree. Not that he had many friends. It was difficult being a small town's only policeman and being popular.

The breeze ruffled his hair. Wallis breathed in deeply, savouring air that was cool and, at this time of the morning, clear of flies. He examined the town. It was a strange place. Free and easy and full of mateship and yet loaded with gossip and petty jealousies and class consciousness, like most towns he had been to. Only this place was different, because of the way it was compartmentalised. There were four groups.

There were the old hands, who regarded themselves, in a crusty and rough way, as the elite. Their fathers and grandfathers had come up this way and endured fearfully hard times. They had endured so much, Wallis reflected, that their descendants didn't dare leave in case all that pioneering effort would be wasted.

There were the government employees in their government houses who worked here because they couldn't get jobs anywhere else. Was that a fair assessment, he wondered? So many people persisted with jobs because they were terrified of being out of work, or of not belonging to some sort of group, that they had no alternative but to keep in that job all their working lives. He thought of the railway workers, who were the largest single group in town. And he thought of himself, now committed to being a policeman, not through a consuming sense of duty or devotion to the law, but because it was too late for him to become anything else. John Black was the same. He was serving time in Marree, like a prisoner ticking off the years before his release; and turning his wife mad in the process.

Wallis looked across the railway line, to where the other two groups, the Afghans and Aborigines, lived. He liked the Afghans. Honorable, quiet people, they had been brought here for a purpose which no longer mattered. Who the hell wanted people who were good with camels these days? The Afghans made Eric Wallis feel sad, because they made him feel vulnerable.

And the Aborigines. They stayed out of everyone's way, lived with dogs and lived like dogs, dreamed of the past, and got drunk on cheap liquor. They made everyone feel guilty or ashamed and, therefore, many of the most guilty reacted badly towards them. The trouble with the blacks, Eric Wallis thought, was not that they looked filthy and got drunk on vile things like metho or plonk, but that they were too damned gentle. They should complain more. Better still, they should get out of town, and the squalor they accepted so quietly, and go back into the bush. Out along the creeks and waterholes, to hunt with dignity and survive in conditions that were too tough for the white man. Fat chance of that happening. They had tasted the worst and most tempting of the white man's offerings and were hopelessly confused, and stranded between cultures.

The sky was a little lighter.

No place for women, Wallis thought, looking about him again. Not that there were many women about. A good looking one, like the Spencer girl, attracted the men and aroused gossip among the women in a way they wouldn't understand down south. If she were a bit of a flirt, like Betty Spencer, she could cause a lot of damage.

Poor Fred. Wallis reckoned his friend had been keen on Betty, even though she was only a youngster and he was a good bit older. She was attractive and there had been any number of suitors and Fred had missed out. He was probably a bit quiet for her and she'd gone for the flashier Spencer bloke. Worst of all, Fred had to call in at the homestead and see her every fortnight on the way up the track. Some of the old women reckoned he was still keen on her and that's why he hadn't chucked the job and gone elsewhere. Maybe so. Anyway, it was Fred's business. Wallis yawned.

Slinging the rifle under his arm, he walked to the front of the vehicle and looked up and down the street. A rooster crowed from somewhere to the east, but otherwise the town slept. A faint light was glowing through a window of the post office bungalow. John Black would have been asleep hours ago, he guessed. He remembered how John had come searching for him with the message that the Adelaide detectives were on their way by car. A fat lot of good a carload of detectives could do, the morning after the men had been seen. The time to catch them was last night. And he'd failed, even though they'd searched the train and checked all the homes in town again. He had driven all the way to the railway camp in case they'd jumped the cook and his mate on the way home from the pub. But all had been quiet at the camp. Still, the men there had promised to keep an eye out for them. The cook and Clarrie, the bulldozer driver, had seen the two men and would recognise them and that was a help. South was the way the fugitives would almost certainly be making, and the more people down that way who knew what they looked like, the better.

Wallis had come back and driven ten miles to the north but there was not a sign of them. He'd gone back to John Black and got him to wire a request that the train north be searched at all stops, just in case they'd managed to get on board. Goodness knows, the train was long enough and it had been dark enough for them to slip by the searchers.

At Fred's suggestion, he'd even gone out along the Birdsville Track for a few miles. Their headlights had stabbed far into the distant plains but there'd been no sign of the men. Not even a fresh tyre mark or footprint. He had asked Fred to keep his eyes open this morning, just in case. He could count on Fred.

A softly corrugated line of yellow appeared in the sky where a low-lying cloud had caught a ray from the still-hidden sun. Colour was beginning to return to the street. A fly settled quietly on his nostril and he brushed it away. He could now clearly make out the mail truck, parked outside the hotel. He thought of Ivan, asleep in the front. Lucky Ivan. Got drunk in town and worked hard on the track. You could say what you liked about him but he had no worries, and that was something.

Wallis slung his rifle under the other arm and walked slowly towards the truck. He gazed out at the vast plain stretching behind the town. Not a sign of life. Just a mangy dog scratching at some bushes near the hotel. He reached the truck and glanced in the cabin. Ivan was curled across the seats, having laid cushions across the metal frames. Wallis walked around the back of the truck, running his finger idly along the rough edge of the tray, and feeling the ropes. From within the hotel he heard the sound of voices.

'You awake, Roy?' he called, in as hushed a voice as he could manage. He heard the sound of bare feet padding towards him. The half-caste handyman appeared.

'Oh, it's you, Joe. Is the boss up yet?'

Joe tucked his shirt into his unbuttoned pants. 'No sergeant. I'm just off to get him, though.' He looked distressed.

'What's up?'

'Ethel says Gloria hasn't shown up. Been out all night, she says, and it's her turn to get the fire going.' The man was struggling to do up his trouser buttons.

'Oh well, you've got your troubles and I've got mine. When you wake the boss, tell him we still haven't found the two men, will you?'

Wallis left Joe with a worried look on his face and the last button on his pants still undone, and returned to the truck. When he was several yards away he heard the sound of a man coughing.

He walked to the cabin, reached in and gave Ivan's beard a tug. 'What's wrong, swallow a fly?' Ivan stirred. 'Come on, wake up. It's almost midday.'

The Russian opened an eyelid still sticky with sleep. 'What's up?' he mumbled.

'You were coughing.'

Ivan propped himself on one elbow and looked out the doorway. 'Was I?' He tested his throat. He sat up and scratched his back. 'Catch them?' he yawned.

'No. Did you have a quiet night?'

'Didn't hear a thing. Bit uncomfortable, though. Where's Fred?'

'He's over in the Rover. Still asleep. What time do you plan on leaving?'

'Pretty soon, I suppose.' He yawned. 'Fred said we'd shove off once Blackie sorted out the mail that came up last night and once the sister had breakfast. She's going with us, you know.' He smiled in anticipation. 'Nice, isn't she? She'll make going to Birdsville a pleasure from now on, eh?'

Wallis didn't reply. He was examining the back of the truck. 'Got a fair load on this time, Ivan. Did you check it last night?'

'Yes.' He rubbed his eyes to shake off the last traces of sleep and deposited a streak of dried grease across an eyebrow. 'Always check it the night before we go.'

'I mean after Fred told you to bring it here and guard it. Did you check the load then?'

Ivan had tied the tarpaulin in place, but he had not checked the individual items in the load. 'No,' he said simply.

'Well, let's have a decko at it. You get up and take the tarp off.'

Ivan untied the securing ropes and scrambled easily to the top. He headed for the highest part of the load, a tower of truck tyres which rose from the front of the tray. A pair of huge earthmoving tyres formed the bottom of the pile, which rose in a narrowing tunnel to a stack of smaller lug grips. Ivan straddled the top tyre and threw the canvas back to the tailboard. He looked down with interest at the constable, who had pulled the cover clear of the sides and was slowly walking around the truck.

'See anything up there?' Wallis called.

'No.'

'Everything just as you left it?'

Ivan glanced around him. 'Yes. What are you looking for, anyhow?'

Wallis looked up at him, irritably. 'Never mind. Here.' He threw a securing rope to Ivan who caught it without losing his balance on the tyres. 'I'll give you a hand to tie the tarp on again.'

Fred Crawford was awake when the constable and the Russian walked up to the Land-Rover. 'Still no sign of them, Eric?' he asked, in a voice that rasped unevenly through his dry throat.

'No. You two better go and have some breakfast, if you want to get off soon.'

'What are you going to do?'

'I think I'll just circle around the town to see if I can pick up some tracks. You never know. They might have gone bush on foot. They must have. Either that or they got on that blasted train last night, after all. Well, I'll go and see what I can find.' He started up the Land-Rover. 'Thanks for the help, mate.'

'That's all right,' Fred answered. He took his rifle and walked with Ivan towards the post office. The Land-Rover disappeared down the street. The sun, now clearing the horizon, split the billowing dust trail with slivers of yellow and reddish-brown.

When they reached the post office, they could hear a child crying from one of the back rooms. 'There goes John's alarm clock,' said Fred, and knocked on the door.

A sleepy-eyed John Black let them in. He looked a little dismayed to see Ivan enter too. 'Any luck with the search, Fred?' he asked.

'No. Eric thinks they either tried to walk out or they hopped the train. He's out looking for any tracks leading out of town now.

We covered all roads last night without seeing so much as a trace of them.'

Mrs Black appeared from another room, nursing a child. 'Good morning,' she said in a tired voice, and noticed Ivan. Fred thought she might drop the baby. She looked towards the kitchen, and then at Ivan. 'You two have had a hard night by the look of you,' she said, and Fred knew she was capitulating, and that Ivan was staying. 'I suppose the first thing you'll want will be a clean-up. I've never had such dirty men in the house.' She looked pointedly at Ivan, who wiped his mouth with the back of a dust-caked hand.

'Good idea,' said Fred. 'Come on, mate.' He led the other out of the house to the shed which contained the bathroom.

Mrs Black called after them. 'I'll have breakfast ready by the time you come back.'

Barbara Dean was in the kitchen, setting the table, when they returned. The aroma of grilled steak came from the fuel stove. 'Mr Black tells me the policeman had no luck last night. You poor things must be worn out.'

'Oh, we're all right,' Fred said. 'I can always have a sleep at the wheel while I'm driving. There's no one else to run into, out where we're going.' He made his joke shyly and grinned with pleasure as she smiled.

'Breakfast like this is a real treat,' Fred said. 'We don't normally get an invitation to dine with the Blacks. This is a rare occasion.'

'Is that because of me?' she said.

'Well it's not Ivan.'

The Russian beamed. 'All I usually have is a dingo's breakfast.'

'What's a dingo's breakfast?' she asked.

Fred blushed. A piss and a look around. How could he explain that? 'Just whatever you can pick up,' he lied. That settled it. Ivan rode on the top. Fred was offended by any swearing or ribaldry in front of women and while he could accept the prospect of Ivan upsetting the sister by his matted appearance, he could not tolerate the thought of coarse jokes or rough language being used in her presence. Like many bushmen who spent long periods away from the company of women, he tended to put the female species on a pedestal. The more attractive or cultured they seemed, the more elevated the pedestal. And already Barbara Dean was high in his estimation.

'You look mighty fresh this morning,' he said, not knowing how to extricate himself from his embarrassment. 'Nice frock.'

'Thank you,' she said, and knives and forks in one hand, and the skirt of her frock in the other, she slowly turned for his benefit. He forgot about the frock and thought how cool and soft and womanly she looked. Then she was facing him again, waiting for some gesture of his approval.

John Black entered the room. 'What's this, a mannequin parade or something?' he said.

'Mr Crawford was just saying he liked my dress.'

'Well, I'm glad he likes it. He and Ivan the Terrible are about the only two who are going to get a chance to admire it today. You're not travelling on a Sydney bus, you know.' She laughed.

'You're looking forward to this trip, aren't you?'

She nodded excitedly. 'Thrilled,' she said, then turned again to Fred and added worriedly: 'This business last night isn't going to affect the trip. I mean, we're still going, aren't we?'

He grinned. 'Of course. We'll leave other people to worry about those men.'

Three quarters of an hour later, they climbed aboard the mail truck and drove out of Marree up the Birdsville Track.

Eric Wallis was continuing his futile search for tracks, half a mile south-west of the town, when he saw a man hobbling over the stones towards him, waving his arms. It was Joe, the hotel handyman. 'What's up?' he called.

Joe stopped but he was too breathless to reply. Instead he waved for the constable to come towards him.

Wallis bounced the Land-Rover over rocks until he was alongside the man. Joe was standing on one foot, rubbing the sole of the other.

'What's up?' the policeman demanded.

'The boss said to come back into town,' he panted. 'It's Gloria.'

'Who's Gloria?'

'From the pub. You know, the tall one.'

'What about her?'

'You remember. She'd been missing.' He paused for breath. 'Well, I found her under some bushes. Face's bashed in.'

'Is she dead?'

'The boss doesn't think so, but she looks dead.'

'Hop in. Quick.'

He drove across the stones at a speed that bounced them from their seats and shook the dust from the floor in choking clouds.

A small group of people watched him draw up behind the hotel. A dog barked. The publican detached himself from the others and led Wallis to the bushes. A swarm of flies rose as they approached.

'I kept the others away,' the publican said. 'Didn't want to spoil any footmarks. I haven't moved her yet, either. Didn't want to touch a thing until you got here. Only found her a few minutes ago.' He stood back and let Wallis move on alone.

Carefully, the policeman pushed his way into the bushes. The body of the tall waitress lay on the ground, her face bruised and puffed and caked with blood. Ants were crawling on her body. One outstretched arm was near him. He brushed an ant off the hand, and moved the fingers. They bent easily. He felt her pulse. 'She's still alive,' he said.

'Yes. I asked a couple of blokes to fetch the stretcher from the railway station.'

Wallis examined the woman and then spent several minutes closely inspecting the grass and earth around the bushes. 'Looks like our friends,' he announced.

The publican walked closer to him. 'What do you mean?'

'You've kept everyone away from here since Joe found her?'

'That's right.'

'Well there are two men's footprints. Look, you can see them here.' He pointed to a patch of dust. 'And here, too. You can see them all around on this side of the bushes.' He rubbed his chin thoughtfully.

'Was she, ah, was she molested?'

'You mean raped? Don't think so. Her clothing's intact. Anyhow, here comes the stretcher. Let's get her out of the sun and set about getting a doctor to her. And be careful not to destroy those footprints.'

'They're important, eh?'

'Could be. You've given us a good description of both men and now we've got these prints. When the Adelaide detectives get here today, they can compare them with what was found at the Alice. Then we'll be getting somewhere.' He waved the men with the stretcher in to the bushes on a line that took them clear of the footprints. He walked back to the Land-Rover with the publican.

'In the meantime, I'll get John to get in touch with all the people down the line,' he added. 'We've got to warn them that these men are about. They've killed one woman already and it looks as though they've tried to do the same here. Things are getting tougher for them all the time and they know it. Heaven help the next poor bastard they meet.'

CHAPTER EIGHT

The rumbling of the mail truck woke Johnny Parsons. He twisted his aching back and listened to the dull roar of the motor. Once before, many hours ago, the motor had started and they had moved but it was only a short journey, maybe only a hundred yards. And the driver had stayed in the cabin. They had listened to him shuffling in front and had not dared move. Later, Johnny had slept but Frog had coughed and woken him. He had heard voices and a thin shaft of light had filled the rubber tunnel above him. But the light quickly went and so did the voices and he had drifted off into another tormented sleep. He listened again to the motor. Yes, now they were right. They were really on their way to Birdsville.

The two men were curled in the largest tyres, each like a foetus in a rubber womb. Johnny tried to tap Frog's shoulder but found he could not move his numbed arm. He clenched and unclenched his fingers to restore the circulation. It was strange, like operating a hand on someone else's body.

'We're on our way, Frog. We'll soon be out of here.' He paused, awaiting a reply. 'You awake?'

Frog grunted.

'It must be daylight,' Johnny said. He felt the vehicle slow down. 'Hang on, be quiet. We're stopping.'

The truck rolled to a stop. A thumping noise sounded above him and then came the stamp of feet on the ground, and he realised with surprise that someone had been sitting on the load.

There was a strange creaking sound he couldn't identify. The truck lurched forward for maybe ten yards and stopped. Again came that creaking sound, then a slam and the clank of a chain. Of course. It was a gate. They'd passed through a gate.

'Thanks, mate,' said a voice from the front. He heard the sounds of a man scrambling to the top and they were moving again.

'Be careful, Frog,' he said in a voice just loud enough to be heard above the grinding roar of the accelerating motor and the occasional jolt which thudded into the truck. 'There's someone up top. Probably the mad Russian.'

'Can you get off me, Johnny?' Frog's voice shook unevenly. 'It's bad enough when the truck's standing still. It's murder with you bouncing into me like this. Can you move?'

They had not changed their basic positions since squirming into the tunnel of big tyres. Frog had the lower position. He was on his side and lay with his knees tucked close to his body. Johnny was on top, with his limbs spilling from the well of a bulldozer tyre. He was thirsty and the air smelled of his companion's stale body odour.

He tried to move away from Frog, but his stiffened body and leg muscles wouldn't respond. He reached backwards and upwards with his free arm and gripped the bead of a giant tyre. He pulled himself clear, coaxing into life a fresh batch of muscles with each new movement.

After several minutes, he was able to stand inside the tunnel of tyres. Painfully, Frog sat up and stretched his arms. Then he, too, stood, so that their heads were close together and they touched bodies frequently, as the truck bounced and flung them against the beads of the tyres.

'When are we getting out of this hole?' Frog whispered. His throat was so dry he had difficulty in making himself understood. 'It's going to be hot as blazes in here soon. There's not much air now.'

'There's no use our crawling out now, with the Russian sitting up on top. We'd be like sitting ducks, untying the canvas and trying to crawl out. Specially the way the thing's rocking. No, we'll wait. They've got to unload some of this stuff along the way, surely. We'll wait till they do and then step out and take over.'

Barbara Dean was bitterly disappointed with her first view of the Birdsville Track. They had driven over the railway line at Marree, passed an untidy collection of hovels, near which grazed a herd of goats, and gone through a gateway in a fence. Then the truck had weaved through a band of low trees. To her astonishment, she learned they marked the bed of the Frome River. She looked, but saw no sign of a river. Just the trees, and a coating of grass and maybe the suggestion of a few dips in the track. No more than hollows, like you would find in any suburban road back in Sydney. Now they were rolling forward into more open country. The track was graded.

'Where are the sandhills?' she asked, anxiously, as though they were on the wrong road.

Fred Crawford turned and smiled at her. He looked utterly relaxed. He was wearing a wide-brimmed hat, sunglasses, a khaki shirt that was unbuttoned and brief khaki shorts. On his feet were lightweight sandals. The shirt she suspected was a concession to her. Through the unbuttoned gap, she could see a strip of deeply tanned chest and stomach that indicated regular exposure to the sun.

'Don't be too impatient,' he said above the noise of the motor. 'We've still got well over three hundred miles to go. You'll see plenty of sandhills before this trip's over. Actually, the first one we cross is just before the Cooper.'

'What's the Cooper?'

'Cooper Creek. Big river. They call it the Barcoo or the Thompson in Queensland. You've probably heard of it. Runs into Lake Eyre — when it's running that is. Usually comes down when it rains heavily up in Queensland. Floods the track. Gets very wide.'

'Is it flooding now?'

'No, it's been dry for a while. Nothing but grass there now.'

'What do you do when it's in flood? Just wait till it goes down, I suppose.'

'Oh no. We unload and take the stuff across by boat. There's a boat there at the crossing. Sort of a punt.'

'And what do you do when you get to the other side?'

'Load up again.'
'But how do you get the truck across?'
'Don't. I use two trucks. I've got more than one, you know.' He grinned. 'Not all as good looking as this one, of course. We always get plenty of warning when the Cooper's coming down, so I leave one of the trucks on the other side. Then it's just a case of driving to the river, boating the load across and then reloading the other truck. And away you go.'
'That sounds like a lot of work. Is that the only river?'
'No. There's the Diamantina. You've heard of that?' She nodded, and he continued. 'It's only about a mile short of Birdsville. It's up at the moment, as a matter of fact. Unusual for this time of year, but they got some late rain around Winton and it's just coming down. Takes months.'
'Will we be able to get through?'
'Oh yes. There's a ford. It's only a couple of feet deep. It's pretty fast flowing at the moment but it's not over the banks, or anything like that. Nowhere near it.'
'Doesn't it flood like the Cooper?'
'It can come down all right, too, don't worry about that. Spreads to more than a mile wide. When that happens, we go boating there, too.'
'You've got to be versatile, haven't you? Everything from sandhills to flooded rivers.'
'I'm sorry we can't offer you the full variety this time. I'm afraid this is going to be a very tame trip. All we can offer you is the tail end of a flood in the Diamantina. Still, you'll see the sandhills — if you can wait for them.'
She smiled. 'You know, I really am terribly excited about this trip. Going to a new place, meeting new people, seeing new country.'
'Well, it's certainly different to Sydney.'
'You know Sydney?'
'Yes, I was there during the war.'
'How'd you like it?'
'All right. Not keen on the cities, though. Everyone's in too much of a hurry.'
'Have you always lived up here?'
'No, my people come from Perth. I first came up this way just before the war. And then after the war, I bought some surplus

army gear and came back here. Went into business. Got the mail contract. Do a few other things too. You know, sinking bores and making dams and things. Water's the thing that's scarce up here. It's bores that keep this country alive. You'll see quite a few of them along the track. I'll point,them out to you.'

He changed gear to enter a sandy depression, edged with spiky grass. 'Most of the bores on the track were sunk by the government around the turn of the century. This is a cattle track, of course, and so the bores are sunk about a day's walk apart. Not that I'd like to walk it.'

He steered around a depression which was paved with cracking plates of dried mud. 'It's about mustering time now. We probably won't see any herds on the drove. If we do, we just move off the track and give them the right of way. The cattle are a bit wild-eyed up here.'

'Would they charge us?'

'No. We'd probably frighten the daylights out of them. It's just easier for us to go around them, than for the drover to have to persuade them to go round us. There's almost always room for us to wander off.'

Barbara stared through the cracked windscreen at the vast, pebbly plain stretching before them.

'It looks harsh,' she said. 'Big and empty and cruel.'

'Gets under your skin after a while,' he said. 'It's funny, but you can go away from this country and something makes you come back. But you're right, you know, about it being cruel. You've got to fight it to make a living. Lose the fight and it'll break you. Or kill you.'

They drove on for several miles without speaking.

She opened her bag, took out her sunglasses and put them on. It was becoming hotter and the glare was increasing. Away in the distance, she saw a hazy, dark green line. What was it, trees? A thin, low line of trees. And beneath them tiny dark shadows. That would be cattle. So things do live out here, she thought. How lonely. How awfully lonely. She thought of herself being stranded under a tree in the middle of a desert that went from nowhere to nowhere.

The sound of the motor reminded her that the truck was their only link with the sort of life she knew and could bear. Even if it was rugged, like life at Marree, at least there were people who were friendly and lived in the comfort of each other's company. Not like being stranded under a tree, like those cows. Or steers or whatever they were.

'Have we got any water?' she asked, suddenly.

'Yes. Why?'

'How much?'

'Bag on the front, a couple of drums on the back. Why did you ask? You don't go anywhere without water here.'

'That's what I was thinking. I was looking out there and I suddenly realised what it would be like without water.'

'It wouldn't be pleasant and it wouldn't be long,' he said, gravely.

DEHYDRATION, he thought, remembering his dictionary. 'The removal of water from.' A clinical word for a terrible fate. Delirium, hours of agony and then a lightweight corpse, drained of all fluid and with a mouth full of sand. He'd seen it. A kangaroo shooter had gone missing near the southern part of the track a couple of years before and Fred had found his body. The man had holed the petrol tank on his utility. Cruel country. 'The sun gets pretty hot out here,' he added, leaning forward and peering up at a sky slowly being bleached of colour as the day advanced. 'Going to be hot today,' he announced. 'Over the hundred, I'd say. That means a slow trip.'

'Why's that?'

'Tyres. If they get too hot, they'll blow. The faster you go, the hotter they get. It's like driving on a stove. I'll have to pull up every now and then and give them a chance to cool off.'

She glanced at him. He looked completely at home, relaxed, confident. She began to feel brighter. She looked down at his feet. He had kicked off the sandals and was driving barefooted. Yes, he was really at home. She looked again at the distant cattle. They were probably feeling at home, too. It was just a case of what you were used to.

She thought of Sydney, and the leafy streets and terraced houses near the hospital where she had spent so much of her time. It's just somewhere over there, she thought, glancing beyond Fred to the east, but that's impossible. This is not in the same country. This is another world. She breathed deeply and the hot air scorched her throat.

She thought of Ivan, sitting up on top, with no cover from the sun except his hat and she felt guilty. 'Are you sure Ivan will be all right?' she asked. 'It's going to be terribly hot out in the open later on, isn't it?'

'Ivan will be all right. He's a pretty tough bloke. Tough as a dingo,' he said and added under his breath. 'It's all those breakfasts.'

'But I do feel guilty, making him sit up there. I mean, if I weren't here, he'd be able to sit in here, out of the sun.'

'Look, don't worry. Often when there's just the two of us, he gets up there. He reckons there's a bit of a breeze and he gets away from the heat of the motor. We can fit three in the front, though, so if things get a bit uncomfortable up there, he can come in here with us. There's room.' He patted the hump of the transmission tunnel. 'I think he'll stay up there, all the same, unless he wants company. With his hat and all those whiskers, he's pretty well protected from the sun.'

She smiled. 'It's a very practical disguise, then. How long has he been with you?'

'A couple of years, now. He's a Russian, you know, and had a pretty rough time of it during the war. He spent a few years in a concentration camp. Not many of his mates survived the sort of treatment the Nazis gave the Russians. He'll put up with anything, and he's a hard worker. He's taken to this sort of country pretty well. It's a surprising thing, that. Not many new people come up here, now, but most of them are New Australians. Germans mainly, although we've got a mixture of Poles and Czechs and so on. They seem more willing to rough it than the people who've lived in Australia all their lives.'

'Does Ivan do much of the driving?' she asked.

'No. I normally drive all the way myself. He looks after the load. Besides the truck's a little touchy. Doesn't like anyone else at the wheel. Me and the truck are a bit like Alexander and Bucephalus.' He looked quickly at her, longing for a response. But her face was blank.

'Pardon?' she said and he was embarrassed. It was too much to have hoped that she might have understood what he was talking about.

'Bucephalus,' he repeated, and felt an added pang of embarrassment that he might be mispronouncing the word, because he had never heard it spoken. 'That was Alexander the

Great's horse. Only he could ride it.'

Her expression was a blend of admiration and astonishment. 'What's a Greek scholar doing driving a truck up the Birdsville Track?'

'I'm not a scholar,' he said, straightening and clenching his fingers on the wheel. 'I just found the name in a book.' He changed into a low gear to slow the truck for a gutter cutting the track. 'Seemed a strange name for an animal.'

'Yes.' She laughed. 'Imagine calling him over for a bag of oats.'

The track improved and Fred accelerated and changed into top gear.

'You must read a lot,' she said.

He nodded. 'A lot of bush people do. Some of the old timers used to read anything they could get hold of, in the days before radio. Probably helped them stay sane. I met an old dingo trapper who had the most fantastic memory. He could recite hundreds of poems. "The Man from Snowy River". All that stuff.'

'You must have a good memory, to remember the name of Alexander the Great's horse.'

'You make it sound like I used to saddle him.'

They both smiled and Fred felt more relaxed. 'The only war I was in was the last one,' he said. 'I missed Alexander's shindig. Must have been a remarkable bloke. Conquered Greece when he was twenty, only lived till he was thirty-two and yet he ruled a kingdom that stretched all the way from the Mediterranean to Kashmir. He never lost a battle.'

'And only he could ride that horse with the unpronounceable name,' she said. 'Just like you and this truck.'

'Right.' He moved his leg from the gearlever and patted the worn knob. 'Come on, Bucephalus, take us to the outer limits of the empire.'

'Birdsville?' she said.

'Right again.'

The truck jumped out of gear, and the engine snarled as its load was suddenly released. 'Bastard.' Fred muttered, unable to restrain himself, and tugged the lever back into place. The sound of the engine dropped to its normal grind. Again he hooked his left leg around the gear stick but kept his hand on the knob for a few seconds, to make sure the gear was properly engaged. 'Alexander's horse was too good for anyone else to ride,' he said, with feeling. 'This truck's too bad for anyone else to drive.'

'I get the feeling you're very attached to it,' she said, challenging him. 'You like it because it's got character.'

He tilted his head, in a gesture that meant she might have spoken the truth. 'There are better trucks around, but at least I know what this one will do. We've covered a lot of hard miles together.'

Far to their right, a line of white birds rose from the ground and fluttered like a handkerchief in the breeze.

'You like this sort of work?' she asked. 'Driving out here, on your own?'

He nodded. 'It's a living, and better than a lot of others. Roo, on the left.'

His sudden change of voice made her turn. 'Over there.' He pointed to the slim outline of a kangaroo whose upper body rose from a fuzz of grey bushes well clear of the track.

Barbara scanned the area for several seconds before seeing the kangaroo. 'You've got good eyes,' she said.

'No. You just get used to identifying things. It depends where you are. I'd probably get run over in the city because I didn't see a car coming, but I can spot a roo at half a mile. That one's nervous and doesn't know whether to hop away or not. See the way it's ears are twitching?'

'Are there many kangaroos up here?'

'It depends. If it's been raining, you can see hundreds. They chase thunderstorms because they like the fresh grass that grows after a bit of rain. Other times you could drive up and down here for six months and not see one.'

The kangaroo turned, a clumsy shuffle of hindlegs and thick tail, and began hopping parallel to the track. Once in motion, it assumed a flowing grace that swept it across a patch of rough rocks and sand, through more low bushes and then out on to a clear plain. Legs in perfect unison and tail counterweighting the out-thrust body, it moved with a smoothness and at a speed which would have been beyond any four-legged animal covering similar terrain. It was a moving creature perfectly suited to its territory. Then, it stopped and, in stopping, lost the marvellous synchronisation of twin-drive legs and balancing tail, and became again a clumsy-looking oddity, leaning on its tail, like a cripple on a crutch, as it strained for height, to see if the truck were in pursuit.

'No one's after you, young lady,' he said softly, and the kangaroo was lost to his view, as the truck rolled to the north.

'It's a female?' Barbara said. 'You can tell from this distance?'

He nodded solemnly.

'My heavens. What eyes.'

He looked at her and slowly smiled. 'It's the colour.'

'You're serious?' She looked at him intently.

'Red for boys and blue for girls.'

'Now you're joking.'

'You've heard of blue flyers? They're the women out here. Actually, they're a grey blue, and smaller than the males. The big reds grow to six feet or more. That was a female. You saw the colour.'

She had noticed nothing but the kangaroo's shape and the way it moved for it was the first time she had seen such an animal outside a zoo. She twisted in her seat, to catch a final glimpse of the kangaroo, but it was hopping away to the west, and dust from the truck had drifted across to obscure her view.

'I feel like a real city slicker,' she said.

He changed gear to ease the truck through a rough patch.

'You were saying you liked this work,' she said, eager to keep him talking.

He nodded.

'Better than the other things you do?'

He glanced at her. 'You mean the dam sinking? No, as a matter of fact, I think I like that better.'

The truck shuddered as it crossed a series of ruts. She braced herself against the dashboard until the shaking ceased.

'Why?' she asked, resettling herself in the seat. 'I would have thought that was very hot and dirty work.'

'Oh it can be,' he said. 'But at least you're making something. You know, shaping something that's got a purpose and is going to be around for a while. There's good money in it, but this isn't good country for dams, so there aren't enough people who want blokes like me to sink dams for them. So I do the mail run as well.'

'I'd have thought storing water would have been very important up here.'

'Water is important. Storing it is the problem. The trouble with dams is evaporation. The sun up here is so hot and so constant that a shallow dam will lose all its water in a couple of days.'

'So what do you do?'

'Build very few dams.' He laughed.

'And you take the mail to Birdsville?'

'Spot on,' he said. 'I drill a few bores as well. Underground water is what keeps this country alive. There's more of it, and it doesn't evaporate, way down below us, out of the sun.'

'There are some people who want dams — around the homesteads and so on, where they can keep them filled from bores — but making a living just building dams in this country would be on a par with selling refrigerators to the Eskimos in Alaska.'

'Speaking of natives, what about the Aborigines?' she asked. 'Are they as bad as Mrs Black was making out? She seemed to be frightened of them.'

'Eve Black is a silly woman.'

Barbara expected him to continue. She waited for several seconds. 'Silly about the Aborigines?'

'About most things,' he said. 'She's not the sort of woman who should have come to this country. She gives John a bad time. When she has a problem, instead of seeking help, she seeks revenge.'

After a long pause, Barbara said. 'Are the Aborigines likely to be dangerous? I mean, do they get violent?'

'Look,' he said, turning to her briefly. 'Most of your patients are going to be Aboriginal and you'll find they're the least violent people you could meet.'

'They do seem dirty.'

'There isn't much water around.' Again, he was silent.

'You like them.' It was a statement, not a question.

'Yes. Not that I'd pretend to know any Aborigine very well. They're secretive people. They're not good workers, but that doesn't mean they're stupid, like some people reckon. Maybe they've got more brains than all of us white twits who work our tails off so we can make money for the tax man. The more time I spend out here, the more I think the Abos are the ones who know what life is all about and we're the ones who are mixed up.' He looked at her sharply. 'I hope you're not a converter?'

She looked puzzled.

'You know, someone fired up with a ton of missionary zeal. Out to change them, or to save them?'

She shook her head. 'I'd just like to keep them healthy.'

'Good,' he said. 'That's good.' He smiled at her. Thank God for that, he thought, and rubbed a thumb self-consciously around the rim of the steering wheel.

The track meandered towards a large hill, a flat-topped mesa that lay on the plain like a straw hat tossed on a table. Its sloping sides were paved with stones, debris from the sheer walls that rose like the ruined ramparts of some ancient fortress. On the northern side, a section of the wall had succumbed to the ceaseless savaging of time and weather and turned to sand, which spilled gently down the slope. A brief wind squall plucked at the sand. It streamed from the ramparts like whispy curtains flapping through an open window.

Beyond the decaying hill was the first homestead. 'That's Lake Harry,' Fred said, pointing to a distant clump of palm trees beside a group of low buildings on their right. Well behind them, a weather-worn ridge shouldered its way out of the plain. The hills wore a speckled coating of hazy purples and pinks.

As they drew nearer the homestead, Barbara could see the lake, its shimmering white surface stretching away towards the low hills. 'Is it salt?' she asked.

He nodded. 'They almost all are up here.'

'Like Lake Eyre?'

He nodded.

'We must be fairly close to Lake Eyre,' she said, pivoting in her seat to look the other way. 'Where is it from here?'

'You can't see it. It's over that way.' He jerked his thumb to the left. 'About thirty or forty miles.'

'It seems awful that the biggest lake in a continent should be dry,' she said. 'Is it always dry?'

'No, it filled up several years ago. We had regular rain for a couple of seasons and the rivers flowed down and it filled up. It was a wonderful sight.' He looked briefly at her. 'Grass and flowers sprang up on the banks. We'd never seen that before. Ducks and all sorts of water fowl came there. But it went dry again. No grass, no flowers, no ducks. Just salt. Miles and miles and miles of it.'

They were level with Lake Harry homestead now. 'Aren't you

going to stop?' she asked.

'No.'

'Why not?'

'No one lives there. It's an out-station for Muloorina. Over that way.' He jerked his thumb to the left. 'They just use it for shelter when they're working over this way.'

'Well, where do we stop first?'

'Dulkaninna. That's thirty-four miles on. Should make it in time for morning tea. No sense hurrying.'

'Oh, I don't mind,' she said. 'As long as I get to Birdsville in three days. Not all city people are in a perpetual rush, you understand. I want to look around and meet some of the people.'

'I'm afraid you won't meet a great number of people. There are only half a dozen homesteads on the way. Quite a few of the menfolk will be out now, too, mustering. Still, those folk who are about will give you a great welcome. Quiet, but very sincere.'

'I'm sure I'll like them.'

'They'll like you, too, that's for sure.' He smiled again at her, a shy smile that set his mouth crinkling at the ends and then suddenly developed into an unsuppressed yawn. ''Scuse me?' he said, before he could properly close his mouth. 'I'm not used to such late nights.'

'You must be feeling awfully tired.'

'I'll be all right after tonight. I'll be asleep as soon as that sun goes down.' He jerked his head back. 'I wonder how Eric is getting on back there.'

'Eric?'

'The policeman. I wonder if he's found those blokes yet.'

'Oh, I'd almost forgotten about them. What's the full story about them? Mr Black told me a little about it last night but everyone in the house was in such a dither after you went that I couldn't quite grasp the details. Apparently they murdered a woman in Alice Springs and now they're trying to escape through Marree. Or at least, they think they are. Is that right?'

'That's about it. Eric was telling me last night that they stole some opals, apparently pretty valuable ones, that had been mined at Coober Pedy — that's a couple of hundred miles over that way.' He pointed past her to the west. 'They belonged to some American. He'd left them in the hotel safe and was taking them out of the country. Quite a few Americans go to Coober Pedy.

Interesting place. Country's very much the same as here. Gibber plain, you know, hardly any grass and no trees. Practically everyone lives underground in little caves. Got them all furnished out with kero refrigerators and everything. I believe they're quite comfortable and they're certainly a lot cooler than a hut out in the sun would be. It'd be as deserted as this,' he indicated the country ahead of them, 'if it wasn't for the opals. You know, it's amazing what people will put up with to make a living.'

'Like you for instance?'

He laughed. 'This is a bit different to living in a hole in the ground. Anyhow, to get back to the story. Eric said the police reckon this woman interrupted these two fellows cracking the safe and they killed her. Beat her to death.'

'How horrible.'

'Mmm. You know, they must be mad. Eric was worried last night that they might have got into one of the homes. Never know what they might do. They must be desperate, especially now they've got this far, and things are closing in on them.'

She suddenly looked alarmed. 'Do you think they might come this way?'

'I shouldn't think so. Apparently they haven't got a vehicle any more and in any case they'd be battling to make it up the track, without knowing it. Besides,' he smiled reassuringly at her, 'Eric's pretty sure they're heading south. Seems obvious. That's the way they've been heading so far. I bet things will be busy now around Marree and down Leigh Creek way. There's an airfield there, you know. Eric was saying that if the two men were still missing this morning, he'd probably get an aircraft from there to fly over the country all around Marree. There's not much cover and if they were trying to walk away, they'd soon be spotted.'

He thought of Eric and of the detectives driving from Adelaide and of the homesteaders to the south all seeking two fugitives, and suddenly felt sorry for the men. Strange that, he reasoned. He knew they were killers and yet he could feel sorry for them. Maybe it was just the thought of them being so outnumbered. You needed help to get by out here.

'They'll need to be good to get away,' he muttered, but she didn't hear him above the roar of the motor.

The sun was higher now, and they drove on towards a simmering horizon.

The tall thin man stood on the verandah of Dulkaninna homestead and watched the mail truck approach. He had been watching its billowing trail of dust for several minutes. Now he could clearly make out the familiar shape of Fred Crawford's truck, laden so high that it looked like a double-decker bus. It approached the thin line of coolibah trees, wound and bumped its way through the creek bed and then turned off the track towards the homestead.

It was only a small building, parched by the sun and whipped by sand-laden winds since this man's parents had built it and begun to fight the dry land for a living. He stepped from the shady verandah and the flies pounced on him in a sticky-legged swarm. Mechanically, he began to brush them away, each stroke of his hand timed by a lifetime's experience to return across his face just before the flies did.

The truck shuddered to a stop. The dust trail which had been pursuing it swept on, engulfing it in a haze of yellow-brown grit. Ivan scrambled down as Fred helped the girl to the ground. Enveloped in dust, she began coughing.

Fred and the tall man from the homestead stood awkwardly, waiting for her to finish coughing. When she had controlled her breathing, Fred introduced her to the man. He offered her a gnarled hand and said he was pleased to meet her and invited them in for a cup of tea. She liked him. His voice was quiet and gentle and he had the natural grace of one of the coolibahs down by the creek.

They went through a flyscreen door into the kitchen and, in the restful grey light, drank tea.

His wife was quiet, too. She had a sun-reddened face and hair that was shot with grey and pulled back severely into a bun. She explained that this was a busy time of the year for them with the men riding out around the waterholes, mustering cattle. She asked Barbara if she knew the sister who used to be at Marree before they closed the nursing home and Barbara said no and they drank more tea.

The men left to unload drums of kerosene and oil and the vegetables, papers and mail. Half an hour later, Fred returned.

'Ready to go?' he asked Barbara.

She nodded and said goodbye to the woman and her husband and with Fred's help, climbed back into her seat. She sat there, gasping, for the heat hit her like the sudden lick of an opened furnace. And the flies. She tried to brush them from her eyes and nose and ears. She prayed for Fred to start the truck so that the breeze might blow them away.

Ivan was re-securing the tarpaulin to the tail of the truck. 'Fix the rest when we're moving,' Fred called out. He was anxious to start, for he could see Barbara was distressed.

Barbara called goodbye and the man, standing in the sun, touched the brim of his hat and his wife waved from behind the wire kitchen door. The truck swung away along the track.

For several minutes, Ivan sat still, enjoying the cooling effect of the breeze. Dulkaninna homestead disappeared from view.

The increasing velocity of the wind ruffled a corner of the tarpaulin's loose front edge. It billowed and flapped towards the tail. Gingerly, Ivan edged his way towards the rear to catch the flicking rope. He was trying to grab it when he saw a tyre bounce beside the truck. It was the lugged tyre he had been sitting on. It had fallen off. He cursed. Fred hated stopping for things like this.

He turned to crawl to the front so he could rap a signal on the cab. He stopped and tightened his grip in surprise. Where the tyre had been, the head and shoulders of a man had appeared. And he was pointing a gun at him.

CHAPTER NINE

The look on the bearded man's face told Johnny Parsons that he recognised him and was frightened. The Russian, crouched on the swaying load, watched in silence as the figure emerged from the hiding place in the tyres. Johnny tried to stand but a sudden jolt sent him pitching head first, so that he sprawled towards Ivan. He lost his grip on the pistol but frantically grabbed it again. He looked up, expecting some movement, some challenge. His muscles still ached and he felt slightly travel sick. But the Russian hadn't moved. His shocked eyes had seen Johnny lose the gun but his body had made no move.

Breathing deeply to rid himself of the nausea, Johnny pushed himself back to the tyres, gun levelled at the staring Ivan. He told Frog to come out.

Slowly, painfully, Frog climbed from the dark hole that for the past three hours had been a shaking, pounding, stinking prison. He saw that Johnny was in control and allowed himself the delicious luxury of a stretch. He sneezed twice to rid his nostrils of the dust that had gathered there.

Johnny waved the pistol. 'You, Ivan,' he called, and his voice was almost swept away in the wind. 'You know what this gun is?'

Ivan's eyes flitted from the gun to Johnny's face and then back to the gun.

'You know what I'll do unless you do just what I say. I'll kill you. Follow?'

Ivan licked his lips and nodded.

'Good. Remember that.' He twisted around and examined the country sweeping past them. The earth was flat and reddish and studded with green-grey salt bush and lonely clumps of straw-coloured spinifex. He turned back. Behind them, a wire fence ran away at an angle. It ended in a dancing, gaseous horizon. In that vaporous zone, he could make out the blades of a windmill, and a faint line of trees. The glare was intense and he rubbed his eyes.

'Lonely enough for you?' he asked Frog who, with one eye closed and the other screwed up to overcome the glare, had also been taking his first view of the country along the Birdsville Track.

A hawk, startled by the noise of the truck, rose from its perch on a stunted bush and lazily shrugged its way into the sky. There was no other sign of life.

Johnny turned to Ivan, who had now pushed himself into a sitting position and had clutched the flapping tarpaulin. 'Have you got a gun up here?' he demanded.

Ivan said nothing.

'Not talking today? I said, have you got ...'

'No.' Ivan shouted the word. 'There's no gun up here.' He shook his head vigorously and the effort seemed to clear away the shock that had stunned him. 'How did you get here? I know all about you two now. They're looking for you back in Marree. What are you doing here?'

'We hid in the truck.'

'But I was with it all night, you know.'

'We were here first ... you know.' Johnny mocked the Russian's accent. He smiled at the sound. 'Nice and cosy wasn't it? You in the front and us in the back.'

'But we looked. This morning.'

'You just didn't look far enough. We had a good hiding place, that's all.' He turned to Frog. 'Thank heavens we're out of it though, eh?'

Frog nodded and tried to speak but his dry throat refused to let the sound pass. He coughed and said 'Yes.' The voice sounded strange, so he coughed and repeated the word. 'I could do with a drink,' he said.

Johnny wiped his parched lips with the wrist of his gun hand. 'Where's the water?' he demanded.

'Down front. In a water bag.'

'Haven't you got some up here?' Frog asked.

Ivan thought of the drums on the back but shook his head.

'Let's stop the driver and get a drink, Johnny,' Frog said. 'I'm just about dying of thirst.'

Johnny twisted and surveyed the empty land. 'There's not a soul in sight, so we might as well take over here as anywhere. In any case, the sooner I get out of the sun, the better. You.' He waved the gun at Ivan. 'Who's down in the front?'

'Fred.'

'Who else? Come on. We heard voices back there when you stopped.'

'Only a girl. A nurse.'

Johnny's eyes narrowed. 'A nurse? What's she doing on this truck?'

'She's going to Birdsville.'

'Why? What's wrong? Someone sick or something?'

'No.' Ivan permitted himself a slight smile at the other man's ignorance. 'There's a mission hospital up there. She's going there to work, you know.'

'And who else is down there? Any other men?'

Ivan shook his head.

'Only the three of you, eh. How come I heard so many voices back at that last stop?'

'We were at a homestead, you know. There's only Fred and myself and the girl. True.'

'Does this Fred carry a gun?'

Ivan gazed down and wondered what he should say. Fred always carried a .303 rifle with him, but he didn't like the thought of that powerful weapon in these men's hands.

'You heard me. Does he carry a gun?'

'I, well, I don't know.'

Johnny narrowed his eyes in disbelief.

'I mean, you know, he's got a gun but he doesn't always take it with him. I don't think he'd of brought it this time, not with the girl on board. Might make her nervous, you know.'

'I think you're lying. Look, mate, if you lie to me, I'll kill you. You know that, don't you?'

Ivan wet his lips. 'I don't know whether Fred's got it or not.'

'Well we'll act as though he has. Get him to stop the truck.' He turned to Frog who was holding on tightly with one hand and shielding his eyes with the other. 'You ready?'

Frog nodded.

Johnny motioned to Ivan with the gun. 'Come on. Do like I said. Get him to pull up.'

The Russian began to crawl towards the two men. 'Just a minute,' Johnny warned. 'Hold it there. Where do you think you're going?'

'To stop Fred. I've got to kick on the roof, you know.'

'Well you stay where you are. Frog, you kick on the roof.'

'How many times, Johnny?'

'How should I know. Just kick it until he starts to pull up.'

Frog turned and lowered himself to the top of the cabin. He braced himself to counter the swaying of the truck and then stamped hard several times. The truck began to slow. The motor revved as the driver changed to a lower gear and the sudden jerk almost caused Frog to lose his footing.

Fred's voice called out: 'What's up?'

Johnny waved his gun at the Russian who took it as a signal for silence and said nothing.

The truck was in a lower gear now and gradually whining to a halt. Frog noticed that the driver was slowing it through the gears. The brakes hadn't been applied. Right at the end he heard them, a brief, rubbing noise, and then the truck was stopped. The motor continued idling with a ragged beat. The driver began to climb out, putting on his sandals as he got out of the cabin. 'What's up, mate?' he called, and squinted above him.

At first he saw only Frog, standing with his legs wide apart on top of the cabin and staring down. 'Who in blazes are you?' Fred said, and stepped clear of the truck to get a better view of the stranger.

'What's wrong?' Barbara called.

'There's some cove standing on the roof,' he said. He looked up again and for the first time saw Johnny Parsons. His head and shoulders were clear of the load and he was pointing a gun at him.

Two men. He looked at both strangers. Even before he compared their appearance with the descriptions he had heard in Marree, he knew who they were. Barbara was saying something to him but he didn't hear her words. He gazed up at the man with the gun and said: 'Where's Ivan?'

Johnny Parsons scrambled down to the roof of the cabin. He turned and spoke to the Russian. 'Jump down and show him you're okay.'

He trained the gun on the mailman as the Russian joined him. 'Right, now both of you walk away from the truck.'

Barbara's voice, sharp with anxiety, came from inside the cabin. 'What's going on Fred? Who is it?'

Fred hadn't moved. 'It's the two men we were looking for last night,' he said.

'That's right,' said Johnny. 'Now do like I told you and get clear of the truck. And get your lady friend to join you. I think you know I mean business.'

The mailman stood where he was. 'How in blazes did you get up there?' he demanded. 'Don't you know that . . .'

'Will you do as I tell you,' Johnny loudly interrupted. 'I'd just as soon shoot you now, mister. It's up to you. Hey you,' he cut in, noticing Barbara climb from the other side of the truck, 'walk around the front and join your boyfriends.'

She backed away, staring up at the two strangers. She opened her mouth as though to speak, but instead hastily walked in a wide circle around the truck to Fred and Ivan.

'Right,' Johnny called, 'now the three of you walk well clear of the truck.'

'You're not going to leave us out here, are you?' Barbara asked, a sudden horror in her voice.

'Not if you behave. Now just get clear so's we can get down.'

Slowly the two men and the girl backed away from the truck. Barbara's eyes darted from the two strangers to the shimmering emptiness surrounding them. Instinctively, her hand gripped the loose flap of Fred's shirt, like a frightened child holding on to a parent.

Fred knocked her hand away. 'For God's sake don't get panicky,' he snapped. He swallowed awkwardly and then added in a whisper: 'Look, I'm sorry, but don't hang on to me like that. We'll be all right.' He knew he was frightened and he felt a surge of shame that he had exposed that fear to the girl. He stumbled on a stone. 'Let's walk normally,' he said, and turned his back on the men. They walked on, his mind racing to take in the situation.

Fifty yards from the truck he stopped. 'This is far enough,' he said, softly enough for his companions only to hear, and turned to face the men on the truck. He felt calmer now.

'How's this?' he called. 'Game enough to come down now?'

He saw the two men speak to each other but couldn't hear what they said. Then the tall one called out: 'Just stay there until I tell you to move.' The fat man dropped to the ground first and walked straight to the front of the truck and began to drink from the water bag. The other one joined him.

While they drank, Fred whispered to Ivan. 'What happened on the back?'

'A tyre fell off and when I turned around again, the tall one was pointing a gun at me. They'd been hiding somehow down under all the tyres.'

'Did they say what they intend to do?' Fred said.

'Yes,' Barbara said. 'What did they say?'

'How do you mean?'

'Did they say where they're making for, or what they were going to do with us?' Fred said.

'No. The tall one, Johnny, said he'd shoot me, though, unless I told him the truth.'

'About what?'

'Hey.' The sudden shout made them look towards the truck. Johnny Parsons had just lowered the water bag and was breathing deeply with satisfaction. 'Stop the talking,' he continued, his voice loud and authoritative. 'You, Whiskers, walk over there.' He waved his gun to the right. 'Get so far away you've got to shout to hear each other, so's I can hear too. You, Nursie, walk in the other direction. Go on.'

'Do like he says,' Fred advised the girl. 'We'll be all right.'

Johnny drank again as they spread out. He wiped his mouth and examined the thin streak of mud left on the back of his hand. He rubbed it against the stubble of his chin and made a conscious effort to relax. He gazed about him. The very emptiness of the desert seemed friendly. He transferred his gun to his left hand, deliberately wiped the palm of his right hand on his hip and then took back the gun. Frog was crouched in the shade of the truck, eyes on him. He joined Frog and then studied the three figures watching him from their separate positions.

Ivan was standing awkwardly, transferring his weight from

one leg to the other. His wide brimmed hat cast a deep shadow over his bristly features and, from this distance, Johnny couldn't make out his face. He guessed it would look frightened. He allowed himself a little grunt of pleasure when he remembered how numbed Ivan had been at his appearance on the truck. The Russian must have noticed him staring at him now, for he nervously dropped into the squatting position of an Australian bushman, rubbed his face and then stood up again. He shifted his feet and then adopted a military 'stand-easy' position. Johnny remembered then that this man had been a prisoner of war, and was used to taking orders. He'd be easy.

He examined Fred Crawford. This man could be a different proposition. He didn't look an exceptionally strong man but he was tough, there was no doubt about that. He had a lean and leathery look about him. As Johnny watched, the mailman dropped into the squatting position but there was no nervousness about his action. For him, it was just easier than standing. He began to trace patterns in the sand with a finger, but Johnny could see that he was still looking at him. This was the vital man in their escape plans. Johnny wondered how far he could be forced, how much he would react to threats.

What of the girl? She was a complication he hadn't expected. She was standing with her hands clasped in front of her, breaking the grip only to brush away flies. She kept glancing at the crouched figure of the mailman. She was frightened at the moment but that would probably soon wear off, Johnny reasoned. Then what? She looked as though she had plenty of life in her. Good looking, too.

Slowly, Johnny stood and left the shadow of the truck. 'Postman,' he called.

Fred Crawford's hat tipped back slightly.

'You see what I've got here?' He held his gun aloft, turning it. 'Do you all see it?' He paused, to make sure they were all watching. Hand still high, he walked on until he was near them.

'This is very important,' he continued, his voice loud and slow. 'This is why I'm in charge here and why you'll all do what I say from now to Birdsville. If you do what you're told, I won't have to use it and we'll have a good trip. If you don't do what I say, I'll kill you.'

Again he paused. He looked at each of them individually. 'I've already had a chat to Ivan and we understand each other.'

'What are you going to do with us?' Barbara called.

'That depends on you. Do just what I tell you and nothing will happen to you, I promise.'

Fred stood up. 'Are you the bloke who killed an old lady up at Alice Springs? Do you expect us to take any notice of what you tell us?' He looked from one man to the other. 'Or maybe you didn't kill her. Maybe it was your fat mate?'

Back at the truck, Frog scrambled to his feet but stayed in the shade. The engine still idled, sending a regular pulse of vibration buzzing through the frame.

'Never you mind what happened back there,' Johnny shouted. 'Look mister, you better take care what you say and do. I'd just as soon shoot you now as later. I could get on fine without your company.'

'It's a long walk to Birdsville,' Fred said and rolled a small stone under one foot. He played with it for a few moments, like a soccer player teasing an incompetent tackler. 'Or maybe you plan going back to where all the search parties are.'

'We're not walking and we're not going back. We could take that truck on without you're help, mister.'

'Could you?' Fred folded his arms and kicked the rock away. 'Have you ever been up here before? And do you know how far you'd get trying to find your own way.' He tilted back his hat. 'You wouldn't make Birdsville.'

'I can follow this road as well as you.'

'Sure you can follow this road. Anyone could — as far as the Cooper. This is a highway compared with the track on the other side. And there's the best part of three hundred miles of it from there on. You'll find more tracks than you could count. You'd probably end up dingo-bait in the middle of the Stony Desert. Of if you go off to the west, you'd end up in the Simpson Desert. No one's ever driven across that from this direction. Maybe you'd like to be the first to try.'

Johnny looked to the north, as though the hazards might be on view.

'Of course,' the mailman continued, 'you might fluke it and stick to the track for a couple of hundred miles. And then you might take the dry weather route instead of the wet weather route.' He paused. Johnny was watching him intently. 'Reckon you could pick the right one? Take the wrong one and you'd end up in Goyder Lagoon. Quicksand and stuff like that. Maybe you'd fluke finding the right route and get stuck on Dead Man Sandhill — that's if you could get across the dozen or so sandhills before.'

'Look,' Johnny began but the mailman continued.

'Maybe you can't even drive a truck like this.'

'That heap!'

'No, now just a minute, it's not just an ordinary truck, you know. It's got a few mannerisms that make it kind of personal to drive. The sand's chewed out most of the brakes, for instance. And there are no lights. And it'll only cross the sand if you take ...'

'Oh, shut up,' Johnny said and stepped forward. 'You've had your say, mister. But what I said still goes. You're all going to do exactly what I say. You know,' he said, smiling suddenly and staring at the mailman, 'you're a good salesman. You've just convinced me I need you to get to Birdsville. But if you do one thing wrong, just one thing, I'll shoot your mate here and then I'll shoot the girl. You know we don't mind killing women, don't you?'

Slowly Fred nodded. Ivan and the girl were looking at him. 'There's one thing you've overlooked. We're not alone out here, you know.' Johnny glanced quickly around him.

'Oh I don't mean right now. But we've got to go through another four stations yet and they're all expecting Ivan and Sister Dean and me. If one of us doesn't turn up, they'll ask questions and your game will be up.'

'You're bluffing, mister. None of these homesteads are in radio contact with Marree. I made a few enquiries. I know.'

'So what! They all know Ivan and I are due. Every fortnight, we come. And they've known the sister is coming for months, now. That's big news, up here.'

'But they don't know for sure you're on your way today or that she's with you. Not for sure they don't.'

'You're wrong. We had morning tea at Dulkaninna back there. These homesteads may not be in touch with Marree but they're all in touch with each other. Get very gossipy on the radio. Right now, Dulkaninna will be talking to them all, telling them about the sister. And they'll all follow us through from station to station. You might have a gun but you can't afford for anything to happen to any one of us. The way things are back at Marree, anything suspicious is going to bring those search parties up here like a shot.'

Johnny turned and began to walk back towards Frog. As he moved, Fred called after him. 'You might have a gun but you're in a hell of a spot. You can't afford for anything to happen to us. You'd be better off if we just left you here and you just headed for the scrub. You'd have a day's start on anyone. I can give you some food.'

Johnny whirled. 'No way,' he yelled. 'We're going on that truck. Maybe I'd find trouble if anything happened to one of you. Maybe not. But listen, all of you. I'm in trouble already. A little bit more's not going to make much difference. I'm going to travel on this truck to Birdsville, whether you all come along or not. Hear that? I'm not going to let any one of you foul things up for me, not now. Maybe people will ask questions if one of you doesn't turn up. So Fred, or whatever your name is, you've got my word that you'll be last to die if you try to ruin things for me. But if you care for your mate or the girl, don't try. Understand? They go first. And another thing. You said people might ask questions. It's up to you to make sure they don't. I've got plenty of bullets to go round. Every time you do something wrong, someone gets hurt. I don't care whether it's the girl or Whiskers or some joker out here. I'm getting through and I don't care if there's not a living soul left along this lousy track.'

CHAPTER TEN

Johnny walked to the truck. Frog, his face creased in anxiety, stepped from the shade to meet him. 'What now?' he asked.

'Look in the front and see if you can find a gun,' Johnny ordered. Frog rummaged behind the seats and reappeared almost immediately with a .303 rifle. He gave it to Johnny, who rolled it in his hands and then returned it. 'You keep it,' he said. 'But use it only when I tell you, understand? See if you can find the cartridges for it.'

Frog searched and found a box of bullets with the cleaning kit for the rifle. He put the tin in his pocket. He gripped the rifle firmly in both hands and felt better.

'Now get back up on top,' Johnny said.

'But ... why?'

'To keep guard, that's why.'

'Are we going to move on now?'

'Sure.'

'But I'll be up on the back, out in the sun.'

'So will Ivan. You've got to keep an eye on him.'

'But why me?'

'You've got the rifle.'

'Yeah ... but.' He looked in dismay at his new possession. 'Johnny, I can't stand too much of this sun. I've got no hat.'

'Well, take the Russian's.'

'Oh geeze, you can imagine what'd be running around inside that.'

'Well, go without. The choice is yours. Now get up there and keep your rifle on them. We've wasted enough time here already.'

He waited until Frog began to climb on the truck, and then called to the three figures who were watching in silence. 'You can all see what Frog's got and you all know what he'll use it for. Now, we're going to get moving. You, Nursie, come over here first.'

Barbara hesitated, then began to walk towards the truck. Her shoes kicked up little puffs of dust as she picked her way through the spinifex. Johnny inspected her closely but her eyes avoided his until she reached the edge of the track. 'Well?' she demanded.

He waved his head towards the cabin. 'Get in the middle.'

He examined her body closely as she passed him and climbed into the truck. Then he turned to the Russian. 'You next. Get up on the back again.'

'What about his hat, Johnny?' Frog called down softly.

Johnny didn't bother looking up. 'If you want it, you ask for it. Come on Ivan, hurry up.' He waited until the bearded man was climbing to join Frog before ordering Fred Crawford to move. The mailman sauntered across to him and said: 'All right, we're all here. Now what are we going to do?'

'You're going to get in there and drive us to Birdsville. We'll just carry on as though you're on a normal run. I'll be sitting on the other side of the girl, so if you try anything, she's nice and handy to my gun. Follow?'

'How am I going to explain you two when we stop at the homesteads?'

'That's your problem.'

'Oh great. I give a story you don't like and you start shooting.'

'That's right. Tell them we're hitchhikers or dingo trappers or something. You know what sort of story they'd believe up here.'

'Well, they wouldn't believe either of those. There are no such things as hitchhikers up here and you're not dingo trappers, that's for sure.'

'You'd better think of something, then.'

'You'd better just be friends of mine I'm taking along for the ride. Tell them you used to know me when I lived in Perth. You came over here to see me. If they think you're my friends, they're less likely to be curious and get hurt.'

'Good, You're catching on. Frog and I are friends of yours from the west.'

'What's your name?'

'Johnny.'

'Johnny who?'

'Just Johnny, to you.'

'Look, if I'm to introduce you to people, I've got to give you some name.'

'Smith. You can call me Johnny Smith.'

'How about your partner.'

'Frog? You can say he's my brother.'

'You don't exactly look alike.'

Johnny permitted a brief smile to break through. 'Thank you. Better make him my stepbrother then. Let people think my father had poor taste the first time.'

'All right. Johnny and Frog Smith it is then. Wait on. *Frog* Smith.' Fred repeated the name with a show of distaste. 'I can hardly call him that. What's his real name?'

Johnny shrugged his shoulders. 'Wouldn't have a clue. Call him Frog. Everyone does.' He stepped away from the truck to see the man on top more clearly.

'Hey, Frog. What's your name?'

The fat man looked down in astonishment. 'What do you mean?'

'What do you want to be called?'

'What?' He looked at the bearded Russian sitting near him, as though Ivan could interpret the question.

Ivan shrugged his shoulders. Bewildered, Frog turned once more to his companion on the ground. 'Are you all right, Johnny? I'm Frog.'

'Oh for Christ's sake.' Johnny said, and walked back to the mailman. 'Call the silly prick what you like.'

'Frog Smith,' said Fred. 'But let's get one thing clear. I'm willing to play along with you only so's people won't get hurt. I'm not doing it to help you. I don't like you or your fat mate. Clear?'

'I couldn't care less what you think of us. I don't like you, either, for that matter. You say too much. But just don't say the wrong thing at the wrong time and we'll get along okay. But come on, we're just wasting time out here in the sun. Wait till I get in the other side and then you get in and drive on. Don't try anything. There are two guns on you now, you know.'

Fred waited until Johnny signalled to enter. As he climbed in, he glanced up at Frog, sitting up front, clutching a rope with one hand and the rifle with the other. 'You all right, Ivan?' he called.

'Okay, mate.' The call came from the back of the truck.

Fred climbed in. He twisted in his seat. 'Tell me one thing,' he said to Johnny. 'Why Birdsville?'

'What do you mean "Why Birdsville"?'

'Well, it's about the last place on earth I'd expect anyone like you to head for.'

'That's good, then. I reckon I should go to a place no one would expect me to.'

'But why come with us?' Barbara said, her voice resentful.

'Let's just say you were the only way out of Marree.'

'I get it,' Fred said. 'You had no intention of going this way then. Things were getting a bit too hot for you back there.'

'Now then I didn't say that. I always work to a plan and that's why I've always been successful. I don't just rush in and do stupid things on the spur of the moment. Going to Birdsville's part of my plan now. It's just that going with you was something I hadn't originally scheduled. But now I think it's going to work out nicely.'

'What are you going to do at Birdsville?' Fred said. 'Do you plan retiring there or are you moving on somewhere?'

Johnny waved the gun at him. 'You're a nosey sort of bloke, aren't you? All you need to know is that we're going to Birdsville. You take us up there just as though it was a normal run. No delays, nothing like that. That's all you've got to do. Don't go worrying about what we're going to do once we get there. Just get us there.'

Fred shrugged his shoulders. 'I've got to go there anyhow. A lot of people depend on this truck getting through on time.'

'You do that. You get us through on time. How long does this trip take?'

'Three days.'

'Three days? The signpost back at Marree said, three hundred and twenty five miles. That wouldn't take you three days.'

'Well it does. You forget, I've got calls to make and things to unload. Besides, the track gets a lot worse soon. Low gear work for most of the way. And in any case, the sign's wrong. The one at Birdsville says four-twenty to Marree so try and work that out. I've heard blokes swear it was five hundred.'

'Well how far is it?'

'Our way it's three-seventy or three-eighty miles, something like that. And it takes us three days to do it.'

Johnny pulled himself into the seat. 'Okay. Three days then. Now get moving before we start to cook in here.' He waved the gun. 'Come on. Move.'

Fred snicked the lever into low gear, revved the idling motor and drove off. Barbara sat close to him to avoid touching the other man. She was using the sleeping bag Fred had lent her as a cushion. Fred changed into top gear and, continuing the motion of his hand, reached down and patted her clasped hands. 'Okay?' he asked, concern in his voice. She smiled at him and nodded.

Johnny squirmed in his seat, so that he was three-quarters facing them. 'You'll pardon me. I trust, Miss, er Miss . . .'

'Dean,' she answered coldly. 'Sister Dean.'

'Oh, of course. You'll pardon me, Sister Dean, if I don't offer you my seat. It's just that it's so much more convenient this way. Easier for me to watch you both. I'd feel too much like the meat in the sandwich between you two. Besides, I'm sure you'd much prefer to be next to the postie.'

'Much.'

'Yes, I thought so.' He leaned back and smiled and again began fondling the case beneath his jacket. After a while, he said 'Where's the next stop, Fred?'

'Etadunna.'

'How far's that?'

'About an hour. Bit less maybe.'

'What do you do there?'

'Unload a few things.'

'Take long?'

'No.'

'How long?'

'Maybe half an hour. Depends.'

Johnny looked at his watch. 'Be about lunchtime. Where do you eat?'

'There, sometimes.'

'Yeah, well not today. Got food on board?'

'Some.'

'Well, it better be enough, cause we're not eating in any of these places. We'll eat out in the open where there's just our own little family to worry about. If you haven't got enough for all of us, get some somewhere.'

'We'll get by.'

'Good. Always prepared, eh? Carry spares for a rainy day.'

'Don't get many of those out here.'

'You just expect trouble, that it?'

'You always expect trouble out here. If the sand's bad, you can spend a couple of days plating your way across one sandhill.'

'What's the sand like now? Good?'

'It was all right last trip. But it can change. Especially when the weather's hot, like this. Takes the moisture out of the sand and it doesn't bind together. The wheels spin in it. You've got to dig yourself a path across, then, and lay metal plates. What are you like on a shovel?'

'I won't be doing no shovelling.'

'If you're in a hurry, you will, unless you'd rather sit on your tail for a few days.'

'Look, Freddie boy, don't try and put the wind up me about these sandhills. We'll take them as we find them. You just stop talking and try and drive this crate a little faster.'

'You were asking the questions.'

'Yeah, well now I'm telling you to shut up. You do just that.' He folded his arms, burying the gun beneath his armpit.

Barbara looked sideways at the driver and noticed he was smiling. She smiled too.

They knew they were near Etadunna a long time before they saw the iron roofs of the station buildings shining among the trees. The country changed. Ridges of eroded hills appeared and the grass grew thicker and the bush more plentiful. They saw cattle and fences. Occasional flocks of birds wheeled overhead. Lines of well-worn wheel ruts ran off the main track. And when they came down the slope and round the bend towards the knot of buildings, there was even a signpost, with big black letters on fresh white paint, pointing back to Marree. The country was still hot and dry, but it had the look of land that held life.

Etadunna consisted of two houses and a scattering of sheds. As they rolled to a stop, a big man on a small horse came riding towards them from a stockyard on a hill. A woman and two boys walked from the main building. The man on horseback arrived first. He grinned a welcome and dismounted.

'Hello, Denzil,' Fred called.

'G'day, Fred,' he drawled, in a well-worn voice. 'You started a bus service, or something, eh?'

Fred managed a laugh. 'Looks like it doesn't it? No, there are a couple of people I'd like you to meet. You too, Mrs Leary.' He touched the brim of his hat as the woman reached them, and nodded to the boys. They nodded in reply.

'This is Mr and Mrs Leary,' he said. 'And this is Sister Dean. You know, the new sister for Birdsville ...'

They nodded in recognition and each shook her hand.

Fred indicated Johnny, who was standing slightly behind him, with his left hand in his pocket. 'This is an old friend of mine from Perth, Mr Smith and that's his stepbrother up there with Ivan.'

Denzil Leary moved forward and shook Johnny's hand.

'They came up to see me so I decided to give them the works and bring them along for the ride.'

'Good idea,' said Leary and he touched his hat in greeting to Frog. 'You apparently plan on doing some shooting,' he called.

Johnny swung round and saw Frog was still clutching the rifle.

'Well,' Leary was continuing, 'you might get a shot at an emu or a roo just north of the Cooper. There are a few about right now. Nothing much else, except for an occasional dingo. Had any luck so far?'

'Not yet,' Johnny answered for Frog. 'We didn't realise the country would be quite like it is. Nothing much about, is there?'

'No,' said Leary and changed the subject. 'Will you all be staying for lunch, Fred?'

'I don't think so, thanks all the same, Den. I promised to show them a bit of the Cooper and I thought we might eat up there.'

'Whatever you like. Well, let's get these things unloaded. You brought everything, I suppose.'

Fred nodded and called Ivan down to help him. Leary told the two boys to lend a hand. Mrs Leary invited Barbara inside but

Johnny was beside her and she declined. Mrs Leary raised her eyebrows, excused herself and walked inside. She was proud of the way she kept her home and it was the first time any visitor had refused her invitation. And yet the sister had gone inside at Dulkaninna. Mrs Leary went back to her work, looking forward to the afternoon session on the radio. She'd have a few observations of her own to make about Sister Dean.

Outside, the men worked for twenty minutes unloading the Etadunna items. Johnny worked with them, staying close to the mailman all the time. Frog had climbed down, drunk more water from the bag and was now resting beneath the shady branches of a tree. He had the rifle across his knee.

When the work was finished, they resumed their places in the truck and drove away, up the hill and past the stockyard.

'That was good,' Johnny said, when the iron roofs had disappeared behind them. 'Just keep that up and we'll all have a good trip. How many more stations to go?'

'Three,' Fred answered.

'What's the next one?'

'Mulka.' He slowed as the truck approached a fence with a closed gate. 'You want to open that?' Johnny shook his head. 'Get Whiskers to do it.' 'Ivan,' Fred shouted, and the Russian jumped down and opened the gate.

'Mulka. How big's that?' Johnny asked, when they were through the gate.

'Pretty small. Country's fairly dry, there.'

'Sounds great. How far?'

'Not far. Bit under thirty miles. We've got to cross the Cooper first and a couple of sandhills.' The track was now driftsand over clay, and the ravaged tyres hummed on the smooth surface.

'The Cooper. That's where you said we were having a meal. How far's that?'

'Not far. About a dozen miles.'

'What is it, this Cooper?'

'A creek.'

'Can we have a bit of a wash and a clean up there?'

'It's dry.'

Johnny paused for a few moments and then said: 'What about the sandhills? Where are they and how bad are they?'

'There's one just up ahead before the crossing and one after it, a much longer one. We won't know what sort of condition they're in until we see them.'

They drove on without speaking until Fred said: 'You can see Kopperamanna up ahead now.'

'What's that?' asked Barbara.

'The sandhill. That's what they call it.'

They were approaching the sandhill from an angle. It ran across the horizon, like a long, speckled lizard sunning itself on the land. Stunted bushes in a mottled variety of greys and greens and sombre yellows dotted its surface, softening the reflective glare of the sand. Away to the left, it disappeared in a blur of trees.

A smokey haze rose near the trackside. 'Is that a fire?' Johnny asked, his voice alarmed. 'A campfire or something.'

'No need to panic,' said Fred. 'It's not smoke, it's steam. There's a bore there.'

'An artesian bore?' Barbara said. 'But why the steam?'

'The water's almost boiling. It comes from a long way down, where things are hot. So there's steam.'

There was also a strong aroma of sulphur, which grew more sickly as they approached. The bore head was a confusion of pipes and taps, arranged in the shape of a lopsided T. A jet of hissing, bubbling water spurted from the longer arm of the pipe and splashed into a pool. From that near-boiling reservoir, a drain ran to the west, its path marked by clumps of spikey green grass. The edge of the drain, the ground beneath the pipe and the pipe itself were encrusted with soda.

'I didn't think a bore would be like this,' said Barbara.

Fred began to slow the truck. 'What did you think it would be like?'

'Oh, I don't know. Different.'

'Want to have a closer look at it?'

She looked at him. He pulled up.

'Just a minute,' Johnny cut in. He tapped on the windscreen. 'Is that where we cross the sand?' He was pointing to a spot a hundred and fifty yards ahead where the track swung to the right at the base of the hill. There the road petered out into a flat blanket of sand, only to reappear as twin furrows which cut a deep path up the white slope. 'Is that it?' he repeated.

'Yes, that's it,' said Fred.

'Can we cross *that*?'

'It's only twenty feet high, at the most.'

'But it's so steep. You'd be battling to walk up that.'

'We'll give it a go. There are some worse ones yet. Anyhow,' he turned to the girl, 'as I was saying, Barbara, would you like to have a closer look at the bore?'

'Skip it,' said Johnny. 'Let's get over the sand first.'

'Now look, it's only going to take a minute and I promised to show her a bore. Back in Marree. What's the harm?'

'This is no tourist bus. Keep moving.'

'It'll only take a minute. Look, Johnny, don't spoil this trip for her altogether. It's probably the only time she'll ever travel up here. Be a sport, for once in your life.'

Johnny looked surprised at the changed tone in Fred's voice. He shrugged his shoulders. 'All right. Go ahead. If you want to stand in the sun and look at some hot water, go ahead. But I'll be watching. And only a minute, remember.'

Fred jumped to the ground and raised his arms to help the girl down. He could see a puzzled expression on her face as she extended her hand.

'You'll find this interesting,' he said, in a loud voice. 'This bore shoots out just on eight hundred thousand gallons of water a day. Comes from three thousand feet down. There are bores like this all along the track, about a day's walk apart, for the cattle.' He led her around the front of the truck towards the steaming pool. 'Some of the bores are sixty years old. They've been going like this all that time. Must be a lot of water down below, eh?'

He reached the edge of the pool and pointed along the bore drain. Then in a whisper, he said: 'I'm going to have a go at getting away from them.' He saw her stiffen. 'Don't look back or do anything that might make him suspicious.' He raised his voice again. 'Yes it goes on like that for miles. The cattle drink it downstream, where it's cooler.'

'What are you going to do?' she whispered.

'Pretend to get bogged on the sand. Get them out of the truck and drive away. If he makes you get out, stay near the door. Think you can jump on when it gets moving?'

She drew a deep breath. 'What about their guns?'

'I hope they'll put them down when they start digging. If you get down in the cabin and keep your head out of the way, you should be right.'

'Hey.' It was Johnny calling. 'School's over. Let's get moving.'

They turned and began to walk back. 'Fred,' Barbara whispered, with an urgency that almost stifled the sound. 'What about Ivan?'

Fred touched her arm in what he hoped she took as a gesture of assurance. 'Well, what did you think of it?' he asked loudly.

'Wonderful,' she said. Her voice trembled.

'How are we going to cross the sand,' Johnny asked when they were inside.

'Just drive over,' said Fred. 'Get ready to hop out, though, in case we slow down.'

'What for?'

'To give a push, that's what for.' He engaged four-wheel drive and hooked his leg around the lever.

'Do you think we'll get stuck?'

'Hope not. But if it starts to slow down, and I yell out, get out and push, quickly. And get your mate off the top to help, too. Every little bit helps in sand. Ready? Here we go.'

Johnny started to speak but his voice was engulfed by the sudden roar of the motor and deeper whine of the transmission. The truck lurched forward, gathering speed as it neared the hill. It reached the first thin layer of windblown sand and the rumble of the tyres died in its soft smother. Then the front wheels pushed deep into the twin ruts, gripped and the truck began to grind its way to the top. Fred heard a cry from the top and guessed Frog had lost his balance. He kept his foot hard down. His left leg was locked around the vibrating lever. The gearbox shrieked. The left wheels dipped into a series of hollows and the truck rocked. They were halfway up now. Fred tugged the wheel to the right so that the tyres tried to climb the steep ridges bordering the tracks. It was futile and he knew it but it gave the impression that the truck was labouring. He eased his foot off the accelerator.

'She's slowing. Sand's worse,' he yelled above the scream of the gears. He glanced quickly at Johnny and saw him bracing himself in the corner. He turned the wheel to the right, then left, then right and eased the accelerator again. They were on top now, ploughing their way along a flat ridge that ran for thirty yards. Ahead of them, the wheel tracks, a foot deep, ran through an avenue of saltbush.

'Keep it going,' Johnny screamed.

'Can't,' Fred yelled back. 'Sand's too soft. Jump and try pushing before she stops altogether.' He put his head through the doorway and called up: 'Jump off, quick, and give us a push. QUICK.'

He turned to Johnny but he was still there, one arm stiffly braced against the dash. 'For Pete's sake, get out,' he yelled.

A thumping sound came from the roof and then Ivan leaped to the ground. He fell to his hands but straightened quickly and ran alongside the driver, jerking his thumb back along the track and trying to make himself heard above the roar.

Fred could catch the words 'fallen off.' He looked quickly back across the cabin but Johnny was still there, eyes blazing excitedly. He wasn't going to jump, that was certain. Fred cursed and let the truck jerk to a halt.

'What's happened?' Johnny's voice was unnaturally loud in the sudden silence.

'We're stuck, that's what happened.'

'Where's Frog?' Johnny leaned across and waved the gun at Ivan who was panting beside the driver's door. 'Where's Frog?'

'He fell off.' Ivan pointed back along the track. 'He lost his grip and landed flat on his back in the sand.'

'All out,' Johnny ordered. 'Come on you two, quick.' He dug the barrel hard into Barbara's ribs, so that she gasped in pain. 'Out.'

He waited until they were standing beside the truck before he himself climbed out. He looked back in time to see a winded Frog stagger to the top of the sandhill. He still clutched the rifle.

When he saw them, Frog stopped, spread his legs and leaned on the rifle. 'Thank Christ you stopped,' he gasped and bent lower, one arm folded across his aching middle.

Johnny glanced through the cabin at the others and then ran to his companion. 'How in the blazes did you fall?' he said.

Frog sank to his knees and rolled his eyes at Johnny. One side of his face was covered with sand. 'I thought you weren't going to stop,' he said.

'How did you fall off in the first place?'

'I was changing hands on the rifle. Wanted a better grip. It's hard holding on up there, oh geeze, it's hard.' He swallowed noisily. 'I wasn't ready when it hit the big bump. Geeze, I hit hard.'

'Next time, hang on,' Johnny said. 'Come on, up on your feet.'

Back at the truck, Fred was talking quickly to Ivan. 'They're coming back,' Barbara said softly.

They waited in silence until Johnny and Frog reached them. 'No harm done,' Johnny announced. He nodded at the truck. 'What do we do now?'

'We dig,' Fred said. 'She's not bad and at least she's on the flat. If we can just clear some of the sand that's piled up in front of the wheels, we should be able to get rolling again. First of all, though, the motor's stopped. Ivan, give me a crank, will you? You other two can start digging at the back, to save time.'

'Who's giving the orders around here?' Johnny demanded.

'I'm just trying to get us moving again, that's all.'

'Yeah, well maybe you are, but just to make sure you're not playing tricks, the girl stays alongside me. Understand? Now Ivan, do like your boss says and start the motor.'

Ivan flashed a brief, hopeless look at Fred and walked to the front. He had to scoop away sand from the high central ridge to allow the handle to turn fully and then, with one practised swing, cranked the motor back into life. He rejoined the others.

Fred had taken his place behind the wheel and was blipping the throttle. 'Okay,' he called. 'If you want to get out of here, you'll have to start digging.'

'Where's your shovel,' said Johnny. 'Your boy can use the shovel and we'll watch.'

'Shovel be blowed. You can use your hands. The sand's soft enough. And if you two help, we'll be out of here three times quicker.'

Frog looked at Johnny for direction. 'All right,' Johnny said after a long pause. 'We'll help. Frog, give me your gun and lend Whiskers a hand.' He held out his hand for the rifle.

Frog clutched the rifle in both hands. 'Johnny, I feel crook. That fall shook me up. And I can't take this heat. It's all right for you. You've been in the front. I feel crook. I really do.'

Johnny looked at him contemptuously. 'You're getting to be a bit of a load, Frog.' He pushed the pistol into a trouser pocket. 'All right, have a blow. Think you've got enough energy to keep the rifle pointed at Whiskers and the girl here?'

Frog flopped down near the back of the truck on the side farthest from the driver.

'All right Whiskers, let's go,' Johnny said. 'You take this wheel,' he pointed to the side nearest Frog, 'and I'll take the other. And you, Nursie, stay near Frog.'

The lower parts of the wheels were hidden in the deep channels of sand. To clear them, the two men had to lie on their stomachs and reach down with one hand to scoop away the sand. Ivan felt around the tyre and knew the driver could move the truck whenever he wanted. He looked under his free arm at the girl and, behind her, the man with the rifle. Frog had put the gun across his knees and was busily brushing the sand from his clothes. Fred was still blipping the throttle, waiting. Ivan nodded to the girl and mouthed the word 'now'. She bent down and scooped up a handful of sand. With it, she edged towards Frog. He looked up but continued brushing his clothing. Ivan began to squirm clear of the wheel. He could just make out Johnny on the other side, regularly tossing up a handful of sand. Slowly, he rose to his feet.

The unexpected movement caused Frog to look up. Barbara stepped closer and flung the sand in his eyes. Frog bellowed in pain. She turned and ran. Ivan took two hesitant steps towards the rifle but heard Johnny shout and turned and ran after the girl.

'Now, Fred, now,' she called as she reached the front. She tried to jump in the cabin but slipped. The truck began to judder forwards. Ivan grabbed her by the hips and shoved. Fred slipped to the outer edge of the seat to make room for her sprawling body. The truck had accelerated to walking pace now. Fred saw Ivan scramble aboard amid the tangle of Barbara's bare legs.

Johnny had rolled clear when he heard Frog's shout. He stared at Frog, who was rubbing his forearm crazily across his eyes, and then at the truck, gradually bumping away with its spinning back wheels showering him with loose sand.

Johnny started to run but fell in the churned-up surface. In a frenzy of arms and legs, he clawed his way to the edge of the track and began to run through the low saltbush, using the growth to give his feet grip on the sand. The truck was slowing, its wheels spinning. The tail slewed in a looser patch. It almost stopped and he was level with it, shouting. The wheels bit into firmer sand and the truck jerked forward. He could see the driver now, close to him. Fred turned just as Johnny sprang at him.

One hand clutched Fred's flapping shirt and almost dragged him from the wheel. The truck was poised on the edge of the descent. Fred tried to jab his attacker loose with his right elbow but missed. Johnny hooked his arm in the elbow and swung him away from the wheel. His foot slipped from the running board and he began to fall. With his left fist, he pounded at Fred's head, knocking his hat clear. He clutched at the exposed hair, jerking the head back.

Barbara screamed. She saw Fred start to slide out of his seat as the truck dipped down the sandhill. She grabbed his shirt but it tore. She tried to seize his leg but the jerking knee struck her a numbing blow on the shoulder. Then they were gone and Ivan was reaching across, gripping the wheel.

The two men landed with sickening force on the sand. The bouncing impact broke Johnny's grip. They began to roll down the hill, flattening the saltbush and flailing the sand with their arms and legs.

Giddy and choking for breath, Fred slid to a stop. The bushes had scratched his face and all but torn off his shirt. He pushed himself to his hands and knees and saw Johnny, ten feet away from him, lying on his back and frantically delving in a pocket for the gun.

Fred scrambled to his feet and threw himself at the man. He could see the gun coming out of the pocket. He closed his eyes as he fell on top of him, elbows drawn up to hurt as much as possible. That's what he wanted. To hurt this man. He heard the violent 'oof' of escaping breath as his elbows dug deep into the stomach. Then they were fighting in a choking cloud. He was astride Johnny, both his hands gripping the hand that held the gun. There was a sharp pain in his side and he realised Johnny was biting him. He let go with his right hand and hammered his elbow into the side of Johnny's face until the biting stopped. The face was snarling at him through a thin layer of blood. He punched with a savage relish until the face turned red and the eyes closed and the hand holding the gun relaxed. He saw the gun fall into the sand.

Fred shook his head. A thin mixture of blood and sweat was dripping from his chin on to his chest. He heard someone running behind him and began to straighten. He started to turn his head but something hit him behind the ear. A white pain seared his eyes and jagged through his teeth. He began to fall and the sand turned red and then black.

CHAPTER ELEVEN

Fred could smell the truck. It was that hot, burning-oil smell he knew so well. But there was something wrong. The smell was above him. That was wrong, but he couldn't remember why. And there was none of the noise, none of the shaking of the truck. Just the smell. He tried to puzzle it out but his head hurt too much. One eyelid flickered and he realised with surprise that his eyes had been closed. The eye opened fully and he stared up at the sump of the truck's motor. He tried to open the other eye but couldn't. He rubbed it and heard the buzz of startled flies. The lid felt sticky and the lashes were matted and glued together. With all the concentration he could muster he began to pull the lashes apart. His head hurt and he groaned.

'He's awake.' It was Barbara's voice. He felt her hand upon his shoulder and then her face was close to his. She looked pale and frightened, even in the shadow beneath the truck. That's where he was, beneath the truck. And then he remembered the sandhill and the truck and the fight. 'You all right?' he said weakly.

She nodded. 'How do you feel?' Her voice was soft and concerned. 'Fine,' he said and rubbed the back of his head. 'What hit me?'

'The fat one,' she whispered. 'With the rifle.'

He took a deep breath and winced. 'Ow. My ribs. Did he hit me there too?' He rolled on his side and looked at her, lying on her stomach with her body and legs stretched out in the glare of dust beyond the truck.

'No,' she said. 'The other one kicked you.'

'I don't remember that.'

'You were unconscious. You must have knocked him out and when he woke up, he kicked you. It was horrible.'

He rubbed his ribs and looked about him. Ivan was crouched near the front wheel, eyes anxiously peering at him. Fred rolled over and looked back beneath the truck.

Johnny and Frog were sitting in the shade of the tray, eating. The remains of the lunch Mrs Black had packed were at their feet. Between them was the empty water bag, flat and misshapen like a deflated balloon. Beside it was an open carton with three empty beer bottles. Johnny was sitting side on, gazing at the bottles. He had taken off his jacket and folded it across his knees. His face was puffed and his nostrils were rimmed with caked blood.

Frog saw Fred move and picked up the rifle laying across his lap. Johnny turned his head. 'Well,' he called to Fred, 'you're awake at last. You've been out for an hour or more. You must be a bit soft, Postman.'

'Soft!' cried Barbara, squirming clear of the truck and rising to her knees. 'He beat *you* fair and square. He didn't kick you when you were unconscious. You're a . . .'

'Oh shut up,' Johnny yelled, slapping his thighs in emphasis.

Satisfied that she had obeyed, he stood up, picking his teeth with a fingernail as he studied the three at the front of the truck. Gun in hand, he strolled up to them. He stopped short of the girl and the Russian and kicked a stone under the truck. 'Come on,' he said, stepping back a few paces, 'get out of there and on your feet. You've had your rest in the shade. There's something I want to tell you and I want to see your face when you hear it. Come on.'

He waited as Fred painfully dragged himself out into the sun and sat up next to Barbara and the squatting Ivan.

Johnny spread his legs wide apart and tucked his thumb into his trouser belt. 'I told your friends and now I want you to hear it,' he said. 'I told you I'd kill your pal Whiskers if you tried anything. Well you tried all the same, didn't you?' He paused and rubbed the gun against his pants, enjoying the hypnotic way in which the movement attracted their eyes. 'The Russian's still alive, isn't he? You tried to dump me back there and your hairy mate's still alive, despite what I told you. Do you know why? Want to know?'

Fred licked his lips and waited.

'What you did back there deserves something very personal,' Johnny continued, raising the gun until it pointed at Fred. 'So I'm going to kill you instead.'

Slowly and audibly, Fred sucked in his breath.

'Lost your voice?' Johnny taunted. 'Don't tell me you're too scared to talk.'

When Fred spoke his voice was soft. 'What about Birdsville?' he said.

'What? Speak up, Postie.'

'I said how will you get to Birdsville? You couldn't drive there.'

'Oh, but I'm not going to kill you right now. I need you until Birdsville. But when we get to Birdsville, you're going to go. I'm going to kill you.' A thin trickle of blood had begun to run again from his nose. He wiped it away and examined the back of his hand. 'You don't do that to me and get away with it. What I said about the others still goes. Try anything more and they cop it. But you're going to get it anyhow. You've got two days to live, mister. You signed your own death warrant back on that sandhill.'

Slowly Fred rose to his feet. His body swayed slightly as he stood, feet wide apart, facing Johnny. For several seconds the two men looked at each other. One corner of Johnny's mouth began to crinkle in a grin. 'That's something for you to think about, isn't it? Maybe you'd like to try something right now? I don't think you will, though. For two days, you'll know I'm going to kill you anyhow, but I bet you hang on to life as long as you can. That's good. I'm going to enjoy watching you. I'll bet you plead with me when the time comes.'

'You're mad,' Barbara said. Her voice was matter-of-fact, as though she were discussing someone who was not present.

Johnny waved the gun at her, like a person wagging a finger in reproval. He wet his lips several times as he sought the right words. 'Look,' he said. 'I've just about had enough of your nagging. You're a good looking girl but that means nothing to me, and unless you shut up, you'll end up dead with your friend here.' He paused to let the full effect of the words sink in. 'Ever since we stopped, you've done nothing but talk. Now I let you talk and I let you have your own way, like putting him under the truck in the shade. I let you do that. But no more. You hear? You get under my skin any more and watch out. You just watch out. I've got nothing to lose by killing one extra. And you're liable to be that one. You think about that. Now you,' he pointed at Fred, 'get back in that truck and let's get moving.'

Fred felt the side of his face. The blood from the bush scratches had run into one eye and congealed. 'Give me time to clean up, first. If I go into Mulka looking like this, what do you think they'll say. Especially with you looking the way you do, too. They'll put two and two together.'

'No they won't. We're not calling in, that's why. You're just going to drive on now until I tell you to stop.'

'We'll need some water and how are we going to get it unless we call in at Mulka?'

'What about the bores you were talking about? You said they were all along the track. Get some water from one of those.'

Shaking his head in frustration, Fred turned and asked Ivan to get the empty water bag and hook it on the front again.

While Ivan fetched the bag, he took off his tattered shirt and carefully folded it over his arm. He wanted time to think. His head and whole body ached but he knew he had to think and think clearly. He felt he had woken during some crazy, rambling dream. As he carried out the useless routine of folding his torn shirt, he tried to sort out the pieces of that dream.

His ribs ached. So the man called Johnny had kicked him. Fred had known other men who would put the boot in when an opponent was down, but he had never heard of anyone doing it to an unconscious person. But then he'd never met a murderer, and this man had bashed an old woman to death. Fred glanced across at him. Johnny was watching him through narrowed eyelids. His eyes. They were so strange. His face was normal enough but Fred had never seen such eyes. They seemed to be able to flash hot or cold. When Johnny had threatened his life, they had been hot, blazing hot. Fred looked away. With a show of great concentration, he patted a crease in his shirt, and went to his bag behind the driver's seat. He took out his one spare shirt, and put the torn garment away. Would this man really kill him when they reached Birdsville? Maybe he was just bluffing. Fred found the thought encouraging. Johnny was probably a tired and frightened man. He'd been on the run for a couple of days. Being chased like that would probably make any man act crazily. Could even explain why he'd kicked him like that. It could have been just reaction from the fight and fear of being caught. After all, he would face a murder charge. Murder. Don't forget, this man has already killed. And Eric Wallis had said that it was the most brutal killing they had seen around Alice. Fred's mind became a jumble of doubts and fears again.

He turned and faced Johnny. 'Aren't you worried about what'll happen if we don't call into Mulka?' he said. 'They're expecting me. I'm supposed to deliver stuff there.'

Johnny shrugged. 'Let the next mailman take care of that.'

Fred put on the new shirt. The pain from his ribs made him wince. He folded his arms gently across his chest. He shifted his feet so that all his weight was on one leg. 'You mean that?' he said.

'Mean what?'

'About killing me.'

'Sure.' His voice was flat, matter-of-fact.

'Do you really think you can get away with all this?' He let his lips part in what he hoped looked like a taunting smile.

'Why not? I'm doing all right so far.'

'Maybe. You've still got a long way to go, though.'

'I'll make it.'

'What about your mate?' Fred nodded towards Frog, who looked up with interest. 'Isn't he going with you?'

Johnny's eyes darted quickly from Frog to the mailman. 'I don't get you.'

'Well, you're always saying I and not we. I thought maybe he wasn't going with you.'

'Don't try and get smart. We're in this together. Aren't we Frog?'

The fat man didn't answer.

'Too bad for him,' Fred said. 'That means two hangings instead of one. They still hang in this State, you know. You remember that.' He nodded at Frog.

'And you remember that they can't hang you more than once.' Johnny said. He shifted the position of his thumb in the belt. 'We've got nothing to lose by another killing. We could kill the whole lot of you and it wouldn't make any difference.'

Frog moved uneasily.

Fred glanced from one man to the other before answering. 'No difference, eh? You must be pretty used to killing. Tell me,' he turned to Frog, 'was that your first murder back at the Alice?'

The fat man shook his head vigorously. 'Don't look at me. I didn't have nothing to do ...'

Johnny interrupted: 'I'm getting sick of hearing your voice. What say we start making tracks.' His eyes were beginning to light up again.

Fred flicked at a fly. 'I didn't realise you'd be so touchy about it. From the way you've been talking, I thought killing didn't mean a thing to you. Maybe you're just a bag of wind, eh? Talk a lot, but no good when it comes to action. Maybe your mate does all the work for you and you do all the talking. You certainly weren't doing so good by yourself back on the sandhill.' Barbara stirred nervously. 'Fred, please,' she said softly.

Johnny jerked his hand from his belt.

'Who killed the old woman, anyhow?' Fred continued.

'Never mind who killed her and stop talking about it,' Johnny said. 'You hear me? Stop.'

Fred shrugged. 'No need to shout. Sound travels a long way here. You can just talk normally and I'll hear you. Just 'cause you're frightened you needn't start yelling your head off.'

'Frightened! Who said I'm frightened.' He gripped his wrist tightly, pointing the gun firmly at the mailman's chest. 'Like to see who's frightened?'

'Oh I'm frightened,' Fred said, and grinned. He brushed his bloodied eyelid. 'Tell me, who was the more frightened back in Alice Springs. You or the old woman? Or maybe she didn't see you. Maybe you hit her from behind. Was that how it happened?'

'Shut up.'

'Or maybe it was a fair fight. Although I don't think it could have been fair, if you won, not by your form back on the sandhill. I don't think you'd be much good without that gun in your hands.'

'Well, I've got it,' Johnny hissed. 'You just keep talking and you see if I can use it.'

Fred wet his lips and decided to keep on. 'You use it and you won't get to Birdsville.' He paused to make sure the other man understood.

'You're asking for a bullet,' Johnny said.

'You do that and you won't get up the track. You're in a tight spot. Sure, you've got the gun but you can't afford to use it. Shoot me and you won't get ten miles in the truck. You can't touch the girl because everyone who lives up this way knows she's coming. Harm any of us, and they'd start talking over the radio and you'd find all of Birdsville waiting for you. That wouldn't suit you, would it? You might have the gun but you daren't use it. Not if you want to get through.'

'Don't push me too far. We could take that truck by ourselves if we had to.'

'Bull. Do you think you'd get by all the homesteads without them asking questions?' Fred shook his head. 'You can't do it without us.'

'Look, I told you I'm sick of you talking. Get in that truck and start moving. We've wasted enough time.'

'And if I don't you'll shoot. Ha. Don't make me laugh.'

Barbara moved forward and gripped Fred's arm. 'Don't,' she said. 'Please stop before he does something.'

'He won't,' Fred told her, in what he hoped sounded like a calm voice.

The two men stared at each other in silence for several seconds. Ivan, who had been listening at the front of the truck, coughed.

Johnny turned at the sound. 'He's next,' he said, pointing the gun at the startled Ivan. 'I'd shoot him and have no trouble thinking up some good excuse for him not being with us. Now if you want to see how good I am at that, just try something. Just try it. I'm not bluffing. I wouldn't lose any sleep about putting a bullet through him. The only things that'd miss him would be the bugs in his beard. You do one more thing wrong, Postie, and Whiskers gets it. The same goes for the girl. Understand?'

'You're a brave one with that gun. Care to put it down and see how good you are?' Fred challenged. 'You weren't doing so good back there. They tell me you did your best fighting after your mate had clobbered me on the head with the rifle butt. A good man with the boot, eh? Like to keep going where we left off?' He pushed Barbara away from him.

'You keep back.' Johnny extended the gun. 'Frog, keep that rifle on him.'

'Come on, put it down for a minute and we'll see how good you are.'

'Fred, don't,' Barbara called, moving forward.

He put his arm back to restrain her. 'Stay back,' he said. 'This is between me and him. I don't like people to kick me.' He lifted his arms and began to circle Johnny, like a boxer in a ring.

Johnny followed him with the gun. 'Try anything and you're dead.'

'You're yellow.'

'Get back or I'll shoot.'

'Yellow.'

'Shut up.'

'You're yellow.'

'SHUT UP.'

Barbara dashed forward. 'Fred, don't, please,' she pleaded.

Johnny turned quickly at the sound of her voice. Barbara saw him grab at her and tried to move away but he was too fast. He seized her arm and pulled her in front of him, so that she shielded him from the crouching mailman. Johnny bent her arm behind her back, pressing up so hard that she was forced to stand on tip toe. She cried out in pain.

'Now,' Johnny shouted, his voice triumphant, 'now what are you going to do?'

'Let her go,' Fred said.

'No, sir.' He jerked hard on the wrist again, making her gasp. He was smiling at Fred over her shoulder. 'Not until you get back to the truck.'

Fred dropped his hands. 'What sort of bloke are you? Let her go.'

'Get back first.'

'You bastard. You crazy, savage bastard.' Fred mouthed the words slowly and deliberately.

Johnny laughed, a short, shrill laugh that contained no mirth. 'I beat you, didn't I?' he said. 'Now do as I say, or do I break her arm?'

His face white, Fred walked in a wide half-circle around them until he joined Ivan at the truck. All the time, Johnny watched him closely, pivotting the girl so that she was always protecting him from any sudden lunge.

'That's right,' Johnny said, as though soothing an animal. 'That's the way. Just do as I say.' Still he retained his grip on the girl. Her head was flung back, with her mouth wide open in pain.

She rolled her eyes appealingly at Fred.

He stepped forward. 'Well, for heaven's sake let her go,' he shouted, thumping his hands together in emphasis.

'Okay,' Johnny shouted back at him. 'But just remember this.' He wrenched at her arm, so that she screamed. *'I mean what I say.'* He let go the wrist and, planting the palm of his hand against her shoulder, pushed her towards the others. She stumbled and sprawled in the dust at Fred's feet. He bent quickly to help her. She was crying.

'All of you remember that,' Johnny was continuing. 'When I say something, I mean it. And right now, I say we get moving. You, Whiskers, get the motor started.'

'Do it yourself,' Ivan answered sullenly.

'Better do as he says,' Fred advised, looking back at his friend.

'Well, listen to that,' Johnny said. 'The mailman's got some sense at last.' He smiled maliciously at Fred. 'So you know who's the boss. That's good. It seems to me that at last you've learned something that's going to do you a lot of good.'

'I certainly have,' Fred said, holding the sobbing girl.

The girl pushed herself away from him. 'Why did you go on like that?' she said. 'You could have got everyone killed. He's crazy, you're crazy.'

'I wish to hell you weren't here,' Fred said.

Australia's inland rivers are geographical conundrums. Unlike most rivers of the world, they rise in accessible regions and finish in remote, unlikely places. They begin well, but finish badly. Many have deep reaches of permanent water in their early stages, but as they cover distance they lose strength, not gain it as they should. Their problem comes from the worn face of Australia, for they are doomed to roam a flat country. Not for them the nourishment of broad tributaries, rushing down from a passing range of mountains. They enter deserts and meet dry channels and become dry themselves. They head for destinations they rarely reach and dissipate their waters in arid wilderness.

Of the conundrums, the greatest is Cooper Creek. To begin with, it is a river, not a creek. The explorer Charles Sturt chanced upon it in 1845, during his attempt to probe the centre of the continent. Sturt met the Cooper far from its source, when he was travelling in the vicinity of the present-day north-south border separating South Australia and Queensland. He named the stream after his friend, a judge of the fledgling colony of South Australia, and, while he described it as a 'fine watercourse', he gave it the lesser appellation of creek because he could distinguish no sign of a current to justify the title of river.

Yet the Cooper is a river, and one of the mightiest of the inland. It begins life in Central Queensland and ends its run on the desolate shores of Lake Eyre. Only after heavy rains, enough to cause abnormal flooding in its headwaters, does the Cooper system ever flow its entire length. When it does, the flood comes down in a slow, wide surge of brown water. Denied a deep bed, the Cooper spreads. It trickles through a maze of shallow channels, fills lakes scattered like the links of a broken chain and spreads fifty miles wide or more into the thirsty desert. It is more a flood seeking a river than a river in flood.

After the flood, the deeper hollows remain as waterholes. Some are permanent, sustained by their depth and protected from high rates of evaporation by the shade of friendly trees. Others, broader and shallower, survive only a few years before they are swept dry by sun and wind. Fish burrow into the mud to plant their eggs, and die. The mud dries and buckles. Weeds grow and wither. And the lake waits for the next flood.

The permanent waterholes are mainly to the east, in the Cooper's earlier stages, for only the rarest, most devastating floods penetrate to the western channels, beyond the Birdsville Track, and allow the Cooper's load of brown silt, born from the plains of Queensland, to stain the white salt bed of Lake Eyre.

Cooper Creek is the sum of two rivers, each discovered and named separately before their connection with Sturt's stream became known. The westernmost is the Thomson River, which itself originates from creeks that join near Longreach. As the name of that town implies, the Thomson has a long stretch of deep and permanent water near the town. The other fork is the Barcoo, which begins near the towns of Tambo and Blackall. The two rivers merge near Windorah. From that point, the stream becomes the Cooper and flows to virtual oblivion. It winds south through some of the most wretched country in Queensland, before turning west, to enter South Australia near the ghost town of Innamincka.

Unhappily, ghosts are familiar spirits to the Cooper. It has a history — at least in modern times — of tragedy and disillusionment. It saw the death of Sturt's dream of an inland sea, for along its course he found only waterholes in a region of appalling deserts. On its banks, the explorers Burke and Wills perished in 1861. Those who followed found distinctive tribes of Aborigines flourishing along the watercourse. They were taller and lighter-skinned than normal, and friendly to the white man. Their numbers were estimated to be as high as ten thousand. They lived on fish and duck, the plentiful nardoo seed, and the game attracted to the water. But the coming of the whites spelled death to the blacks. The Europeans brought disease, new animals and new beliefs and the combination destroyed the tribes. From the first touch they withered. So drastically did they decline that not one descendant of the ten thousand survived the first century of exposure to civilisation.

Within a decade of the tragedy of Burke and Wills, German missionaries had begun establishing stations along the Cooper, suffering terrible privations in their zeal to save a lost people from the eternal vacuum that awaited non-believers. With the passing of the tribes, the missions were abandoned. Their ruins dot the western path of the river. The roofs have collapsed, the walls of mud and straw bricks have crumbled, and drift sand — the only regular visitor — has covered the floors, causing the buildings seemingly to shrink in height. Once tall doorways, their timber frames still firmly pinned together by hand-fashioned wooden nails, diminished to dwarf size as the level of sand rose.

One such mission, part-buried in the sand dunes overlooking Lake Kopperamanna, was only a few miles to the left as Fred Crawford drove on to the flood pan of the Cooper. He knew the place well. He often went to the lake to fish, baiting a trap with meat and feasting on the sweet callop that fluttered in his snare. The lake was a couple of miles long and kidney shaped, but shallow and inclined to dry-up after a couple of years of drought. He had fished in it one year and driven across it the next, which was typical of Cooper country. There was water in the lake now, so he swung off the track until he had reached the lake.

'What are you doing now,' Johnny said, as the truck slowed.

'I'm going to wash,' Fred said, getting down from the truck. 'You should too. You've got blood on you. Don't drink the stuff, but it's all right for washing.'

So the two men waded through the muddy water at the edge of the lake, and bathed, but stayed well apart. The mission ruins were nearby, but Fred didn't go near the buildings, for these men would foul the site.

His ribs ached, his head felt as though it were on fire and the cuts on his face stung as he washed the dried blood away. And his mind was stained by a terrible fear, a certainty of doom, a sense of having no control over his own fate.

When he returned to the truck, he drove with the despair of a man crossing a long, long bridge that he knows must collapse.

He was a man of patience, but of no great subtlety or intellect. He could see no solution to his problem. Back at the sandhill, he had tried to resolve the dilemma in the only way that seemed reasonable to him: to get away from them or overpower them. He had tried to do both. He had almost succeeded. But he had failed and from now on, any action would be harder to take. Only one thing was becoming clear and that was that the main threat came from the tall man, not his companion. Johnny was indisputably the leader and, equally clearly, he posed the main threat to their lives. He meant to kill, the other man seemed frightened by the prospect. The two men were together, yet opposites. Together, and armed, they would be too strong for them. The incident at the sandhill had shown that. Fred touched the back of his head in recollection.

The girl glanced at him and instinctively he lowered his hand. She worried him. Barbara Dean was a stranger and now he was responsible for her life. He had almost gone too far back there. He felt ashamed of that. If only he and Ivan were the only ones on the truck, he'd tell these men to go and get stuffed or have another go at them. The girl complicated things, giving the other men an advantage they shouldn't have and burdening him with restrictions he didn't enjoy and extra responsibilities he didn't fully comprehend. But he liked her and felt bad for having spoken to her roughly. He would have preferred to have spoken to her now, to offer comfort or to apologise, but he didn't know what to say. So he kept silent.

He let his left hand rest on the gear lever. He felt again the buzz of the gearbox and the violent shaking of the engine in its worn mountings: all familiar sensations. Assured by the touch of a mechanical friend, he felt better.

They spent ten minutes crossing the Cooper. There was no water, nor an easily defined river bed. The Cooper was a low place, where trees grew and the grass was denser and showed green tinges. The single track broke up into several, each meandering along twin lines of crushed grass through the trees. Fred chose one path to the right. The truck weaved a course through white-stemmed trees, jogging and rocking on the hidden bumps and dipping in patches of loose sand. Once, away to the right, a kangaroo thumped through the grass. They saw a few cattle which had grown fat and sleek.

Fred looked about him. The Cooper always affected him. It was a green thread in the desert tapestry. The river, even its dry bed, was a symbol of life in a huge area where living was hard, and dying easy. Here was grass and cattle with glistening, bulging hides; beyond was sand and bleached bones. He looked about, and wondered if he would see the Cooper again.

He had punted over this crossing, when it lay submerged beneath fathoms of swirling brown water, hundreds of yards wide. But now it was quiet and the trees and the grass rested and waited. The water might come again next year or the year after or the year after that. But it would come. It always had. Rivers were inevitable. He felt vulnerable. Frail. For the first time since the war, he felt capable of dying.

Fred engaged low gear in four-wheel drive and began the long haul out and over the sandhills guarding the north. This was harder going than Kopperamanna but he kept the truck churning through the sand. They swayed round bends with the gearbox shrieking its song of mechanical agony, his hand holding the main lever in place, his leg hooked around the four-wheel drive lever, and the tyres biting deep in their fight for grip. He prayed the truck would continue moving. He could guess Johnny's reaction if they genuinely became stuck.

'The Natarannie Sandhills,' he shouted to Barbara. She nodded, glad of his voice.

'I once spent a week getting across them,' he continued, and saw Johnny flash a menacing look at him. 'Sand was very dry and soft then. We had to plate every inch of the way.' He changed gear. 'You know, drive on to a couple of metal strips, then put another couple in front of them,' he changed back. 'Then drive on to those, go back for the first lot, lay them up ahead, and so on.'

They were running downhill through the sand now. Suddenly the truck dipped down to a marshy plain. 'Oldfields Leap,' he called, as they slid down the steep slope. 'It's a beauty when you're going the other way. Practically stand on your tail.' They thumped on to the plain and the truck shuddered with the impact.

Johnny Parsons bounced heavily in his seat. 'How far to this next place?' he called.

'Mulka? It's at the end of the hill. About half an hour away.'

Johnny turned to examine the sandhill. It was on their left now, high and massive looking as it ran in an unbroken line to the north, and wearing a thick fuzz of the stunted bush that seemed to flourish only on the sand.

They were following a sinuous track through a swamp, curling between clumps of water grass and dodging the creamy edges of sour, evaporating pools. A flock of long-legged birds broke cover and flapped frantically for a hundred yards, until they buried themselves in fresh shelter.

The swamp ended and more sandhills closed in on them from the east, too. They were a speck of movement in a static ocean of sand. 'Christ, what country,' Johnny said. 'Okay. Call in to this next place. It's got to be better than this. But no tricks.'

High on the back, Frog surveyed the surrounding hills anxiously. The fewer times they crossed sand, the better he liked it. Travelling out in the sun and wind, balancing like a truckie's dog, was bad enough but when they crossed sand the steady swaying suddenly changed to a violent pitching and shaking. He'd almost been thrown off again, when the truck had taken that final sharp dip down the last sandhill. He cursed the truck and he cursed the track and, as an afterthought, he cursed the opals. Most of all, he cursed the opals. If it hadn't been for them, Johnny wouldn't have dragged him into this whole mess. He had a feeling growing inside him that they weren't going to get to Darwin. He looked at the ridges of sand surrounding them and shuddered. This looked like a short cut to hell.

He had been thinking a lot about that woman in Alice Springs. The way Johnny had hit her, with an eagerness, almost a relish. He thought, too, of the way Johnny had attacked the waitress at Marree and he wondered if she, too, were dead. And then back there on the sandhill. That was different, he supposed, but if he hadn't intervened, Johnny could have kicked the unconscious mailman to death.

And Frog thought of the way Johnny had looked at him after he'd fallen off and he felt a little more frightened. Lonely, too. Oh my God, how lonely he felt. He was travelling with a man he was growing to fear and three other persons who hated him because of that man. And out here, of all places. He looked about him and felt like screaming. This wasn't his country. He was from another world, a world of pavements and buildings and people, lots and lots of people. A place that had shade and was cool. Cool. Even the thought was blurred like a confused memory of childhood.

He put down the rifle and wiped his forehead. Ivan, from his perch four feet away, watched with interest. 'Have you got any water up here?' Frog called to him.

Ivan shook his head.

Frog looked for the opened beer carton but it was down at the tail of the truck. He dared not let go the rope.

'Get me some beer from the back,' he said. 'Please. I can't stand this heat.' He could feel the wind whisking the moisture in his eyes.

Ivan was shaking his head slowly. He slid across, until he was almost sitting beside Frog. 'That stuff will do you no good, you know. Make you sick like a dog. You've had too much water and grog. That's why you feel so crook. You do feel crook, don't you?'

Frog nodded. 'I don't know how you stand it. The heat and the country and everything.'

'You get used to it, you know.'

The truck bounced over a ridge of sand and Ivan grabbed Frog's arm to steady him. Frog nodded his thanks but said nothing.

'Was it you killed the woman?' The question from the Russian shocked Frog.

'No,' he said. 'No, believe me, I never killed her.'

Ivan nodded slowly. 'I thought it was the other one,' he said.

'All I did was pinch a ute and open the safe. He's no good at things like that. That was all I was supposed to do. He promised me I'd get half the money. He killed the woman. I had nothing to do with that. We didn't plan on that. I'd never do nothing like that. Johnny reckons we're in this together but I never had nothing to do with the killing. I was just in the same room with him, that's all. I didn't do it. You believe that don't you?'

Ivan nodded gravely. 'How'd you get mixed up with him in the first place?'

Frog shrugged. He held out his right hand and deliberately rubbed the thumb against the two fingers until little rolls of dirt had collected on the tips. 'My fingers,' he said, and looked sideways at the puzzled Russian. 'Because of my blasted fingers. I'm good with them. You know, opening safes and things. Anything. I've done some good jobs in my time and Johnny knew it, so he asked me to open this safe for him. Said it would be worth five thousand to me. We got the opals, but look where we are. Oh geeze, I feel crook. You sure there's no water?' He wrinkled his eyes in appeal.

Ivan shook his head. Fred hadn't told these men about the extra drums, so neither would he. 'I don't think your friend cares whether you have water or not, you know. I don't think he cares about anyone, except himself.'

Frog licked his cracked lips but said nothing. The truck hit a series of deep ruts, and both men steadied themselves. When the track became smoother, Ivan said: 'Did you know he was a murderer when you went with him?'

'No.' Frog shouted the word. 'All I knew about him was what he told me. Come to think of it, that wasn't much, either. He just told me he'd been in Coober Pedy and that some Yank was going to take a fortune in opals up north. He wanted someone who could open a safe and pinch a truck, and a mate in Adelaide put him on to me. He'd worked out a plan for the whole thing. Perfect, or so he reckoned. Anyhow, everything went wrong and here we are. If he hadn't killed that woman, we'd have probably been all right. Now everyone's after us. He just went crazy when she came in. He just hit her and hit her . . .' He rubbed his fingers harder.

'Why didn't you split up?'

'What?' Frog asked the question weakly. 'I'm not going to hang for him. If I'd have left him, I'd have been gone a million. He had our escape worked out and I had to stick with him. You can understand that.' He looked hard at Ivan, seeking the sympathy that other man rarely gave him. 'If I'd broken away, they'd have probably caught me and blamed me for the killing. Besides, he kept all the opals.'

'You don't reckon he's going to share them with you, do you?'

Frog arched an eyebrow. 'He couldn't have got them without me. All he did was find out where they were. I got them out. I did all the work.'

'And he hangs on to the opals. Have you seen them yet?'

Frog, trying to dredge up moisture for his throat, coughed and didn't hear the question.

'Has he shown you the opals?' Ivan said.

'What do you mean?' Frog shuffled closer.

'Well, you said you were getting five thousand but I heard people saying the opals were worth a lot more. I forget how much now. Fifty thousand or something like that. So I was wondering if you'd seen them, you know, actually laid your eyes on them. Seems to me like your mate's dudding you. You know, cheating you, because five isn't half of fifty, is it?'

Frog didn't answer. He turned his face into the breeze, away from the Russian. Ivan, feeling contented with the conversation, slid back to his original position.

The heat became intense and the horizon danced with vaporous puzzles. Around the five people on the truck, the distant land was converted to raw stripes of colour and inverted, hazed images. Ahead of them the track dissolved, literally, into thin air. First it would rise in layers, projected into the sky in a series of fractured steps. Then it would disappear, swallowed by the contracting ring of heat.

The sign materialised gradually. At first it was tall and wavering, a vertical scar in the shimmering layers. As they drove closer, it solidified into a squat post with a crude arrowed sign at its top.

'Mulka 2 m.' The post was planted in the gibber plain, a mast of wood rising from an ocean of stones. It had been fashioned from the trunk of a small tree and leaned drunkenly, having shifted in its supporting base of heaped ironstones. The sign was at a fork in the track. One set of ruts went straight ahead. The tilted sign ignored it and instead pointed left towards wheel marks that ran past the skeleton of a steer that had perished the previous summer. The dead animal was a scrap heap of bones and hide and sand. The beast's hindquarters were given a vestige of shape by fragments of hide which covered the hip bones like a decaying tent, but the skull, with its two probing horns, had already been picked clean by birds and ants, polished by the wind, and bleached by sunshine. The barrier of bones had trapped driftsand, turning the dead beast into a mound, a growing island. That was the way dunes began, collecting the wind's deposits on a foundation of low bushes, heaped stones or dead animals. The steer was unlikely to amount to much. It, and the faltering post, were the sole foreigners in an immense colony of gibbers. There was no other protrusion to catch the wind. The ironstones — shattered into head- and fist-sized lumps by a constant succession of hot days and cold nights and then polished smooth by the wind — stretched like a glistening red pavement to the horizon.

'The cobblestones of Hell,' Fred said and turned left, off the Birdsville Track.

The heat had begun to have a stupefying effect on Johnny Parsons and he jumped at the words. 'What?' he shouted.

Fred was aiming the truck along the twin ruts through the gibbers. 'That's what Sturt was supposed to have called this place. This is part of his Stony Desert. The cobblestones of Hell. Good name. He and his men rode and walked across that.' He jerked a thumb out the doorway. 'Tough men. They were out on that trip for a couple of years. He went blind, with the glare I suppose ...'

'Spare us the history,' Johnny said straightening himself in the crude seat. A cut on his face had begun to bleed again. 'Where's this next place?'

'Just over the ridge.'

'What ridge? It looks flat to me.'

'There's a low ridge up ahead. You'll see the homestead when we get beyond it.'

The rise took half a minute to materialise. It bubbled from the rim of the heat haze, a low hill immensely worn. The track curved right, over its brow. A tall radio mast came into view.

Then, as though being dragged out of the vapours that shrouded the limits of their view, a homestead rose, to attach itself to the mast. The homestead was surrounded by a high fence of corrugated iron. Trees grew around the fence.

'Mulka,' Fred announced. 'They used to have an old store here, but it's just a cattle station now. Run by Tim Sanderson and his family. Lived here all his life.'

'Just them?' Johnny asked. Fred nodded.

'Good.' He had a closer look at the homestead. A ridge of sandhills ran beyond the buildings. 'How big's the family?'

'Tim and his missus and three kids.'

'How old are they?'

'How would I know for sure? Tim'd be in his late forties, I suppose and Mrs Sanderson'd be ...'

'The kids, I mean. What are they and how old are they?'

'Two boys and a girl. The eldest boy's about twenty. The other's seventeen or eighteen and the girl's a good bit younger.'

'Big boys?'

'Look, if you're planning to start trouble here, let's just keep going, like you said first of all. These are nice people and you've got no reason to hurt them.'

'Who said anyone's going to get hurt? You just act like you did at Etadunna and no one's going to get into any trouble. Have you got much stuff for them?'

'Not a great deal. Should have it all off and ready to go again in an hour or so.'

They were slowing down now, as they followed the gentle curve of the track past a square stone outhouse near the homestead. They stopped beside a weathered utility truck, parked beneath a tree outside the homestead's iron fence. Two thin dogs ran out, yapping.

Johnny leaned across and tapped the barrel of his gun on Barbara's knee, causing her to move it in pain. 'Just a reminder,' he said, smiling into her hostile eyes. 'I'm putting this in my pocket now, but it'll be nice and handy. Do the wrong thing and I'll use it.' He pocketed the gun and straightened his back. 'Remember now.'

A short, thick-set man with a long nose appeared at Fred's door. He must have walked from the outhouse behind the truck. His sudden appearance startled Johnny.

'G'day, Fred,' he said, in a soft voice. He noticed Barbara and Johnny and raised his hat. The movement revealed a bald head as red and polished as a desert stone, yet there was plenty of hair on the rest of him. His chin bristled with a grey stubble and his exposed forearms were covered in a thick, hairy coat. Great tufts of curly hair pushed their way through the open collar of his shirt. Barbara thought he looked like a bald-headed collie. Then the wide-brimmed hat dropped back into place and the illusion was gone. One of the dogs jumped up and, with a casual swing of his leg, the man kicked it away.

'This is Tim Sanderson,' Fred said, as he began to climb out. 'Tim, meet Barbara Dean, the new sister for Birdsville, and a friend of mine, Johnny Smith.'

He nodded greeting, and then quizzically examined the two men's faces. 'Don't look like you've been friends too long,' Sanderson said. 'What happened to you?'

'Ah, it was just an accident, Tim.'

'Sure,' said Johnny, pushing Barbara so that she got out through Fred's door. He followed her. 'We're both pretty lucky really, aren't we Fred? We were unloading at the last place and some crates fell on top of us.'

'We'd appreciate a bit of a clean up, Tim.' Fred touched his scratched cheek. 'Feel a bit of a mess like this.'

'Of course. You were lucky all right, weren't you? If the whole lot had come down it'd have buried you.' He gazed up at the load, and nodded at Ivan, who had begun to scramble down. He noticed Frog. 'Who's the bloke with the rifle?'

'Oh, it's, ah, Johnny's brother. Stepbrother. I used to know them years ago before I came up here. They're just travelling with me for the trip.'

The man's eyes lit up with interest. 'Where are you from?' he asked Johnny.

'We've been around a bit,' Johnny answered. 'Adelaide was the last place.'

'Bit different to Adelaide, here eh?'

Johnny nodded. He said nothing and the awkward pause embarrassed Sanderson.

'Well,' Sanderson said, scratching his knee. 'Let's stop magging in the sun. How about some tea.'

'Wonderful idea,' Barbara said and they walked towards the house. 'I believe you've been here all your life,' she said, as they stepped into the shade of the verandah.

Sanderson smiled at her. 'Love it here,' he said. 'Probably seems strange to you.' He waited for her polite protest and then continued, turning so that he could point beyond the tin barrier to low sandhills. 'This probably looks like the last place on earth you'd like to live, but stay here for a while and the country sort of gets into you. I've been to the big cities a couple of times but I'm always glad to get back. There's something about it that makes you want to come back all the time. Anyhow,' he grinned sheepishly, 'you'd rather have a cuppa than listen to me mag. Mother,' he shouted. 'Visitors.'

He opened the flyscreen door and beckoned Barbara through. A spindly-legged girl of ten, who had been watching them from the shadows of the kitchen, backed away shyly.

'That's my daughter, Margaret,' he explained. 'Where's your mother, love?' he asked in a louder voice. 'Tell her the sister and some friends of Mr Crawford's are here.'

The girl spun on her heel and disappeared into another room. Barbara smiled. 'She's a pet,' she told Sanderson.

He beamed with pleasure. 'She's a great help around the place. Anyhow, take a seat and we'll soon have a cuppa for you. Fred, you know where the bathroom is. Take your friends with you and get cleaned up before the missus gets here.'

'Good idea,' said Fred, and began to leave the room.

Johnny turned to Frog, who was standing just inside the door. 'Why don't you sit down next to the sister till I get back,' he suggested, and followed Fred.

When they returned, Mrs Sanderson had begun pouring tea, made from a kettle constantly simmering on a huge stove. She was a tall woman, taller than her husband and with a face that, even now, was strikingly attractive.

'The folk along the track are gossiping about you already, sister,' she was saying. 'A new sister is a big event, especially when she's travelling with such a good looking young man as Mr Crawford.'

'I ought to warn you, Sister,' said Fred, defensively, 'that Mrs Sanderson has been trying to marry me off since my first trip up the track. She doesn't understand that I'm a misogamist. But definitely not a misogynist.'

'There he goes,' Mrs Sanderson said and her eyes twinkled. 'Each trip Mr Webster, the talking dictionary, gives me some new word I've never heard.'

'And she never asks what they mean.'

'I'd be frightened to. Goodness knows what shocking words he might be saying to me.' Her eyes narrowed. 'What's wrong with your face? Have you scratched yourself?'

'He and his friend were very lucky, really, mother,' Sanderson cut in. 'Some of the load fell on top of them back at Etadunna. You should have seen them when they arrived. Faces all covered in blood. You'd have thought they'd been fighting like deadly enemies instead of being old friends.'

'Etadunna?' she said and there was such doubt in her voice that Fred spoke quickly.

'Just after Etadunna. Some of the load was loose. We stopped to tighten things and, bang, down it came.' His hands fell around his ears. 'Only small stuff luckily.'

'Goodness me,' she said, and her face became creased with anxiety. 'You could have been killed with some of the heavy things you carry. Are you sure you're all right now?'

Fred said 'Sure.'

'And how about you?' she turned to Johnny and for the first time studied him closely. 'Forgive my husband for not introducing us but I'm Mrs Sanderson. You're Mr Smith, this other gentleman's brother, I presume.'

'That's right,' said Johnny and shook her outstretched hand. 'Pleased to meet you.'

'Can I get something for you. Your poor face looks sore.'

'No. I'll be okay thanks. I wouldn't mind a cup of tea, though.'

'Of course,' she said and passed him a cup and saucer. 'Your brother tells me this is your first time up here. I suppose you find it a bit different to where you come from.'

Johnny nodded and sipped his tea. 'Nice brew,' he said.

'Thank you. How do you like yours, Sister?'

'It's fine, thank you Mrs Sanderson.'

'Do you drink much tea?'

'Love it.'

'I thought maybe you weren't very fond of it.'

'Why no, this is a lovely cup.'

'No, I didn't mean that. I meant tea generally. Mrs Leary said on the radio you wouldn't have a cup when you were at Etadunna and I thought you probably weren't terribly keen on tea. You know how it is with some folk. I know you had tea at Dulkaninna and *that* made Mrs Leary just a bit more upset. Oh, not that she was complaining, or anything like that. It's just that visitors are so few and she likes to have a bit of a chat. You know how it is. Especially when someone as talked about as you comes along and ...'

'Fair go, Kath,' said her husband. 'I don't know, Sister, when the womenfolk get on the radio they're like a lot of parrots.'

'Oh Tim, be quiet. Sister knows what I mean. I just thought she mightn't like tea because she didn't have any at Etadunna. You know what I mean, don't you, Sister?'

'Of course I do, Mrs Sanderson. No, it was just that Fred was in a bit of a hurry and I didn't want to delay him.'

'You see, Tim.'

Sanderson drained his cup. 'Less talk and more tea, please Kath.'

'Sometimes I think the only reason you married me is because I make a good cup of tea,' she said, as she passed the teapot.

'Go on with you,' he said. 'You know why I married you. Because you don't mag like other women.' He burst into a laugh so deep that the forest of hair on his chest quivered. 'Oh well,' he said when he had finished, 'less talk and more work. Let's go and get the things unloaded Fred.'

'Just take a bit more care this time,' Mrs Sanderson advised.

'Don't worry,' said Fred, standing up and putting his hat on, 'last time was just a fluke. Thanks for the cuppa. You coming Ivan, Johnny?'

Johnny nodded. 'Tim,' he said, 'I believe you've got a couple of boys about the place. Are they around?'

Sanderson paused at the door. 'No, I'm sorry about that. They'd have liked to've met you all. They went out this morning after some cattle. Won't be back for a few days.'

Fred said: 'If the boys aren't about, your brother had better give us a hand, eh Johnny?' Frog shuffled his feet uncomfortably.

Johnny seemed to ignore the question. 'How about you, Sister?' he asked. 'Going to watch?'

'Now why would she want to watch?' Mrs Sanderson said, smiling. 'You men leave us. The sister's probably had enough of the sun for one day, anyhow.'

'Good idea,' said Fred.

'Might be an idea if my brother stayed too, if you don't mind Mrs Sanderson,' Johnny said. 'He doesn't look too good. He's been out in the sun on the back of the truck all the time.'

'That's right,' Frog cut in, glad of the chance to stay in the house. 'I haven't been feeling too good. I think it must be the sun.'

'Just as well to stay indoors while you can, then,' said Mrs

Sanderson. 'The sun's a bit severe if you're not used to it. It was ninety six in the house at lunchtime, but it still seems a lot cooler than outside, doesn't it?'

'It sure does,' said Frog and sat down again.

The four men went outside, leaving Frog with the two women.

'Would you like some more tea, Mr Smith,' Mrs Sanderson said. Frog accepted and took the cup and sat down at the far end of the room.

'Are you feeling all right?' Mrs Sanderson asked.

Frog nodded and waved his hand vaguely near his head. 'Just the heat,' he said. 'I just want to sit down and have a bit of a spell.'

'Well, if you're sure, then,' she said, and studied him anxiously for several seconds. Then she turned enthusiastically to Barbara. 'He should be in good hands with you to look after him, Sister.' She smiled and then launched herself into conversation. 'They're really looking forward to your arrival up in Birdsville. Mrs Thomas is due to have her baby any day and they're wondering who'll arrive first, you or the baby. Always has trouble, she does. This'll be the eighth. She lost the last one, poor thing, so I can imagine how she's feeling. Apart from the baby, they tell me things are pretty quiet at the moment. I understand this is your first time in a place like this — the mission hospital, I mean.'

Barbara nodded and said a belated 'Yes' as Mrs Sanderson continued. 'You'll certainly find it different to Crown Street. A niece of Tim's had her baby there, so I've heard of it. Oh I know all about you being in Sydney,' she explained as she noticed the surprised look on the sister's face. 'Beth gave us all a word by word account of what you said at morning tea at Dulkaninna. I know you were at Crown Street for the last couple of years, and that you had a flat at Elizabeth Bay with a view of Sydney Harbour, and that you're twenty-six — you shouldn't have told Beth that; everyone within four hundred miles knows now — and let me see, what else.'

'Goodness me,' Barbara said. 'What else is there?'

'Well, Beth didn't say whether you were engaged or anything like that. You're not married, of course?'

'Heavens no.' Barbara laughed.

'You wouldn't be engaged then?'

'No.'

'I didn't think so. No girl who was engaged to some handsome doctor would rush off to a place like Birdsville. I hope you don't mind me asking, but how come a girl like you hasn't found herself a nice young man? There must be scores of them around Sydney.'

Barbara seemed flustered. 'Well,' she said, groping for an answer, 'I've been too busy, I suppose. To tell the truth, I hadn't worried much about it.' She spread her fingers on her chest and with mock anxiety, asked: 'Am I starting to look like an old maid?'

'Goodness me, no. It's just that if you'd lived around here all your life, you'd have gone off nine or ten years ago. Got married, I mean,' she added hastily.

She leant forward, confidentially. 'There aren't too many white girls left up here. All sorts of strange things happening.' She reflected for a moment. 'Not many eligible males, for that matter, either. All you'll find at Birdsville will be a handful of married men. There is a school teacher, though, but he'd be too young.'

'Well,' said Barbara, 'I hadn't thought of taking a husband back with me.'

Mrs Sanderson looked at her and laughed uncertainly. Frog walked to the table and deposited his empty cup. He mumbled thanks and returned to his chair.

Mrs Sanderson waited until he was well settled, before continuing. 'Fred's a nice man, isn't he?' she said.

Barbara nodded. 'He seems very nice.'

'As good a man as you'd meet. Should have had a wife to comfort him and look after him years ago. There's quite a sad story about Fred, you know.'

'Oh?'

'Yes, people reckoned he was very keen on the little girl who lives up the track.' She indicated the direction with her head. 'Betty Spencer. You'll meet her tomorrow. Nice enough girl, but not really in Fred's class, I'd say. Anyhow, Fred was apparently keen on her. Poor man, there aren't many women of the colour he'd be interested in, living out this way. She grew into a pretty little thing and Fred had his eye on her but she upped and married this chap at Clifton Hills. He's a bit of a smart type. You know. Dresses up like one of those cowboys you see in the magazines. Fancy hat and fandangles and things. Goodness knows what the cattle think of it all. Anyhow, Betty must have liked it because she married him and now they've got a little baby. Bit tough on Fred. He's a very sincere type and I think he still likes her a bit. And just between you and me, I've heard that Betty's had a think or two since she got married. Still, too late now.'

Barbara pushed her cup and saucer towards the teapot. 'I wonder if I could have a little more tea.'

Mrs Sanderson poured as she spoke. 'Fred's a good deal older than her. He's about thirty-five or so. More your age.' She wrinkled her nose as though she had passed on some secret information. 'Not Betty's. She would have been too young for him, anyhow. Didn't know her own mind, and now she's beginning to regret it, I'd say. Not yet twenty-three and a mother already. That's what I meant about them starting young out here.'

'Yes, I see,' Barbara said, and was surprised, for she thought of all the girls she had known who were much younger mothers than this Betty Spencer. The hardened fifteen-year-olds. The frightened girls with pale-faced husbands who had not begun to shave, and who sat in the hospital waiting room, hoping people wouldn't look at them. How little of the world this woman must know. The thought startled her. Until this moment, Barbara had regarded herself as an innocent, entering a region of wiser and infinitely more practical people. But this woman, she realised, was shielded from the world, and spent most of her life behind a tin fence. Suddenly, Betty felt sorry for Kath Sanderson, who was smiling brightly, waiting for her visitor to say something. 'Tell me, how long ago did all this happen?'

'The wedding? Oh, she married young Spencer about eighteen months ago.'

That would have been a big event out here, Barbara thought, and recalled the weddings in fashionable Sydney churches, where radiant brides popped through archways, like white sausages emerging from a production line. On Saturdays, while she worked, and attended to the after effects of such a system.

'Surely Mr Crawford would have got over it by now.'

'How? There's no other white woman to help him forget. There are two things wrong with his job. He's got to call in at Clifton Hills every trip and be reminded of her, and he gets too much time to think. His job's too lonely. The only person he spends any time with is Ivan and he's hardly the sort to take your mind off a pretty girl. It's not the life for a man like Fred. You know, living in a truck for most of the time with only someone like Ivan to talk to. Not that there's anything really wrong with Ivan. He's a good worker and he's very loyal to Fred. It's just that he doesn't wash.' She laughed but covered her mouth, as though embarrassed by the daring of her remark. Barbara laughed too, being anxious to make the woman feel at ease, and Mrs Sanderson lowered her hand. 'Fred's a cut above a lot of people you meet. He's got a good head on his shoulders and he'd be worth a lot of money today. A lot of money.'

'He does more than just handle the mail contract. Maybe he told you. He's got a few vehicles and some other men working for him. He does all sorts of contract work, like sinking bores and building dams and so on. He knew there was some money to be made up here, and believe you me, he's making it. He's not just a rough old inlander like some of us.'

They talked for another twenty minutes and then walked out on to the verandah to watch the men working. Frog followed them.

The four men unloaded the mail, drums of oil and fuel and the food. They stacked all except the mail and some crates of fruit in a shed and returned to the homestead verandah. There, Mrs Sanderson began shuffling through the mail while her husband carried the fruit inside.

'Can I go to the bathroom now?' Frog asked Johnny. Mrs Sanderson looked up at his words.

'Yeah, I'll show you the way,' Johnny offered. He opened the wire screen for Frog and led him to the far end of the room. Sanderson, having deposited the fruit, walked past them with a nod and went on to the verandah. Johnny waited until the door had slammed. 'Listen, Frog,' he whispered urgently. 'It's down the end of this corridor. On the way you pass their radio. It's a two-way job. Put it out of action. Okay?'

Frog looked puzzled. 'I suppose so. But why?'

'We don't want them talking to the world about us. And when you get outside see if you can do something to stop their utility from travelling too far. Okay? Now hurry.' He gave Frog a sharp push and returned to the verandah. Five minutes later, Frog joined them. He nodded to Johnny.

Barbara spoke to Mrs Sanderson. 'I hope you don't mind us all trooping through your house, but do you mind if I just pop in to your bathroom and powder my nose?'

'Course not,' she said, putting the mail down on a cane table. 'I'm only sorry you're all going to push on so soon.'

Barbara took her bag and went to the bathroom. She closed the door carefully behind her and took out her lipstick. She went to the cream wooden shaving cabinet and wrote on the mirror in thick red letters: 'HELP. MEN ARE MURDERERS. TELL POLICE MARREE. WILL KILL US.'

She stood back and read the message. Then she hurriedly applied a smear of lipstick to her lips and left the room. She hoped they would leave immediately.

Fred was already beside the truck when she reached the verandah. Sanderson had refilled the water bag and was hooking it on the front. Near him, Frog appeared to be examining the station's utility truck. Mrs Sanderson, with Johnny standing nearby, was waiting for the sister at the fence.

'It's been lovely having you,' Mrs Sanderson said and took both Barbara's hands in hers. 'I hope we see you again.'

'You've been so kind,' Barbara said. She looked at Johnny, eyeing her impatiently. 'I'm only sorry we've imposed on you so much. I'm afraid we've made an awful mess of your bathroom.'

'Oh that's nothing dear. It's wonderful to see so many people at one time.' She stood beside the tin fence and watched Barbara join the others at the truck.

'Say goodbye to Margaret for me,' Fred called out.

'Good heavens, I'd forgotten about her,' Barbara told him. 'Where did she get to?'

'She's a quiet little mouse,' he said, as Ivan cranked the motor. 'She goes and hides when visitors come. Not that that's often.' He pushed the lever into first gear. Ivan climbed on, as the truck began to roll forward. The dogs chased it, barking furiously.

Tim Sanderson joined his wife at the fence and the pair of them waved until the truck had rolled past. They walked clear of the house and watched it head northwards.

Mrs Sanderson felt a small hand grip hers and smiled down at her daughter. 'Well, so you've come out at last, eh,' she said. 'They've all gone now.'

'Daddy,' the girl asked, looking up at her father with pale blue eyes. 'What did the man do to the radio?'

'What do you mean?' he asked. 'Do what to the radio?'

'Take something from it. Why did he do it?'

'Who? What man?'

'The little fat one.'

'Now just a minute, child,' her mother said. 'What's all this about. How do you know he took something from the radio?'

'I saw him. I was hiding and I saw him. I don't think he wanted anyone to watch him because he kept looking around.'

Sanderson stared open mouthed at the distant trail of dust and then wheeled and walked briskly inside.

'This is crazy,' he muttered, as he pulled open the wire door. 'No one'd do a thing like that.' He turned on Margaret. 'You must have seen things.'

The girl looked upset. 'I didn't,' she protested. 'He took something.'

'Then why didn't you say something?'

The girl stared down at her shoes.

'Let's go and have a look,' Mrs Sanderson suggested.

He led the way into the radio room and stood back to examine the large grey set. 'Can't see anything wrong with it,' he said and walked over to switch it on. He waited several seconds, then turned several knobs. He turned to his wife, his face white. 'It's not working. He did something to it, all right. Now why in the name of . . . it was working all right at the last session, wasn't it?' His voice had an accusing tone.

'Perfectly,' she said.

'Well he did something to it then. Look at it.' He waved his hand at the set. 'Dead. Completely dead. Margaret.' He looked down at the girl. 'What did he take? Do you know?'

She shook her head.

'Well where did it come from?'

'Up there.' She pointed. 'From the back.'

He kneeled on the desk supporting the set and peered in the back. 'He took something all right,' he thundered, sliding his legs back to the floor. 'The thing's practically empty back there. What's wrong with the man? What would he want with the guts of a radio?' He glared angrily at the girl. 'Why didn't you tell us about this? You've got a tongue in your head. This man's gone away now and he's taken everything.' He threw up his hands 'We're as good as cut off from the world.'

Mrs Sanderson shook her head. 'I didn't like the look of him from the start. Or his brother. Not that they looked like brothers. I've never seen two men look less alike in my life. Tim, there's something strange about those two men. I've never heard Fred mention them before and he's told us about most of his friends. And did you see the way they were going on all the time. Why, the fat one even asked the other one if he could go to the bathroom.' She paused. 'The bathroom! Sister said it was dirty. She went in after him and she complained it was dirty. Why that filthy little wretch.' She began to stride towards the bathroom. 'If he's dirtied this place ...'

She flung open the door.

CHAPTER TWELVE

North of Mulka, some sand ridges and small hills rose from the stony plain. They were low and flat, minor eruptions that scarred and pimpled the face of the desert. The sun was low in the sky. The wavering heat hazes had gone, and the land was dappled by shadows. In place of mirage, there was now an awesome clarity that stretched the horizon to an immense distance.

It was the time of the day that Fred Crawford preferred, and this was one of his favourite places. He loved the hills, and the secret colours they revealed only at this time of day. He turned off the track, towards a raw cliff stained purple in its folds. He headed towards a rise where stood the remains of a homestead, Here, they would spend the night. The building was a plain rectangular structure of mud bricks, still partly roofed but with only gaping holes where the door and windows had been. Isolated clumps of spinifex and the twisted trunks of a few long-dead trees shared its loneliness.

Fred helped Barbara to the ground. She examined the scene more closely. She felt as though she had intruded upon some long-forgotten and private burial ground. 'People used to live here?' she asked, incredulously.

'A long time ago,' he grunted, as he lifted his box of provisions from the truck.

'How awful for them. How could they live? I mean, in a place like this.'

'They couldn't. That's why they left. Here,' he called to Ivan, who had jumped down, 'give me a hand with this.' Together, they carried the box to the building where Johnny was waiting.

Barbara stayed where she was, examining the landscape. 'But why did they come in the first place?' she asked. Fred had disappeared around the corner of the building, and didn't answer her question.

'He didn't hear you,' said Frog. He leaned against the front of the truck with the rifle slung in his arms. He smiled at her. She turned her head away and began to follow Fred to the building.

'You can at least talk to me,' he said, softly, as she passed him. She quickened her step.

'Rude bitch,' he muttered. He waited until she had disappeared behind the building, then followed the others.

As Frog turned the corner of the hut he heard Barbara cry out. A laughing Ivan came bursting through the doorway, swinging a large lizard by the tail. He swung it around his head several times and sent it flying in twitching cartwheels through the air. 'And don't come back until we're gone,' he shouted. Still smiling Ivan walked past Frog to collect their sleeping bags from the truck.

Frog walked to the door. Inside, sand covered the floor and sloped more than a foot deep against the far wall. A thick grey-green bush grew in one corner. In the opposite corner Barbara was bent over, smoothing the sand with her hands. She had claimed her territory for the night. Frog leaned against the doorway and watched the way her skirt tightened as she worked. Finally she straightened, saw him, and walked outside to where Fred was filling a billy can with water.

The shadows had spread and merged into one by the time Fred had put the billy on his small spirit stove. He began to boil some frankfurters. Barbara cut slices from a loaf of bread and buttered them. She placed them in a neat pile beside the stove and then stood back, gazing into the flame. Her thoughts drifted back to Mulka.

She wondered whether the Sandersons had seen her message yet. Help might be on the way already. The thought comforted her. By the morning Fred's policeman friend from Marree could be here and this whole nightmare might be over.

For the first time since the men had appeared, she felt the warmth of confidence in her body. Even the flame bursting from the stove seemed cheery. And there was something about Fred, bending over the billy as though his only worry was whether the frankfurters cooked properly, that was reassuring. Almost comical. Fred, the man who made his living in a job most men would find too tough, was fussing over his stove for all the world like some nervous city housewife. She watched him for a while, smiling to herself.

What was this other girl like, the Betty who lived at Clifton Hills? How much of Mrs Sanderson's tale had been true and how much gossip? Barbara found herself curiously eager to know the answers. Her mind tried to form images of this young girl who supposedly had broken Fred's heart. With a start, she realised she must have been staring oafishly at the flame. She patted her hair in a quick, unconscious gesture and moved closer to Fred. She knelt beside him. 'How's it going, cook?' she asked.

He tilted back his hat and smiled at her. 'Hungry?'

'We all are,' Johnny said. He was lying back, propped up on one elbow, with his outstretched feet pointing at the base of the stove. The hand holding the gun rested lazily on his lap. 'What are you trying to do with those starvers? Turn 'em into soup, or something?'

'Just keep your shirt on,' Fred said. He turned to Barbara again. 'There aren't enough plates to go around so we'll eat them in the bread. Just no one drop any crumbs on the tablecloth.' He grinned at her.

They ate the frankfurters and as the land around them faded away into night Fred made tea and they ate more bread with apricot jam. Fred turned off the stove and sudden darkness separated them.

'No one move,' Johnny's voice snapped. He sat up and fiddled in his pocket for his torch. Its light, weak and yellow now, probed the circle. 'Christ it gets dark quickly.'

'You're jumpy, aren't you?' Ivan said.

'Yes I am, Whiskers, and you'd better remember it. I'm liable to pull this trigger. You, Fred,' the light stabbed at the mailman, 'why'd you turn that thing off?'

'I can't let it burn all night. Why don't you go and collect some timber and make yourself a proper fire. Then you won't get frightened of the dark.'

'Don't call me frightened, Postie,' he said. 'I just want light so's we can see each other, that's all. You.' He flashed his torch at Ivan. 'Go get some wood. Enough to keep a fire going all night. Frog, go with him and keep an eye on him. Just remember, Whiskers, you start anything out there and the girl gets it. Okay, now go and get some wood.'

Frog stood up and backed away from Ivan, who pushed himself to his feet. 'Give us another bit of bread and jam before I go?' Frog asked.

'Have it when you come back,' Johnny said. 'We want that fire.'

'Come on,' Ivan said to Frog. 'There are a couple of dead trees over this way.' He disappeared into the darkness and Frog began to feel his way after him. He took out his torch and picked out the Russian making his way surefootedly up the slope. He jogged after him until he was alongside.

'Nice night,' he said, gazing up at the few stars beginning to wink in the heavens.

'I don't know why you put up with him,' Ivan said.

'What do you mean?'

'Well, he just bosses you around as though you were dirt, you know.'

'Who, Johnny?'

'Yeah.'

'Hell, someone's got to get the wood, I suppose.'

'Well, why you? Why not him? He hasn't done a stick of work since he came. He's made you do the lot. Even made you sit out in the sun all the time. I notice he hasn't offered to give you a break, you know.' Ivan stopped and began urinating on the dirt. 'I know I wouldn't take it,' he continued. 'He reckoned you were partners, didn't he? Funny sort of partners, you know. You do all the work and he keeps the opals. I wouldn't trust him, I wouldn't. Anyhow, he's going to get you into more trouble unless you stop him.' He finished and began walking on.

'Stop him. What do you mean?'

'I mean all this talk of his about killing people. Next time he kills, you're up for murder, too, you know, no doubt. Unless he kills you, you know.'

'Me?'

'I've seen him looking at you with that crazy way of his at times.

I'd look out for myself if I was you. You got a gun, you know. I'd be inclined to use it on him before he shoots you. It's just what he's likely to do, you know. Here's some wood. Hold out the light, will you?'

Frog's brow crinkled in thought as he illuminated the timber for Ivan.

'You're in a pretty bad spot, you know,' the Russian continued, as he straightened with an armful of timber.

'How do you mean?'

'Well, everyone's looking for you. That means they're all against you, you know. And all because of what the other bloke done, not because of what you done. They're after you because of him. It'd be different for you, I suppose, if you could trust him but you can't even do that. If I were in your shoes, I wouldn't be game to go to sleep tonight. C'mon, let's get some more wood.'

He led the way to the top of the rise. Frog stared thoughtfully back at the faint light coming from the torch at their camp. His eyes were more used to the dark now, and he switched off his torch and followed the moving shadow that was Ivan.

He hurried to catch up. 'Johnny wouldn't do nothing to me,' he said. 'He needs me to help get up to Darwin.'

'I don't reckon he needs you from what he was saying today.'

'What was that?'

'Oh, I'd better not say or you might go straight back there in a temper and try to shoot him.'

'What are you talking about?'

'Look, I heard him say a few things when you weren't close handy. That's all. I'm not going to say anything more. Just trying to give you a friendly warning, you know. Switch your torch on, will you? There should be a bit of wood about here.'

Frog held the light while Ivan pulled a dead branch from a stunted tree. He sat on the pebble-strewn ground and rested the rifle across his lip. 'What did he say?'

Ivan, his back to Frog, smiled at the question. He felt pleased with himself. 'I can't tell you,' he replied. 'But if I'd been you and I'd have heard it, I'd have shot him on the spot.'

'Oh, you're crazy.'

'He's the crazy one. Saying things like that about a man who's stuck by him. I wouldn't let him do what he's trying to do to you.'

'Do what? What are you talking about?'

'Blame you for killing the woman.'
'What?' Frog jumped to his feet. 'Blame me for it?'
'Sh. Keep your voice down, mate. Sound travels a long way here. See, I knew I shouldn't have told you.'
Frog felt a cold fear rising inside him. 'He killed her. Not me. He can't blame that on me.'
'Well, that's what he's doing, you know. He reckons if they catch the two of you together, you'll swing for it, not him.'
Frog switched off the torch and stared about him at the shadowy loneliness. He felt like running somewhere.
'We all believe you,' Ivan said. 'We believe he killed her, not you. But if anything happens to us and you get caught, it's just his word against yours. Even if they hang him, he'll make sure you hang too. While he's about, your life's not worth a crumpet. If you two do get clear, he won't share with you. He'd kill you for sure. And if you get caught, he'll see that you hang.'
Frog clutched the rifle tightly. 'He *can't* blame that on me.'
Ivan lifted the last of the timber. 'He is, you know.'
'I don't believe you. This is some kind of trick.' His voice had changed tone and he snapped the words out.
'You know what sort of bloke he is. He's crazy, you know. Do you trust a crazy man? I wouldn't take my eye off him, if I were you. Anyhow, let's get back before he shoots through and leaves us here.'
At the suggestion, Frog ran to the top of the incline and stared down. There was no light and he had difficulty making out the shape of the building and truck.
'Johnny,' he called. 'You there?'
'What's wrong?' Johnny's voice came back out of the darkness. 'Where's the Russian?'
'He's here.' There was a sigh of relief in Frog's voice.
'Well come and get this fire started, my torch has had it. And stop yelling out. There might be someone about. You never know. Come on.'
Ivan had joined Frog. 'He's still giving you orders, you know,' he said shyly, and walked down to the others, carrying timber in one arm and dragging the longest piece of wood with his other hand. Frog followed at a distance, picking up small pieces the bearded man dropped.
Ivan lit a small fire near the doorway.

Fred stood up and stretched his arms. He rubbed his shoulders. 'Beginning to get a bit cool,' he yawned. 'Think I'll take a walk and put something warm on and then get some sleep. I'm tired.'

'What's this about taking a walk?' Johnny said, standing up, too. 'You forget where you are. You can sleep for all you're worth, but you're not going walking. I've got a feeling you might keep on going.'

Fred gave Johnny a pitying look. 'You don't understand people much, do you? I want to take a walk for very natural reasons. Either I walk somewhere else, or I answer nature's call at your feet. What's it going to be?'

'Very funny,' Johnny said. 'You've got ten minutes. And don't go near the truck.'

'I want to go near the truck to get a jumper. I'm getting cold.'

'Okay then, Frog,' Johnny called and gesticulated with his thumb. 'Go with him. Keep the rifle on him all the time.'

Ivan glanced quickly across at Frog who had begun munching a slice of bread. The Russian nodded, as if to say 'I told you so.'

Johnny watched the two men disappear into the night and then strolled to where Barbara was sitting, her arms looped around her knees. He crouched beside her and closely examined her face, rigidly aimed at the flickering fire.

'It's not so bad now, is it?' he said, in as soothing a voice as he could manage. She ignored him.

'I think it would pay you to be friends with me,' he continued. 'I'm in charge here, that's something you should remember.' She turned her head away from him.

'I'm talking to you,' he said, his voice rising. Her head didn't move. He reached out and grabbed her hair, twisting her head round until she faced him. Her teeth were clenched.

'When I talk to you,' he grated, shaking her head to emphasise each word, 'LISTEN.' Her eyes had filled with tears, but she made no sound.

'Hey,' called Ivan, 'cut it out.' He began to walk towards Johnny, but the gun waved him back.

Johnny let go the girl. He stood up and faced the Russian. He could see Ivan's teeth glinting through the tangle of hair around his mouth. 'You got something to say?'

Ivan hesitated. 'Just don't hurt her,' he said in a subdued voice. 'She's not harming you, you know.'

'What are you going to do about it?' said Johnny, his eyes suddenly eager. 'I'd like you to do something, because I think I'd enjoy shooting you. Now, what are you going to do, eh?' He was waving the gun slowly from side to side, and swaying in rhythm with it.

'Nothing,' said Ivan. 'Just don't hurt her.' He walked to the edge of the fire and put another stick on. He squatted down and stared helplessly across the flames at the girl.

'I'm all right, thanks, Ivan,' Barbara said. She pushed her hair back into place. She glanced briefly at Johnny. 'You're certainly a brave one with that gun,' she told him.

'Just don't forget that I've got that gun. You're very silly,' he added in a gentler voice. 'You should be nice to me, I might decide to do the same to you as I'm going to do to your friend, Fred. You want to remember that.'

'If you want to be nice to me, you can leave me alone,' she said and turned her head until he moved away.

Johnny walked well clear of the fire and waited there out of sight until Fred and Frog returned.

Fred was wearing an old navy jumper, loosely hanging outside his shorts. 'Where's our friend?' he asked. Johnny walked slowly back into the circle of light cast by the fire. Fred said: 'I thought maybe you'd decided to leave us.'

Johnny rocked his head from side to side. 'You're a real comic, aren't you. You know, you're wasting your talent out here. Pity you're not going to live to entertain other people.' He smiled.

Fred turned his back on him. 'I'm going to bed, Ivan, Barbara,' he announced, nodding at each. 'Didn't get much sleep last night. Might be an idea if we all turned in.' Barbara stood up and he put his hand on her shoulder. 'A good sleep will make you feel a lot better. Your sleeping bag's ready. Is there anything else you want?'

She shook her head. For the first time, he noticed her red-rimmed eyes. 'Are you okay?' he asked.

'I'm fine Fred,' she said. 'Don't worry about me. I'm just tired.'

'Try not to worry. Things'll work out.' He walked into the hut and, in the entrance, turned, so that one side of his face was brightly lit by the fire. 'You know,' he said, 'you chose a lousy time to travel up the track.' He grinned, and the stark shadows broke into a fresh pattern on his face.

Barbara smiled back. She waited until Fred had disappeared within the building before wiping her eyes and facing Johnny. 'I presume you'll be trusting enough to allow me to go for a walk — on my own.'

Johnny nodded. 'Up there,' he pointed away from the truck. 'And don't be too long.'

He watched her leave and then ambled over to Frog. 'We'll have to take watches during the night,' he said. 'I'll take first turn and you get some sleep. Give me the rifle.'

Frog hesitated. 'Well come on, you're not going to take it to bed with you, are you?' He reached out and took the rifle. Tucking it under one arm, he walked twenty paces from the hut and slowly peered into the ocean of darkness surrounding them.

Ivan walked past Frog. 'I see he's taken the easy watch for himself,' he muttered. 'Now you got no gun, either.' He continued into the building and lay down. Beside him, Fred was stretched out on his back, hands clasped beneath his head. A flicker of light reflected from the wall.

'You okay, mate?' Ivan asked.

'Bit sore. How about you?'

'I'm okay, you know.' He lowered his voice to a whisper. 'I got the fat one a bit frightened,' he confided. 'He thinks his mate's going to turn on him.'

'Oh?'

'Yeah. Might do us some good, don't you think, Fred?'

'Could do. What are they doing out there now?'

'Gonna take turns watching us. Fat one's sleeping first.'

'Has he still got my rifle?'

'No. The other one took it.'

'Where's Barbara?'

'Just gone for a walk. Johnny had a go at her while you were gone.'

Fred sat up. 'What do you mean?'

'He pulled her hair.'

'What? What for?'

'She wouldn't talk to him or something. I don't know what it was all about. He's nuts, I think.'

'No doubt about that.' He lowered himself on to one elbow. 'So he's got a bee in his bonnet about Barbara now. Ivan mate, we've got to do something but I'm blowed if I know what.' He lay down again, and stared at the reflected firelight dancing on the mud wall. Soon, he closed his eyes.

Ivan studied his friend's face. Fred was under sentence of death and yet if he tried to save himself someone else would die. Ivan or the girl. Maybe they'd all die, anyhow, once they got to Birdsville. Someone had to do something before then. Fred couldn't, because if he failed, someone else would die. The girl couldn't. That left him. He had tried to turn Frog against Johnny but that mightn't work. He rolled on his side and thought about it.

Barbara came in and went to her sleeping bag in the corner. 'Are you awake, Fred?' she whispered. Ivan knew by Fred's breathing that he was asleep but said nothing. He heard her sigh and sit down. In the shadows, he could see her take off her shoes and comb her hair. She unzippered the bag, put her legs in but apparently decided it was too warm and took them out again. She sat there for some time, fingering the buttons at her hip, but then lay down as she was. She twisted to one side, turning her back towards him. Ivan stared curiously at the unfamiliar outline of a woman. Funny how the hip sticks up, he thought.

Voices sounded outside and he rolled over. Frog entered. Ivan saw him place the folded tarpaulin from the truck in the corner near the doorway and lie on it. Outside, he could hear firewood being broken and then Johnny came to the doorway and sat down, leaning against the bricks.

Johnny was the dangerous one. Therefore he'd wait until Frog was on duty. Then he'd try something. It had to be tonight. He was sure now. The longer he waited, the more dangerous for them all. He closed his eyes and waited for Frog to take over the watch.

Ivan shivered and woke up. He'd been asleep. It took him a few seconds to accept the fact. He was cold, so he must have been asleep for some time. He pushed himself on to one elbow and looked at Fred. He didn't appear to have moved, and was breathing deeply, with the faint rustling hint of a snore. Ivan sat up.

The fire must have gone out because there was no glow from the doorway. He could see a shadowy figure there, hunched as though sleeping. Slowly, and as quietly as he could manage, Ivan stood up. At first, he had trouble steadying himself and his foot crunched on a stone. He held his breath and waited for a challenge, but none came.

He crept forward until he could see through the doorway. The moon had risen and the land outside glowed like pale skin. Silhouetted in the opening was the guard, his outline unmistakable. It was the fat one, Frog. Propped against his hunched shoulder was the rifle.

Ivan wondered if he should wake Fred and get his help. But Fred might make some noise in awakening and that could rouse Frog. No, he could do it himself. Besides, he wanted to do this himself. A lot of people back at Marree poked fun at him. Wait till they heard about this. His body began to tingle with excitement.

Carefully he approached the sleeping Frog. He reached the doorway and steadied himself by bracing the open fingers of his right hand against the wall. With the other hand, he felt for the rifle. Slowly, he entwined his fingers around the barrel. Still Frog slept. Ivan moved his hand from the wall and took a second grip on the gun. With both hands, he pulled hard.

Frog grunted in surprise. The rising rifle butt clouted the side of his head and he sprawled in the dust, gasping. Ivan slipped his hand into place on the rifle and leapt outside into the moonlight, hurdling the body. Behind him, he could hear the sudden rustle of canvas. He turned and pointed the rifle at the doorway.

'What's the matter?' It was Johnny's voice, slurred with sleep. 'What's up?' He blundered through the doorway and stood over Frog, who was rolling on to his hands and knees. Then he saw the Russian. He took a step forward, saw the rifle and hesitated.

Ivan saw him fumble in his jacket pocket. The gun; he was going for his gun. Ivan lifted the rifle. He felt a burning elation. This man he hated. He aimed and squeezed the trigger.

The hollow click seemed to echo back through the stock. He slammed home the bolt and pressed again. Click.

Empty. It was empty. You fool, Frog, you bloody fool. He was shouting these words silently to the man on the ground. You've carried this gun all bloody day and you haven't bloody well loaded it.

Johnny had straightened up and, very slowly, was removing his gun. With a frantic swing of an arm, Ivan hurled the rifle at him and turned to run. Three paces and he stopped and looked back. Johnny had fallen forward, the rifle tangled in his legs. He was shouting. Ivan began to move towards him but Johnny pushed himself to his knees and raised the pistol. Ivan turned again and ran. If he could make the rise. He tripped on a loose stone and stumbled on to his hands. He heard the angry snarl of a bullet rushing past. Oh my God. If only there was no moon. He glanced back. Johnny, feet spaced wide apart, was aiming again.

Ivan stumbled on, darting first to one side, then the other. Why wasn't he shooting again? He thought of the war, of Russia, the last time people had shot at him. Only it had been snow, not sand. Why wasn't he firing? Maybe Fred ...

Quickly he looked back. He didn't hear the crack of the gun. There was just the numbing kick, high up on his body. The hammer-blow force spun him into the ground. He was on his back, staring up at the moon, but still moving. He could feel his legs pushing him. Then the moon had gone and he was back on his feet, running. He'd been hit. The thought worried him more than the pain. He'd been shot. As though from some strange hand, fingers clawed at his chest. He was over the rise and he fell again.

He heard Johnny saying 'Look after them with this' and then the soft pad of moving feet. Desperately, he looked about him. The country ran in soft undulations with a sprinkling of stunted bush and spinifex, towards the long ridge of a sandhill, several hundred yards away. Ivan got to his feet and ran towards it. He covered fifty yards before crouching for shelter behind a bush.

'I can see you, Whiskers,' Johnny shouted. 'You're hurt aren't you?' His voice had the edge of triumph. 'How far do you think you can go?'

Desperately, one shoulder drooping and his breath now rasping through his throat, Ivan ran on.

'I'm going to kill you, Whiskers. Coming, ready or not.'

Oh my God, it's a game to him, Ivan thought and tried to run faster. If only Fred would help. Fred. He stopped and summoned all his breath. 'Fred,' he shouted.

He heard Johnny laugh. 'Fred can't help you. There's a gun on him and the girl back there.'

'It's not loaded,' he tried to shout, but another shot interrupted him. With a whine, the bullet bounced off the ground beyond him. He ran. Again that laughter. He glanced back and saw the man's grey shape farther away now, walking after him. Not running, walking. Curse the man, he was following like a hunter certain of catching his prey.

Ivan stumbled on. If he could build up a lead and get to the sandhill, he had a chance. Might even turn the tables. He could feel definite pain in his chest now. His hand felt wet, too. He dropped into a shallow hollow and scrambled one handed up the other side. He fell once more.

Stop falling, he told himself. He rubbed his hands against his thigh. It was moist. And sticky. Blood. My God, it's blood. Oh my leg. He wiped his hand across his stomach. Wet. I'm covered in blood. He began to weep. He stumbled and nearly fell. He dropped both arms and turned to face his pursuer. Johnny was a hundred yards behind him, slowly picking a path through a dense circle of spinifex.

Ivan felt the hate for this man blaze inside him again. If only Frog, stupid, stupid Frog, had loaded the rifle.

He tried to run but could only walk. Still, he could make the sandhill first. The sandhill. Glinting frostily at him, it had became a symbol of life itself. He fell twice more.

The sand was close now, but it was getting darker. What was wrong? Had the moon gone? He looked up and fell. The ground was soft and cooler. The sand. That was it. He was on the sand. He felt like smiling, but he couldn't open his eyes. 'Oh, don't go to sleep,' he called aloud and began to crawl. Funny, his chest didn't hurt any more.

Moving was harder now. He was going uphill, that was why. Of course, he was on the sandhill. It was very important to get to the top. He must get to the top. He could feel his face being scratched and then his chest. Damn it, he'd gone to sleep again. He opened his eyes. He was crawling over a bush. Crawling? What am I doing crawling?

He tried to stand up but he fell. Over and over he was rolling. It was good and he thought of when he was a boy. He had stopped now and he could hear someone coming. He was sleepy but he didn't care now. Someone was beside him and he tried to smile.

He heard the sound of a gun and it echoed and echoed and echoed.

CHAPTER THIRTEEN

Fred stiffened at the sound of the shot. He waited for another laugh, a shout, some sign that Ivan still eluded Johnny. There was an awful silence. He began to move away from the wall of the hut.

'Stay there,' Frog ordered, his voice panicky, and he thrust the rifle hard against Barbara's stomach, pressing her against the bricks. Fred retreated to the wall.

'For the love of heaven, point that thing away from her,' he said. 'You're so jumpy it's liable to go off any time.' Frog stepped back. Once more Fred looked towards the ridge and tried to picture the scene out there. It was so quiet now. Fred still wasn't sure what had happened. He had woken to the sound of shooting and there had been a shot. It wasn't from his rifle, so it must have been Johnny's gun. By the time he had reached the door, there had been no sign of Ivan. The fat one had been covering him with the rifle and Johnny had been limping up the rise. Limping? Ivan must have attacked him and hurt him. But where was Ivan now? He remembered Ivan's voice, strange and pitiful, calling his name and his scalp began to tingle as a terrible fear grew inside him.

He turned to Barbara, her back pressed against the wall, eyes fixed on the rifle which Frog gripped as though about to lunge forward and stake her through the middle.

'For God's sake, take that rifle off her,' Fred said. Frog warily lifted the barrel. 'Don't you try nothing,' he ordered.

Fred turned his head. He could hear the scratch of footsteps on the other side of the rise. He waited in silence.

Johnny walked into view, a deathly colour in the moonlight. He glanced back for a moment and then limped down to the hut. Ten feet in front of Fred, he stopped and rubbed his shin. Then he lazily began reloading the automatic, extracting rounds from his jacket. He glanced up and smiled as he pressed the first cartridge into place. 'Aren't you going to ask me what happened?' he said.

Fred had begun to shiver, not with the cold but with the rising fear and anger inside him. 'Where is he?'

'Who, the Russian?' Johnny answered almost absent-mindedly. 'Oh, he's still out there.'

Fred covered his eyes with his hand. Barbara missed the gesture and said, eagerly, 'Then he got away from you.'

Johnny shook his head. 'Maybe you didn't think I was serious today about killing Whiskers. Well, now you know I was, don't you?' He walked over to Barbara and gripped her wrist. Her eyes were wide with shock. 'You don't want to die, do you, sweetheart?' He twisted her arm behind her back and began to drag her away from the wall. 'That's it,' he said, turning her so that she faced Fred. 'Let him get a good look at you. Beautiful girl, isn't she Fred? Wouldn't like her to die, now would you?' He slipped his arm around her and stroked her chin with the gun barrel. 'Nice face, don't you think Fred?'

Fred watched, silent and slightly crouched, like a small animal awaiting its chance to strike at a more powerful enemy.

Barbara turned her head angrily from the barrel and buried her chin in a shoulder. Johnny drew up her bent arm and pushed her away from him. She stumbled and Fred moved forward to help her. He drew her back with him to the wall.

'What happened out there?' Fred asked, his voice cracked and uneven.

'He thought he could take over,' Johnny said. He bent down and rubbed his shins. 'You know, the dirty little Russian even threw things at me.' He straightened up. 'Now he's dead.'

'Where is he? Let me see him.'

Johnny jerked his thumb over his shoulder. 'Back there. He can stay where he is. He's dead all right. There's nothing you can do for him.'

'Let me go out,' Fred protested. He had begun to tremble, so that he shook the girl, too. 'You can't just leave him there. If you've never done a decent act before ... There are dingoes and ...' His voice trailed off.

'You can bury him in the morning,' Johnny said. 'You know, Frog and I played a bit of a joke on you tonight, didn't we Frog?' The fat man looked up blankly. Johnny walked to him and took the rifle.

'Joke?' Fred asked flatly.

'Yeah.' He raised the rifle, aimed it at Fred and pulled the trigger. He saw Fred duck, pulling the girl with him, and laughed. 'Yeah, joke,' he said. 'It was empty all the time.'

He handed the rifle back to Frog. 'Load it now,' he ordered. 'From now on, Fred, it'll always be loaded. You stayed here tonight with nothing but an empty gun holding you back. Thanks for being so helpful. It made it much easier out there.'

Slowly, Fred uncoiled his arm from around the girl. He stared, unbelieving, at Johnny for several seconds. From somewhere beyond the ridge, a dingo howled.

Light from the moon was piercing the ruins. Fred concentrated on the ghostly beams, for he was trying to stay awake. It wasn't right that he should sleep. He blamed himself for Ivan's death. His eyes closed and he shook himself awake. He shouldn't sleep with his friend lying dead outside, but his head ached and his body hurt and he was desperately tired. Half dreaming, he began to think about the shooting. Where had Ivan been shot? He wondered whether his friend lay with a red hole in his chest or with half his head blown away. With moonlight streaming through the open doorway, he imagined his friend's body lying on the cold rocks, bathed in the faint glow that was softening the whole desert. He saw images of Ivan in various grotesque poses. Face down, with legs and arms splayed wide, as though skewered to the ground. The body rolled on to its back, and Ivan grinned at him. Only there was no mouth. Just a curving gash of blood which suddenly erupted into a welling fountain of gore.

Fred sat up. He had been sleeping. He mustn't. He should think. He had to work out some way to stay alive, to save the girl and himself. But his mind was out of control, whipped into aimless, erratic wandering by shock and weariness.

The shaft of moonlight reached gently into the ruins. It reminded him of light under water. He had seen that once, in an aquarium. A soft, thick beam of light that projected into a tank of water. You looked through windows below the surface. Fish swam lazily through the light. Weed floated in the water. It was unreal, a scene from another world, viewed from the outside. Not real.

He lay down. Oh God. Why?

He liked the desert at night, or he had. That was when the heat went, and the flies disappeared, and a man could rest and think. He and Ivan used to talk at night. He thought of a camp on the shores of Lake Kopperamanna on a winter's night when the two of them had been so cold they couldn't sleep and had torn down the dead branches of trees and kept a huge fire burning until dawn. The wood was so brittle they had broken the limbs with their hands. It was a huge fire, far too big for their needs, but they had been cold and the blaze added comfort because of its size. They had talked a lot, and drunk tea. But it had been a bad night. So cold. They had almost stripped four trees, snapping off the branches and leaving the dead trunks to glow naked in the reflection of the fire.

Why was he thinking of that night by the lake? They hadn't slept because of the cold, and in the morning, mist had hung above the water and drifted through the trees. Mist that floated, soft and unreal, like the light coming through the doorway.

That had been a bad night. He should forget it. He tried to think of a pleasant time he had shared with Ivan. He tried hard, staring at the shaft of light angling through the entrance to the ruins, but couldn't. He couldn't think of one happy, pleasant happening. Just hard work. Poor Ivan. All Fred had given him was hard work, and the chance to have a few beers when they reached the pubs at Marree or Birdsville. Poor dirty, bewhiskered, hard working, lonely, dead Ivan. Fred sniffed to stop his nose running. His eyes were moist.

He shuffled his body towards Barbara. 'Are you asleep,' he whispered.

She turned, and in the faint light he imagined he could see her opened eyes. 'I want you to know I like you and care about you,' he said. 'Just in case anything happens to either of us, I wanted to tell you that.'

It's important that you know, he said to himself. He reached out, and found her hand waiting for his.

She held his hand until she felt the fingers relax and curl in sleep, and then she herself dozed. When she woke again, it was still dark. Her hip hurt, and she shifted position. Her mind was galloping through thoughts. One moment it was the mind of a professional nurse, used to death and seeing people suffer, and accepting that such things happened; the next, the mind of a young woman in alien territory, and afraid.

First the nurse. Fred Crawford would be in a mild state of shock, with his condition exacerbated by extreme tiredness. He had also been injured in the fight. He was extremely fit and resilient, but she would have to watch him closely tomorrow ...

Then the woman. Even the hut in which they slept was frightening. Spooky. Decaying walls, a collapsed roof, bushes growing through the sand. And lizards to be grasped by the tail and thrown away. She thought of Ivan. They'd shot him, just as they'd threatened. And they'd said they would shoot her. What would that be like? Quick? Nothing? Or an awful burning, terrible pain, such as she'd seen other people suffer. What a ghastly place, eerie in the moonlight, with the man with the rifle standing at the door. The executioner ...

A good night's sleep should help Fred. Maybe a rib was broken, although she didn't think so. Bruised and painful but not broken. The scratches on his face had washed up remarkably well. The main cut that had filled his eye with blood was in the hairline and couldn't be seen. Scalp wounds always looked worse than they were ...

His hands were so rough and yet his touch gentle. He was a strange person, full of contrasts. She had imagined the driver of the mail truck that was to take her to Birdsville would have been a rough diamond. Tough and capable of coping with any mechanical or natural disaster, and probably not able to string three words together. Instead she had found, what was it, Mr Webster? A man who knew the name of Alexander the Great's horse. She struggled to recall the name, and couldn't. A stone was grating in her back, and she moved ...

An intelligent mind. He would probably be more affected by

what had happened tonight than someone with less imagination. The shock would be greater. What was the term the tutor had used, all those years ago? A fine blade is more liable to be damaged by a stone than a blunt one? Something like that. She must watch him, check in the morning for signs of delayed shock. Ivan had been his friend ...

He was somewhere out there, stiffening in the ghastly pose of rigor mortis. My God, what would he be like by sun-up. Fred had been worried about dingoes. Now, what had she read about Burke and Wills? One of them — Wills? — had died on his own and when they found him, much of the body was missing, taken by wild dogs. The hands, certainly. Was it the head too? He'd died near here, less than a hundred years ago, on the Cooper. She'd read about Burke and Wills. Someone had given her a book about the explorers and their fatal expedition. Here, read about the country you're going to. Big grin ...

Was Ivan truly dead? People could survive terrible injuries. Those not used to injuries or death could assume that extensive wounds and massive haemorrhaging meant a person was dead. That man with the gun might have been mistaken and left Ivan out there, bleeding, unconscious but alive. She analysed the possibility but her mind, temporarily agitated, slumped back into a drowsy, lethargic acceptance of Ivan's death. He had seen it. Correction. He had caused it. He would check. He wouldn't be squeamish, or shocked into running away. She pictured him turning the body with his foot, studying his handiwork. He had come back calm, even pleased with himself. Butcher. There were cold ones in the hospital, but none like that ...

She rolled more on her side and stretched her arm until her fingers could touch Fred's hand. He had hair on the back of his fingers. The skin was softer there, not calloused like the pads. I'd like to be close to you, she thought, and was ashamed, feeling such thoughts after what had happened. And then was not ashamed ...'

People *do* react in strange ways in a crisis or moments of extreme stress. A fact. Well known. And if they had a feeling for a person, even the beginnings of some emotional involvement, it could be intensified. An acceleration of a process. Like putting a flame under something ...

Still it was shocking. She was being stirred by a warm feeling, an intense desire. Just like that other time. That awful time when those people had been killed. She and Peter had been driving at night and it was raining and this other car came around the corner at high speed and hit them, and then Peter's car had rolled on its roof and by the time they had crawled out, with the rain wetting their necks and backs, the other car was over the bridge and into the river and the people were drowning. Three of them. The lights of their car had shone under water. She thought the lights would have gone out but they had shone, like candles for the departing souls. Only two candles for three souls. The police had arrived before they were properly out of the car because the police had been chasing the other car. One policeman and Peter had gone in the creek to attempt rescue but the water was deep and the doors were locked or jammed or something and the creek was so murky they couldn't see, even with those ghostly lights burning. The police had driven them to Peter's flat and he had changed into dry clothes and then kissed her and then they had made love. Wildly, as though celebrating the fact that they were alive and the others were dead ...

No, that wasn't why. She opened her eyes wide and gazed towards the broad shaft of moonlight penetrating the hut. Gazed, but saw nothing in the blur of memory. She and Peter had *liked* each other. Certainly it had been wild, and maybe it had been like that because the reaction had been triggered by shock. But it wasn't animal-like, an orgy, a lustful celebration of life and its enduring symbolic coupling as portrayed by those still alive. Not that at all ...

No? Well, right now, after this shocking day, she felt a longing for Fred. Not the same as that other night, but a desire to be near him. To touch and be touched. To comfort and be comforted. Could feelings be stimulated by a shocking occurrence? All the preamble to the mating game swept aside by some happening so sudden, so upsetting, that it threw you together, condensing weeks into hours? Double six, jump twelve places and throw the dice to win the game ...

Calm down. You're being silly. Look at this sensibly. Do you like the man? Yes. How? I admire him. That's not enough. Well, give me time for God's sake, I've only known him for a couple of days! And you want to sleep with him. I *am* sleeping with him, Games, games, you're only playing with words. No, I am sleeping with him. He's just there, I'm here. He's sleeping and I'm not sure whether I'm asleep too.

He seems a decent man. Decent. That's a good word. Old fashioned but good. You see, you like him too!

You should sleep. You'll be on duty soon. On duty, on duty. I hope he's all right when I make the morning rounds.

Nurses' hours didn't suit Peter. At least, that's what she imagined caused it. She didn't see him much after that night. I wonder where he went?

She opened her eyes. The man in the door moved, so that his body divided the beam of moonlight into angled shafts, that glowed, soft and faint, like lights shining through water ...

Tim Sanderson and his wife spent a restless night at Mulka. Sanderson had tried to repair the radio. He carried many spare parts and his life at Mulka had made him a resourceful improviser, but too much damage had been done. Eventually, he decided to wait until dawn, before setting off for Etadunna in the utility. He could leave no earlier as the lights on the vehicle were poor. Besides he dared not leave his wife alone in the dark, in case the men returned.

A cold grey light had begun to spread through the sky as Sanderson handed his wife the loaded rifle, kissed her goodbye and threw into the old utility a pack of sandwiches and a water bag. It was less than thirty miles across the sandhills to Etadunna, but only the foolish or ignorant ever travelled in this country without emergency provisions. Parts of the Birdsville Track were studded with the bones of those who had tried.

He peered into the back to check that the spare cans of petrol and oil were there. He took the crank handle and started the motor on the fourth swing. At the sound, the two dogs cringing behind him wagged their tails and leapt into the back. Sanderson ordered one of them back to the house. It jumped out and slunk away. The other dog barked joyfully, revelling in such favoured treatment.

'You'd better keep Bluey with you, Kath,' Sanderson called. 'No one'll get near the place without him letting you know. I'll try and be back by nightfall.'

He waved goodbye, slipped into the seat and reversed out on to the track. He turned to the south and headed towards the low shadows that were the Natarannie Sandhills.

The chill air swept into the cabin. Sanderson pulled up his shirt collar for warmth. Shivering, he peered at the lightening sky and knew it was going to be warm soon, too warm. All but the brightest stars had now faded, although the moon still glowed, pale and weak, as though aware that the sun would soon rise and burn it from the scene.

Sanderson drove slowly. He was not a fast driver either by instinct or ability. Nor would the ute go fast. It had long since churned out its heart on a diet of dust and sand.

Driver and vehicle were well teamed. One couldn't and the other wouldn't go fast. Even the urgency of the mission failed to push Sanderson beyond his normal pace. He had been reared in a land where time is critically measured in seasons, not minutes. In any case, his stern common sense told him there was no sense risking a buckled wheel or a rock through the sump. The important thing was to get to Etadunna; a few minutes earlier didn't matter.

The sun was clear of the horizon as the ute slogged its way through the first sandhills. A flock of white galahs rose in a curving cloud from the track ahead, giving the illusion of a monstrous tent billowing free in the wind. Sanderson smiled as the cloud thundered away from him. He liked birds. He watched the flock wheel off at a tangent. It was hard to tell if they were frightened by his approach, or just joyful in their powers of flight. They turned again and their wings flashed white in the sun.

Then he heard his motor cough and he forgot about the birds. The motor misfired again, running unevenly for perhaps twenty yards before it caught momentarily. Then it stopped again. Sanderson pulled up. He was familiar with the symptoms — a blockage in the fuel system.

He took some tools and disconnected the petrol pipe at the carburettor. The dog jumped down and excitedly began chasing the distant cockatoos, now just a glinting line of white.

Forty-five minutes later Sanderson had cleared a black, gritty sediment from the filter and the whole fuel line between the tank and the petrol pump. He wiped his hands on his hips, ate a sandwich, sipped some water and whistled the dog, which was pawing at something a hundred yards from the track.

With the crank handle, he wound the engine to suck petrol back to the carburettor. Then he switched on the ignition and spun the motor into life. At the sound, the dog jumped into the back.

Sanderson drove another two miles and the motor coughed and stopped. Again he cleaned out the fuel line. The blockage was worse and took longer to clear. Twice more he was stopped by fuel blockages. On the last occasion, he drained his petrol tank and refilled it from the spare drum of petrol. Then he dismantled the carburettor and cleaned it thoroughly.

By noon, he had reached Naterannie Swamp. He still had half his journey to cover. Ahead of him lay the sharp climb of Oldfields Leap. The sand looked soft and he accelerated. The ute lurched up the climb, covered ten feet and then shuddered to a stop, motor racing and an ominous metallic rasp coming from the back.

Sanderson switched off the motor. The dog jumped down and ran to the door, excitedly wagging its tail. Sanderson swore loudly and emotionally at the ute for a full minute. It had broken its axle. And he had no spare.

He got out and glared balefully at the back wheels. He kicked a tyre a couple of times and felt better. With hands on hips he surveyed Oldfields Leap. Ahead of him lay the softest section of sand. He had no chance of fixing the truck. This was going to be a bootleather and sweat job.

He thought briefly of returning home, but dismissed the idea. It was essential that he get to Etadunna with the news about the men on the mail truck. The only way to get there now was to walk. He knew it was 120 degrees or more on the sand and he had a lot of it to cover. Still there was no other way.

The heat from the sand licked at him like tongues of flame. He pulled his hat low over his forehead, gripped the water bag and began the long walk over the dunes to his neighbour's homestead.

The dog slunk beside him, trying to compress itself into the shadow cast by its master. Sanderson changed his grip on the water bag and, with his free fingers, scratched the dog behind the ears.

CHAPTER FOURTEEN

At dawn, Fred had taken the tarpaulin and a shovel from the truck and gone to the sandhill to bury Ivan. Johnny seemed in a good mood and stayed back on the rise above the hut, the rifle carelessly placed across his knees. He began to shave, using Fred's gear.

A number of hawks flapped into the air as Fred approached the dead man. He brushed away a vast swarm of flies and wrapped the body in the tarpaulin. He kept only Ivan's hat. He walked a few paces from the sand and began to dig in the rock-hard red earth.

He worked for more than an hour, scraping out a shallow grave. In it, he placed the canvas bundle and then gently began replacing the soil. That done, he shovelled up all the wind-polished gibbers within twenty yards and with them formed a rocky crust over the now vulnerably soft earth. He knew that dingoes were about.

He took off his hat and with his arm wiped the sweat from his face. He studied his work for several seconds. 'Rest in peace, mate,' he said. 'I promise you'll get a proper burial later.' He put on his hat and turned to walk back to the others. He fixed his eyes on Johnny. 'And I promise that he'll pay for it,' he added. He walked towards the rise.

Johnny, clean shaven and hair neatly combed, was examining

something spread out on the ground before him. He looked up, as though he was pleasantly surprised to see Fred approaching. 'Oh, you're back, eh?' he said. 'Everything fixed?'

Fred didn't answer.

'Put down the shovel and come over here,' Johnny continued, standing and making a beckoning motion with the rifle. 'You'd probably like to see these.' He pointed at the opals spread on a cloth at his feet. 'Nice, aren't they?'

Hands on hips, Fred looked at the opals. 'They must mean a lot to you,' he said. 'You reckon they're worth killing for.'

Johnny shrugged and bent down to pick them up. 'Once you've started something, you can't stop. Stand back.' He gestured with his rifle. Lovingly, he wrapped the opals in the cloth and placed them in the case. He put the case inside his jacket and stood up.

'They're worth a lot of money,' he said. 'Worth taking a few risks for.'

'Risks!' Fred bent down for the shovel and began to walk to the hut. 'Where's the risk in shooting an unarmed man? This is the second time you've killed now for those things, isn't it? Doesn't that worry you?'

'Why should it?' Johnny said, sauntering behind him. 'After the first one it doesn't matter much, anyhow.'

So Ivan didn't matter, Fred thought to himself. Ivan didn't matter! He dropped Ivan's hat and gripped the shovel in both hands. He turned to face the other man.

Johnny stopped walking and raised the rifle. 'Just calm down now,' he said in the same affable manner. 'Look, there's no use getting het-up over it. He was just a hairy little wog who didn't wash. No one's going to miss him.'

Fred stood, indecisive, for a moment. He noticed a strange, zestful look of anticipation growing on Johnny's face. He relaxed his grip on the shovel and picked up Ivan's hat. Dusting its brim against his leg, he turned and slowly walked down to the truck.

'That's a good fella,' Johnny called after him. 'May as well be friends while you're still with us.' He laughed. 'Hey, Frog,' he called to his companion, lounging in the doorway, scraping dirt from beneath his fingernails, 'you can have Whiskers' hat now. Fred brought it back for you.'

Frog shook his head. 'It doesn't matter.'

'Course it does,' said Johnny who had reached them. 'You

don't want Frog getting sunstroke, do you? Give it to him.' He pointed the rifle at the girl and waited.

Fred threw the hat at Frog's feet. Frog looked at it, as though it were some repulsive creature.

'Well, go on,' Johnny said, walking over and picking up the hat. He slammed it on the fat man's head. 'You wanted it before. If the Russian was good enough to leave it to you, you should be big enough to wear it.' He smiled and examined each of the three silent faces looking at him.

He asked the mailman: 'What's the plan for today. How far will we make?'

Fred shrugged. 'That's up to you. Normally, somewhere around Clifton Hills.'

'That's a homestead, isn't it?'

Fred nodded.

'How many others on the way?'

'Just one.'

'What's that, and how far?'

'Mungeranie. Less than an hour away.'

'You mean to say you brought us to this ruin,' he swept his hand towards the hut, 'when we could have spent last night as someone's guests?'

Fred eyed Johnny for several seconds before answering. 'Look, Johnny whatever-your-name-is, get this clear. I'll take you up to Birdsville because I've got no choice, and I'll even play along with you when we call in at the stations. But I want to keep you and your fat friend away from other people as much as possible. I don't want you hurting anyone else.'

'Very noble of you but I was only pulling your leg. Can you imagine some cocky letting Frog sleep with the sister so's he could keep an eye on her all night.'

Barbara reddened and Johnny laughed.

'You're in high old spirits this morning, aren't you?' Fred said.

'Murdering seems to suit his liver,' Barbara said.

Johnny stopped smiling. 'Well now, Sister, don't you start provoking me again today, or I might dispose of you and then I'd become a real riot. Anyhow, we're wasting time and it's getting too hot out here. Start packing up. We're moving on. Have you got any stuff for this next place?'

'No,' Fred lied.

'Nothing? How come?' He was eyeing Fred suspiciously. 'I thought you brought all their food?'

'They got big stocks last time. They didn't order any more.'

'What about mail? You're a mailman. You must have something for them.'

Fred shook his head. 'That's not unusual. They get very little mail.'

'You're not trying to put something over me, are you?'

'We can stand here all day arguing about it if you like. It suits me.'

'Okay. We'll miss Munga-what's-its-name. But don't tell me there's nothing for Clifton Hills because the name's scrawled all over those tyres on your truck back there. I know because I spent some time among them, remember? How far from this next place to Clifton Hills?'

'Ninety odd miles. Nearly a hundred.'

'What's the track like?'

'Get's worse. We're in for a slow day.' He looked up at the sky. 'Going to be hotter than yesterday so we'll have to pull up every now and then to let the tyres cool.'

'Well they're cool now so let's get going. You and the girl pack up. Frog, are you ready to move?' Frog grunted.

Johnny gave him the rifle. 'Take this and keep an eye on them. I'm going to have a leak.' He sauntered away from the hut and disappeared behind the truck.

Barbara moved close to Fred and looked in his eyes. 'What's up,' he said, smiling at her. She was concentrating on one eye, and then the other.

'Look the other way,' she said.

'Why, what are you going to do?'

'This is Sister Dean speaking.' She wagged a finger. 'Look to the right. Thank you. Now left. Good.'

'Good?' Fred bent to pack the stove.

'Yes. I don't think you have concussion. I was just checking.'

He looked up. 'You'll send a bill?'

'Free service. Hey!' Frog had pushed her.

The fat man put his fingers to his lips. He whispered to Fred: 'I'm sorry about last night.'

The mailman looked up. 'So am I.'

'Sh. No, I mean it.'

'So do I. What are you trying to say?'

Frog looked back to see if Johnny was in sight. 'I didn't know he was going to kill him. I didn't want that to happen.'

'You could have stopped it. You kept me back here by a trick.'

'But I didn't know he was going to kill.'

'You were with him when he killed before, weren't you?' Fred accused. 'Save your breath. You're just as guilty as your mate.'

Frog could see Johnny returning. 'Has he been telling you I killed the sheila,' he whispered. 'Well, I never did. Don't you believe him.'

Johnny returned and the rest of the packing was done in silence. Three hawks were circling high beyond the ridge as they drove away.

The cluster of sand ridges and low hills dropped behind and they entered a vast stony plain. The heat rolled on them with a dry, scorched breath.

Again, the horizon became a shimmering, mysterious blur of images. From the haze, a black object emerged. It was directly in their path, an expanding and contracting mirage of great bulk, appearing from the zone where the twin wheel tracks vaporised in the layers of rising hot air. As they drew closer, the mirage solidified into a large black bull. It was standing hoof-deep in a muddy puddle of water.

Fred pulled up fifty yards short of the beast. He began rolling himself a cigarette. 'Why the stop?' Johnny asked, squirming in his seat to face the driver. 'You could soon push that thing out of the way.'

Fred pointed with his tobacco pouch towards the bull. 'He's not going to move for us. There's plenty of space to go around him.'

'Well why pull up?'

'I told you before. The tyres. They're hot by now. Anyhow, this is as good a place as any to have a break. Not often you have company out here.'

The bull, legs spread apart, watched them intently.

'What's he doing out here by himself?' Barbara asked. 'And where did the water come from.'

Fred lit his cigarette. 'They had some late rain up this way a week ago. Must have been heavy here. That bull probably strayed away from the bore and went from puddle to puddle. Then the holes began drying up and now he's stuck here.'

'He looks mean,' she said.

'He's a bit weak. Probably been standing in that puddle for a few days. There's no feed about and he daren't leave the water.'

'But it's almost dried up. What'll happen when it's gone?'

Fred drew deeply on the cigarette. 'He'll perish.'

Johnny laughed. 'The great stupid thing. Why doesn't he walk back to the bore.' He leaned out the doorway and thumped the side of the truck. 'Go on, get out of there,' he yelled.

The bull swished its tail.

'You won't move him,' Fred said. 'Even if you chased him away, he'd only come back to the water again.'

'Can't we do something?' Barbara asked.

Fred nodded and began to get out. 'I'll let them know at Mungeranie. They'll come back and lead it back.' He strolled around the truck, examining the tyres, and then climbed back in. He drove in a wide semi-circle around the animal, skirting the muddy area adjoining the track. The bull's head turned to follow them, but it did not move from the water.

They drove on until a thin line of scrub and some low hills signalled the end of the stony plain. They drove through two sandy creeks and then came upon Mungeranie station. It was a low building with a tin roof and a wide verandah around it. An Aboriginal stockman was walking towards the house when he saw the truck. He turned and leaned against a wire fence, running beside the track, and waited.

Fred pulled up alongside him. 'G'day Charlie.' He nodded. 'Tell the boss there's a big bull perishing about twelve miles back down the track.'

'Twelve mile,' the Aborigine repeated, and waited for Fred to climb down.

Fred saw a white man appear around the corner of the house and wave to him. He revved the motor to drown any call. He nodded farewell to the black and moved off. Looking back, he could see the white man waving furiously. Fred could guess that he was shouting. Johnny had not seen the man and Fred kept going.

'Close on a hundred miles to the next place now,' he said, above the roar of the motor. 'You might as well settle back. It's going to be a long slow trip.' He leaned forward and pushed the open windscreen as far out as it would go. 'Might as well have full air-conditioning.' He glanced back once more. The white man had joined the Aborigine at the fence. Fred made a mental apology to them and hoped that he would get the chance to explain sometime.

They drove towards a cluster of sand-topped hills, passed through Mungeranie Gap, and moved on to the open plain again. The heat became intense.

For three hours they headed north, stopping every hour to let the tyres cool. The track was fainter here, just two dusty wheel tracks dividing a high, central ridge crusted with stones. In places, the tracks forked into two, sometimes more, paths, and each meandered in seemingly aimless loops before rejoining the other.

At one of the stops, Barbara wandered about fifty yards from the track. She noticed with a shock that, standing side-on, she was unable to make out the track at all. It was only when running with the track that its twin grooves stood out clearly.

She told Fred. 'I know,' he said. 'It can be a real trap. I met a couple of blokes from Port Pirie who came up about this far a few years ago. They were shooting roos. There were a few about then, after a couple of good seasons. Anyway, these blokes were in a jeep and they spotted a roo off the track and chased him across country for about a quarter of a mile. They spent three-quarters of the day trying to find the track again.'

They had lunch on the fringe of a cane grass swamp and then continued. The land became sandier and swamps more frequent. And it was slow going. Once Fred was able to snatch top gear for a brief romp across a claypan, but for the most of the afternoon, the truck ground its way to the north in low gear.

The sun was well in the west and blazing in through Johnny's open doorway when Barbara noticed the mirage effect of trees above the horizon to the left. She nudged the driver and pointed to them.

'That's the Warburton,' Fred told her.

'What's that?'

'A creek. Or a river. Call it what you like. Runs on to the lake.'

'What, Lake Eyre?'

He nodded. 'Clifton Hills is just up ahead. The Warburton

starts near the homestead. It's supposed to be a sort of continuation of the Diamantina. The river ends south of Birdsville in Goyder Lagoon. You probably knew that.'

Barbara shook her head. 'No, I didn't. It's hard to imagine a lagoon up here.'

'It's a big one,' he said. 'At least it is at the present time, when the Diamantina's running, like it is now. The river spreads itself out in the lagoon and then goes underground. I suppose it helps to fill up the bores. Anyhow, if there's any water left over, it comes out again in the Warburton. Which is not very often.'

Barbara re-examined the hazy reflection of trees, floating on the edge of the earth. 'What's it like on the other side?'

'I can see you're one of those people who've always got to climb the next hill to have a look-see.' He smiled. 'Beyond the Warburton's the Simpson Desert. You've heard of that?'

She nodded.

'It's largely unknown. Different country to this. Sand's much redder and the hills drift about quite a bit. It's one of the few unexplored parts of Australia left.'

'You mean to say no one's been in there?'

'Oh, a couple of people have crossed it, or reckon they have. A fella did it on camels before the war, after a particularly good season when there was a bit of feed on the sand. Occasionally a horseman'll go a bit of the way in, after straying cattle. A couple of characters claim they crossed it in Land-Rovers just for the heck of it. Did it from the west to the east, of course. That's the way the wind blows the sand. You couldn't do it the other way. The sandhills are smooth on the western side and drop away sharply on this side. Like waves coming into the beach.'

Waves on sand. She thought again of Sydney, and the surf at Bondi and Coogee. Her beaches, where she swam on her days off. Memories of past summers intruded, seeming out of place in this hot, empty, baking wilderness. Sunburned shoulders, cream on the nose and sand sticking to her oiled skin. Crashing waves, shouting children, salt in the mouth, water in her ears. There were waves in the Simpson Desert, but not the waves she knew.

A sudden flood of homesickness washed over her. Or was it fear? She felt an urgent longing for the security of familiar places, and old friends — and even for those wretched, pitiful, gossipy women with whom her mother played tennis. She inched away from the man on her left, who frightened and repelled her, and who brought back vivid memories of the night, and its terrible happenings. But the night had brought her closer to Fred Crawford. Could you fall in love with one man, while hating another? Would one emotion be fired by some counter-balancing mechanism in the mind?

Stop being a fool, she told herself. But looking at the man behind the wheel she realised there was nothing foolish about her feelings for this man. She smiled. 'What's on the other side of the desert?'

'Here we go again. If you kept on this way,' Fred pointed north-west, 'You'd bowl into Alice Springs. It's a pity our passenger didn't try taking a short cut when he left Alice Springs in the first place and headed straight for here. He might have made history. You know, become a sort of Burke and Wills.'

Johnny shifted in his seat. He had pulled his jacket over the left side of his head to protect himself from the sun. 'You'd be a sensation as a teacher,' he said. 'Why don't you stop yapping and get us on to this next place.'

'If you took your head out of that bag, you could see it now.'

Johnny slipped the jacket back on to his shoulders. Ahead and to the right, he could see the flash of sunlight on a roof. 'Thank Christ,' he said. 'I'm sick of being cooked in here.' He studied the flat, grassless area on which the station stood. 'Where are the hills?' he said eventually, his voice puzzled.

Fred glanced across at him. 'What hills?'

'This is Clifton Hills, isn't it?'

'That's right.'

'Well, where are they? This place is as flat as a pancake.'

'The homestead used to be further to the north, where there really are hills. They built a new place down here next to the Seven Mile Bore but they still call it Clifton Hills. Too much sand and too little water up at the other place.'

Barbara asked, 'Do the same people still own it?'

'The owners don't live here,' Fred said. 'A manager looks after the station. This is one of the really big properties in the world. I think it's number three in size in Australia. Covers about eleven thousand square miles.'

'Eleven thousand *miles*.' Barbara said.

'They're a long way from neighbours,' Fred said. 'You know

how far back it is to Mungeranie? Well that's the closest station. The next place to the north would be Pandie Pandie, and that's only seventeen miles from Birdsville. And the way we're going, Birdsville's a hundred and fifty miles or so from here. Long way between neighbours, isn't it?"

'What do you mean "the way we're going"?' Johnny asked. 'You get us to Birdsville the quickest way. Understand?'

'We'll get to Birdsville the *only* way,' Fred said. 'The low river track's covered by Goyder Lagoon. That's the shortest way but we couldn't get through. No hope while the water's up.' He was silent momentarily as he steered through a particularly rocky section. 'There are two detours. The outside wet weather track or the extreme outside wet weather track. We take the last one.'

'Why? Are you up to something?' Johnny's voice was suspicious.

'We take it because the outside wet weather track's still a bit sticky in places. So we take the extreme outside wet weather track.'

'Those are fancy names. What do they mean?'

'We take the track that detours furthest to the east. It's drier.'

Johnny digested this information as he watched Clifton Hills draw closer. He could see two large unpainted iron buildings facing each other. Near them were a few trees. Towering behind the main building were the blades of a windmill. Wisps of steam from the bore rose above the homestead.

Fred drove by the smaller building and stopped the truck opposite the wired-in verandah of the homestead. A short, plump woman with white hair opened the wire screen door and stepped down. She wore old-fashioned wire-frame spectacles and with one hand shielded her eyes from the sun. She waited for Fred to get out and walk over to her.

'G'day, Mrs Spencer,' he said. 'Got some visitors for you.'

'Hello, Fred.' There was a hint of a smile on her wide, thin-lipped mouth. 'I know. Heard all about them yesterday. You've no idea the amount of talk you've been causing.'

'Like what?' he asked, his voice apprehensive.

'About the sister and your friends,' she said. 'You know how we love to have someone new to talk about.'

Fred looked around him. 'Where's George?'

'He's out mustering. Left over a week ago.'

'I, ah, suppose he took all the men with him?'

Mrs Spencer nodded, and smiled towards the sister, who had just walked around the front of the truck.

'Just you and Betty here then,' Fred said, his voice hushed.

'And the baby,' she said. 'Introduce me to your friends, Fred.' She wiped her hands on her spotted apron in anticipation. She greeted each of them with a nod and handshake. Her voice had a soft, tired drawl, but behind it lay a hint of mocking humour. Her hair was pinned back in a severe, masculine style. Behind the apron she wore a simple cotton frock that hung loosely over her dumpy frame.

'Are you here by yourself, Mrs Spencer?' Johnny asked pleasantly.

'No,' she said, clasping her hands in front of her and squinting at him through her unshaded glasses. 'My daughter-in-law and her baby are inside. My husband and son and the other men are out mustering.'

'Oh. Will they be back soon?'

Again the smile played around her mouth. 'Depends what you call soon, Mr Smith. About another four weeks or so. They've got a big area to cover.'

'That means we're not going to see them. What a pity.' Johnny smiled.

Mrs Spencer turned to Barbara. 'Not much sense in us all standing out in the sun. Come inside, Sister. You look as though you'd appreciate a cup of tea. I suppose the rest of you would like some, too?' She walked up the steps and opened the wire door. 'No need to ask you, Fred. I know you and Ivan from old.'

They all entered the house and she looked outside. 'Where is Ivan?' she asked.

'He's not here,' Fred said, adding hastily, 'How about this cuppa you promised.'

She walked from the verandah into the kitchen. 'I thought maybe he'd washed and I hadn't recognised him.'

She smiled at the sister, probing for a response. Mrs Spencer lived in a man's world and had moulded herself to be tougher than most men. She had a sharp wit, which she honed on the hides of unfortunate males. Inevitably, she lacked allies in her self-imposed battle to prove women could be as strong or durable or clever as men and her main weapon, her tongue, had made her a much feared adversary. Now her eyes watched Barbara's face closely. The sister returned her smile. She seemed genuinely amused. Maybe sympathetic? At that moment, Amy Spencer decided she liked Barbara Dean.

'What's wrong with Ivan?' she said, suddenly puzzled as she tried to recall earlier conversations with the women further down the track.

'He didn't come this time,' Johnny said, not allowing Fred time to answer. 'There was no need for him with my brother and myself going along.'

Mrs Spencer took a kettle from a fuel stove that was flooding the room with heat. She glanced up at Johnny, and then at Fred and the others, but said nothing.

'Been very hot, hasn't it?' Fred said.

Barbara took up the conversation. 'I'm nearly dead from the heat and the noise of the truck. Honestly, I don't know how Fred stands it all the time. I hope it's not going to be hot like this all the time up at Birdsville.'

'Gets a lot hotter in summer,' Mrs Spencer said not looking up. She poured the tea and opened a tin of homemade biscuits. 'I hope no one minds eating in the kitchen.'

They shook their heads. All sat down except Fred, who held his teacup and leaned against the doorway.

'What happened at Mungeranie?' Mrs Spencer asked.

Fred, standing behind Johnny and Frog, waved his hand at her in what he hoped she would take as a signal to drop the subject. Johnny turned to hear the answer.

'Just a bull perishing on the track,' Fred said. 'A pretty valuable one by the look of it. Got lured away from permanent water by the rain. Did you have much rain here?'

'No,' she drawled, eyeing Fred strangely. 'More up north. Birdsville and further up got heavy falls. Last Saturday's plane had to be cancelled and the field's still closed.'

'Where, at Birdsville?' Fred asked in surprise.

She nodded. 'We normally only get about four or five inches of rain a year,' she explained to the sister, 'and Birdsville got that in two days last weekend. You never know what to expect, as you'll find out.' She turned again to Fred. 'The place is having a bad trot. The storm must have put their radio out of action, we haven't heard from them for a day or so.'

'Will we be able to get through?' Johnny asked anxiously.

'With Fred you will,' she said. 'Or at least, you should. I haven't heard, so I don't know what the track's like further north. It's all right down here, though.'

'But isn't there a river or something?'

'Oh, I don't think rain at Birdsville would affect the Diamantina much, would it Fred?'

'No,' said Fred, shaking his head. 'Not unless they've had rain further up.'

'No, well I don't think they have,' she said. 'Who's ready for more tea?' She offered the teapot.

Barbara nodded. 'Goodness me, things have been happening in my new home town,' she said. She tried to speak casually but her voice surprised her by emerging at a higher pitch. Her hand trembled, and the cup she was offering rattled in the saucer.

'Yes,' Mrs Spencer agreed. 'The radio will be your worry, too. It's in the mission hospital, as you know.' She looked at Barbara, to make sure she did know.

'You'll find everyone starving for news when you get there. With no radio and no plane, the place's really cut off from the world. That reminds me,' she waved her cup at Fred, who walked to the table and poured himself more tea, 'was Mulka having radio trouble when you went through?'

'Well I don't know,' said Fred straightening up. He exchanged glances with Barbara. 'They didn't say anything about it. Why? Are they having trouble?'

'I haven't heard from them today, that's all. They were all right up till yesterday afternoon.'

Barbara looked shocked. 'You mean they haven't sent any messages?'

'No.'

Fred noticed Johnny smiling. 'Well, they didn't mention anything to us about the radio,' Fred said. 'So I suppose it was okay when we were there.' He took a long sip from his cup.

Footsteps sounded on the verandah and a young woman appeared. She was holding a baby against her shoulder. 'This is my daughter-in-law,' Mrs Spencer explained. 'She's been feeding the baby.' She introduced the visitors and then poured a fresh cup of tea.

Betty Spencer was tall and slender with broad, angular

cheekbones and large brown eyes. She wore a simple white blouse and a floral skirt. Johnny eyed her with interest and, briefly, she returned his frank stare.

Barbara stood up and walked over to her. 'What a beautiful baby,' she said, and held out her arms. 'May I take him — or her?'

Betty Spencer gingerly handed over the baby. 'Him,' she said. 'Glenn.'

'Betty reads the movie magazines,' Mrs Spencer explained. 'I've never heard of the name.'

'I think it's nice,' Barbara said, cradling the boy in her arms.

'He's still got wind,' Betty said. 'You'd better hold him up.' Barbara lifted the baby and began massaging its back.

'I can see you've had experience,' Mrs Spencer said.

'I'm rather used to babies. And you're a beautiful baby.' She nuzzled the boy. He began to cry.

Fred laughed. 'You might be all right in the city but you haven't got the Birdsville touch yet.'

'Stop bullying her,' Mrs Spencer said. 'The young fellow's just overwhelmed by the crowd. He's never seen this many strangers in his life.'

Betty sat down beside Frog and began sipping her tea. 'Tell us about the search for the two men at Marree, Fred,' she said. 'All the stations were talking about it this morning. And what happened at Mungeranie this morning? Why didn't you stop?' Her big eyes looked at Fred with an innocent excitement.

Fred coughed and desperately sought some way to evade answering the question. He saw Johnny stand up and casually saunter on to the verandah and pour himself a cup of water from the long, cylindrical water bag hanging near the door.

'Nothing for them,' Fred said. He moved to the table and put down his cup and saucer. 'That was fine thanks, Mrs Spencer. Right now we better get all your stuff off the truck. Not too much daylight left and we've got to shove off again soon.'

Mrs Spencer sprawled back in her chair. She eyed Fred intently. 'Now what's all this about, Fred? You've been acting queer since you got here. You're not trying to tell me that you're going to take the sister and these other folk out into the sand for the night.'

'It'll do me here,' said Frog, who was fanning himself with Ivan's hat.

Fred turned to him. 'Look, I know Mrs Spencer's hospitable

but I also understand her position. She doesn't own this place and the company has very definite rules about not putting up visitors.'

'They won't miss a bit of extra meat for one night,' Mrs Spencer said.

'Well, you're not supposed to and I know what George would say. Besides, you and Betty have enough work to do around here on your own without having us on your hands.'

Johnny had returned and was standing in the doorway. One hand was in his pocket, fondling the concealed gun.

Mrs Spencer looked at him intently for several seconds and then faced Fred and shrugged. 'Whatever you say, Fred.' She seemed about to say something else but shrugged again and said, 'Whatever you think's best.'

'Oh Mum,' Betty cut in. 'You can't let them go on tonight. We were counting on them staying here and you know it. What's going on, anyway? Fred looks as though he's seen a ghost and no one's saying anything.' She looked around at the faces staring at her. 'Well, what's wrong with everyone?'

'Hush,' Mrs Spencer said. 'Fred wants to get the truck unloaded. Let him get on with his work. You and me and the sister can go into the lounge where it's a bit cooler while the menfolk start unloading.'

Johnny stepped forward. 'No I'm sorry, Mrs Spencer, but you won't be able to do that. Thank you for the invitation to spend the night, Miss.' He turned to the girl, now staring at him with her mouth open. With a slow, deliberate movement, he withdrew the gun. 'We accept.'

Betty dropped her teacup.

'There's no need for anyone to get frightened,' Johnny said. 'Frog, go outside and get the rifle.'

Betty stood and backed towards the sister. 'Who are you?' Her voice was trembling as she reached for her baby.

'I think your mother-in-law has a fair idea,' Johnny said. 'She's been giving us a few strange looks, haven't you Grandma?'

Mrs Spencer looked up at Fred. 'These are the men they've been searching for. It that right, Fred?'

Fred nodded. 'Don't take any chances with them,' he said, stepping behind Mrs Spencer and resting his hands on her shoulders to prevent her rising. 'They're desperate. They have no scruples about shooting.'

'That's right, Grandma,' Johnny said. 'Just do as you're told and you won't get hurt. Same applies to you too, girlie.'

Betty held the baby tightly against her body. It began to cry again.

'What happened, Fred? How did they get with you?' Mrs Spencer asked, tilting her head up at the mailman.

'They hid on the truck at Marree. No one saw them. They came out just after Dulkaninna.'

The verandah door slammed and Frog returned with the rifle.

'That explains why Dulkaninna and Etadunna were arguing about the number of people on the truck,' she mused. Mrs Spencer examined Frog. 'That's Ivan's hat you've got isn't it?'

Frog tilted his head as though to hide it from her eyes.

'Sure it is.' Johnny answered for him. He walked across the kitchen and peered into the darkened dining room. Inspection finished, he turned around with a smile.

'Where is he?' Mrs Spencer said. 'What's happened to Ivan.'

'I'm afraid he's dead,' Fred said. 'They shot him.'

Mrs Spencer moaned softly and momentarily closed her eyes.

'Don't say they,' Frog protested. 'He shot him, not me.'

Johnny looked sharply at Frog. 'What's it matter who shot him?' he snapped. 'He didn't do what he was told and he got killed for it.' He flexed his shoulders, as though relaxing himself, and continued more evenly. 'Now you ladies have nothing to worry about if you just do what we tell you. That applies to everyone.' He glanced at Fred. 'All we want to do is spend the night here in a bit of comfort and in the morning, we'll move on and you'll be none the worse off.'

Mrs Spencer touched Fred's hand. 'Where did it happen?'

'Ivan? Back at Ooroowilanie. Last night.'

'What say we just forget about that,' Johnny said. 'Just remember that if no one causes any trouble, no one'll get hurt here. That's the main thing.'

'Do you think I'd let a couple of murdering men stay here?' Mrs Spencer said.

'You've got no choice, Grandma,' Johnny said. She tried to stand but Fred pressed down on her shoulders, holding her in the chair.

'Don't argue with him,' Fred advised.

Mrs Spencer looked up at Fred. 'What's happened to you, Fred?' she demanded. 'These men kill your mate and you tell me to do nothing.'

'You don't understand,' Barbara said. 'Fred's not thinking of himself. These men have threatened to kill me if he does anything.'

'We will, too,' Johnny said. 'Now we've got a couple of extra women to make sure he behaves.'

'You pair of murderers,' Mrs Spencer said.

'I'm no murderer,' Frog said, with great precision. 'I've killed no one. Stop saying that.'

Johnny critically examined the fat man. 'You're talking too much, Frog. The sun's got at you.'

'Well I notice you haven't taken a turn on the back. It's all right for you in the front out of the sun all the time.'

'Will you shut up, you great slob.'

'Why should I?'

'Because I tell you, that's why. If it hadn't been for me you'd have been caught long ago. Now just do what I say. And I'm telling you to shut up.'

Frog tightened and relaxed his grip on the rifle in a series of quick movements. For a moment, Fred thought he was going to turn the rifle on Johnny but instead he let the barrel drop to the floor. 'Just don't say that I killed anyone, that's all,' he grumbled and sat down. ''Cause I never.'

'All right, we heard you. Let's forget all about what's happened and settle down for a nice quiet night as guests of these two ladies. Now, Grandma, first thing we should do, I suppose, is see that Fred unloads your things from the truck. I feel a very strong sense of gratitude to you for ordering so many big tyres this trip. They helped make a terrific hiding place. Now what say we all go outside while we unload?'

'What do you mean, all of us?' Mrs Spencer demanded. 'You don't expect us', she indicated Betty and Barbara, 'to help unload the tyres, do you?'

'Of course not, Grandma. It's just that I don't trust anyone of you in here alone with your radio. I know from what you told us that you do have a radio and it's working. I'd hate you to send a message that might embarrass me, while I was outside. Understand? So we'll all just stick together. Don't make me do what we did at Mulka.'

'Did you put their radio out of action?' Fred asked.

'Not me personally.'

Fred turned to Frog who shrugged his shoulders apologetically and said, 'He told me to.'

'What did you do to it?' Fred said.

'Just took some bits and pieces and chucked them out when we were a few miles from their place. Didn't harm anyone.'

'Didn't harm anyone?' Fred echoed, his dream of help from Marree fading. 'Do you two realise what radio means to these people out here? Supposing someone gets sick or hurt? That's the only way they can get help, that radio.'

Johnny interrupted him. 'Stop making such a fuss about nothing. We don't want them gossiping about us and that's all there is to it. I wouldn't worry too much about their health,' he added sarcastically. 'I've never seen two healthier looking people in all my life.'

'In any case,' Fred argued, 'it was a dumb move. The first thing Tim Sanderson'll do when he discovers you've tampered with the radio is hop in his ute and drive to the next station and report it. People will soon put two and two together and where will that get you? I thought you didn't want anyone to know you were heading this way?'

'He won't get very far in that old heap of bolts,' Frog said softly.

'Far enough.'

'No he won't. I put enough dirt in the tank to stop the Queen Mary.'

'Dirt in the tank!' Mrs Spencer exclaimed. 'That's a criminal thing to do out here. You're a great one to be protesting about how innocent you are. You're every bit as bad as your partner.'

'Well, he told me to do it. Don't blame me. It wasn't my idea.'

'Just because you haven't got any brains doesn't mean you can't be just as guilty as him,' she said, spitting the words at him.

Frog flushed. 'Who are you saying hasn't got any brains? I got the opals for him, didn't I? Where would he have been without...'

'Oh for Christ's sake, shut up,' Johnny snapped. 'I'm getting a bit sick of the way you've been talking, Frog. You either stick with me or, brother, you've had it.' His words were loud and menacing. 'Understand?'

For a brief moment, Frog stared defiantly at him. Then he lowered his eyes and gave a couldn't-care-less shrug with his shoulders.

'You'd better understand,' Johnny said. 'You try and buck me and you won't know what hit you.'

The others listened to this exchange in silence. Now Johnny glared at them. 'Well, what are you all staring at. I told you all to get outside. Come on, Grandma. Get moving. Or would you rather we kept on going tomorrow with all your things still on board. I'd just as soon dump them on some sandhill.'

Mrs Spencer stood up. 'That's the spirit, Grandma. You lead the way and we'll all follow.'

'Let my daughter-in-law stay inside,' she said. 'You wouldn't expect the baby to go outside in this heat, and with all the flies?'

'Now look, I'll tell you what I'll do. She can stay with the baby on the verandah where I can see her all the time. But if she tries to sneak inside I'll come after her.' He pointed his finger at the girl. 'Got that?'

Betty Spencer nodded, her eyes still wide with fright and followed the others on to the verandah.

Fred worked until dusk. Occasionally Frog or Johnny — never both together — would help him lower a particularly heavy item to the ground.

When they came to the tyres, Johnny walked over to Mrs Spencer and said, 'How many vehicles have you got here?'

'None at the moment,' she said.

He looked about the homestead, searching for a sign of some vehicle.

'What do you mean, none? You must have some. Where are they?'

'There's only two vehicles on the station and the men have taken them with them.'

'Come off it, Grandma. Only two with all those big tyres? You're not just trying to dodge having us put some dirt in your tanks, now are you?'

'We've only got a Land-Rover and a truck. All those big tyres are for a team of geologists, or whatever they call themselves. They're drilling for oil. They've got all sorts of big equipment. Bulldozers. You know.' She drew the shape of a big wheel with her hands. 'Huge tyres on them.'

'Where are they?'
'A hundred and fifty miles or so to the north-east.'
'Why didn't you tell me about them before?'
'Why should I have? I didn't know you were interested in looking for oil.' She smiled slyly at the sister, to share her small triumph.
Johnny was not amused. 'Do they come in here often?' He asked the question slowly, flatly, in the manner of one who is tolerating a fool.
'No.'
'But what about the tyres. Someone'll be in for those.'
'I shouldn't think so. The boss bloke ordered them months ago. He'll be in to collect them in his own good time. You're pretty nervous, aren't you?'
Johnny spent several seconds apparently examining the pattern of her apron. 'You know, Grandma,' he said, lifting his eyes slowly until they met hers, 'I just hope for your sakes that this character doesn't come bowling in looking for his tyres, because if he does and he starts any trouble, you or the sister or that girl are going to cop it first. I need Fred to get me to Birdsville. But I don't need any of you ladies. Just remember that.'
He stabbed his finger at her, as though adding an exclamation mark to the sentence, and then walked away, to stand by himself until the work was finished. When the goods were stored, he ordered everybody to re-enter the homestead.
Betty Spencer had put the baby to sleep in a cot on the verandah. Johnny sent her inside to help Mrs Spencer prepare tea. He left Frog to guard them and wandered through the house, inspecting it. Entering a doorway off the far end of the verandah, he found the bedrooms and a large bathroom with a septic tank toilet system. He tried it out, washed, and then followed a corridor running along the other side of the house back to the living room, one corner of which was dominated by a huge radio transmitter and receiver. Briefly he examined it, glanced at some old magazines lying on a table in the opposite corner and wandered into the dining room. Betty was setting places at the large wooden table.
She stepped back in fright when he entered. 'No need to be scared,' he said.
'I didn't hear you coming,' she said. She was balancing plates

on one trembling arm. The plates were rattling.

'You'd better put those things down before you break them,' he said.

She placed them in a pile on the table, and then stood back, staring at him like a rabbit transfixed by a snake.

'Well, go on, put them out properly. I'm not going to bite you.'

She wet her lips and continued setting the table.

'Must be lonely for you here,' Johnny said.

'You get used to it,' she said, without looking up.

'Does your husband go away often?'

She paused before answering. 'Pretty often.'

'I wouldn't if I were him. You're too nice a girl to leave home all the time.'

She looked up and he smiled.

'I don't mind,' she said. 'He's got his work to do.'

Johnny walked around the table and picked up a fork she had just set down. He examined it as he spoke. 'How old are you, Betty? Nineteen? Twenty?'

She had finished at the table and pressed herself against a cabinet. 'More than that. You shouldn't ask a lady her age.'

'How old's the baby, then?'

'Five months. Why all the questions?'

'Oh, I'm just wondering what a girl as good looking as you would be doing stuck out in a place like this. Where do you come from? You know, where were you living before you got married?'

'Marree.'

'Marree? The big smoke, eh?'

She nodded and saw him smiling and began to smile, but stopped herself. 'I'd better get back in the kitchen.'

'No, don't go.' He reached out and touched her arm, gently. 'I want to talk to you.'

She looked at him shyly from beneath lowered eyebrows.

'You're not frightened of me, are you?'

She looked down at the floor. 'I suppose not.'

'Good. That's good, Betty. So you're from Marree, eh? Like it there?'

She moved her arms from behind her back and spread them along the cabinet. 'I suppose so,' she said.

Johnny studied her young, slender body. 'Travelled much?' he asked.

'A bit.'

'Been to any big towns?' His eyes were following the outline of her brassiere through the thin blouse. He rested an elbow on the cabinet.

'I've been to Port Augusta,' she said. She followed the direction of Johnny's eyes and folded her arms. She wasn't embarrassed; it was a defensive act. She was used to men staring at her, only they were different — the station hands and drovers and ringers whose appearance and manners had been roughened in this bitter country and who might spend six months without seeing a young white woman. They were either as direct as a bull, or painfully shy. This man was different but his eyes had the same hungry look. 'I suppose you've been around,' she said, a statement of fact rather than a question.

'Oh yes,' he said. 'Sydney, Melbourne, Brisbane, Adelaide; you know, all the big places. That's the sort of life I like. That's the sort of life a pretty girl like you should have.'

She unfolded her arms. 'Mrs Spencer's been to Adelaide and she didn't like it much. Said the people weren't as friendly as they are up this way.'

Johnny shrugged his shoulders and moved closer, so close that his breath could ruffle her blouse. 'That's probably so, but that's not everything. I can see you're friendly. A lot friendlier than most of the girls down Adelaide.'

She stiffened and slid away from him. 'I better be going back to help,' she said.

'No, stay,' he said and touched her shoulder.

She hesitated. A tingle of excitement began to spread through her body.

'What do you do at nights?' he said.

She shrugged her shoulders. He let his hand slip down the front of the blouse. She turned her eyes to look at him.

'Not much,' she said, speaking softly. 'Listen to the radio. Play cards sometimes.'

'Doesn't sound like much fun.' He let a finger play with a strap beneath the blouse. 'Do you get many visitors?'

She shook her head, and studied the floor. She glanced briefly at the man, who leaned closer.

'What are you doing tonight?'

Her body glowed with warmth. Confused, she turned her head

away from him. Through the doorway to the kitchen, she saw Fred looking at them. She pushed the man's hand away.

'Tonight,' he breathed, and touched her again.

She slipped from under his hand and walked quickly through the room into the kitchen. Fred watched her. So you're still the same, he thought.

Betty headed for the verandah, glancing quickly at Fred as she passed by. Her eyes smiled. Was it a look of triumph? Yes, you can win any man in this part of the world, he thought, and concentrated on the floor.

In the other room, Johnny Parsons examined himself in a mirror, adjusted his hair, and entered the kitchen.

The aroma of cooking steak greeted him. He took a deep breath. 'Smells good,' he said. No one answered him. Mrs Spencer was busily inspecting the meat. Frog sat near the other door with the rifle pointed towards Fred.

'Where's the girl?' Johnny asked.

'Checking on her baby,' Barbara said. 'And now that you're back, would you mind telling that watchdog of yours over there to let me go to the bathroom and clean up. I feel as though I'm covered in dirt.'

'And tell him to stop pointing that rifle at us,' Fred said. 'The condition he's in, it might go off.'

Johnny walked to the verandah door. The girl was bending over the cot. He breathed deeply and turned. 'Sure, Sister,' he said. 'It's up the other end of the house. Go this way,' he pointed along the verandah, 'and come back the same way. Just a quick wash. Don't be too long, or I'll come looking for you.'

'Would you like a bath or a shower, Sister?' Mrs Spencer asked.

'Later,' Johnny said.

'Thanks, but I don't think I'd have time before tea,' Barbara said, as though he hadn't spoken. Mrs Spencer was delighted at such a show of resistance, particularly when it related to a matter so fundamentally affecting the house, which was her territory.

'Ask Betty to get you a towel,' she said.

'And don't be long,' Johnny reminded her.

Mrs Spencer ignored him. That, she decided, was the best way to deal with him.

Ten minutes later, the sister joined them in the dining room as Betty was putting the last plate of food in position. They ate steak, tinned tomato and bread and butter. The bread was a wrapped loaf from Whyalla, more than five hundred miles away. Fred had brought it.

'About the only thing we can grow here is meat,' Mrs Spencer explained to Barbara, talking as though the two intruders were not present. 'I daresay beef's a great delicacy in some places, but you get a bit sick of it, meal after meal.'

They finished dinner with tea and powdered milk and then sat around the table for several minutes, saying nothing. Fred played with the spoon in the sugar bowl and Barbara gazed around the sparsely furnished room. Frog seemed intent on something under the table and Johnny smoked a cigarette and stared at the girl. She and Mrs Spencer exchanged glances.

From out on the verandah, the baby cried and Betty stood up and left the room. Mrs Spencer rose and said, 'I'll clear up.' Barbara offered to help.

Johnny looked at his watch. It was almost seven o'clock. He seized Mrs Spencer's wrist as she reached to clear away his plate. 'Grandma,' he said, 'does that radio in there pick up the news?'

She wrenched her arm free.

'Well does it?' he asked.

'You can get the ABC on it,' she said.

'Well come on and tune it in for us,' he said. 'I want to see if we're on the news.'

He followed her into the living room, where she switched on the set. She turned a dial and stood back and waited. Suddenly, music came pouring from the set so loudly she had to turn down the volume.

'That's a good wireless,' Johnny said. 'What station is it.'

'It's the ABC in Adelaide,' she said. 'Relayed through Port Pirie.' She spoke as though relating the obvious.

At half a minute to seven, the music stopped and a voice announced the time and the fact that they were listening to the ABC. There was a pause. The time signal pipped and Mrs Spencer glanced at her clock. The news fanfare followed, so loudly that she lowered the set's volume once more. Johnny sat on a small table and squirmed nervously. Frog waited at the far end of the room, rifle still at the ready.

The announcer said 'Here is the News' and read four overseas items. Fred rolled a cigarette. The announcer then read about a strike in the steelworks at Newcastle and about a fishing boat missing off the east Tasmanian coast. And then everyone in the room stiffened as he said:

'In South Australia, the State's biggest manhunt continued today as hundreds of police and volunteers searched for two men wanted for the murder of a woman in Alice Springs last Sunday night.

'The search has been extended to all parts of the State, and police throughout Australia have been issued with descriptions of the wanted men.

'Roadblocks have been set up on every major highway in South Australia and police are keeping a constant watch on railway stations and airports.

'The search intensified on Tuesday night after two men, believed to be connected with the murder, were sighted at Marree, four hundred and fifteen miles north of Adelaide.

'However, a thorough search of the Marree–Port Augusta area failed to reveal any further sign of the men and police have now widened the search to include all major towns in South Australia.

'The murdered woman was Mrs Agnes Ruby Charles, sixty-eight, owner of the Centralian Hotel, Alice Springs. Police believe she was beaten to death when she disturbed thieves stealing opals valued at more than forty thousand pounds from the hotel safe.'

Frog changed his grip on the rifle.

'Today the South Australian Commissioner of Police, Mr Fortescue, said it was believed the men would attempt to leave the State to dispose of the opals and every endeavour was being made to apprehend them.

'He gave the following description of two men police wish to interview. The first man is about thirty years of age, about six feet tall, well built, with dark hair and with a long scar on his forehead.'

Johnny stood up and touched his forehead. 'Scar? What scar?' Frog hissed at him to be silent.

'. . . is about forty to forty-five years of age, short and thick set, swarthy complexion, and long dark hair. Both men were wearing slacks and weatherproof jackets and are believed to be desperate.'

'I'm not that old,' Frog protested. Johnny waved him into silence.

'The men are alleged to have attacked a hotel waitress at Marree, fracturing her skull. They have not been seen since the incident.'

The announcer paused, then continued. 'A one hundred mile strip of the Queensland coast is tonight being lashed by a cyclone which has followed a week of unseasonal monsoonal rains in western and northern parts of the State. In Bowen ...'

Johnny leaned across and switched off the radio. 'What's this about a scar,' he said, walking into the next room to examine his forehead in the cabinet mirror.

'What's this about a waitress?' Fred said.

'It was a girl Johnny hit,' Frog said. 'Thank heavens he didn't kill her.'

Johnny returned to the living room smiling. 'It's where I banged my head on the dashboard when you ran into the creek,' he told Frog.

'What creek?' Fred asked.

'Not you. It was before we even got to Marree. Way back before Oodnadatta. Frog almost wrecked us in a creek. I cut my forehead. There's practically no sign of it now.'

Frog was pale. 'The girl's not dead. Did you hear that? I suppose she gave them our descriptions.'

'I should have hit her harder. Anyhow, the bloke in the pub could have described us. Wasn't a bad description was it?' he asked the others. 'But scar on the forehead. That's great. Everyone'll be looking for a bloke with a scarred forehead and this thing' — he wiped his brow — 'will be gone in another day. How did you like Frog's description? Fat and greasy.'

'He didn't say that,' Frog protested.

'That's what he meant.' He laughed. 'We didn't get a bad run, did we? So they've given away looking for us around Marree. That's good. We've got a clear run from here right up into Queensland. And Birdsville can't even hear the news anyhow, because their radio's on the blink. Perfect.'

Mrs Spencer shuffled from the room. 'Where do you think you're going?' Johnny called after her.

'To do the washing up,' she said. 'Unless you'd rather do it.'

'You can do it, Grandma. And good luck to you, too.' He laughed again. 'Well, what do you think of us, Freddie boy?' He leaned towards the mailman. 'We've really got them running around in circles, haven't we? And they're not even close.'

'I think all this publicity's turning your head,' Fred said. 'I'd have thought publicity was the last thing you'd have wanted.'

Johnny waved his hands in the air. 'That's the price of fame, I guess, eh Frog?' He turned to his companion.

'I'd rather do without it,' Frog said. He looked worried.

'Oh you just didn't like the description they gave of you.'

Frog hunched his shoulders, as though to help repel criticism. He was used to people joking about his appearance. 'It's not that,' he said, turning quickly. 'What's this about forty thousand. That's not what you told me the opals were worth.'

'Yeah, I heard that. They're not worth anything like that. Probably just the American trying to make a profit from his insurance company. Christ Frog, what a villain he must be. He'll make more from this than we will.'

Frog tried to digest this information. He needed more time so he changed the course of the conversation. He said, 'They're looking everywhere for us. How do you think we're going to get clear once we get past Birdsville? They'll probably have the cop there alerted.'

'They couldn't have. They think we're moving south. Anyhow, even if they thought we might be heading that way, how could they tell him? The radio's not working. There's no other way of telling him. They couldn't even fly a plane in with a message, because the field's closed. Stop worrying, Frog. Things went wrong first of all because you put us in that creek.' He saw Frog open his mouth to argue. 'Now you know that's right. You spoilt my plan. It wouldn't have gone wrong otherwise. It was perfect. Well, anyhow, we'll forget about that. Things are right now. Better. They're perfect again. No one knows we're here. No one at Birdsville even knows about the business back at Alice Springs. I tell you Frog, everything's going right for us again.'

'What about when we get past Birdsville? How are we going to get past all the cops on the way to . . .'

'You're talking too much,' Johnny interrupted. 'We don't want people around who can talk to the world later on and tell where we're going. Too many people know too much about us already.' He looked meaningfully around him, and walked out to the kitchen.

CHAPTER FIFTEEN

After helping Mrs Spencer wash up, Barbara showered and changed her clothes. The shower was outside the house, in a small, square building with its roof supporting a tank of bore water. The water was hard and difficult to lather but to Barbara it felt heavenly after two dusty days on the track.

Guided by the light from a lantern, she returned to the house. From somewhere close by, a dog barked at her, and she jumped in fright. She found the steps to the verandah and saw a shadowy figure sitting at the top.

'It's all right.' It was Frog's voice. 'It's only me.'

He stood and held open the wire door for her. 'What are you doing out here?' she asked.

'Just making sure you come back in.'

Barbara stepped on to the verandah and he closed the door. 'Thank you,' she said. 'You don't think I'd go wandering away out there, do you?' She indicated the pitch blackness beyond the house.

'Johnny just thought I'd better stay out here,' he said. He put the rifle against the wall and poured himself a cup of water from the water bag. 'Care for some? It's tank water.' She shook her head and he began to drink.

'Do you always do what he thinks?' she asked. 'He's got you

into the worst kind of trouble that way.'

'What can I do?' he said, rehanging the cup on its hook. He wiped his lips and picked up the gun. 'He's still got the opals and I earned my share of them.'

'But don't you see,' she whispered, a sense of urgency in her voice, 'he probably doesn't mean to share them with you and no matter whether he does or not, if you keep going along with him, you'll be blamed for all he's done. You've got the gun there. It would be so easy for you to ...'

'Look,' he said. 'I know what sort of position I'm in but I know what you're trying to do. That Russian reckoned he was my friend and he said the same sort of things you're saying. And what did he do? He almost killed me to get the rifle. I know who you're thinking of and it's not me. Now let's get inside.'

'You're being a fool.'

'C'mon, get inside with the others.'

'I've got to put these away first.' She held up her soiled clothes and the towel.

'Well put them away and come on in. And don't try and turn me against Johnny. I know what he's like. I can think for myself. Just give me credit for a bit of sense. I know what you'd do to me once you got rid of Johnny.'

The others were sitting in silence when Barbara and Frog returned to the living room. Johnny was drinking from a bottle of beer he had found in the refrigerator. He glanced up admiringly at the sister.

'I'd hardly recognise you,' he said. 'You look about three shades whiter than when I last saw you. Nice frock.' He reached across his chair and lifted the hem, rubbing the material between his thumb and forefinger. She pulled it away from him and he giggled.

'You're too touchy,' he said. 'Wait till you've been among the Abos for a couple of months and you'll chase the first white man you see.'

'Come and sit down over here,' Mrs Spencer said, as though the man had said nothing. She indicated a chair near her. 'How do you feel now?'

Barbara stepped cautiously around Johnny. 'Much better, thank you. It was beautiful under the shower.'

'I think I'll have one,' Betty said, standing up. 'Will you listen for the baby?' Mrs Spencer nodded and the young woman walked from the room.

Johnny twisted and called after her. 'Don't be too long.' He turned and smiled at the others. 'Nice girl, that.' No one answered. He finished the rest of the bottle and stood up and stretched. 'I think I'll get a bit of fresh air. Frog, you keep an eye on these people here. Don't let anyone touch the radio. Stay here unless I call you.'

They watched him stroll from the room, hands in his pockets. 'He looks as though he's going for a walk around the block,' Barbara said. Mrs Spencer gave her a half smile. 'Wish he would,' she drawled. 'This is a big block. Take him months to get round.'

Johnny Parsons sat on the steps leading from the verandah. The glow from the kitchen cast his shadow across the faint moat of light that ringed the house and protected it from the black immensity that lay beyond. A dog growled. It was somewhere to his left, in the dark beneath the house. He sat still, trying to distinguish objects, and the dog became quiet.

A sliver of light showed from the roof of the shower house. He could distinguish the faint outline of the building and, as the seconds passed, the shape of the water tank on the roof grew clearer. He became aware of noises. Insects buzzing and slapping against the screens. A scratching sound, that was probably the dog clearing a resting place for itself in the dust. The distant shuffling of horses moving in a stockyard. The creak of a windmill. A deep rumbling and hissing sound, coming from the far side of the house. That would be the artesian bore. Its acrid perfume hung thick in the night air, stinging his nostrils with a bitter reminder of minerals washed from the depths of the earth.

From the shower house came the sudden splashing of water and a small cry of surprise, as though the girl had found the water too cold. He gazed intently at the light escaping through the crack in the roof, and, as a person stares into a fire and dreams, so he conjured images. First her skin would be tightening under the splash of cold water. He thought of her body quivering for the first few seconds, and then relaxing. Now she would be soaping herself, making her brown skin slippery to touch. She had hair on her arms, bleached fair against the tanned skin by constant exposure to the sun. He liked that. He remembered a Sydney girl with hairless arms and shaven legs that prickled his skin, and he thought of summer nights he had spent with her and other girls on beaches, when the sea turned black and disappeared into the night as completely as the country facing him now had faded into shadows. The memory of warm, salty bodies, of sunburned shoulders, and oiled, prickly legs entwined around his, came to him and he left the steps and walked carefully towards the shower house.

The girl began to hum, and he stopped, surprised at the intimacy of the sound. Maybe she was thinking about him. He had no doubt she was attracted to him because of the way she had behaved in the house. He knew women, and knew the signs. Or so he thought, with the absolute certainty of a man who had never cared for a woman. He was interested only in the chase, and in the snaring of the game, and had learned the rules. Some poor men went through life without knowing what it was all about. They spent their time in crude and declared pursuit of the female, in the erroneous belief that the chase was one sided and, as a result of such ignorance, had fared badly. Not Johnny Parsons. He had started that way, as one of the pack, but had quickly learned that women were driven by deep emotions too, and were just as much hunters as men. The discovery had amused him. He had become a trapper, playing with emotions, reading the signs, and catching lots of women. He did well, he reminded himself, although it had been a long time . . .

Walking softly, he moved beyond the small building until he was facing the closed door. Four slits of light outlined the doorway. She must have a pressure lantern in there, he thought, for the light seemed brilliant.

He tiptoed towards the door, until he was so close he could imagine her standing beside him. He pressed his body against the door and closed his eyes. The last woman had been older and worn, not like this young one. He opened his eyes and tried to peer through a crack at the hinges. He could see nothing. The sounds were maddeningly close, but he could see only an intense white light. He moved to the other side and pressed his face to the gap between the door and the wall. He could see across the room. There was no sign of her body. Then came the blur of an arm. He was breathing heavily now.

The water stopped so suddenly that it startled him. She must hear the sound of the air rasping his throat! He held his breath and saw a towel, her hand, a blur of hair. The light on the wall moved and the doorknob shook. He stepped back. The door swung open, jerking unevenly on misaligned hinges.

She stood there in a dressing gown, brilliant lantern in one hand, the other grasping her clothes and towel. She saw him and stepped back in surprise. Her dressing gown fell open.

She stared at him, mouth open but saying nothing. He recalled how he had touched her near the breast, and she had not flinched. In fact she had looked at him with the same strange expression he thought he saw in her eyes now. He had known another girl like this one. A mad case. One touch on the breast and she was helpless with lust. He reached out and touched her.

The scream rang clearly into the house. In the living room, Fred jumped to his feet. There was another scream and a dog began barking furiously.

'It's Betty,' Mrs Spencer shouted. They were all standing now. Fred began to run to the door.

Frog, closer to the door, swung the rifle at him. 'Back,' he ordered. 'Back or else.'

Other dogs had joined in the barking and through the confusion of noise another scream sounded. Fred began to move. Frog thrust at him with the rifle butt, knocking him back against the others, and then turned and ran to the verandah. 'What's wrong?' Frog called. He could hear a scuffling sound outside. He pushed open the screen door and moved down the steps.

Behind Frog, Fred reached the doorway. 'Stay back,' Frog yelled. He moved back, up the steps and pressed himself against the door to keep Fred inside.

To their left, two long shadows stretched from behind the shower house. The man and the girl, hidden behind the building, were struggling. Then came the sound of savage growling and a man's voice crying out in pain. The lantern appeared from around the corner of the shower house and the girl, gown streaming behind her, ran towards them. She reached the steps and saw Frog there, rifle in his hands. She stopped, paralysed with fear. A frenzied growling made her look back. Johnny had appeared, a dog attacking one leg. He bent down and a shot rang out. The dog howled and began writhing on the ground, biting at its back. On the verandah, the baby started to cry.

'Come back here,' Johnny shouted at the girl. She looked at the immobile Frog, blocking the steps and ran along the side of the house towards the bore. Johnny stumbled after her, shouting.

Fred put his foot against the door and lunged with all his power. The force sent the fat man sprawling down the steps. Fred bounded over him, stumbling on the lower steps and pitching on his hands and knees. Near him, the dog was howling piteously. Fred stood up, in time to see Johnny reach the corner of the house, his body silhouetted in the glow from the girl's lantern. Fred ran after him. He heard Frog shouting, but ran on.

When he reached the end of the building, Fred saw both the girl and her pursuer and stopped, halted by the ghostly unreality of the scene. Two wraith-like figures could be seen through the steam rising from the artesian bore. Betty was at the edge of the water. Being unable to run any further, she had stopped and was now unmoving and rigid, as though frozen in a gesture of surrender. She had dropped the lantern and covered her face with both hands. Behind her the bore pipe gushed near-boiling water into the pool.

Johnny ripped the gown from her shoulders. The water bubbled and hissed. Johnny looked at her semi-nakedness, and tore the gown from her body. The action spun her around. The brilliant light from the fallen lantern cast grotesque shadows across the rising clouds of steam.

'No!' Fred shouted and ran towards them. Johnny began to turn. He still had the gun in one hand, but Fred reached him before he could level it, and tackled him side on. The impact drove the other man to the ground, jarring the gun from his hand. Tangled together, they slithered through the dust.

The force of the charge took them into the girl's legs, throwing her on top of them. She fell across Fred. He was aware of a sudden and ridiculous contrast. One body, warm, soft and smelling of soap, lay on top of him. Another, hard, foul smelling, and violent, squirmed beneath him to get free of his grip.

The gun had come to rest near the edge of the pool. Johnny Parsons reached for the weapon, trying to carry the weight of the man and the woman with him. Fred locked one arm around the other man's throat to hold him back, and their bodies arched sideways. Betty slid across them. Fred felt her belly and then one soft breast drag across his face. He tried to thrust her clear but the movement allowed the other man to roll on top. Dusty clothing ground into Fred's face. His head was locked between the man's arm and chest, and through his nostrils, compressed painfully against a ridge of muscle, came the stench of stale sweat, rancid and overpowering in its closeness.

The grip eased as Johnny lunged for the gun. Fred grabbed him by the hair and pulled him back. He saw Betty run towards the house. Her buttocks and one thigh were stained with mud from the pool's edge. He had never seen her naked before.

He got to his feet and dived for the gun. His fingers fumbled to grip it and then with awful force, Johnny landed on top of him, hands grasping for the weapon. In desperation, Fred swept at the weapon with his open hand and saw it spin towards the pool. Knees ground into his neck as the other man crawled over him in a futile effort to stop it. With a hissing splash, the gun dropped into the water.

Johnny flung himself at the edge and plunged his arm into the water in a wild clawing motion. With a cry of pain, he snatched his hand out of the pool and flapped it wildly in the air.

Fred pushed himself to his knees and crawled to the bore. He lifted Johnny's shoulder and hit him flush on the exposed cheekbone.

Johnny shook his head and then thrust himself up at his adversary. Eyes blazing, he wrapped his arms around Fred's body. Fred cried out as the other man squeezed his injured ribs. He fell back, near the edge. He could hear Johnny grunting like a maddened animal, as he twisted and thrust him towards the pool. The sulphurous fumes from the bubbling water stung his lungs and he coughed in a racking, violent way that brought the taste of vomit to his mouth. Johnny was on top of him, bulldogging him towards the edge. Then Fred's shoulders were in the pool's border of mud and grass and he could feel the heat on the back of his head.

He beat on Johnny's back but couldn't break the grip. Johnny pushed him closer. In despair, Fred grabbed a handful of hair and pulled as hard as he could. He jerked the head back and with his other hand tried to smother the mouth and nostrils. Johnny bit him and he let go. With both hands now, Fred pulled at the hair until he thought it must tear away from Johnny's scalp.

Johnny was screaming and suddenly the bear hug relaxed. Fred rolled away from the pool. As he rose, he caught a glimpse of Frog with the rifle, and the three women nearby. Mrs Spencer was trying to wrap the torn gown around the naked Betty.

Then he was on his feet and Johnny was lunging at him. Fred ducked and swung wildly. He missed and felt a sharp blow on his shins. He fell to his knees and Johnny was kicking at him again. He grabbed the swinging foot and twisted. For a moment, Johnny was airborne before crashing heavily at his side. Fred fell on top of him. He pounded away blindly. A knee jarred against his chin and he toppled backwards.

Both men scrambled to their feet. Fred saw Johnny's face, white in the lantern light, and he hit it. He felt a blow on the shoulder and then he hit the face again and it was gone. Through a blur of red, he saw Johnny on the ground. He felt his feet tugged and he crashed on top of the other man. They were on the brink of the bore again. Both were coughing.

Johnny staggered to his feet and tried to kick Fred over the edge. With his legs, Fred lunged and caught Johnny on the chest, bowling him backwards in a cloud of steam and dust.

Johnny got to his hands and knees. 'Stop it,' he gasped. 'Stop, or the girl cops it.'

Slowly, Fred stood up and looked at the circle of white faces, watching from their position closer to the house. Frog was staring at the fallen Johnny but the rifle was swaying across the group of women. Nearest him, Betty was sobbing, hands pressed to her face.

In a sudden movement, Johnny began to scramble to his feet. Fred swung a long uppercut that sent him sprawling towards Betty's feet. Johnny lifted himself on one elbow. Blood was streaming from his nose. 'Shoot her,' he called to his companion. 'Shoot her, shoot her.'

Barbara ran forward and pulled the girl away. 'For heaven's sake, no,' she cried, and turned the girl behind her.

Fred stayed where he was, panting with exhaustion, not daring to move. Frog's eyes were round with fear.

'Shoot her, damn you, shoot,' Johnny shrieked. He pushed himself to one knee and grabbed for the gun, trying to wrench it from Frog.

Frog pulled the rifle away.

Barbara turned with Betty and ran towards the house as the two men tussled with the rifle. Fred staggered over to Johnny, pulled him away from the other man, and with all that remained of his strength, punched him hard on the jaw. Johnny fell to the ground as though dead.

For almost a minute, Fred stood hunched, arms braced on his knees, regaining his breath. Slowly the women returned and stared down at the unconscious figure.

Painfully, Fred straightened and weakly patted Frog on the shoulder. 'Good boy,' he said. Frog shook his head, as though to sharpen his brain, and peered at Fred.

'No need for the rifle,' Fred said, holding out his hand. 'We've got this bloke at last.'

'No.' Frog snapped the word and pointed the rifle at Fred. 'No. You get over there with the women.'

'But this is your chance,' Fred said. 'You and all of us.'

'No. I know what you're trying to do and I'm not going to fall for it. You're not going to trick me. Now get over there.'

Eyes on the rifle, Fred slowly walked to the women. He was conscious again of the wounded dog howling. 'He shot it in the back,' Mrs Spencer said. 'Can you imagine a man doing such a thing?'

Fred nodded, and took several deep breaths. 'Okay?' he asked Betty, now huddling between Barbara and Mrs Spencer. Betty didn't reply. 'She's all right, isn't she?' he asked Barbara.

'I think so. She's had an awful fright though.'

'Stop talking,' Frog called.

'Look,' Fred said, walking towards him again. 'If you let him take control again . . .'

'No more talking,' he repeated.

'But can't you see he's going to commit more murder? You side with him now and he'll kill the lot of us. You'll hang too.'

'Shut up.' His voice was high. 'I'm no fool. I know what you'd do with me if I gave you the gun. Now you just stop talking.' He shouted the words.

Fred turned to Barbara, despair in his eyes. 'Oh my God,' he said. 'The fool. The blind, bloody fool.'

Tim Sanderson and his dog walked into Etadunna homestead two hours after dusk. Sanderson had had a slow journey, resting and sheltering from the fierce heat whenever he could find shade.

It was easier going when the sun went down, but he had stumbled on a stone and twisted his ankle. When he reached his goal, his legs and feet were aching, his ankle was burning with pain and his body was dry and exhausted.

He told Denzil Leary and his family about the message on the mirror. Leary suggested putting through an emergency radio call to the Broken Hill Flying Doctor base, for it to relay a telephone message to Marree. Sanderson disagreed.

'Fred and the others could be at Clifton Hills tonight and they might hear the message go through,' he said. 'We shouldn't risk that. Do you mind if we take your car and drive to Marree. I reckon that would be better.'

Mrs Leary spoke. 'Of course Den will do that. But first, you're going to have something to eat and drink and I'm going to bandage that ankle for you.'

Sanderson nodded. 'Do you mind doing something else for me. Could you have a look at the dog and see if he'd like some tucker. He was walking those last few miles like his feet were on fire. Poor blighter just made it.'

At ten minutes past midnight, Denzil Leary's dusty Plymouth sedan rattled across the railway line at Marree. He and Tim Sanderson drove to Sergeant Eric Wallis' house. He wasn't there, so they went round to the post office where a light still burned.

John Black answered their knock. The postmaster's pipe dangled unlit from his mouth. 'Do you know where Eric Wallis is?' Leary asked, dispensing with any formalities.

Wallis, sitting on the edge of the table beside another man, twisted to see them. 'What are you fellers doing here at this time of the night?' he asked. His face was heavily scored with fatigue lines and his voice was slurred.

'G'day, Eric,' Leary said. 'I brought Tim Sanderson down with me.'

Wallis nodded acknowledgement of the fact, rubbing his eyes in the same motion. 'What's up? Must be important.'

'It is. Tim walked in to my place tonight and I wanted to send you a message but he thought it best to drive down rather than risk having them listen in.'

'Hold on,' the policeman said, shifting his position on the table edge. 'Let's take this slow. Tim, you tell me what this's all about.'

Sanderson explained about the mail truck and the two strangers and the lipstick message, the broken radio and his walk to Etadunna. Wallis smoked a cigarette and listened intently. When Sanderson had finished, he asked him to describe the men to him.

'Well, that's them all right,' he said. 'I don't know how it happened, but in some way they got on board Fred's truck. So that's where they got to.' He slid off the table. 'What was the message she left on the mirror again.'

Sanderson handed him a slip of paper, hobbling forward on his injured ankle. Wallis read aloud. 'Help. Men are murderers. Tell police Marree. Will kill us.' He repeated the last three words. 'Will kill us.' He slapped the table and swore aloud. 'How in blazes did they get out there? Did they give you any idea?'

Sanderson shook his head. 'All I got was the message.'

'If only we'd found out earlier.' He shouted the words.

'I got in as soon as I could,' Sanderson said, his face flushed. 'I tell you, that walk through the sand was no picnic.'

'Oh no, look I don't mean that, Tim,' Wallis said. 'You did all you could. What I mean is if only we'd known a couple of days ago when Fred first set off. We could have done something then. The mail truck would still have been close and there were any number of bods to help. Half the detective force from Adelaide was here day before yesterday. No use to us now, though, they're all back in Adelaide.' He thumped a fist into the palm of his hand. 'No wonder we couldn't find them anywhere around here. We combed every blessed place along the road and railway line. We even had Gus here flying around.' He indicated the other man sitting at the table. 'Oh, you fellers haven't met Gus have you. This is Gus Cochrane. Flies a Cessna.'

Cochrane nodded a greeting.

'The sister must have been pretty desperate to write a message like that,' Wallis continued. 'Will kill us. Christ! We've got to do something to help them and do it pretty quick-smart.' He tilted his head back and closed his eyes, mentally picturing the Birdsville Track. 'Let's see, tonight they should be at Clifton Hills, or somewhere about there. And then Birdsville tomorrow.' He looked at his watch. 'Birdsville today, that is. Doesn't give us much time, does it? Let's see now. The bloke who can get to them quickest is the constable at Birdsville. John,' he turned to the postmaster. 'Let's get the line open and make a start to relaying a message through to him.'

Leary shook his head. 'No use. You can forget any help from Birdsville.'

'Why?'

'You couldn't get a message through. Birdsville's been off the air for a couple of days.'

'What's wrong?'

'Dunno, Eric. I think the radio must have been damaged in the storm they had up there. Had a pretty bad one because the airfield's still closed.'

Gus Cochrane stood up. 'That lets me out then,' he said. 'I was thinking, Eric, maybe I could fly you up there in the morning.'

'Wait on now,' Wallis said, discovering an idea. 'That might be the way. You may not be able to land at Birdsville itself, but you could probably put down in a claypan or something like that along the track.'

'I suppose so,' Cochrane said. 'That's providing the ground's not too wet.' He turned to Sanderson. 'Do you know whether there's been much rain up along the Birdsville Track itself?'

'There were heavy showers in some places,' Sanderson said. 'They were all to the north of my place, though. I don't think it's been too bad, has it Denzil?'

'No,' Leary said. 'From the radio, Birdsville got it worst. The really heavy rain was there and further north.'

'Well, it's worth trying then,' Wallis said. 'First thing in the morning, Gus and I'll take off. We should have no trouble spotting that truck of Fred's and then we'll put down somewhere in front of them.'

Wallis paused, contemplating what he could do at ground level to rescue those on the truck. He turned to the postmaster. 'John, see if you can get me a line through to Adelaide. I better let them know what's happened. We could do with some sort of follow-up and they might be able to send another plane up.'

Cochrane shook his head. 'I think they'd find it hard to get another light plane at short notice. There's only one Cessna in the whole state and I've got it. Ideal country for aircraft, but people haven't woken up to it, yet. Might be a couple of Austers or Moths down south, but they're not much good. A DC3's no use unless the strip at Birdsville's open and if that's not, you can forget it.'

Wallis stamped in frustration. 'They might just as well be in a foreign country instead of heading up a road out of town. Christ!'

He made one circuit of the room. No one else spoke. 'Never mind,' Wallis said eventually. 'We've got Gus' plane here and that's a real stroke of luck.'

'Eric and I are old mates,' Cochrane explained. 'I just stopped here on my way back to Adelaide. Delivered some stuff to a geologist's camp up near the border. They reckon there's a lot of oil or gas around. Looks terrible country, although it was dry enough at their strip to land.'

'That's the mob Fred was taking those big tyres for,' Wallis said. 'They're operating somewhere out of Clifton Hills.'

'Oh a long way out of there,' Cochrane said. 'Well to the north-east.'

'Near the Track?' Sanderson asked.

Cochrane shook his head. 'Maybe a hundred miles to the east, right up near the border.'

'Never mind them,' Wallis said. 'The point is we've got to get up there as quick as we can. Anyhow, here's my plan. Gus and I leave at dawn and fly up there ...'

Sanderson interrupted. 'Could you drop me off at my place. I'm a bit worried about Kath. It's just possible they might have come back. In any case, she'll be pretty worried. She was expecting me back last night.'

'Is there anywhere to land?' Cochrane asked.

'I reckon you could put down all right within a half mile of the homestead. Just gibbers. Small stuff.'

'Okay,' Wallis said. 'It's probably just as well to check there. You come with us then Tim, and we'll drop you off at Mulka. Could you handle that Gus?' He turned to the pilot, who nodded. 'Good. Maybe we should check at Mungeranie, too.'

'No need,' Leary said. 'They didn't stop there. Harry was complaining about it on the radio yesterday. Fred apparently just shot straight through.'

Wallis said: 'Have you heard anything from Clifton Hills?'

'No, wouldn't hear from them normally until the first session tomorrow, or rather this morning. There's only Mrs Spencer and her daughter-in-law there at the moment. All the men are out.'

'In that case, we'll call at Mulka and drop off Tim and then we'll call at Clifton Hills. You should be able to land somewhere about there, Gus.' The pilot nodded agreement and Wallis continued. 'We'll send a message back from there.'

'That's if their radio's still working,' Sanderson said.

'That's right, by George. If they pulled yours to bits, they'll probably try the same thing with the Spencer's. Anyhow, after Clifton Hills, we'll fly on until we see the truck and then land at the next place ahead of them and stop them. Sort of hide in ambush, if we can, to get the drop on them. Right?'

They nodded. It was his plan, and he would have to make it work.

'Now just as a follow-up, I'll get Albert to drive up in the Land-Rover. I'll go and haul him out of bed now, and he can push off before dawn.'

'That's that Abo of yours,' Sanderson said, with doubt in his voice. 'Do you reckon he's got the nous to get up there on his own?'

Wallis lit a cigarette. He took much time in striking the match. 'For Christ's sake, Tim, he's a good bloke. Tell him to do something and he'll do it. I trust him. Good enough?'

'Sure. Sure.' Sanderson answered hastily.

The constable examined the glowing end of his cigarette. 'He's a darned sight more used to this country than most of us.' He was beligerently defensive, a habit he had developed when talking about his offsider to the people around town.

'Would you like me to join him when he gets to Mulka?' Sanderson said, anxious to make amends. 'I could take my rifle. Two of us would be better than one.'

'That's not a bad idea, Tim. You've had a pretty rough trot, though. Do you feel up to it?'

'Oh I'm okay. I'd like to do it, Eric.'

'Good on you. Okay, you join Albert at Mulka. I'll go and rouse him out now and get the Rover packed up. You fellers may as well get some sleep. There's not much of the night left now. John, if you could get that line to Adelaide through for me, I'll just go round and dig old Albert out of bed, and by the time I get back, you should have the number.'

He stepped outside into the crisp night air. He rubbed his hands together. Much of the tiredness which had dogged him all day had left him. He had been humiliated by the futile search in Marree. Now he looked forward to the dawn.

CHAPTER SIXTEEN

Johnny regained consciousness and sat up. He tried to stand but fell down again. He held his hands over his eyes for several seconds until his head cleared and then he looked about him. The bright light from the lantern made him blink. Near it, he saw Frog, bent in a crouching position, leaning on the rifle for support.

'Where is he?' Johnny mumbled. Frog pointed towards the house and Johnny saw Fred, standing alone and watching them intently. 'Where are the others?'

'I sent them inside.' He moved closer, to help Johnny to his feet.

'How long ago? How long have they been inside?'

'Just a minute or so. The girl was cold. Why?'

Slowly, Johnny began to slap the dust from his clothes. 'You great fat idiot. Did you think of the radio in there?' He straightened his body painfully. 'No I bet you didn't. Here,' he reached out, 'give me that rifle.'

Frog stood back.

'Well, give it to me.'

'No, I think I'd better not, Johnny.'

'What do you mean you'd better not.' He grasped the rifle and wrenched it from Frog's grasp. 'Bring that light and follow me. You, Postman, get inside too. Quick.'

Fred turned and began to saunter towards the verandah. 'Faster,' Johnny ordered, and rammed the barrel between Fred's shoulder blades. Fred stumbled forward and broke into a trot. 'That's better. Now keep moving like that.'

They jogged to the steps. The dog was twitching on the ground. The house was in darkness. 'Frog, hurry up with that light. Get inside there with it quick.' Frog climbed the steps. 'You too.' Johnny jabbed Fred.

Inside, the verandah and kitchen were deserted. Johnny took the lantern and ran through to the dining and living rooms. No one was at the radio. He put the lantern on the table and with the rifle butt hammered at the set. It shook and began to sway. With his fingers he wrenched at it until, with a splintering crash, it fell across the room, trailing wires and coloured cables.

He picked up the lantern, leaped over the fallen set, and ran into the hallway. At the far end, he saw the three women, grouped around an open cupboard. 'All right,' he called, 'up here, all of you.'

He noticed Mrs Spencer make a sudden movement towards something shiny inside the cupboard. He pounded along the corridor. Mrs Spencer began to level a shotgun at him. He reached her and kicked at the gun, sending it spinning high from her hands. It smashed against a window and fell in a shower of broken glass at his feet. The three women backed away from him.

'You sneaky old bitch,' he muttered, with venom in his voice. Slowly, eyes on Mrs Spencer, he bent down, carefully placing the lantern and rifle against the wall and picking up the shotgun. From the crouched position, he suddenly lunged towards them, grasping the gun by the barrels and swinging it viciously in a downward arc. It cracked the floor only a foot in front of Mrs Spencer's feet. Gasping with fright, she jumped back, stumbling against Barbara who clutched at her. Betty, now wrapped in a blanket, began to scream.

Holding the gun limply, Johnny straightened up. His mouth took the shape of a smile but there was no suggestion of humour. 'So you'd pull a gun on me, Grandma,' he breathed.

Twisting quickly, he swung the gun over his shoulder and smashed the nearest window. He glanced at Mrs Spencer to make sure she was watching. 'Here's what I think of you and your gun,' he said, and strode down the hallway, breaking windows, grunting with each blow, immersed in a fury of cascading glass.

He reached the end of the hall and turned. The gun was still intact so he stamped back towards the women, beating the wooden stock against the wall until it shattered. He bashed the last splinter from it and then wildly threw the barrels out through the broken window.

Panting heavily, he stooped to pick up the discarded .303 rifle. 'Pull a shotgun on me, will you?' he said. He saw a segment of glass left in the window beside him and belted it out with the butt. 'All right,' he continued. 'If that's the way you want it, I can be rough too. Now all of you get back in the living room. Come on, move. You too, girlie.' He prodded at Betty.

'Don't try and touch her again,' Barbara said.

'She bit me,' he shouted.

Mrs Spencer stepped in front of the girl. 'Good on her. You're nothing but a mad dog. You should be treated like one. And you're a fool with guns.'

Johnny stopped, recognising a switch in her tone.

'That shotgun was loaded,' she said. The old woman was struggling to cope with the happenings of the night. They were beyond her range of previous experiences, but mishandling a gun was something more familiar, a deep sin that offended any inlander. 'I've never seen anyone do anything so stupid.' She screamed the words. 'That could have gone off any time while you were doing all that.' She waved her hands at the devastation around them. 'And you were holding the barrels. You could have blown your head off.'

She was chiding him, like a schoolmistress. Johnny felt a fresh surge of anger, a hatred for this old woman. He looked about him for an unbroken window. He found one near the end of the corridor. He turned to make sure Mrs Spencer was watching and splintered it with the butt. He looked at her again, and then pounded at the window until the whole frame collapsed and fell outside. He walked towards them, smashing every window frame until the side of the house was torn and splintered. Satisfied, he stopped and grinned at Mrs Spencer. 'See,' he announced triumphantly. 'That's what I think of you. You're nothing but an old dog yap yap yapping. You're an old bitch.' He laughed. 'You look silly, Grandma. Silly, do you hear me?'

He spun round quickly, on a sudden impulse. Frog and Fred

were watching him from within the living room. He relaxed. 'All right,' he said. 'All in there together. Now move.' He slashed the air with the rifle to indicate speed.

Barbara walked past him and then the girl, cowering against the wall. He pushed her roughly as she went by. 'You've got nothing to make you so proud,' he called after her. 'I've had better women than you.'

Mrs Spencer was level with him. 'You filthy beast,' she said.

He shoved her hard against the broken wall. 'Go on with you, Grandma, get in there with the others.'

Fred moved out into the hallway. 'You've had your fun,' he said. 'Stop pushing the women around.'

'Get back,' Johnny told him. 'I'd like to cut you in half right now but after what you did tonight I've got something better planned.' He grinned. 'I'm not very worried about you at the moment. You're time's coming tomorrow. I'm saving you up for something special. Just don't press me too far or I might forget and blow your brains out in front of these *ladies*.'

'If you want to get to Birdsville, you can't do without me and you know it.'

'Oh for shit's sake don't keep giving me that line. You're too cocksure, Freddie boy. I've watched you drive that bomb of yours and I reckon I could handle it. So just don't push me too far.'

'You'd get stuck or lost. You'd never make it.'

'Oh balls. Anyhow, what's it matter. You're going to take me to Birdsville.'

'Why should he?' Barbara said, from within the room.

'Because if he doesn't, your next. And don't you get any idea about pretending you're broken down or taking wrong roads. You get me to Birdsville by tomorrow, Freddie, or your girlfriend gets it. I might even decide to have a little sport with her first of all, if you know what I mean.'

'You bastard.'

'Oh, sticks and stones, Freddie. I've got you by the balls, haven't I. You get to Birdsville tomorrow and you die. You don't get to Birdsville and she dies. What's it going to be? I'm sure you'll appreciate the game, Sister.'

'You're crazy— stark, raving mad,' she said. She spoke slowly emphasising each word.

'Oh now now Sister, you know that's not true.' He was calm

again now and enjoying the restoration of his command. 'Besides, it's an unkind thing to say to your travelling companion. It's just that all this is worth a lot of money to me and I've got to protect my investment. Haven't I, Frog?'

The fat man looked at him uneasily.

'And we're partners, aren't we?' Johnny said.

'What about my share?'

'Oh now, Frog, don't worry. We'll share just as I planned.'

Fred said: 'I know what his share will be.'

'Now you just shut up. Frog stood by me out there and I won't forget it. Thanks Frog,' he said. 'We stick together and we'll be right. Just remember that. I'll look after you. This mob would throw you to the wolves.'

He pushed the group into the room, past the wreckage of the radio set. 'The baby's crying, Betty,' Barbara told the stunned girl.

'Well she can just let it cry,' Johnny said. 'We're going to all settle down here and have a nice quiet night. Keep an eye on them for a moment, Frog, while I just go and have a wash and get a few things from the kitchen.'

Johnny returned a few minutes later with two opened bottles of beer and a long, pointed butcher's knife. He gave one of the bottles to Frog.

'What are you going to do with that knife?' Mrs Spencer asked.

'Nothing if everyone behaves.' He swallowed a mouthful of beer. 'I sort of feel lost without the little gun any more. I thought this'd be handy.'

He rotated the knife in his hand. There were red marks on his fingers from their contact with the scalding bore water, but he ignored them. The long blade had his total attention. 'Looks nice and sharp, doesn't it? This is for tomorrow, Sister, unless we get to Birdsville. One tit at a time, right off,' he looped the blade through the air in a series of simulated incisions, and then once across the throat. 'How about that?'

He glanced casually at Fred. 'You'll take me there, won't you?'

At dawn, Mrs Spencer cooked some more steak and they ate breakfast. No one spoke. Johnny seemed to have developed a fondness for the carving knife. He touched it incessantly, except while he ate, during which time he reverently placed it on the table beside his plate.

Soon after seven, they went outside to board the truck. The dog had died during the night and lay in a tormented shape near the steps. Johnny kicked it aside and walked to the truck.

He used the knife as a baton to indicate to Barbara that she should get in. Again, Frog climbed on the back, but most of the load had gone and he was able to sit on the edge of the tray, with his legs dangling over the side. Johnny took the rifle with him.

Fred pumped some fuel into the tank, topped the radiator, started the motor and clambered into his seat. Betty and Mrs Spencer, lazily flicking flies away from their faces, watched in silence. Fred signalled the older woman over to the truck. 'Mrs Spencer,' he called, above the throb of the motor, 'if anything happens to me, will you see that Ivan gets a decent burial. It's only a shallow grave I dug for him.'

Mrs Spencer's eyes blinked behind her glasses as she nodded.

Fred reversed the truck back on to the track. He nodded again to Mrs Spencer and lifted his hand in a static wave to Betty. Barbara noticed the gesture. It was like a salute, a final farewell.

Fred pushed the lever into first gear and the truck lurched forward. Barbara had to steady herself against the dashboard. She watched Betty Spencer as the truck rolled past. She was standing by herself, arms clasped in front of her, a young, pathetic figure. She hadn't spoken all morning and now the sun seemed to have drawn all emotion from her face. Mechanically, her eyes followed them as the truck rumbled between the homestead and the steaming bore.

On one side, water being delivered from the bowels of the earth hissed and splashed. On the other, two women watched in silence, unmoving, as though carved from stone. Absurd thoughts crowded Barbara's mind. Of women, farewelling ancient warriors heading for a war in which they were certain to die. Of spectators lining the path to the guillotine. Only Betty was in sight now. A woman watching her lover being taken to the firing squad. Had Fred loved her? The truck bounced over a pipe laid across the track, and the girl disappeared from Barbara's view.

She eased herself back on the seat and saw Fred looking at her. She felt embarrassed that he had seen her staring at the girl. 'She still doesn't look well,' she said, hoping he would believe that it was a case of professional interest. 'She's had a big shock.'

'She'll get over it,' Fred said unemotionally and seemed to return his concentration solely to driving.

But he thought of Betty Spencer. She might get over it but he doubted if she would change. Often, as he left Clifton Hills, on his regular runs to Birdsville, he thought of her. It had been a painful experience in the past but today, despite all that had happened, he felt less concerned because now, at last, he felt he understood. She was weak. She was good looking and she could stir the loins with the way she walked and stood and looked at you, but she was uncertain of herself and had no more control than a wayward cat. Any man came along, *any man*, and she had to see if she could tempt him to take his pants off. He pictured the scene of Betty and Johnny in the dining room. You can't help yourself, he told her. Stir the bloke. Not that you'd do anything. Just flirt and give that come hither look to test yourself out and then fob the fellow off and wait for the next bloke to come along. A deadly type to be living in such an isolated, woman-starved part of the world as this. You're weak, Betty, he thought, and, for the first time since he had known her, Fred felt sorry for her rather than for himself.

He felt relieved. But because the track was particularly rough at this point, no sign of emotion emerged through his mask of concentration. Right now, he was just the Birdsville mailman, intent on delivering his load.

He drove through a long, sandy creek. His driving fascinated Barbara. His eyes moved constantly, watching the sand disappearing beneath the nose of the truck, flitting ahead to size up the ruts and hollows that lay twenty yards beyond, returning, glancing quickly at the side of the track, up ahead again, then back, moving, sizing up, all the time. His left hand regularly sought the gear lever and thrust it into the correct gear with a wristy decisiveness. His hands played on the steering wheel, sometimes gripping it, other times almost fondling it. The truck, the noisy, hot, shaking truck seemed part of him and she liked it better for the thought.

Most of the time his left leg stayed bent across the shorter lever that held the transmission in four-wheel drive. Once, while he was depressing the clutch, the lever jumped out of engagement and they almost stopped. His feet danced on pedals, his hands thrust at levers. Back into four-wheel drive. Main lever into first.

Left leg back into place, securing the shorter lever. The cabin shook with the grinding vibration of the motor working at full throttle.

Then they were through the sand and Fred relaxed and the sound of the engine subsided into a monotonous throb. 'I'll have to fix that,' he said, more to himself than to Barbara. 'Bastard of a thing.'

He turned to her. 'Sorry. Didn't mean to swear, but sometimes the old truck gets me down.'

They bounced through a sequence of gravelly wash-outs and the violent shaking pitched her towards the roof. 'Hang on,' he called, and grabbed her knee. She put her hand on his, and they drove that way for several minutes. Eventually he spoke. 'Can't have you breaking your neck on my truck.' And he took his hand from hers and gripped the steering wheel.

They jolted over the track for half an hour and then came to a fork where the route divided into three. An abandoned truck tyre lay on the middle track. Fred slowed and swung to the right.

'This is the extreme outside wet weather track I was telling you about,' he said. Johnny waved the knife to acknowledge the information. He seemed in a pleasant mood again this morning and happily played with the knife, spinning its handle in the palm of his hand or frequently picking at the seat with the long point. Barbara now sat well away from him, so that she was pressing against Fred.

The countryside worsened. Gradually, even the stark vegetation that had grown around Clifton Hills gave way to flat, stony desert. Once the noise of the truck disturbed a dingo, a hundred yards to their right, and it slunk into the wastelands.

The day became hotter. After an hour, Fred let the truck roll to a stop. Johnny flashed the blade. 'What's the stop for? Tyres?'

Fred nodded and began to roll himself a smoke. 'Tough on tyres out here,' he remarked. 'Whose going to stretch their legs?'

'You can, but stay in front of the truck where I can see you. The sister and me are going to stay side by side all day, aren't we?'

She looked at the knife. Johnny with the gun had been frightening enough, but the relish with which he wielded the knife sent shivers of fear through her. It was a new toy, and he seemed eager to use it.

Frog got off and sat in the shade beneath the vehicle's tail.

At the front, Fred unhooked the water bag. 'Anyone care for a drink of water?' he asked. 'How about you, Barbara?'

'Yes please.' Fred walked to Johnny's side.

'Not this way,' Johnny said, tilting the knife so that its blade pointed towards Barbara's ribs. 'Round your side and pass it through to her that way.'

Fred walked around and handed her the bag. She drank from it and then Johnny took it from her and quickly swallowed three mouthfuls. All the time his eyes were on Fred.

'Frog,' he called, 'do you want a drink?'

'Yeah,' Frog called. 'Get him to bring it around to me. This sun's too much for me. I've had it.'

Fred reached for the water bag. 'You stay where I can see you,' Johnny told him. 'Come and get the drink here Frog. I'm not taking my eyes off this character today.'

Grumpily, Frog walked up to the cabin. 'Geeze, I feel crook out in the sun,' he told Johnny.

'You'll be right when we get moving. Hurry up and finish so's we can get going again. We've got a timetable to keep. Birdsville's the deadline tonight, isn't it Fred?'

'We'll make it,' Fred said, his voice flat.

'Oh now, don't sound so disinterested.' He squirmed in his seat to find a more comfortable position. 'You know, if you do this properly, I might even change my mind about you. You remember,' he waved the knife, 'what I said I was going to do to you. I mightn't kill you if you get me there on time and you don't try to put something over me.'

Barbara looked at him hopefully. 'See, the sister likes that, don't you, dear?'

She looked at him with a pleading expression on her face. 'If you get to Birdsville, you're in the clear. There's nothing we can do to hurt you. Don't harm him. Please.'

'I told you I'd think about it.' He leaned forward so that he could see Fred clearly. 'Just get us to Birdsville on time and you've got a chance. I don't feel a bad bloke today.' He smiled at Barbara, and she drew away from him.

Fred restarted the truck and they juddered into motion on the long, easterly detour into Sturt's Stony Desert.

Long before the aircraft reached Clifton Hills, Eric Wallis saw the smoke. It was rising vertically from the horizon, staining the pure sky like a thin charcoal smudge on bleached fabric. At first, he feared it was the homestead burning. But as the Cessna drew closer, he could distinguish the smoke rising from flames beyond the cluster of buildings. The oily black column suggested rubber burning. He wondered if it were the mail truck, but a low sweep across the house revealed the blazing pile of tyres and the waving figure of Mrs Spencer.

Gus Cochrane landed on the gibbers near the house and Wallis ran to the woman.

'I couldn't think of anything else to do,' she said, apologising for the crackling, dirty bonfire. She was much less calm than she had been during the night, having been engulfed in a late wave of shock. Her eyebrows were singed and above the acrid aroma of burning rubber the policeman could identify the pungent smell of burnt hair.

'I dragged a few tyres over there and poured petrol on them,' she continued. 'Must have used too much. It went up with a terrible whoosh.' She touched her scorched hair and brittle strands fell away. 'I didn't know what else to do. We had no radio. There's no car on the place with the men gone. I didn't know what to do but I had to do something. There are a couple of new tyres in there,' she added, as though seeking forgiveness for a wrong doing. 'I didn't mean to burn them, just the old ones, but we needed more smoke.'

Wallis could see Betty Spencer, baby in her arms, watching from the verandah. She was surrounded by debris: broken glass, shattered walls and window frames. Wallis was appalled.

The old woman told the sergeant of the night's happenings and confirmed that the truck had gone towards Birdsville along the most eastern loop of the track. 'I didn't expect anyone in a plane,' she said, still in shock. 'My only hope was that the men from the drilling site might come in. Although, I think I've burned a couple of their tyres.' She covered her eyes with both hands. For her, destroying someone else's property was close to ultimate sin. 'They're due in here any day. I didn't dare say anything last night for fear of what that creature might do, but I know the geologists are keen to get their big tyres. They've had to wait weeks. I thought they might be close so I lit the fire to hurry them up.'

Suddenly, uncontrollably, the old woman began to cry. And the black smoke poured into the sky.

Several times during the morning, Fred stopped the truck to let the tyres and the engine cool. The motor was now boiling when it pulled hard in soft surfaces, and he made regular stops to let the engine temperature ease back to a safe level. The heat was so intense that all of them climbed from the vehicle and sat in the shade while Fred checked the vehicle, and passed the water bag.

Gradually the track swung to the north again, and when the sun was at its zenith, they rejoined the outside wet weather track — the shorter of the detours — at a long sandhill. They followed the hill for several miles and then swung away across Dead Man Plain. Here, there were signs that heavy rain had fallen. The plain was spotted with brown, where pools of water had dried into buckled layers of mud, and occasionally the wheels sank in soft patches of clay.

Johnny had stopped playing with the knife. He had taken off his jacket and was clutching it on his lap. He had undone the front of his shirt, to let the warm breeze lick at his perspiring body. Every few minutes he lifted himself from the seat to prise his trousers away from his sticky legs. Occasionally, his eyes closed and his head lolled back.

At first Barbara watched him in case there was some opportunity for her to do something. Push him out. Grab the knife. Something. But now she was feeling both hot and sick. The desert and its overwhelming, nostril-searing heat had sapped her initiative and she merely hoped that the man with the knife would spare Fred. Spare them both.

Fumes from the motor, made more volatile and noxious because of the terrible heat, filled the cabin and she feared she would be violently sick. She let her head slump against Fred's shoulder and left it there, despite the constant jarring as he steered and changed gears.

They left Dead Man Plain and entered a long, stringy chain of dunes running to the north. They crossed several short claypans. On these, Fred avoided the track and skirted wide around the edges, seeking firm going. The claypans appeared dry but a thin, cracking crust hid a gluey bog just below the surface. Fred knew the truck would sink to the axles if he tried to cross them. He thought of bogging the truck deliberately; he could do it so they would never get out. And he thought of the way the man with the knife would react and kept on going.

He was climbing into the sandhills from such a claypan when he heard the aeroplane. At first he thought it was a different sound in the truck's motor. Then he saw it: a small, high-wing monoplane banking low on their left-hand side. It was so close he could make out two figures in the cabin.

Johnny saw it too and instantly shook off the heat-induced lethargy. He reached down for the rifle and rested it between his knees. The plane flew out of sight behind a sandhill.

Johnny watched, to see if it would reappear and then glanced quickly across at the driver. 'Who was that?' he asked. 'Do you know?'

Barbara had been dozing and she woke with a start. She straightened up. 'What happened?' she asked.

'A plane just flew low over us,' Johnny said, peering out over the hills. 'Who was it, Fred?'

Fred licked his parched lips before answering. 'Honestly, I don't know,' he said. 'There aren't any planes up here that I know of.'

'Well it must have been someone who knows you. They came down so low.'

'That doesn't mean anything. Any aircraft would come down low to see us because we're probably the only vehicle they'd see for three hundred miles or so.'

'Yeah, but what were they doing here in the first place?' He grabbed Barbara's arm and pulled her close to him. 'Look, if this is part of some trick you're trying to work on me ...'

'Keep that knife away from her,' Fred said. 'If we hit a decent sized bump, you could put that thing right through her accidentally. Just calm down. I don't know who it was any more than you do. For all we know, it might just have been some geologist doing an aerial survey or something. There was an aircraft down at Marree doing one of those a couple of months ago. Could be the same thing up here.'

Johnny slackened his grip on Barbara's arm. 'They wouldn't be doing a survey in a small plane like that.' He put the rifle back on the floor where he could quickly reach it. He flourished the knife. 'Don't forget I've got this,' he said. 'Now take it easy when we get to the top of this next hill. If anything goes wrong, anything, she gets the knife in the ribs and I ask questions afterwards. Understand?'

The truck bumped its way through twin ridges of sand to the

crest of the sandhill. There was no sign of the aircraft.

'Where's it gone?' Johnny said, more to himself than as a question to the others. One eye screwed up against the glare, he searched the sky.

Fred changed gear, followed the winding path between rows of saltbush, and drove on to another small, flat claypan.

'Where could it have got to?' Johnny asked. 'It couldn't have flown out of sight in a minute or so.'

'Well, apparently it has. And for the love of Heaven, stop flashing that knife about. The plane's gone and that's all there is to it.'

Johnny leant out the doorway and looked behind them, in case the aircraft had circled. 'I'd like to know what they were doing up here,' he said. 'Take it easy up this next sandhill. I want to have a good look from the top.'

Fred drove off the edge of the claypan and climbed the next hill, a long, winding ascent. Near the top, the track flattened out and Johnny waved to him to stop.

'You stay here,' he said, as Fred braked the truck to a halt. 'I'm just going to walk up to that mound over there and see what I can see. The girl comes with me.'

He jumped out, laid the rifle on the ground and put on his jacket. Barbara hesitated. He motioned her to get out of the truck with a suggestive flash of the knife.

'What's up, Johnny?' Frog asked. He slipped off the tray and flopped into the shade beneath the truck.

'I saw a plane a few minutes ago.' He looked at the fat man, who had rolled on to his back. 'Didn't you see it? What's wrong with you?'

'I feel crook,' Frog groaned. 'It's the heat.'

'Get yourself a drink of water. Come on, Sister, you and I are going to have a looksee. You first.' He pointed towards a high sandy mound ahead of them. From it, he would command a view of miles of country.

'Johnny,' Frog called out after him, 'get me the water bag before you go. I haven't got the strength to move. It's the sun. It's got me.'

Johnny turned. 'If you were thirsty enough you could get it. Stop snivelling and just wait till I get back.' He followed the girl to the base of the mound. He put the rifle against a saltbush and gripped the girl's hand in his.

'Can't you put that knife away,' she pleaded.

'No.' He began to climb in the loose sand and yanked her after him. She stumbled and fell. He pulled her roughly to her feet and together they scrambled up.

They reached the top and Johnny let out his breath in a hiss. Ahead of them, the track wound down into another, much larger claypan. On it was the aircraft. It had attempted to land and the wheels had broken through the shallow surface crust, tipping the plane on to its nose. Its propeller blades were bent and covered in mud. In the shade beneath the wing were two men. One was lying on his back, as though injured. The second man bent over him, occasionally glancing anxiously towards the track. He was holding a rifle.

'Stay where you are,' Johnny whispered to the girl. He slid down the sand and returned with the rifle. 'So you didn't know anything about the plane, eh?' he muttered.

'No, I swear we didn't,' she said.

'That's why he's got a gun, eh?' He lifted the rifle and took aim.

'What are you going to do?' she said.

'What's it look like?'

'You can't shoot them.'

'You keep your voice down or I'll cut your throat. Let me handle this.'

He squeezed the trigger. The rifle barked, loudly and powerfully. A puff of dust rose from the crust of clay just behind the men. The man with the gun spun round, searching the hills for the marksman. Johnny fired again and the man threw himself on the ground, beside his companion's body.

'You down there,' Johnny shouted. 'I've got you pinned down so listen to me. Can you hear me?'

A voice floated up to them. 'Who are you? Show yourself.'

'Not on your life,' Johnny yelled. 'You know who I am. Now you do as I tell you or the mailman and the girl are going to get hurt. Do you understand?'

'Where are they?' the voice called back.

'Right where I want them. We're going to drive past your plane in a minute. You attempt to stop us and the girl gets killed. Do you understand?'

There was no answer.

'Did you hear me.'

'I heard.'

'Well?'

'How do I know you've got the sister?'

Johnny turned to Barbara. 'Stand up,' he told her. She stood on the crest of the mound.

'Are you all right, Miss Dean?' the voice called. 'This is Eric Wallis.' She waved an arm. It was more a gesture of despair than reassurance.

'All right, get down,' Johnny told her. 'There you are,' he called. 'Now are you going to let us through or would you like me to cut her throat here?'

'You're bluffing,' Wallis shouted.

'Am I? Would you like me to prove that I'm not.' He grabbed Barbara's hair and wrenched her head back. She screamed.

'Miss Dean,' Wallis called.

'She's all right but *she* knows I'm not bluffing.' Johnny heard a sound behind him and looked down. Fred was at the bottom of the mound. 'Back to the truck,' Johnny ordered, 'or the girl will get it now. Do like I say.'

'Oh please, Fred,' Barbara pleaded. 'He will, I know he will.'

Fred backed away. Johnny watched him until he had reached the truck.

'Are you all right, Miss Dean?' Wallis was calling.

'She's all right. Now are you going to do what I say?'

'What do you want?' His voice was resigned.

'That's better. You and your partner stand up and walk out in front of the plane. I won't harm you.'

He saw Wallis slowly push himself up. 'My partner can't move. He's unconscious. He was knocked out when this happened.' He waved his hand at the plane.

'Well, you move. Now drop your rifle.'

Wallis hesitated.

'Go on,' Johnny shouted. The rifle fell at Wallis' feet.

'Good. Now march away from the plane to the far side of the claypan.'

He watched him pick a path over the cracked surface. When Wallis was a quarter of a mile clear of the track, he said to the girl: 'Come on. It's time we moved.'

They returned to the truck. Its motor was still idling. Fred was leaning against the doorway.

'Get in quickly,' Johnny told him.

Fred ignored the order. 'Are you all right Barbara?' he asked.

'No time for gossip now,' Johnny said. 'We've got to move quickly. She's all right. Get in both of you. And you, Postie, when you drive this buggy this time, make it move. We're going to get out of here in a hurry.'

He bundled Barbara into the cabin and put the rifle on the floor. He began to climb in when he remembered Frog. 'Are you all right?' he called. There was no answer. 'Frog, are you on the back?'

He jumped down and ran to the rear. Frog still lay on the sand beneath the truck and directly in the path of a wheel. His eyes were half closed.

'Frog, for Christ's sake get up on the back. We've got to get out of here.'

'I feel crook, Johnny,' Frog muttered. 'I don't think I can stand up.'

'You'll soon get up,' Johnny said. He slipped the knife into his belt and dragged Frog by the jacket into a seated position. 'Come on, on your feet.' He pulled him upright and flung him against the side of the truck. 'Now get up, quick.'

'I can't.'

'Oh, for ...' He grabbed Frog around the hips and lifted him until all but his legs were on the tray.

Suddenly, the truck jolted forward. Johnny pulled out the knife and raced for the front. He reached it and jumped aboard just as the truck was gathering speed. He noticed the look of dismay on Barbara's face. He swished the knife at her viciously, so that its point scratched her bare arm. 'So, you two were trying to leave me,' he snarled.

'You said you were in a hurry,' Barbara shouted back, holding her wounded arm.

'Lies,' he screamed. 'You tricked me with that plane and now you try to leave me out here.' He pulled her towards him and thrust the point of the knife against her back.

'I've had enough of your lies and trickery, both of you,' he said. 'Postman, you drive us straight across this next claypan and up over the next hill as fast as you can. Try anything and this knife will go in so deep you'll see it come out her belly.'

The truck had passed the mound and for the first time Fred saw the crippled Cessna, and the unconscious man beside it. He could pick out Eric Wallis standing a long way from the aircraft.

They thundered down the hill and on to the claypan. He swung the wheel to the left and began to follow the solid edge around the pan. Barbara gave a little cry as Johnny pressed harder with the knife. 'Where do you think you're going?' Johnny said. 'Why are you leaving the track?'

'Because we'll get bogged if we stay on it. You can see what happened to them.' Fred's mind was in a turmoil. Help was so near and here he was racing away from it.

They skirted the claypan with the truck jolting and bumping its way over the uneven surface. 'Faster,' Johnny screamed, as they approached the curving ascent up the sandhill.

Fred hit the hill at a speed that he would normally never attempt. The vehicle reared and bucked, throwing them all clear of their seats. Barbara cried out in pain again as the knife dug into her.

From the back, Fred heard another call. 'That's your mate,' Fred yelled to Johnny. 'What's happened to him?'

Johnny glanced back through the doorway. Frog was slipping off the side. As he watched, he saw Frog lose his grip and tumble into the sand.

'He's fallen off,' Johnny said. Automatically, Fred eased his foot from the accelerator.

Johnny looked back across the claypan. The man beside the Cessna was now sitting up and the other man was running towards him. Johnny saw Frog try to stand up, but fall again, grasping at his leg.

'Keep moving,' he said. Fred stared at him in disbelief.

'I said keep moving.' He looked back. Frog was shouting and waving both hands frantically. He stood up and attempted to hop after the truck but fell again.

A thought suddenly struck Johnny. 'My God, he'll talk,' he said and picked up the rifle. He twisted out of the doorway and took aim. The truck shuddered on a bump and the shot went wild. Then they had swung around a bend and Frog had disappeared.

Frog watched the truck drive away. He shouted Johnny's name

again and again but the truck did not return. He could hear its motor gradually growing fainter. He tried to hobble up the hill but he had injured his ankle in the fall and he had to sit down. Now there was no sound of the truck.

He heard a shout and looked back. One of the men from the plane was standing near the edge of the claypan, a rifle at the ready. 'Put up your hands,' the man called again, and began to climb the sandhill.

Tears were running down Frog's cheeks when Eric Wallis reached him. 'Stand up,' Wallis said.

'I can't,' Frog sobbed. 'I've busted my ankle.' He looked up at the man towering above him. 'He didn't stop. He didn't stop for me.'

Frog looked at the crashed plane, its tail rearing high above the clay, and at the rim of sand surrounding them. 'Are we going to die out here?' he asked.

Wallis grunted. 'You're not going to die yet. There's a Land-Rover coming up the track. We'll just sit and wait until it gets here. May take a day or two, but we'll be all right.'

Eric Wallis helped the injured man over to the aircraft. He was rough because he was in a foul mood, and he felt that way because he had failed. The high ridge of sand beside the track should have given him perfect shelter for an ambush, he reasoned, trying to justify the disaster.

The plane had touched down properly and run truly for the first hundred yards and then suddenly the clay had buckled, snagging the wheels and sucking the propeller through the thin crust and into the mud beneath. Wretched country. You could never trust it.

Frog was lying on his side in the shade of the aircraft, holding his ankle and moaning. Wallis ignored him. Cochrane was propped against the fuselage, holding a red handkerchief against his broken nose and breathing noisily through his mouth. Wallis stood up.

At that moment the big truck arrived. It came from the east, away from the track, bush bashing its way through the spinifex and low scrub until it reached the edge of the claypan. There it stopped, a big white Leyland that Wallis had not seen before.

'Is it safe to come out to you? Would we sink?' the driver called out. There were two men in the truck.

Wallis began to run, limping because one leg was bruised and sore. He waved, indicating a way to the opposite side of the clearing. He suddenly felt excited. 'Go that way,' he shouted. 'Keep to the edge. It's treacherous out here.'

As though to illustrate his point, his feet cut through a patch of clay where the surface had crazed into a pattern like soup plates. One ankle squelched in mud and he stopped, stepping back and circling towards the track, to await the newcomers.

The two men were more intent on the aircraft than the man. They glanced at Wallis, recognising him as a policemen and seeing that he clutched a rifle, but even as they spoke to him, their eyes were on the aircraft. It lay on the vast expanse of clay like a broken toy.

'No one hurt badly,' the sergeant said, answering their first question. 'The pilot's got a busted nose, but otherwise we're okay. What the hell are you doing here?'

'We saw you coming down. We were over there,' the older man jerked his thumb over his shoulder, 'and cut straight across country. Well, not straight across. We've had a few sandhills and one other claypan to dodge. We were up on a ridge when we saw you coming down. Lucky we were up high or we wouldn't have spotted you at all. We've come a good twelve miles since. Been slow going.'

He spoke with an American accent. His hair was grey and cut close to the scalp, so that no strand could point anywhere but straight out. The top of his head looked, Wallis thought, like a shorn brush.

'You from the oil camp?' the policeman asked, still bewildered by their arrival.

'Don't know if there's any oil out there, but we're from the camp where they're trying to find it,' the man said, and smiled. His younger companion began walking to the aircraft. 'We were on our way to the homestead at Clifton Hills to collect a few things the mail contractor was going to deliver. Big tyres, hence the big truck,' the older man continued. He tapped the white Leyland. 'We've got a supply road that runs from the camp and joins the Birdsville Track maybe another twenty miles south of here. Comes in where the track goes wide to dodge a big sand ridge down there.'

The American had eyes of an exceptionally pale blue. He

focused them on the aircraft. 'What was it? Motor trouble?'

'No. Nothing was wrong. We were trying to land.'

'What the hell for?'

'I'll tell you the whole story if you'll do something for me. What's your name?'

'Ross. Frank Ross.'

'Look Frank, this is a matter of life and death. I'm Eric Wallis, sergeant of police at Marree and I want you to leave your mate here to look after things and I want you to take me north towards Birdsville. How quickly will this thing go?'

Ross was confused. 'This truck? It's empty and it's fairly new, but I don't know.'

'Well, let's find out. We've got another truck to catch before it crosses the Diamantina.'

'And what the hell happens if we don't catch it?' But Wallis was already hurrying to the aircraft to collect his prisoner and tell Cochrane that he had hitched a ride towards Birdsville.

CHAPTER SEVENTEEN

At four o'clock, the mail truck entered Queensland. It crossed the State border when it drove through a gap in the rotting fence that ran down from a sandhill. Last century, this had been the site of a customs post, a checking point for the herds of cattle moving down from the grazing lands to the north. Occasionally the cattle still came but the customs men had long since gone, swept away by the Federation of the States. Just the fence remained, a decaying symbol of an attempt to divide a land that offered man the common miseries of heat and loneliness.

Fred would have welcomed customs men now. Any men, for that matter. Having to drive away from Eric Wallis had left him with the wretched feeling that defeat was inevitable. Wallis, the most competent man to help them, had failed. Now, there was no one else he could count on. Carl Davis, the constable at Birdsville, was a good man but with the outpost's radio damaged, he was ignorant of their need. Maybe, by chance, he would be waiting for them at the river. Maybe several of the townspeople would be there, knowing the mail was due. The thought welled up inside him, bringing him a new hope, a new confidence. It *was* possible. The town was so starved of news the people might travel down to meet him at the river, to see him cross and catch an early glimpse of the new sister.

What would he do then? He wasn't sure. But the sight of a crowd at the river must confuse Johnny and upset whatever plans he had made. And if he could rattle Johnny, he had a chance.

Fred took his eyes from the track for a moment and glanced across at the other man. The sun was blazing at Johnny through the doorway, draining all the moisture from his sprawling body and evaporating it instantly. The man seemed close to exhaustion. His head hung back and his eyes gazed unfocused towards the roof. His teeth were clenched together so that he hissed as he gulped in the hot, thin air.

If the two men had been together, Fred would have attempted a sudden swerve, some sort of attack. He was used to this heat, to the way the air scorched the nostrils and flowed raw down to the lungs. Johnny was not and he was suffering. With just the two of them. Johnny would have been vulnerable. But stretched across his chest he held Barbara's arm and pressed against the wrist was the knife. His body seemed impotent with fatigue but his arms were locked in an attitude of sheer menace.

Barbara. If only she hadn't been on the truck. If only he could get her safely away from Johnny. He gripped the wheel in frustration and realised just how deeply concerned he was for her. Johnny mustn't be allowed to hurt her. Quite suddenly, with the thought of something happening to Barbara, the loneliness that had lurked within Fred for years became a real and frightening thing. Why couldn't this woman have chosen some other time to travel with him? Why this time, when everything was so different, so deadly?

Barbara was leaning as far from Johnny as his grip would allow. Her head was tilted away from him so that she touched Fred's shoulder with every bump. The truck crashed through a series of wash-outs and she lifted her head. With her free hand, she pushed back her hair, then shifted her position slightly. She glanced at Fred and saw him looking at her. She tried to smile but her dry lips wouldn't part. She leaned against Fred once more and with her outstretched hand, gently covered his left hand on the steering wheel. She left it there for several seconds until, finger by finger, it slipped away.

Fred thought of Barbara for a long time. The truck rumbled on.

The track began to twist towards a wide spread of trees and Fred knew the river was near. They drove over a slight crest. On the horizon, he saw the flash of a distant roof and the stationary blades of a windmill. Birdsville. Just the river to cross. So this was it. The end of the journey up the Track.

Fred reached for Barbara's hand. He gripped it and she lifted her head and looked at him. 'Birdsville,' he said, softly so that Johnny would not hear. The noise of the motor drowned his voice. With exaggerated lip movements, he mouthed the name. She nodded and sat up straight, peering ahead for some sign of the settlement, but they had driven down from the crest and Birdsville lay hidden beyond lower ridges and the trees that marked the edge of the Diamantina.

Johnny stirred, noticed the trees, but missed their significance and closed his eyes. His head rolled to the left and rested against the pillar.

'Can you swim?' Fred mouthed the words for Barbara. She narrowed her eyes, not understanding him. He released his grip on the wheel and mimed a swimming stroke. She nodded. He gripped her hand again. 'Be ready,' his lips said.

Again the hope that someone might be waiting at the river grew inside him. He released Barbara's hand as he changed into a lower gear. He would know soon. The truck curled through the timber, topped a gentle slope and there, one hundred yards ahead, was the water.

The Diamantina was fifty yards wide, a brown, surging torrent that twisted and swirled and frothed as it raced over its stony bed. The track, eroded and scoured, ran down gradually to the water. It emerged on the other side among rearing sandbanks, the wheel marks lost beneath the crumbling sand. Further back, broad trees formed a line parallel with the river bank. From several of the trees rose flocks of birds, disturbed by the truck. Otherwise, the far bank was deserted. No one was waiting for them. Fred had a crushing, illogical feeling of disappointment. His eyes searched the bank for someone.

Barbara pressed his hand and he looked at her. She was staring at him hopefully, expecting something. Fair enough. If she was game, he was ready to try.

Fred made sure that Johnny still had his head turned. Then he reached across Barbara, sliding his left hand along her arm until he had a firm grip near the wrist menaced by the knife. He glanced at her and she nodded to indicate she was ready.

The truck was on the final run down to the river. Fred waited until they were within twenty yards of the water. He let go the steering wheel. In the same instant, he flicked off the ignition and jammed on the brakes. He wrenched at Barbara's arm.

The jarring stop hurled Johnny towards the dashboard. He dropped the knife and threw up his hand to protect himself. His other hand released its grip on the girl. Fred tumbled out the doorway, hauling Barbara after him. The truck, still in low gear, was juddering to a halt.

The girl fell on top of him and they both sprawled on the ground. Fred jumped up and pulled her after him. 'Run,' he shouted and dragged her towards the river. He was pulling too hard and she fell again.

Johnny scrambled out of the truck.

Fred helped Barbara to her feet. He ran behind her, glancing back. Johnny was reaching inside the truck for the rifle. He called to them to stop.

They were in the water now, but it was too shallow to dive and the stones hidden by the brown water were large and slippery and both of them crashed to their hands and knees.

Fred stood up, body dripping. Johnny had the rifle and was running towards them. He was only a few yards from the water. They had no chance now. Not both of them.

Barbara splashed out into thigh-deep water. She turned. 'Go on,' Fred shouted, waving her away from the ford towards deeper water. 'Go with the current and keep under.'

She hesitated. 'Go on.' He flung his arm at her in a desperate signal and turned to face the other man.

Johnny was at the water's edge, waving the rifle and shouting.

In that instant, Fred decided he was going to die. He had surrendered his life for Barbara and, with the decision, his mind held no fear of death. If, in dying, he could distract Johnny's attention for a few more moments, she could reach deep water and be swept to safety.

Johnny, face flushed with heat and anger, was waving the rifle towards the girl. 'Tell her to come back,' he yelled at Fred.

The two men stood, ten feet apart, eyeing each other. Fred began to pick his way across the rocks towards the bank.

'Tell her,' Johnny called.

Fred lunged at him but his foot slipped on the slime and he fell with a splash. Instinctively, he rolled to one side, expecting to hear the bark of the rifle. The rocks hurt his side. He winced, and slipped further. As he moved, his eyes caught sight of Barbara. She had stopped, a crescent of water surging around her waist as she looked back at them.

Fred pushed himself up and moved between the rifle and the girl. 'Go,' he shouted. 'Before he kills you.'

Still there was no rifle shot. Fred turned around. He did it slowly. Dead men have no need to hurry, and he felt like a man who, being committed to die, was no longer alive.

Johnny had the rifle high in his hands, as though about to hit him. 'This isn't what I planned,' he screamed. 'Make her come back.'

Fred lunged at him but again his feet slipped on the wet rocks and Johnny easily dodged his sprawling dive. He pointed the rifle down at Fred's back.

'Come back now or your boyfriend gets it,' he yelled. Barbara hesitated, straining to hold her position against the current.

Fred turned his head. 'For God's sake, get out of here,' he called.

'Come back or I shoot him,' Johnny said.

Fred began to push himself up. 'What's it matter? You're going to kill me anyhow.' With the last word, he sprang at Johnny. It was futile, and he knew it, but he sprang. Johnny saw the attack coming and with the rifle butted him on the back of the neck. Fred slumped at his feet. His legs were in the water. A wave rippled across one foot. Johnny waited, poised for another attempt, but Fred lay still.

'Now you,' he called to the girl, who had begun to retreat with the current, 'come out here or I shoot him. Now.'

Barbara looked wildly behind her, as though trying to sum up whether she should attempt escape or not.

'Come out here and I won't shoot him.'

She stared at him disbelievingly. Her hands paddled the water, as she tried to retain her balance in the strong current.

'I could shoot both of you right now if I wanted to,' he said.

'How can I trust you?' she called.

He lowered his rifle so that the barrel touched Fred's back. 'You've got no choice. If I wanted to shoot you both, I'd do it now.'

She began to push her way back towards the bank. The water

curled high around her body. When she could stand more easily, she called, 'What are you going to do with us?'

He beckoned her to come right out. 'Just leave you here on this bank. Alive. Now come on back here.' He was breathing more easily.

Slowly, eyes not daring to leave Johnny, she stumbled through the shallows, her frock dripping and clinging to her body. Johnny backed away from the prostrate Fred as she reached the edge. She knelt down to examine him.

'That's it,' Johnny said, still backing away. 'You stay with him there. Don't try getting away again.'

He edged around to a reed-filled pocket of water beside the track and put down the rifle. He dropped to his hands and knees and drank copiously from cupped hands. He splashed his face and neck and then picked up the rifle and walked to the truck. He returned with two lengths of rope, one of them long and dirty with use. He retained it and threw the shorter rope to Barbara.

'Tie him up,' he said.

'Tie him up? You said you were going to leave us here unharmed.'

'Just do as I say.'

'But why this?' She held up the rope.

'Tie him up now and I won't have to hit him again. I'm not going to shoot him but he probably doesn't believe that. So unless you tie him up, he'll rush me again. Then I'll either have to hit him or shoot him. So tie him up.'

She pulled nervously at the rope. 'What are you going to do with me?'

'I'm not going to shoot you.' He smiled at her. 'I'll just tie both of you and drive away.'

She glanced at Fred. He was still unconscious. 'But why tie me too?'

'Now be fair, Sister. Give me a bit of a start. If I left you free you'd have him untied in a jiffy and then you'd both be across the river. Next thing, there'd be people chasing me. Now you know I don't want that.'

'But you can't just leave us here. What if no one comes?'

'Sister, suppose you start tying his hands together. You're not in much of a position to argue.' He lifted the rifle. 'If I were you, I'd take the chance. Now do as I say. Tie him up.'

For several seconds, she looked up at Johnny, her mind undecided. He wagged the rifle at her. She moved slowly, looking up anxiously all the time as she swung Fred's legs clear of the water. Pushing some large stones, she created a space into which she rolled his unconscious body.

His mouth was beginning to move and she knew he would soon be conscious. She placed his wrists across each other and quickly roped them together. She began to stand up, holding the unused loops of rope.

Johnny waved her back. 'Now his feet,' he said. 'Carry the rope down to his feet and tie them together.' She did as he said and then turned, waiting for a further instruction.

'Good,' he said. 'Now get over there.' He indicated the side of the track, just in front of the truck. He waited until she had moved and then walked down to Fred, grabbed the rope below his wrists and used it to drag him clear of the track. 'Hate to run over him,' he said, releasing him near the girl.

Fred had begun to stir. Johnny picked up the loose rope trailing from Fred's feet and began to coil it. 'Your turn now,' he told the girl. 'Sit down beside your boyfriend.'

'Are you sure you're going to leave us here unharmed?' she said.

'You've got my word,' he said and smiled. Her face whitened, and she backed away from him.

'Oh now come on,' he said, his voice sharper. 'I can't spend all day arguing with you. Sit down.' He stepped towards her and she sat down so hastily that she almost rolled on to her back.

Johnny pulled the rope, swinging Fred's feet close to hers. Quickly he bound her ankles and then her wrists. He stood back and surveyed them. He laughed.

CHAPTER EIGHTEEN

Johnny Parsons did not hear the first rifle shot or the snarl of the passing bullet. The sounds were lost in the boom of water rushing over the crossing. The second shot hit the front of the truck near him, gouging paint and metal from a battered mudguard. At first, he turned towards the truck and stared at it in bewilderment. It took him several seconds to realise someone was shooting at him.

He spun around, expecting to find the marksman nearby. The track was deserted. He stepped backwards, retreating from the unknown.

'Throw down your gun,' a voice called. The sound was indistinct, muffled by the roar of the Diamantina. 'I could have hit you with either of those bullets. Drop your gun.'

The voice was to the right of the track, where a group of leafy coolibahs climbed a slope. Behind them was a sand ridge. A set of footprints curved down through the sand towards the trees. Very slowly, Johnny lowered his rifle. He put it down gently, reluctantly, his eyes all the time searching the trees for the man who had fired at him.

Eric Wallis stepped from behind the speckled trunk of the nearest coolibah. He was about one hundred paces away, and difficult to distinguish against the shadowy bark of the tree. He held a rifle with both hands.

'You all right, Fred?' the policeman shouted.

'No, he's not.' Barbara screamed the words. 'This madman attacked him.' She shuffled closer to the unconscious mailman. With rescue at hand, and the sight of Johnny Parsons disarmed and dazed beside the truck, she began to cry. She felt ashamed, but couldn't stop. Tears gushed from her eyes. Because her hands were bound she couldn't wipe her face, and she shook her head violently.

'Fred's not dead?'

'No. No.' She shook her head all the more violently.

'Are you okay, Sister?' Wallis called, concerned at the girl's sudden show of agitation. He began to move from the tree and then hesitated. He wanted Johnny Parsons to walk well clear of the truck and his two trussed victims. He had no way of knowing whether the man carried any other weapons. The policeman wanted him in the open before he himself left the security of the trees. And that was his mistake.

Only Johnny Parsons saw the other man limping down the sandhill behind the policeman.

'Are you okay?' Wallis shouted again, his attention still focused on the people at the river. The girl nodded. Fred was stirring, and jerked his wrists against the resistance of the ropes.

'Yes,' she said. 'Yes. I'm not hurt. Fred is, though. That man killed Ivan.' And in a torrent of words, she began to call out all the things Johnny Parsons had done since they left Marree, but her voice was lost in the rumble of the river and Wallis could not understand.

When Barbara had finished, he waved the rifle at Johnny Parsons. 'All right you,' he shouted. 'Move away from there. Come towards me.'

'I can't hear you,' Johnny lied. Wallis' gesticulations left no doubt as to the message, but Johnny was fascinated by the progress of the second man, who had now shuffled much closer to the policeman. It was not possible to distinguish who he was, because the man was hunched and leaning heavily on a large stick, but it was obvious he was trying to keep out of the policeman's sight. He moved slowly, limping from the shelter of one tree to the next.

'You can hear me all right,' Wallis boomed, using his sternest policeman's voice. 'Step away from those people and come towards me.' He moved a little further away from the tree trunk and waved his rifle to emphasise the urgency of the instruction.

Wallis was short of breath from the rush to reach the river and the shouting had been an effort. He was sore and stiff, too. The aircraft crash landing had bruised him and the American Ross had driven the big Leyland so fast over the rough track that his bruises had taken a fresh pummelling. One leg was now so painful he had difficulty in walking. Despite the pain, he had hurried more than a quarter of a mile from the place where Ross had parked the truck. Now that he stood still, and the emergency seemed over, his leg ached with a blazing intensity.

Johnny Parsons was slow to move. The man with the stick was almost behind the policeman.

'Come on,' Wallis ordered. He took a step and almost fell from the pain in his leg. And for the first time, he heard the man behind him. Had he been able to move freely, he may have avoided the blow but he was off balance, and slow. He had time to turn, raise one arm and call out in surprise.

Wielding the branch he had used as a crutch, the other man struck Wallis a terrible blow across the body. The branch broke. The impact drove the policeman against the tree, his body bent like a long, soft cushion that someone had slapped in the middle. The tree was forked at ground level, and he slid between the trunks, arms one side, legs the other. He hung limply, without a sign of movement.

The other man had fallen. He alone made a noise, for his ankle hurt and he cried out in pain. He lay on the ground for several seconds. He was by nature neither an aggressive nor a brave man, and he was fearful the policeman might move. But Wallis was as still as the tree his limp form now divided.

Eventually the man stood, doing so with difficulty and balancing on one leg. He let go the remains of the broken branch, picked up the police sergeant's rifle and, using its butt to support his weight, limped from the shadow of the tree.

'Frog,' Johnny called in astonishment, when the man was clearly visible in the sunlight. The fat man hopped towards him, keeping his hands on the rifle barrel and using the weapon as a walking stick. He was in a hurry to reach Johnny Parsons, but there was no welcoming smile on his face.

Johnny picked up his gun. 'How the hell did you get here. And who was that?'

'Some cop from Marree. He was in the plane. Remember the plane?'

Barbara tried to stand. 'Have you killed him?' she cried out. Being bound, she lost balance and sprawled across Fred. He groaned loudly.

The fat man ignored the girl. 'I came in a truck,' Frog said, intent only on Johnny. He was in pain. His eyes were glazed with the enduring shock of the day's happenings. 'Why the hell did you leave me back there?' he said.

Johnny ignored the question. 'Where's the truck now?'

'What? Oh, over the other side of the hill. You're a bastard for what you did.' He moved closer.

'Anyone else come with you?'

'Oh, for Christ's sake, yes, there was another bloke but I belted him over the head, too. He's all right. Flat as a pancake on his back in the sand.' Frog stopped, and confronted his partner. 'You left me to cop the lot, didn't you? I do all the work, you keep the opals and then you try to knock me off.'

Johnny waved a hand in the air, as though dismissing the protests. His mind was racing, trying to absorb the changed situation.

'Is the copper dead?' Johnny pointed his rifle barrel towards the crumpled figure at the tree.

Frog's thoughts stumbled over the question. The present had lost reality for him. His mind was still on the scene back at the claypan, where he had been abandoned. It took much concentration for the fat man to recall what had happened in the last few minutes.

'The sergeant? No, I don't think so. I just flattened him. He's all right. He won't move for a while. Christ, my leg's sore. I've busted the ankle.'

'Can you walk on it?'

'Not without a stick or something.' Frog shifted his weight and leaned more heavily on the up-ended gun. 'Did it when I fell off the truck. Why didn't you stop for me? You had plenty of time.'

Johnny Parsons turned his back on Frog. He needed time to think and couldn't with that fat fool jabbering at him. The mailman was now conscious and trying to sit up. The girl was kneeling beside him, her face stained with a mixture of river mud, tears and sand, and her eyes were anxiously studying the two men. Johnny scratched his head, as though the action would stir his mind out of the daze that the last few minutes had produced. He had been so clear as to what he should do, and now he had Frog back, crippled and unable to move quickly, and two other men who had come with him. The policeman was wedged in the tree and another man was lying on the sand, somewhere over the hill. It was this heat and the damned country. Together, they conspired against rapid thinking. Johnny struggled to grasp all the elements of the predicament.

'What about this other truck,' he said, turning to face the other man. 'Does it go better than the mailman's heap?'

'Yes, it does, and I've hidden the key if you're thinking of taking off and leaving me again,' Frog said. He was swaying with pain but his voice had a defiance Johnny hadn't noticed before.

'You can start a truck without a key,' Johnny said.

'You can't.'

Johnny tried to laugh. 'Oh look, talk some sense. We're in this together, remember? Look mate, our problem now is that we've got people everywhere.' He waved his hand in emphasis. 'We're not in the middle of nowhere anymore. There's a town just over the river. If the people there don't come to the river now, they'll come some time. Probably soon, if they're expecting the mailman. Someone, sometime, is going to come here so we've got to move quickly.'

He moved closer to Frog, with an arm outstretched in the classical pose of a person seeking a favour. 'Do you think you could walk back and do something about those two blokes you flattened? If they're not dead, it might be an idea to put a bullet into each of them.' He promoted the thought casually, as though suggesting lunch.

Frog stared at him in disbelief, but Johnny was still talking. 'If they follow me — us — across the river and tell the town, the whole show will be up. You just can't leave them there and risk everything.'

Frog shook his head. 'I knew you were like this. I knew it, but I just didn't want to believe it. You did try to shoot me, didn't you? You're a cold, rotten bastard. You were out to kill me back there at the plane. You'd kill anyone. You're only thinking of yourself.

You left me when I fell off the truck and then you took a shot at me.'

Frog shifted his weight to his sound leg and lifted the rifle. Johnny changed his own grip on the .303.

'Balls,' he said. 'I couldn't stop because Fred was driving. He wouldn't stop. You know what he's like. He said something about sand but he just kept on going. What could I do? Shoot him on the spot?'

Frog held the rifle more tightly.

'And I was taking a pot shot at the other bloke, the one at the plane, not you,' Johnny continued. 'Christ, why would I be shooting at you? I would have come back for you, once I knew the way to Birdsville. Well, this is it. Birdsville's only a mile or two across the river. I was coming back. See? I've tied those two up so as I could come and get you.'

'You were just going to ask the copper and he'd have handed me over to you, eh?' Frog's voice was nearly at shouting volume.

'I'd have brought the girl back in exchange. Her for you.'

'Well why have you tied her to the bloke?'

'Shit, will you stop arguing. What's troubling you? Your leg?' Johnny put out his hand once more. 'Here, let me help you sit down. Give us your gun and I'll get a proper stick for you to walk on. The sister can soon fix you up.'

He reached for the rifle.

'You must think I'm a stupid bugger,' Frog said, hopping back a yard. 'I came here and I flattened those two blokes so's I could get my share of the opals. I ought to take them all. I've done all the work. I've had enough of being the sucker for someone else. All my life people have been using me and then treating me like a fool. I do all the work on this job, you cause all the trouble but you do your bloody best to get me involved, and then you plan to piss off with all the money. You must think I'm crazy. I want the opals. I've earned them.' It was the longest speech of Francis Raymond Gardiner's life.

Flying low along the river, a squadron of pelicans glided through the crossing. They passed in silence, haughty birds that ignored the scattered figures near the bank. The two armed men were shouting at each other. As though drawn by the argument, a screeching flight of cockatoos wheeled from the far bank and, like a fluttering ribbon of white, headed for the branches of a dead tree that stood, drowned and naked, in a backwater near the ford. They settled in waves, noisily preening their feathers, fluttering wings and contesting landing rights. Yellow crests and white feathers flashed. For several enchanted moments, they transformed the wooden skeleton into a living, blossoming tree.

On the ground, Frog lost his balance and fell, crying out in pain.

From the branches came the screech of an alarm. The flight peeled from the tree, stripping it of life, and disappeared in a shrill cacophony of protest above the ruffled waters of the muddy Diamantina.

The noise of the birds was the first sound Fred recognised. He tried to move his hands but the rope jerked his bound ankles and he toppled to one side. The birds were still shrieking, but their cries were less strident now and were being drowned by the rumble of the flood. The familiar sounds seeped through the fog shrouding his mind. Now there were voices. Two of them. Sit up again.

'How do you feel?' It was Barbara, so close to him that he twitched in surprise.

'Why did you come back?' he asked. 'You were supposed to get away.'

'I couldn't leave you,' she said.

Two cockatoos, chasing the flock, swept by. Fred watched them with envy. He let his head slump to his chest. His body seemed to be aching all over, but his head and neck felt the worst. He rolled his head, slowly and stiffly. His forehead throbbed. The pain was harder to endure because he couldn't touch his head with his hands. He wondered why pain could be eased or tolerated by something as inconsequential as touch. What a stupid thought! Here he was, trussed like a fowl and his mind was wandering. He should be doing something. His neck ached. If only he could touch it. Why was that important? Stop it. Think. Back to reality. Quick. He tried to think of the appropriate big word. Big words. He laughed. The sound came from his closed lips like an elongated groan.

'Are you all right?' she asked.

He nodded and, for the first time, realised that Barbara, too, was bound and that they were joined to each other. He saw the two men, about fifty paces away. Frog was on the ground, lying back on one elbow like a wrestler who had just been thrown to the canvas. Fred studied the scene intently. As he watched, Frog sat up and tried to stand. Johnny Parsons, using his rifle like a stick, pushed him on his back once more.

'How did the other one get here?' Fred asked. 'What's been happening?'

'I don't know. Sergeant Wallis was there. I don't know where he came from. The other man, Frog, hit him from behind. I don't know how he got there. I don't know. I thought we were going to be all right.'

'Where's Eric now?'

'Over there in the trees.'

From his low angle, Fred could see nothing. 'Is he all right?' he asked, his voice edged with doubt.

Barbara shrugged. It was not a measure of indifference but a slow gesture of despair. When she spoke, her voice was filled with dread. 'He hasn't moved since the fat one hit him but I heard them say he's not dead. They were arguing about him for some reason. I don't know how he is. Oh Fred.' She was crying again.

Fred squirmed around until he could present his wrists to her. 'Try to loosen these knots,' he said, attempting to sound as matter-of-fact as he could. He was watching the men, not her. 'Those two seem to have forgotten us for the moment. Come on, brighten up. We're not dead yet.'

The sound of the rifle shot was clear and sharp. It swamped all sounds but the steady rumble of the flood waters. Barbara's half-sobs, half-grunts as her fingers struggled with the cumbersome knots. The shuffle of Fred's legs on the stones as he tried to maintain balance. The voices of the other men arguing. All stopped. There was no sound but the underscore of the river and the ringing echo of the shot, hushing the area with the violence of its message.

Johnny Parsons stood absolutely still. Dust was rising near his feet, where one leg of the dying Frog Gardiner had rutted the earth in a convulsive final movement. The bullet had shattered the fat man's breastbone. Burn marks ringing the hole in his shirt were disappearing beneath a spreading ooze of blood.

Johnny let the rifle fall to the ground. He arched his fingers, as though the touch of the weapon had been repugnant to him. Turning, he noticed his two prisoners near the truck and immediately bent to retrieve the .303. He walked towards them, stopping several times on the way. Taking this as a danger signal, Barbara moved away from Fred and held her hands well clear. The gesture of innocence was wasted. Johnny was looking her way but not observing any action on her part.

The bough of a dead tree bobbed through the crossing. It swirled close to the northern bank, where steep sand walls reared from the water. Johnny watched the floating piece of wood until it had disappeared from sight. Suddenly he spoke to Fred. 'Where will that go to?' he demanded.

Fred, too, had watched the bough, wondering what was attracting the other man's interest. 'The tree?' he said. 'Just down the river somewhere.'

'Where? What's down there?'

Fred was astonished by the question. He stumbled with the answer. 'There's nothing,' he said, speaking slowly and as evenly as he could. 'It might make Goyder Lagoon. That's where the river spreads out. If there's enough water, it could reach Lake Eyre. It's most likely to end up stuck in some tree.'

'Nothing on the way? No towns or cattle stations?'

Fred shook his head, and winced at the pain the action caused. 'No one'll see that bit of wood again,' he said.

Johnny walked to the river bank, at a point near the crossing where the water was deepest. On a nearby rock, he put down his rifle and waded several paces into the river, until the current began tugging at his trousers. He then left the water and picked his way through boulders and sand to where the body of Frog lay. Flies had settled on the face and open chest wound.

He searched the dead man's pockets, glanced once across at the tree where Wallis lay still, and then walked around the body, not studying it but checking about him, like a dingo circling dead prey to ensure that no rival lurked nearby. That done, he grabbed the body of Frog Gardiner by the heels and began hauling it to the river.

The body dug a wide groove to the water's edge. Johnny rolled the dead man on to his stomach and dragged him, face down, into the stream. The body began to sink. Then it stabilised as air bubbles formed in his clothes. Frog had dirtied himself, Johnny noted with disgust. 'Filthy, fat, stupid prick,' he said, and shoved the body with as much force as he could into the main current of the flood. It stayed afloat for a few seconds, bobbing and spinning, and then disappeared.

Johnny Parsons washed his hands and face before returning to the bank. He picked up the rifle and walked to the bound couple. 'You know,' he said, as though he were resuming an interrupted conversation, and holding the rifle with both hands, 'I never realised what a kick these things give you when you fire them. My wrists are sore. Would you believe that?'

Johnny Parsons inspected the river once more. 'Imagine all this water out here,' he said, talking to himself rather than to his trussed audience. 'Christ, it's hot. What's it like in, Sister?' He spoke without looking at her, then continued: 'You're the only one who's been swimming. You're the only one who's been right under. Except for that fat prick, but he's not going to tell me.' He giggled. She didn't answer and he turned. 'I said what's it like in?'

Barbara shook her head.

'What's that mean? No good.'

Again she shook her head, so frightened by his casual mood that she had difficulty in speaking.

'No,' she said at last. 'It's good. It's very nice in.'

'Ah,' he said, drawing out the sound to suggest pleasure. 'Well, I'm going in. I won't be long, so don't go away.' Again he giggled, and squatted on the river's edge to remove his shoes and socks. They were already saturated but he went through the ritual slowly, and laid his socks neatly on a large rock. Then he removed his trousers and shirt. 'Keep an eye on them for me, will you?' he asked pleasantly, and carefully walked into the river.

'He's mad,' Barbara said. 'He kills his friend and complains about sore wrists.'

'How are the knots going?' Fred said. 'If he stays there long enough we might get free.'

She wriggled closer. 'Please don't try anything again,' she said. 'He said he's going to let us go. Just let him drive away.'

'I don't know whether I could start anything,' he said, grimacing with pain. 'I'm sore all over. A man doesn't have a fight for ten years and then he has one a day on this trip. And gets clobbered on the back of the head most times. Look, I know it's silly, but would you mind rubbing the back of my neck. Just touch it gently,' he added as she began rubbing with her fingers. 'Only a touch, that's all I want.' He sighed with satisfaction.

'Okay. That's enough. Back to the knots.'

What's the opposite to masochist? he thought, and wondered if his dictionary was still intact in the truck.

'Are you all right?' she asked, more concerned about his neck than the knots. 'Does it ache badly?'

He nodded, sorry for the lapse. 'Hurry. He won't be long.'

Johnny Parsons had ventured to where the water was no more than knee-deep and then sat down. The rushing current broke around his shoulders, so that from the bank, his head appeared to be balancing on a bow wave of silvery brown.

'He's enjoying himself,' Barbara said.

'There's just a chance he might drown,' Fred said. 'The rocks are slippery out there, although the way his luck's running, if he lost his grip the river level would probably drop at the same instant. How are you making out with the rope?'

'Slowly. There's still no sign of your policeman friend moving.'

Fred twisted to look at the trees. 'You sure he's not dead?'

'I've got no idea. The fat one just hit him and left him there. He must be badly hurt. I wish I could get to him and see.' Her fingers fumbled with the rope.

'We do that after we get out of this.' He almost added 'if.' His ribs were throbbing and he tried to remember what caused the injury. 'I wish to hell you hadn't come back,' he added. 'If we get the chance to separate, either you get back over the hill and run through the trees, or make for deep water in the river. Let the current take you downstream. That would be best. Get in the river. Keep your head down and just let the water take you away from here. The town's on the other side. Get to the other bank when you're out of sight of him, and walk to Birdsville. It's about a mile from the river. Okay?'

'What about you?'

'Forget about me. If we worry about each other, he'll kill us both.'

'He said he wasn't going to kill us.'

'I don't believe him. Don't tell me you do?' He saw the look in her eyes; not shock but bewilderment. 'Look,' he added more gently, 'I don't know. Maybe he won't. He's off his head and he's just killed a man like some people kill a mouse and I don't know what he'll do next. Just get away if you have the chance, that's all

I'm asking.' He thought again of the night Ivan died.

'Remember the other night I told you I like you? Remember?' He twisted his head to see her eyes answer. 'Well, I'm not good with words but I mean it. I just wanted to let you know. I'm quiet and it's easy for a quiet person to assume people understand what they think, what they really mean. I'm not sure it's true. I've gone through my life not telling people things. You understand? I like someone but I don't tell them. A girl, or a bloke. Same thing. They go off with someone else, or they die and I've never told them what I truly feel. Ivan was a good bloke and I'd have done anything for him. I shared some of the best times of my life with him, and yet I never told him that. Not once. We spent days, months together, and on not one single occasion did I tell him he was a good bloke, or that I liked him.'

'He knew.'

'I didn't tell him and that's important. That's what's wrong. People don't communicate. That's why I'm telling you. This is a rotten time and I'm saying it badly, but I wanted to say it, to let you know how I feel. How's the rope going?' She concentrated on the bonds for a full ten seconds until she said: 'You don't think we're going to get away, do you?'

'Did I make them sound like my last words?' He tried to smile. 'Maybe they were. I truly have no idea what that crazy lunatic is going to do.' Barbara didn't answer and there was such an absolute stillness that he turned.

Johnny Parsons was standing behind her. His underpants hung wet and creased from his hips and his arms grasped a bundle of clothes and shoes. His hair was wet and covered his forehead in untidy wedges, like a string of damp bunting. 'Who are you calling a crazy lunatic?' he demanded, his voice so slow and authoritative that, for one moment, Fred was reminded of an old schoolteacher in faraway Perth.

He hadn't thought of him for years. 'Who?' The question rang through him. What was the schoolteacher's name? Wilkinson. Wilko. He said it aloud.

'Wilko.'

'What?' The answer unsettled the other man. Barbara looked at the mailman with new concern. Fred felt faint. His head had taken about all the hitting it could absorb. Maybe more. Wilko? What was wrong with him, to think of a schoolteacher at a time like this? A drowning man is supposed to see his life in flashback, or so he had read. Maybe the same thing applied to all people who realised they were about to die. He felt as though he was sinking, so maybe it was like drowning.

'Oh, to hell with it,' he blurted, trying hard to keep his body upright while he spoke. He felt terrible. 'You're crazy, mate. As mad as a meat axe.' He didn't care what happened to him now. He couldn't move a yard to save his life but if he proved troublesome enough the girl might get away. He didn't know how. He couldn't think clearly. The ache in his head was appalling.

'You are off your rocker,' he said in a fair imitation of the long-forgotten Mr Wilkinson. Wilko had a bald head, he recalled. Then he fainted.

'He has concussion.' Barbara shouted the words, as though volume would add to the defence of the unconscious man. She knelt over Fred's body, guarding him like a dog defending a sleeping master.

'Can't you see, he didn't know what he was saying. You hit him so hard with that rifle he might even have a fractured skull. He didn't know what he was saying and didn't mean what he said. Just leave him alone.'

Johnny studied the scene with curiosity. He spread his clothes on the truck and wiped his body dry with his hands. 'He looks like a chook, all tied up ready for the chopping block,' he said and pulled on his pants.

'You said you weren't going to harm us,' Barbara said.

'What's that, Sister?' He was concentrating on the task of buttoning his fly.

'You promised to leave us here.'

He put on his shirt. 'I said I wasn't going to shoot you and that I was just going to tie you like that and drive away across the river. And that's right.'

She maintained her watchdog crouch near Fred.

'I mean it,' Johnny said. He put on his socks and shoes before walking towards the river's edge to collect the rifle. He slipped once, and glanced back towards her. She hadn't changed either her position or her doubtful expression. 'You can take that stupid look off your face,' he shouted, and stood up once more. His trousers, which had dried crackle-hard in the sun, bore a slimy stain on one side. He tried to brush it away. 'I'm going to do what

I said I'd do. Have no doubts about that. I'm going to do everything I said.'

Using the rifle, he prodded Fred in the side. He did it gently, just as a person playing with a kitten might use a stick to tease it. 'Come on, wake up,' he said, and kept talking in a soft, persuasive voice until the bound man stirred.

'That's the way,' he said. 'You shouldn't sleep when your guest's about to leave. Come on, sit up.' He pushed harder with the rifle, and Fred lifted himself on to one elbow.

'Time to say goodbye, Fred,' Johnny said. 'I'm just going to take that truck of yours and drive across the river.'

'It's deep,' Fred said. His voice was slurred.

'Well I know it's deep, but it's not too deep. You were going to drive through the water, and don't give me any more of that bullshit about not being able to find my way or not being able to drive the truck. That was all right for a while. You kept me amused with your begging.' He pushed Fred on to his back again to stress the word. 'Begging for your life. Well, now the track's ended and we're at the river and this is where you stay and I go on.'

'You won't get anywhere,' Fred said wearily.

'Why not? Who's going to stop me? You? That copper back there in the tree. Christ, I'd forgotten him. I should put a bullet in him.'

'Good idea,' Fred said.

'What?'

'Fire the gun again. Make a noise. Bring people down to the river.' Johnny looked uncertain.

Barbara spoke. 'For heaven's sake, don't do any more killing.'

'Well, just hang around,' Fred said. 'People should be here soon. They're expecting me in Birdsville. Wait a few minutes.'

'Just go,' Barbara said.

Johnny glanced nervously across the river. The sandy banks were as deserted as when they'd arrived. A mob of cockatoos was settling in a distant tree. 'Only birds,' he said, and turned towards them. 'You speak a lot of crap, you know, Postman. I'm awake to what you're trying. All that bullshit you've been feeding me. "You won't find your way. You can't drive the truck. You won't cross the river. don't make a noise or the people will hear you." Christ. What people? Where is everyone?'

He put down the rifle and cupped his hands to his mouth. 'Hey people, it's me,' he shouted. 'Here I am. Come and get me.' He waited, staring across the river. One of the cockatoos in the far tree fluttered its wings.

'Birds,' he said, and turned to the others. 'What's over there, Sydney? Is this the harbour and someone's taken the bridge? I'll tell you where we are. We're in the middle of nowhere. The big A. The arsehole of the world. And you're in the shit. Not me. You. All your moralising about good and bad and people being crazy. You go on as though this is a normal part of the world. It's not. This isn't the world. This is nowhere. What you do out here doesn't matter.'

Picking up the unused coil of rope, he bent down beside Barbara, so that his head was near hers. 'How would you like your left one cut off,' he whispered. He stood up and laughed, and began walking towards the truck, laying out the rope. 'I could do it,' he called out to her. 'No one would stop me. No one would do anything about it. No one would know anything about it. So if you don't want that to happen, just tell your boyfriend to shut up.'

Johnny reached the truck and began tying the rope to the back axle.

'What did he say to you?' Fred asked.

'It doesn't matter,' she said, but she had raised her arms so that her elbows covered her chest. 'Just don't antagonise him. Please.' Then suddenly she added. 'Oh my God.'

The changed tune in her voice made Fred turn. He could see Johnny Parsons still working beneath the tail of the truck. The girl was looking the other way. 'What is it?' he hissed.

'The policeman. Over there in the tree. He moved.'

Fred shuffled clear of the girl to get a better view. The figure of Eric Wallis, for so long draped between the twin trunks of the tree, had slipped down. He was now on his knees at the base of the tree. As Fred watched, Wallis tried to stand, but fell, and slowly raised himself until he was sitting with his back to the tree. He stayed like that.

'He's alive,' she said, with hope in her voice.

'Just pray he doesn't move again for a while,' Fred said. 'He's in no shape to help us. If this character sees Eric moving, he'll go over there and shoot him. What the devil's he up to anyhow?'

Johnny Parsons had finished tying the rope and stood up. He

was concentrating on removing some grease from his hands.

'Now,' he said, lifting his gaze from his fingers. 'Seeing you two are so keen on swimming, I thought I'd let you get back in the water.' He collected the rifle and threw it into the cabin.

'Worked out what's going to happen to you yet?' He leaned against the bonnet of the truck and asked the question pleasantly. 'I drive across and you follow me in when the rope gets tight. If you're good at staying afloat, you should just about keep up long enough to see me safe and sound on the other side. Then I let you spend a couple of minutes under the water, cast off the rope, and I'm on my way.'

He walked closer, waving a finger at Fred. 'I'm going to enjoy this, Postie. You reckon you're tough. We'll see how tough. See how you go on the end of a rope in that water. What will you do with the sheila. Try and hold her up or stand on top of her so you can breathe?' He lifted his foot to Fred's shoulder and pressed him to the ground. 'So long, hero,' he said, and left them.

'No,' Barbara screamed after him.

Fred rolled on his side and pushed his hands at her. 'Quick,' he said. 'The knot. See if you can loosen it some more. Hurry.'

Johnny had reached the truck. He pulled the gear lever into neutral and swung the crank handle three times before starting the motor. Without looking back at them, he climbed in. He crunched the lever into first gear. The truck jolted forward and almost stalled. He revved the motor and tried again. The truck lurched towards the river. It bumped past them, the driver's eyes rigidly fixed on the racing water ahead.

'I can't loosen it,' Barbara cried, shaking her bound wrists in frustration.

The truck rolled into the water, trailing its slithering tail of rope.

Fred tried to jerk his wrists apart. 'You're making it worse,' she screamed.

He held his wrists still and watched the rope snaking into the river. The truck entered deeper water. Its tyres were disappearing in the brown flood and the body had developed a rolling, lurching motion as the wheels climbed and dropped over submerged stones. The motor was roaring. That's too many revs, Fred thought. He glanced at Barbara. She was extending a loop in the knot, and biting her lower lip in concentration.

The mail truck ploughed towards the deepest part of the crossing, wallowing and spluttering like some giant beast battling the flood. The remains of the load they had hauled from Marree rocked through a wide angle as first one set of wheels and then the other dipped in unseen holes. He's going too fast, Fred thought. He had spent the last dozen years of his life tackling this river crossing and part of his mind — the detached, professional mind of the truck driver — was assessing the new driver's performance. He was driving too quickly and he was slightly off the correct line, but the truck was still moving through the crossing.

Part of the long rope flicked out of the water, trailing spray. Fred felt a sharp tug at his ankles. There was a slight pause in the truck's progress. The rope sagged beneath the surface, then reappeared, quivering spray, to jerk at them and swing their legs towards the crossing.

They began to slide feet-first towards the river. The movement wrenched them apart. Fred grabbed the girl. 'Finish the knot,' he shouted. 'You've almost got it.'

'The rocks,' she said, holding her hands on the ground, so that they acted like a skid. 'They're hurting me.' As though to emphasise her point, she was dragged across a larger stone whose sharp edge peeled back her skirt and gouged skin from the exposed thigh.

They were in the water now, floundering in the greasy shallows and being dragged across slippery rocks. She grabbed his arm to haul herself back to him, and used her teeth to worry the loose loop of rope.

Locked together, with the woman biting at the bonds on the man's wrists, they were hauled into the river.

For an instant, the pressure eased and they stopped their painful slide. The truck had halted. The engine was misfiring. Water on the plugs. Yes, I reckoned you were going too fast, Fred thought. Suck water in the carburettor and you'll blow the motor. Bend a rod or something. Christ, a feller looks after a truck all these years and you get behind the wheel for a few hundred yards and ruin the thing. He hated that man.

'I've got it,' Barbara said. The end of the rope was loose and, frenziedly, she began unwinding the coils around his wrists.

The truck's motor coughed and spluttered as Johnny tried to

clear the misfire. Stationary in the flood, the truck rocked under the pressure of the water butting its side. A wave rode high along the tray and foamed across the back of the vehicle. The engine shrieked, as all spark plugs fired.

You'll ruin the clutch if you ride it like that, Fred thought.

'You're free.'

Fred flung his hands apart and bent to work on the rope binding their ankles. But as he moved, the truck lurched forward, tightening the rope and pulling his body straight. His head slipped beneath the water and he emerged coughing. Barbara grabbed him and, sliding feet first, they both went under.

For several moments, they could do no more than hold each other and try to keep their faces above the surface. As the water deepened, the force of the current began to spin them away from the crossing, sweeping them downstream and towards the middle of the river. With their change in direction, the rope tying them to the truck grew slack. Fred tried to stand, dragging his feet along the bottom in search of grip. His feet slid across sand and rocks until they found a large, flat slab. He hooked his boots against the edge.

'Stand up,' he shouted and pulled Barbara towards him. She stood alongside him leaning into the current. Water curled around her chest. The rope floating on the surface, was bending towards them. The truck appeared more side-on to them now, as it laboured in deep water. A few wisps of spray broke across its bonnet. The wheels were out of sight, churning for grip beneath the flood. Water broke over the truck's tray sending rivulets of brown streaming through the crates and boxes stacked there, and Fred knew that Johnny was off course and straying into deeper water. A front wheel hit a submerged boulder and the vehicle shook, before rearing high as the tyre clawed its way over the obstacle. Then the front crashed into the water, sending a wave through the open windscreen into the cabin. A back wheel struck the same rock, jarring the load and causing the rear of the truck of rise and then slide to one side. The vehicle was now pointing across the ford, towards a flood-ravaged sand bank. The rope, which had bowed loosely across the water, began to straighten as the vehicle, ploughing ahead on its new course, took up the slack.

Fred lunged for the rope. He grabbed it with one hand, flailing with the other for Barbara's arms as the water swept him back towards her. He went under, was grasped by her outstretched hand, found his footing on a rock once more, and emerged from the water shaking his head like a spaniel.

'Hang on to the rope,' he shouted and linked his arm through hers. Like a man readying himself for a tug of war, he held the rope in both hands, bent his knees, and wriggled his feet until his boots were placed more firmly against the edge of the rock. She followed his example. The river burst around their bodies, curving high and away from them like the wave cut by a fast ship's prow. Fred allowed the force to move their bodies back until they were at such an angle that the bow wave was breaking around their faces. The rope, nearly straight now, held them in the current.

'We'll make a fair pair of anchors,' he shouted and then added, more to himself. 'Look where the silly bastard's trying to take it.'

The truck was heading straight for the eroded sand bank. Its front was almost clear of the water. Johnny, not watching where the truck was heading, was leaning across the cabin and looking back to see where they were.

'Don't let go,' Fred told Barbara. 'I want to give the old girl a real jolt.'

The front wheels rolled out of the river and bit into the sand. Johnny Parsons, turning his attention to the way out of the crossing, hauled the steering wheel hard to the left, to try to avoid the barrier of sand.

The rope grew taut. Fred braced his body and wedged his feet more securely against the submerged rock. The truck was partly up the bank. The rope quivered, and began to rise from the water. An awful force tugged at Fred's arm. He heard Barbara gasp and saw her slip beneath the surface as she tried to hold on. He could feel her, locked beside him with her arm still through his. And still holding the rope.

The rope danced on the surface of the river, spraying water as it shivered under the stress of the contest. Barbara's feet slipped. Fred felt her go, saw her emerge from the water with her mouth gasping for breath, and felt the strain increase. Her bound hands were locked around his arm. I'm going to be torn into two pieces, he told himself. Barbara was washed behind him. Still he held on. The truck was scrabbling for grip, the front rearing on the sand, the back wheels spinning in the river shallows.

Then came the sound, a crack like a distant rifle shot, and the awful pull of the rope eased. Fred had never heard the sound from outside the truck before. It was followed almost immediately by the frantic sound of the engine racing at full throttle.

'Bucephalus,' he shouted, and Barbara looked at him not comprehending and thinking he had shouted some profanity. He hauled Barbara close, to make sure her head was above the water, but his concentration was on the truck. 'Good horse,' he said, talking to the truck and gasping the words, for he was short of breath and near exhaustion.

The old truck was rolling back into the river. The front wheels were turned hard left, putting the nose into an arc across the rearing sand bank. Part of the eroded shelf cracked and a slab of sand, bearing the wheels, slid into the water. The motor shrieked. Juddering sideways, the truck hit the rocks and tilted on one side. For an instant, as drums and cartons tumbled from the back, the truck stayed poised with one set of wheels high in the air.

Johnny Parsons fell from the cabin. With a booming splash, the truck rolled on top of him. A brown wave of water swept out but was caught by the raging torrent and curled back at the truck. The motor died in a series of coughing misfires.

Fred let out a roar of triumph.

'What happened?' Barbara was wide-eyed with shock.

'Jumped out of gear,' Fred said. 'We made it happen.' He was breathless from the tug-of-war and had difficulty speaking. 'You put a sudden load on the transmission and it'll always do that. Should have fixed it years ago.'

The truck's wheels hung in the air shedding sand. The rear of the Chev projected into the river, forming a breakwater near a point where the current was most forceful. Around this bulky new obstruction rose a wave which twisted and broke like surf swirling in a violent cross current. Part of the truck's load collapsed, and the tail dipped deeper and swung with the force of the water. A stream of debris rushed towards the bound couple. Cardboard boxes, bottles, pieces of smashed timber and an empty drum bore down on them. The current snatched at a spreading slick of oil.

By contrast, the front of the upturned truck lay in shallow water, near the end of the crossing. The cabin roof was almost exposed. It rocked slightly. From the muddy water beside the roof appeared an arm.

'He's trapped under there,' Barbara cried.

They began to haul themselves towards the truck. A partly submerged wooden box bore down on them, bobbing in a stream of oily brown. Fred deflected it with his arm and lost his grip on the rope.

In the shallows, the hand flailed the water.

Fred grabbed the rope again and hauled the two of them towards the stricken truck. His truck. With his head aching violently, he was hit by an onslaught of conflicting thoughts. A man was drowning in front of him and he was trying desperately to reach him. He hated that man and didn't care if he died. Yet he desperately wanted to haul the owner of that arm from the trap. He thought of himself — anyone — being caught like that, and the thought seemed to supercharge his muscles. The truck was seesawing. Was it the force of the water or the struggles of the man pinned beneath the front? Fred tried to move faster, but the water was impossibly strong and the waves, gushing in a frenzy from the tail of the truck, burst upon him and the girl. He swallowed a mouthful of oily water.

More of the man's arm was showing. It was no longer thrashing the water, but reaching up.

Fred and Barbara scrambled up a shelf in the river bed, and were suddenly in shallower water. Fred slipped on a submerged boulder. The truck loomed above him. The sight of his Chev, upended and undignified with its worn tyres and scarred chassis exposed to the sun, distressed him. It was like an animal that had turned up its legs and died.

They were still in water that broke above their knees when the arm slipped beneath the surface and did not reappear. And at that moment, Fred Crawford, who hated that man and loved his truck, felt an intense sadness for both.

Water ran undisturbed through the roof of the cabin.

Fred could not move. He thought of Johnny under the truck and Ivan under a miserable layer of rocks, and of all that had happened in the past few days and he felt his strength ebb with the running water.

He fell to his knees, and let the river bend his body. He turned his back to the truck. Water cascaded over his shoulders. 'I'm so tired,' he said, looking up at Barbara and seeking her understanding. 'I couldn't lift the truck. Maybe I could try if that was you caught back there but I couldn't for him. Not for that man.'

She sat beside him. 'We might have been able to help if he hadn't tied us like this.'

Fred nodded and, with an immense effort, lifted his hands to begin untying her wrists. 'Retribution,' he said softly, accenting each syllable. 'Evil justly befalling the perpetrator of evil.'

A fresh batch of goods from the truck bobbed passed them. He recognised some of his own possessions. 'I think I'm going to need a new dictionary,' he said and tried to smile.

She grasped his hands. 'I think you do very well without one. You might need a new truck, though.'

I can fix it, he thought, and knew he would take great pride in repairing the truck and putting it back to work. 'This is nice,' he said, squeezing her hands, 'but I can't untie your wrists like this.'

'Don't bother for a minute. Just rest for a while.'

'We should get over to Eric and make sure he's all right.'

'I know. But just wait a minute, please.' He held her hands tightly and they moved their heads until they touched.

From beyond the bank, a cloud of white cockatoos rose from a tree and flew along the Diamantina.